For Max, my dear friend, who walked every step of this journey with me.
(What were you thinking?)

Breaking Reed

For Melissa, my sister,
friend and fellow fighter.
When I grow younger, I
want to be like you. ♡

— Carla

Breaking Reed

Carla C. Hoch

Library of Congress Control Number:		2010916731
ISBN:	Hardcover	978-1-4568-1247-8
	Softcover	978-1-4568-1246-1
	Ebook	978-1-4568-1248-5

This book was printed in the United States of America.

To order additional copies of this book, contact:
Xlibris Corporation
1-888-795-4274
www.Xlibris.com
Orders@Xlibris.com
68338

CHAPTER 1
Beginning from an End

They met while he was still dead. With her death, they said good-bye. Between those two deaths, he learned the difference between living and just being alive.

And here is where I begin again. Among the dead! Reed shook his head at the irony, then took hold of a fresh shoot of grass. He pulled it with a zip from its roots and weaved it in and out between his lips for a moment before biting down on it. The crunch of cellulose felt good between his teeth and, for a second or two, his mind was preoccupied with its noise instead of the silent grave in front of him. The freshly placed squares of sod that laid in repose in front of the headstone looked a bit ridiculous. He wished he could say that their patchwork resembled a charmingly bucolic, organic quilt. But, in truth, it more resembled an ill-fitting, tattered comforter whose clumps of stuffing wouldn't even suit the indiscriminate decor of a doghouse. She had very much liked dogs though so, it was just as well. If nothing else, humorously ironic.

He chuckled to himself and put his hand out for a ladybug to traverse, not hearing the footsteps behind him, until a shadow overtook him. Reed looked up and the shock caused him to gasp and the gnarled blade of grass to fall from his mouth. The ladybug was startled to a complete stop by the massive falling stalk and paused momentarily to gather herself before continuing in her forward press over the thicket of his arm hair.

The girl paused and nodded respectfully before approaching the simple headstone. She kneeled, took the river rock from her pocket, said something under her breath and then placed it beside the numerous other stones on and around the grave. A galvanized bucket caught her eye as she steadied herself to stand. It was filled with rocks, each with writing on it. The most recent was dated that very day and read, "Home soon, my love." That she found disturbing.

Reed had composed himself by the time she turned around and then smiled at her in gratitude.

"What brings you here?" he asked, looking back down at the red-and-black hiker on his arm. The girl shrugged and sat down next to him.

"The clouds in Texas are so weird," she said suddenly, looking up at the blue skies after several moments of silence. "Canadian clouds look like, you know, puffballs! These look like skywriting that has faded!"

Reed laughed and said it was the due to the Gulf Steam and began explaining the phenomena.

"Thank you for apologizing," she said, interrupting his attempt to enlighten her on the wind-current patterns around the Gulf of Mexico. He was altogether too smart. She was glad she had something to say to shut him up.

Reed nodded and thanked her for allowing him the opportunity. The two then sat in silence, each knowing the other was thinking about what had happened and wondering if the other remembered it the way they did. She doubted his recollection was as vivid as hers was. He hadn't even known her name at the time and had made no attempt to learn it afterward.

She moved to rise and Reed grabbed her hand. Startled, she tried to pull it away but her effort only fed his tenacity.

"Don't let anyone else treat you as I did. Please? You are a good woman."

They looked at each other hard for a moment and he couldn't help but think there was something beyond his carnal knowledge of her that made her seem familiar. He felt like he knew her from an entirely different place or world. A dream perhaps.

She looked away as tears welled and he let go of her hand. "How do you know I am a good woman? Just because you *knew* me doesn't mean you know me!"

"Well," he said, watching the ladybug fly away and then sitting back and relaxing himself on his hands, "I know you brought a rock to the grave of a woman you didn't even know who wasn't your patient and was the fiancée of a man that treated you like rubbish!"

"She was a fellow Jew."

"She wasn't Jewish!" Reed laughed. The girl narrowed her eyes at him and asked why there had been a rabbi at the graveside. "How did you know there was a rabbi?"

The girl rolled her eyes and tried to not smile. "I drove by and saw it!"

"Oh! You just 'drove by' through the cemetery?"

She stood quickly and her irritation made him laugh. "You are a good woman, Prudence. Better than you know I reckon."

The girl froze and her nostrils flared. "Prudence! Who is Prudence? You still don't know my name, do you!"

Reed shook his head and looked up at her, one clear blue eye closed in the glare of the sun. "Nope. And, considering our past, I didn't think you would care for me to ask around. Did you really want our colleagues to know I didn't know your name? No matter. I know it starts with a *P*. Stay a bit longer. I'll guess it."

The girl laughed at the absurdity of it all and, in curiosity of whether he actually could guess her name, she sat back down.

"Let's see, you said the other day that your father was a rabbi so I would venture to say that your name is Hebrew."

The girl raised an eyebrow and rested her head on her hand and elbow on her knee.

"Hebrew names with *P*. Hmmm . . . Polly? Is that Hebrew?"

The girl shrugged. That wasn't her name.

"Ritzpah?"

"Umm . . . that's an *R* name."

"Oh, yea. Rumpelstiltskin?"

"Again, *R*, and I am pretty sure that was a guy."

Reed continued thinking, and the girl remembered what she had read on the stone: "Home soon." He seemed to be in oddly high spirits considering his loss. In her expert opinion, he was either "on" something or plotting to "off" himself.

"How are you doing by the way? You know . . ." She motioned with her head toward the grave and Reed was brought back to the present. He looked away, chewed his bottom lip and then shook his head slowly.

"I lost a brother a year ago to cancer and I was a wreck," the girl said with fragile honesty. Reed looked at her a long moment. Her big brown eyes were lined with thick dark lashes. Her brown wavy hair was streaming around her face and he wondered if he had realized back then how beautiful she was.

"I lost a sister close to eight years ago," he said, rubbing his hands over his eyes. "And it nearly killed me. I was 'a wreck' as you said. But now . . ." Reed looked out toward the headstone and smiled. A lump formed in his throat and he cleared it before continuing.

"Someone once told me that faith anchored you. Storms would come and you might be tossed wildly and battered by the waves but, you would always be securely tethered to the object of your faith. And, if nothing else, you would have peace in the certainty of that. So, to answer your question Prunella, I feel wildly out of control, battered to my core and pulled tightly to the limit of my rope. Yet, anchored all the same. Wrecked, yes. But I'll not be left as wreckage."

The girl smiled and wondered how he had navigated the long journey from the offensive thing he once was to the man he was now. She could only assume it to be the deceased that had guided his sails.

"How did you two meet?"

Reed smiled at the question and, to the girl's surprise, he blushed. They had been next-door neighbors, he said. Apparently, one night, in a stupor of exhaustion, he had walked in his sleep, with his pillow and blanket, and bedded down on her driveway. He hadn't been drinking and to his knowledge had never walked in his sleep prior. In fact, for more than seven years, he had hardly slept. Yet on the warm cement of her driveway, sleep took hold of him like a python and had rendered him unconscious for six hours.

"She thought I was dead. She said that only my feet were showing from under the duvet and she thought perhaps someone had tossed it over me to obscure my body." Reed laughed and then scratched his chin.

"I haven't murdered anyone lately, but if I had and was going to hide the corpse, it would be in the boot of a car not out next to its wheels under a duvet in broad daylight!"

The girl laughed imagining the scene and asked how he had been resurrected.

"Well, you know, any other sane human would have called the police but not her! That bird was fearless! I awoke to hear her feet pacing back and forth beside me. Then, she pulled the duvet back and I kept my eyes nearly closed and watched as she looked me over."

He paused and his mischievous smile softened. He remembered her eyes and the look of wonder on her face as she had studied the uncovered portion of him. It was as if she were looking at a painting and her smile showed that what she beheld she found beautiful.

"Anyway, I opened my eyes without saying anything and, when she realized I was watching her look at me, she shrieked and fell backward. She threatened to, as she said, 'shoot my butt off' unless I left the premises immediately. I laughed and fully intended on leaving but, cocky bastard as I was, I decided to stand and have a stretch first. I let the duvet fall and, unfortunately, didn't realize I wasn't wearing any trousers until it was entirely too late! I had on these rather ridiculous pants that had the flag of Ireland across the arse. Anyway, she didn't find it amusing and it really made any effort of apology useless.

"It's difficult to make a good impression on a lass if you are dead the first time you meet her! And no use apologizing for the bad impression if you are nearly naked!"

The girl laughed, imagining the story exactly as he had described it. His eyes remained lit with happiness for several minutes after the telling and it was obvious that he had been in love in a way she never thought was possible. Not for her anyway.

"So how did you get a rabbi to officiate the burial? That's a pretty liberal guy!"

Reed shook his head. It was the pastor of the church the two had attended together who was a Jewish Christian. The man had done his yeshiva, rabbinical study, in Israel and was in fact a rabbi by Jewish standards.

"Except for the whole 'Christian' thing, of course! A Christian rabbi! Give me a break," she said, and Reed laughed at the girl's obvious irritation.

"The two aren't as different as you would think, Patricia."

"Whatever. So are you Jewish Jewish, or is it just one of your grandparents or something?"

Reed smiled. "No, I am Jewish Jewish. Chock-full of 'Jewy' goodness if you will."

"So where are you working now?" the girl asked, changing the subject, slightly offended. She knew Reed had resigned from the hospital. There had been a collective moan from the female staff when he had and she told him as much.

"I'm going home, Portia. I will take a bit of time off with my parents in London but then will go back to Ireland and get a job somewhere doing something."

The girl huffed a laugh. Dr. Ritter Thomas could get a job anywhere and they both knew it. His relatively convincing sense of humility amused her.

"Well, good luck," she said, standing. "Shalom and all that good stuff. If you are ever in Ontario, don't call because I will be here."

"And if I am here, I won't call because I don't know your name."

The girl folded her arms across herself obstinately and then shrugged. "Can't have it all, Dr. Thomas."

"I just want a friend," he said soberly. "And for the record, I know very well that I can't have it all. If I could, I don't reckon I'd be here."

He looked out over the sea of headstones and shook his head. "I am new at being this man. This man has only one friend on earth and that's my housemate, Paul. Is that your name? Paulette? No? Well—" he paused, resuming his plundering of the grass.

"I'm scared. That's one reason I am going back to Ireland. Oh, my mates from London, they knew the man that hurt you. That's the man they would expect to see again, and I'm just not that lad anymore. But, around them, that's the only thing I know how to be. I fear that's who I'd quickly become again.

"In Ireland however, there is mainly just family, although honestly, even they will see this man here as a stranger. I don't know," he said with a shake of his head, losing himself momentarily in an unspoken thought.

"But," he said with a slap to his thighs, "that's my home so even if I am a stranger to those around me, even my own self, at least I won't be in a strange land. That's something, yea? Maybe the place I began will help me begin again.

"So, what I guess I am trying to say, Peggy, is that I need mates. Especially one like you that knew me then, knows me now, and knows I am trying. What do you say?"

Reed held out his hand and the girl looked down. After a moment, she nodded and offered her hand in return.

"Call me Ella," she said as they shook. Reed's face shifted and he looked at her in wonder. "You're Ella?" he said as an affectionate smile crept across his face. "She," he said, motioning to the grave, "spoke of you."

Ella sighed and retrieved her hand. She nodded several times and looked around. She wanted to see him again. But, she wouldn't give him her phone number. That somehow seemed obscene considering the location. He knew where to find her. And now he knew her name.

She walked away and Reed continued smiling as he twirled another blade of grass in his hands.

"Wait!" he yelled. "What's the *P* for?"

"Penelope," she called back.

His head turned quickly toward the grave and tears filled his eyes as he thought back to the last words his beloved had said to him before she died. He laughed and ran his hands through his hair as the tears began to stream down his face.

"Well, Penelope," he said to himself, "Ithaca is just around the corner. And Odysseus is far closer than you think!"

Three months prior

CHAPTER 2

Ritter Gets Caught
with His Pants Down. Again.

Sleep resumed its elusiveness to Ritter. He slept three hours Tuesday night and, by 6:00 a.m., was tired of reading and wasting the hours. He decided to watch the day begin on the front porch in a rocking chair with hot tea and a banana. Sunrises didn't usually draw him but the possibility of catching another glimpse of Cat did and she had given the distinct impression of being an early bird.

He rested his bare feet on the railing of the front porch and rocked himself slowly. His tea was still steeping and he blew on it occasionally. He was careful with the cup as he wasn't wearing a shirt and only thin scrub pants. The just-sub-boiling liquid would leave nothing less than a second-degree burn on whatever bit of his hide was cursed enough to come into contact with it.

Ritter took a bite of banana and caught a glimpse of movement from the corner of his eye. It was Cat coming back from a run. The sun was caught between slumber and sky and what light it gave was caught on a reflective belt she wore. She looked like the last star of night holding on until the morning. Ritter smiled and slid down slightly in the chair hoping to not be seen. He had positioned himself behind a poorly trimmed bush, just in case fortune did smile upon him, and it was aiding him beautifully in his clandestine plan.

Cat slowed to a walk and took off the belt. She was wearing nothing but a sports bra and shorts both of which were soaked through with sweat and humidity. Ritter grinned watching her pant hard to catch her breath half expecting her to blow air through her lips and stomp in place like a mare. She leaned against her truck to stretch and sang with the music coming through her ear buds. Ritter recognized the song and chuckled to himself as she danced slightly to the beat. At one point, she mimicked playing a guitar and Ritter spilled a bit of the steaming tea on the arm of the chair while trying to muzzle his laughter.

Across the street, Isaiah Jenkins, walked out for the morning paper and waved to Cat who reciprocated with a smile and nod of her head. She then started for her house until she heard the elderly man call out, "Wooooo, get chur air gun, Kitty! We got us a copperhead!"

Cat quickly worked the lock on the back of her truck and jumped in, reemerging faster than what seemed possible with a rifle. Ritter sat up on the edge of the rocking chair as the sudden burst of energy from the scene struck him. He was preparing to stand up and call out to her when she took aim and shot.

Cat looked up from the object of her aim, laid the rifle back on her shoulder and both she and Isaiah walked forward to see if the pit viper was dead.

"Look out now, Kitty, it's a writhin' and will bite you still sure 'nuff!"

Cat lifted her heal, brought the hard edge of her running shoe down on the snake's head and Ritter saw the tail draw up and wrap around her ankle. Cat, seemingly unfazed, unwound the snake and slowly brought her foot away. Seeing the thing dead, she picked it up by the tail and looked it over.

"Wow," Ritter said quietly. He exhaled hard, rubbed his hand over his bare chest and thought to himself that what he had just seen was, in some odd way, the sexiest thing he had ever seen!

A bit of banana fell from his gaping mouth and hit his foot with a cool, moist thud. The sensation brought him back to his senses and he leaned down to get it.

"Would you look at that!" Isaiah hooted. "Girl, now that's a shot. Your daddy taught you good."

Ritter looked up through the slats of the porch railing and a thin place in the bush. Cat was smiling and Isaiah was admiring the kill.

"That's the sixth un I seen round here in the past several weeks."

"Six copperheads!" Cat exclaimed in shock.

"Oh, naw, just two coppers. But, amongst us houses here on the cul-de-sac, they've been six snakes, all poisonous. That other copperhead I killed with a hoe in Paul's yard last week. I told him 'bout it. They started showin' up 'bout the time that foreign feller came to town!"

Cat laughed. "How do you suppose he got all them snakes through airport security, Izzy?"

"I do not know," Isaiah said in serious contemplation.

Ritter saw Cat smile and shake her head then, she and the elderly man looked over at Paul's house. He got down low and grimaced for fear they had seen him.

"You met him?" Isaiah said motioning with his head across the street. "That foreign feller?"

Cat sighed. "Not formally, no. Although, I have definitely seen more of him than I should have! Moron was asleep in my driveway on Sunday morning in nothing but his briefs."

Isaiah bumped her arm with the morning newspaper. "He's a good lookin' feller, eh? Got muscles like an ape! I see him runnin' 'bout every ev'nin'. Some mornin's too. And, he's in scrubs all the time. I think he is a doctor." The elderly man then winked at Cat.

"What is your point, Izzy?"

14

"I am just sayin'! He looks like a catch. You think he's nice lookin'?" Cat shrugged in response to the question then threw down the snake and looked at her hand. "Yea, you do. I can see it! He's good lookin' ain't he! Ain't he!"

"Yes," Cat said, wiping her hand on her shorts. "Yes, he is, okay? He is also about a decade younger than me!"

"Aww, Kitty, woman like you's gonna need a young buck to keep step with her. Ain't no man like you your age gonna give you the time of day! You confuse 'em and scare 'em a bit too I 'magine. You ain't what they been 'spectin'."

Cat rubbed her forehead. "Well, thank you for the words of inspiration regarding my prospects!"

"I'm just sayin', Kitty! That'n over there's too young to know he ought to know better than mess with the likes of you!"

Cat glanced at the snake, wrinkled her nose, and then looked over at the porch where Ritter was crouched like a cat spying on a bird. "He's got a girlfriend I think, Isaiah. I have seen her here the past several nights." Ritter bit his lips and smiled. She had been keeping tabs on him.

"Aww, Kitty, you mean that ole Liz Taylor-lookin' girl? Honey, just 'tween you and me, she ain't nothin' but a rental. He's gonna put some miles on her and just send her on back!"

Cat's face twisted. "Oh, thank you for that image, Izzy!"

Isaiah shrugged. "I'm just sayin'! I know I don't look like much now, but in my day, I was tougher 'n a nickel steak, and I know women! That'n, she ain't for keeps. 'Sides, I think she's the one that brung the snakes! I know some things and that girl brung 'em. Like follows like. That's all I'm sayin'!"

Cat shook her head and smiled as Isaiah continued his rant. "She's got nothin' on you, Kitty! Your price is above rubies. She's just an old temple prostitute! Her lips are smooth as oil, but in the end, she tastes like wormwood and is sharp as a double-edged sword. She reduces a man to a crust of bread."

"And on that note," Cat said holding up her hand, "I am going to wash my shoe. I will keep an eye out for snakes."

"Oh, they ain't been in your yard. Been in everybody else's! Them slitherin' evil devils just know better I guess! They know you got the end of days coming for 'em. You a sure shot and got a heavy heel! That's all I'm sayin'!"

Cat turned to go and Isaiah called out to her once more. "Hey, Kitty. Just a rental. I'm tellin' ya!" Cat laughed and Ritter's heart sank hearing her coming closer. He couldn't run, crawl, or slither on his belly to the front door without being seen and he had no idea how he would explain his current location or position in it.

Cat walked to the side of her house, not fifteen feet from Ritter, and turned on the water hose. As she bent over to wash the blood and bits from the shoe that had crushed the viper's head, Ritter's eyes took in the area where the back of her thighs made their way into her shorts. Sweat made her legs look slick and Ritter clenched his fists hoping his body wouldn't give in to instinct and pounce on her.

She straightened and the bands of muscle on either side of her spine made a smooth ravine down to her hips. A thick bead of sweat made its way down the center of her back slowly, viscous from the sweetness of her flesh, and Ritter's lips parted instinctively as if anticipating the taste of it. He lost himself momentarily in the daydream and, as he did, the cup of hot tea shifted in his hands and its scalding contents poured onto his groin.

His eyes opened wide and he held his breath to quell a scream, trying to quietly pull the fabric of his scrub pants away from his body. He looked up knowing that discovery was imminent and wasn't sure which would hurt more: the burn or the embarrassment. The sound of running water however had drowned out whatever noise that he might have created and he remained undetected. Cat leaned over again, deeper this time, and Ritter rolled his eyes. This was too much for any man much less one as weak as he was.

As soon as Cat disappeared behind the fence leading to her backyard, Ritter jumped up and jerked his scrub pants off. He had a bright red burn at the top of his thigh and, as he inspected it, caught a glimpse of Isaiah standing in his front yard across the street. Isaiah waved and Ritter nodded cordially.

"Ya best git, young feller," the old man warned in a low voice. Ritter waved awkwardly in return, not quite understanding what had been said. "Heed the words of the prophet, boy. Judgment's 'bout to be right up on ya!"

Ritter nodded obligingly and then opened the top of his briefs to inspect the damage to his groin. Suddenly, the hairs in his ears quivered as the faint crunch of grass shook them. He looked up, briefs still open, hand deeply inserted, and saw Cat standing with her hands on her hips. Despite the shock she had to have been feeling, her face showed nothing of it. She looked at him as if he were a wall of drying paint. Ritter gasped and then reached quickly for his scrub bottoms.

"Do you just not wear britches?" Cat said with disgust. Ritter held the crumpled scrubs in front of his briefs in the same manner a dog tucks its tail to cover its private parts. He then looked down, closed his eyes, and nodded his head shamefacedly.

"Well, glad to see you are at least a little embarrassed! And I am thankful that you are making an attempt to cover yourself up this time versus prancing around like a buck in my front yard! Why do you insist on walking around in broad daylight practically naked?"

Ritter looked up at the top of the porch afraid to look at her face. "Spilled my tea," he said, breaking into a giggle, which he tried to suppress with a cough.

After a quiet moment of pause, he glanced down and saw Cat's eyes dining on his exposed body. Had Ritter been able to freeze that scant bit of time, he would have. He would have walked to her statue-like body and examined her eyes so that were he to see that glimpse of desire in them again, he would recognize it.

The eyes of the two met. Cat huffed, threw up her hands, and then bent over to pick up the ear buds she had dropped. She raised, gave a last roll of the eyes and shake of her head and Ritter grinned as she once again disappeared into the backyard.

"You want some ala vira, boy?"

Ritter looked behind him to see Isaiah holding a stalk of aloe out to him. Ritter nodded in gratitude, crushed the succulent stem, and began applying the clear ooze to his burn.

"Is there no balm in Gilead? Is there no physician here?" the man said and Ritter smiled. He was still getting accustomed to the American accent, but this had been said plainly and his lack of understanding was with the message itself.

"Pardon?" he said politely and Isaiah smiled. "Oh nuthin', young feller. I know'd you was some kind of doctor and was makin' a joke." The man extended a hand and Ritter shook it as each introduced themselves.

Ritter stepped back into his scrub pants and the old man reached into his back pocket for a handkerchief. He wiped his weathered face and laughed. "She's somethin', that Cat. A real lioness! She could make a shadow move itself back ten steps!"

"I don't really know her, but she does seem rather spirited!" Ritter said with a smile.

Isaiah cackled a laugh and again wiped his brow. "Oh, she's a spirited one! That I'll give ya! Her spirit could be a whole other person in and of its own self! Yes sir-ee, Bob. You could build yourself an image of solid gold and it wouldn't compare. There is no other like her. I'm just sayin'."

Ritter tied the waist of his pants and leaned against the railing. "You seem to know her quite well," he said with a smile. "Would you care for some tea? I believe I will have to make myself another cup."

"No, I would not! I spent most of my years of WW2 in England and I didn't drink it then and I ain't fixin' on startin' it now."

"You were in England?"

The old man nodded, stuck his hands in his front pockets, snorted hard like a pig, then spit. "Ever go to Ireland?" Ritter questioned. Isaiah's face twisted and his shoulders shrugged. "Well, why would I do that?"

Ritter laughed and rubbed his still bed-tousled hair. "Well, do come in and let me fix you some coffee. Paul's just taught me how, and I need the practice."

"Naw, naw, I can't stay long. Thank ya though. Yea, Cat, she's a one and only," Isaiah continued as if the previous conversation of her had not been interrupted. "She'll bring you some peace, boy."

Ritter cocked his head like a bird. "Do I seem restless?"

Isaiah looked out toward his house. "You wouldn't be runnin' with that other girl t'otherwise. I'm just sayin'."

Ritter rubbed his chin and nodded. "Oh, yes. The *rental* as you called her."

"Yep, that's the one. I called her that just for you. I know'd you was over here peekin' out at Cat like a pheasant caught up in the brush."

"With all due respect, sir, you don't know her—"

Isaiah hooted in interruption. "Boy, I ain't got to know that dark haired girl to know she ain't Cat 'cause ain't nobody else Cat!"

Ritter shifted his stance amused at the man's boldness. "Well, perhaps you are the one that should be chatting Cat up."

"Naw," Isaiah said, as if what had been suggested were rational. "She's been set apart for you. Hopefully you will come to see that."

"And you have this on what authority?"

"The final authority." Isaiah said matter-of-factly. He then sighed and spat again. "I got plenty o' time on my hands to talk to God. What you reckon retirement's for?"

Ritter nodded trying to not laugh and be disrespectful.

"I 'magine since you were just a little, fancy-tea drinker you had your mind fixed on what the woman of your dreams would be like. And, I'm 'bout positive Cat don't fit none of that. But you mark my words, she's the one you been a' waitin' for. Yea, she's the one. Queen don't always wear a crown. Just sayin'."

Ritter stretched and interlaced his fingers behind his head. "Well, sir, even if I agreed with your theory, which I do not, we would both be amiss in not acknowledging the fact that she fairly well dislikes me!"

Isaiah shrugged. "You've given her reason to, ain't ya? And, trust me, you'll give her plenty more reasons! You'll break her heart." The old man paused, seemingly overcome momentarily by sadness. "She'll die on account of you," he whispered out of Ritter's hearing. "But," he said loudly, perking up, "she don't dislike you, young fella. She just don't like what you've let yourself become."

Ritter's eyes opened wide. "What I've become?"

Isaiah was heading back home before the words were fully born and seemed not to know anything more had been said. Ritter rubbed his forehead, folded his arms across himself, and walked out onto the driveway.

"So this nymphet has been sent by the gods to save me from myself? Is that what you're saying?"

The old man stopped walking but didn't look back. "No, boy. There ain't but one God and Cat, she ain't your savior. But, she's the divinin' rod that'll lead ya to His cleansin' waters. It is up to you whether or not you drink from that livin' fountain. And from what it seems, boy, you're fairly well parched."

Ritter's face grew serious and Isaiah turned around to see that he had his attention. "Vessel of your temptation can also bear the water of your redemption, son."

Ritter began laughing at the absurdity of all the man had said and, more so, his own intent interest in it. "Wait, wait. You have to expound upon that last 'vessel of my temptation' comment."

Isaiah turned to the side and kneeled down to pick a few stray weeds near Paul's mailbox. "What I'm sayin' is the thing that's led you so far away from what you were meant to be can be the thing that leads you back. I like ya, young feller. I want you to have peace like a river and righteousness like waves of the ocean. I wouldn't be over here carryin' on t'otherwise." The old man stood, wiped the dirt from his hands and started again for home.

"I like you too, Mr. Jenkins," Ritter called out. "Despite your audacity or perhaps because of it. And I will actually consider what you've said even if it does seem like a rubbish bit of senile rambling."

Isaiah stopped and turned with slow deliberation to look Ritter directly in the eye. He paused and looked down for a moment and sniffed. "Then there's hope for ya yet, boy. There's hope for ya yet."

CHAPTER 3
A Pony Changes the Chessboard

The old Jeep Wagoneer pulled up to Cat's house about half past seven on Friday night. Paul's adjoining yard was full of what looked to be nearly his entire rugby team, and Cat wished she could disappear into the floorboard of her truck. To make matters worse, there were about the same number of girls on Paul's porch swooning as the men tossed the rugby ball back and forth, pushing, shoving, showing the thickness of their necks and all but rubbing their antlers against the nearest tree to announce their raw *buckness*. For Cat, climbing out of the truck in front of the young mob was going to feel more like climbing out of a Dumpster.

Juan got out and headed around the front to the passenger door. He held his earth-colored hands up to one of the guys who had the ball, and it was tossed to him. He caught it and sent it back with a perfect spiral before opening Cat's door. The sight of her made him laugh. She sat there, filthy from head to toe, eyes closed and jaw foreword, readying herself for both the physically painful and ego-bruising exit from the truck.

Carefully, Juan helped her from the vehicle and the ruggers in the adjoining yard stopped their play and began wandering toward her like moths to a flame.

"What happened to you, Kit-Cat?" Paul asked, walking forward with his hands on his hips. Cat's right shoulder slumped down out of its normal plane and she cradled the injured limb at the elbow with the other arm.

"A pony threw me but luckily my shoulder broke my fall!" she huffed sarcastically.

Paul looked at her and the shoulder with concern. "Hey, let Ritter look at this . . . Rit, come here!"

"Oh no, not Captain Underpants . . . Pauley! Don't you dare!"

"What? He is an osteopath! He can set this for you!"

Cat peeked around Paul and saw the perpetually smirk-faced man wiggle out of the embrace of a girl and come toward her. It wasn't just any girl draped around him like a flesh blanket. It was Ashton Roth: the *rental* as Isaiah had put it. She was the one Cat had seen come and go quite often and, in person, her beauty was even more overwhelming. She looked like a fecund deity; the sight of her was almost too much to bear. Next to her, Cat looked more like a sixth-grade boy than a thirty-four-year-old woman.

Ritter walked up behind Paul and stood to his side with his hand on Paul's shoulder that was several inches above his own. His eyes were brighter now than they had seemed in their two previous encounters with Cat. His warm brown hair hung down on his forehead in loose, sweat-dampened curls and beads of perspiration shimmered on his nose and on the Cupid's bow just below it.

His too-red lips puckered slightly from their smirk as he spoke. "Well, we meet again. Are you stalking me?" he said in a manner that Cat assumed was deliberately seductive.

She narrowed her eyes and her lips thinned. "I'm glad to see you have pants on this time!"

"You sure 'bout that?"

"What?" Cat said while her eyes watched Paul walk away. He mouthed "sorry" out of Ritter's viewing.

"Are you sure you are happy that I am wearing trousers?"

Cat gave him a chafed look and Ritter's grin became a toothy smile. "I just want to be completely clear on the matter. You seem irritated and if it's because of my wearing trousers I can take them off . . ." Ritter began unbuttoning his pants as if acquiescing to a request.

"Okay, that's enough," Cat said with a sneer and started to walk away. Ritter began laughing. "Okay, okay, love, I apologize. Let me see that shoulder. Come on. I honestly do want to help."

Cat turned back and looked at Ritter with scrutiny. "How old are you?"

"I will be twenty-eight next week. May I . . . ?"

Cat nodded her head hesitantly and Ritter put his warm hands gently on her shoulder. "Why do you want to know my age?" he asked cutting his eyes down at her. "And, may I ask how old you are?"

Cat looked away trying to hide her embarrassment but Ritter saw it and took pleasure in it. "What is it with women and age? It's just a number," he said with a smile and shake of the head before returning all his attention to her shoulder.

After several quiet moments he sighed, "It would certainly help if I could examine you with your shirt off," just loud enough for only Cat to hear. She cut her eyes up at him quickly and saw in his face that he had not meant anything obscene. He had said it professionally and without ulterior motives. Had she looked closer, she might has seen his lips quiver for a tenth of a second as the thought of the naked line of her neck and shoulder flashed through his brain.

"So you are twenty-seven now?" Cat asked skeptically. "No, I'm actually only nineteen but plan on traveling into the future just to see what twenty-eight will be like."

He winked at Cat, and she rolled her eyes. "How do you become an osteopath by twenty-seven? Are you in residency?" she interrogated. The left side of Ritter's mouth curled upward and around, almost circling back to itself. "By being me, and no, I am not in residency. Board certified. They even gave me a little certificate with my name on it! 'Course, it's in French. Do you read French? No? Well, you'll just have to take my word for it then, won't you! I'm Ritter by the way. Ritter Thomas, DO." He narrowed his eyes at her and spoke with a deepened voice, his accent giving him a very theatrical quality. "It's like an MD but more . . . hands on," he whispered.

"I know what an osteopathic doctor is," she whispered acridly in return. "And it's a specialty concentration requiring at minimum twelve, maybe even thirteen years."

He smiled, looking away in concentration. "Well, let's just say I got a head start. You know, in the UK, osteopaths just do manipulation much like your chiropractors. In the US however," he continued, moving his hands on her shoulder as if it they had eyes of their own, "osteopaths are rather eclectic. They perform surgery, basic exams, therapy . . ."

He continued talking and Cat suddenly realized his rambling was for her benefit. She hadn't noticed the pain from the time his voice began buzzing in her ear. "But I studied in France where it is a medical degree like in the States here. Thus, the French certificate. Have you ever been to France? No? Brilliant place. My ma's extended family lives there, and I summered in Provence quite often as a lad."

Cat watched the concentration on his face. He seemed to be focusing on her with all his senses despite his talking. His head was turned as if listening to her bones speak and his eyes seemed to be taking in the view from his fingers.

When he did pause, his mouth remained open slightly as if tasting the scent of her that traveled through his nose. She was oblivious to what he had been saying but completely cognizant of what he was doing. Cat had been around animals long enough to know that they didn't simply encounter an entity; they experienced it. And that was exactly what this seductive creature was doing to her.

"I like the concept of osteopathy," Ritter continued. "It recognizes the interrelation and dependence of all the body systems on one another"—he paused, focusing intently on a spot as if nearing the end of a search for a lost item—"and enhances the body's ability to heal itself." He squinted in concentration, bit his bottom lip and his hands stopped as if having found the item for which they had been searching.

"You want this set, Ginger?"

Cat sighed hard and looked toward her house. "Yes, go ahead. And my name's not Ginger."

He smiled and put his hand tenderly on her healthy shoulder, leaning his head over in the direction of her eyes to bring her attention back to him. "I was referring to your hair color. That's what we call it in the UK. Besides, we haven't been properly introduced, so I am not sure what else to call you. Are you sure you want this set?" He tapped the bottom of her chin with his finger in an expression of what seemed to be genuine affection and concern. "It will hurt fantastically—"

She interrupted him with a raised hand, cocked her head to the side, and gave him a condescending look. "Just do it. It's been a long day."

He smiled and shook his head slightly. She was, despite her size, a formidable presence.

"Look at my eyes, okay?" he said with a soothing, hypnotic tone. Cat tried her best but couldn't maintain contact. Her eyes darted around like wild animals looking for an escape. Ritter didn't waver. His hands grabbed her securely with what she could tell was strength greatly restrained.

"On the count of three, yeah? One . . ."

He surprised her with a pop that sounded from deep within her. The pain shot sharply, nausea slid in around it, and blackness began creeping up her body like a warm blanket.

Ritter saw her pallor and quickly reached for her. "Uh-oh, easy now, Ginger, wait a minute, let me . . ."

He put his left arm around her waist to support her and lowered her to a sitting position. As he did, he saw that she winced hard before laying her back against the muddy wheels of her truck.

Cat closed her eyes for several moments and then looked over at Ritter's face in an effort to anchor herself to the present and not drift into the dark waters of unconsciousness. He sat down beside her and put his hand on her lower back, reminding her to breathe deeply and slowly. Her back was warm and small under her shirt and Ritter could feel the slightly raised line of her spine. He moved his fingers back and forth over its smooth, undulating pattern trying to comfort her and, in turn, found himself somehow soothed as well.

Cat finally came back to herself completely and tried to fill her lungs to capacity. She laughed as she exhaled, knitting her eyebrows and wincing in unison with the laughter.

"Are your ribs hurting you?" he questioned with professional and personal concern. Her eyes closed for a few seconds as his voice echoed in her brain. She then opened them, looked up at the quickly darkening, purple sky and then Ritter. His unsettling eyes seemed cerulean in the soft yellow of the streetlight that was just beginning to glow, and Cat found herself confused as to whether the near loss of consciousness, pain, or his proximity was making her feel weak.

Ritter scanned her face. She was still slightly sallow, but he noticed the color returning to her mouth. She was panting with shallow breaths through slightly parted lips and the unnatural, rhythmic movement of her chest drew his eyes.

"I think you might have a broken rib or two."

His eyes took in her subtle curves and slid down the line of her side. "No," she replied as she closed her eyes and shook her head slightly. "Just bruised."

Ritter moved his hand to her side, and she turned her face away from him. "You look like you are in some considerable pain there, Ginger."

She was. The pain in her muscles and bones paled in comparison however to what she felt in the bit of her heart that lay at the base of her throat.

"Do you mind if I have a look?" he said with a gentle bedside manner as his fingertips moved lightly over the small, rolling hills of her ribs.

With that, it all finally became more than she could bear. His dangerous closeness, his blue eyes, his touch, his warmth, the glow of the streetlight, the bruised sky, the pain . . . it all created a swirling vacuum within her, and she could feel herself sinking and spinning and becoming unhinged. She wanted to bound away like a rabbit from an ensuing predator and yet wanted badly to be ensnared so that he would catch her, devour her, and put her out of her misery.

She rolled away from him, still holding her injured arm against herself, guarding both it and her ribs. Her knees took her weight, and Juan reached down to grasp her up-reaching hand. Ritter grinned and shook his head as a parent does at an obstinate child.

"You need to have that looked at, Annie Oakley," he said as he hopped to his feet.

Cat shook her head and smiled. "No, I'm good. Really. Thank you for setting it." She nodded her head courteously and started walking slowly away from him and toward her front door.

Juan shrugged at Ritter and Ritter turned away, holding his hand up for the ball. "Fine," he said, catching it and tossing it away again. "Don't go to hospital. Then come Monday, you'll perhaps trip or have someone nudge you just right and break it through, puncturing your lung. But, hey, who doesn't need a nice chest tube and a few weeks holiday from work? And by the way, that shoulder could have a fracture as well."

His sarcastic tone grew heavier with every word, the effect being punctuated by his accent and Cat suddenly felt like a bug being crushed under a thumb. She considered what he said however, albeit bitterly, and stopped momentarily. Ritter glanced over at her and could see her face weighing his words against her stubborn will.

Cat rubbed her forehead, sighed, and threw up her uninjured arm in surrender. "Fine! I'll go!"

Ritter smiled and bounded toward her. "Here, I will take you."

"No, you won't!" she shot back, holding her hand up to stop him without even turning to look. "Juan, me puedes manejar? Great. Juan can drive me. Let me get my insurance card."

Ritter stopped with a wide stance, hands on hips, and ran his tongue up and down the inside of his cheek. This was a duel he had no intention of losing and every intention of enjoying.

"You know there is a rugby tournament that began today, right? You go to hospital urgent care and you'll be triaged for hours behind at least a dozen bleeding hooligans. Ugh." He made a sour face. "The smell should be brilliant! Oh, and don't forget that you will also be queued behind any old age pensioner and child with a runny nose. And, I think it is a full moon tonight as well, which is one of the busiest nights of the month in urgent care. I do hope your friend there has a shoulder comfortable enough to sleep on."

Cat looked back over her aching shoulder at Ritter and their eyes locked, each silently acknowledged the battle waging between them.

"Or . . . ," he said as she turned her head back toward her door. He paused and she began biting the inside of her lips in frustration, feeling herself in his crosshairs.

"You could, of course"—his voice again took a soothing tone—"just stop being a child and get in the car with me, walk straight to radiology, let me take a look, bandage you up properly, and be back home in bed in an hour and a half or so. I could tuck you in myself." He put his hands in his front pockets and rocked back and forth on his feet. "Completely up to you, my good woman. You are in charge."

Cat smiled an anguished, tight-lipped smile, feeling helpless as a turtle on its back. She needed to be looked at and were she to go to the emergency room, she would be there past midnight. She was exhausted as it was and had to be out the door by 7:00 a.m. the next morning. There was no option left for her but to surrender and accept defeat graciously.

"Fine," she groaned in a pained, subjugated tone "I still have to get my insurance card though."

Ritter smiled knowing that he had won what he hoped would be the first of many battles between them. "I'll take care of all that later, love," he said kindly. "Let me get you in the car before you change your mind!"

He opened his car door and helped her ease in slowly. She fumbled at the seat belt with her left arm and sucked in air through her teeth as her weight pushed against her right shoulder. Ritter leaned in to assist her and she closed her eyes as his smell wrapped around her like a strong-handed grip, slowly suffocating the little bit of will power that remained in her.

At the sound of the clasp, she opened her eyes. Ritter moved away from her slowly, turning his head slightly so that their noses nearly touched as he went. He inhaled her breath and his grin deepened as he exited the car and closed the door. Cat glared and exhaled a hard growl as it shut.

Paul threw Ritter's wallet and keys to him and Cat watched Ritter in the rear view mirror as he came around the back of the car. She saw him pull his heather gray T-shirt up slightly to put the wallet in his pocket. His jeans were a low-rise and hung loosely below the line of his underwear. His musculature made a deep curve in front of his hipbone down toward his jeans. She gasped to attention and looked away quickly as he opened the door.

Ritter belted himself in and started the car. He looked at her en route to looking over his shoulder and backed the car out of the driveway. The expression on her face was indecipherable, but he knew the wound of defeat was still stinging her pride. He smirked and said with a soothing tone, "You will be fine in my very capable hands."

Cat cut her eyes over at him with false disgust and he winked at her. "Said the cat to the bird," she murmured under her breath.

The car shifted smoothly and the steering wheel slid in and out of Ritter's hands. He and Cat rolled away with a low hum and the beautiful, raven-haired Ashton Roth watched as her plans for the evening drove away. Her eyes narrowed with suspicion and went slowly to Peter who was sitting in the grass and looking over his shoulder in the direction of Ritter's car. It was at that moment, seeing that familiar, deific look in Peter's eyes that the resplendent demon realized what had just transpired. The chessboard had changed. What had seemed like coincidence was the divine strategy of the offense, and Cat was the queen to be maneuvered by the King.

Ashton laughed to herself and Peter looked at her. She grinned malevolently at the angel who in return bowed his head humbly in what she could only assume was prayer. She clapped her ivory-skinned hands quietly in mocking applause to acknowledge the brilliant move and momentary defeat.

Cat. So obvious and yet so unlikely a choice. For all the hopes balanced on her small shoulders, however, Cat was nothing more to Ashton than a minor impediment—easily removed, easily destroyed.

Chapter 4

A Steady Push

The drive out of the subdivision was quiet. The inside of the car hummed like a drone as the road moaned beneath the wheels and the silent, nervous passengers suppressed the cacophony of thoughts in their heads into mute submission. The absence of noise created not only an air of awkwardness, but a heaviness that was almost deafening.

As they pulled up to a Stop sign, the two eyed a young oak tree that had been uprooted and was lying in repose. Dirt hung from its root tendrils like torn flesh off the teeth of a voracious animal.

"Look at that!" Ritter said, bravely stabbing through the quiet. "I knew we had some wind last night but I didn't realize the gusts were so forceful!"

"That wasn't caused by a gust," Cat replied softly as she looked out of the window at the torn mass of wood. "Gusts will tear a tree in two but a steady wind"—she paused, watching the brown, leafy corpse wither in size in the side mirror—"with half the strength will uproot the tree altogether."

Ritter glanced over as she said it. He then looked at the reflection of her face in the passenger window, shifted nervously in his seat and ran his hand through his hair. He had never been so uneasy around a woman. She made him feel disarmed in a way he couldn't describe. He still felt masculine and physically able in all respects but completely vulnerable at the same time. It was as if he were firmly and confidently established on his feet in the unwavering path of a juggernaut. He didn't know her. He had only spoken to her on three occasions, this night being the third, but apparently, that was enough for her to magnetize him to whatever metal she was made. It seemed the wind wasn't the only thing with a steady potency and Ritter wondered if he would meet with the same fate as the uprooted oak.

Several more quiet minutes rolled by. Ritter looked at the clock above the radio, the road ahead, all the display panels on the dashboard, and over at the little, warm, wounded thing curled up in the passenger's seat.

"So is Cat short for Catherine?" he asked. Cat continued looking out of the window and replied no in a polite tone. Ritter raised his eyebrows and ran his tongue along the backside of his top teeth looking for a mental detour after being cut off at the pass.

"Cataclysmic, perhaps?" he mumbled, not expecting her to hear. "Yes," she said flatly, and he looked at her wondering if that in fact was her name. "Well, a more fitting name there's not," he said in a low tone and heard Cat sniff. He looked over to see her suppressing a laugh.

"Well, look at that! The little princess has a sense of humor!" He nodded his head slightly. "I knew I would find a chink in the armor somewhere."

"What does that mean?" she said, feigning offense.

"It means that you are in truth not nearly as impenetrable as you appear." He saw her shake her head and he coughed out a laugh. "What's that? Do you not think you come across that way, or are you disappointed that I found a fissure to pick away at?" Cat rolled her eyes and remained silent in response.

"So, Cat, short for who knows what"—he paused realizing he didn't know her last name—"insert surname here . . . DVM, tell me about yourself."

She shrugged her good shoulder. "My last name is Douglas. And really, there is nothing to tell."

Ritter shook his head. Cat was managing to be aloof without being rude and her skillfulness at it was annoying. He wasn't frustrated that she seemed immune to the inexplicable power he seemed to have over women. He found that somehow refreshing. His irritation was based in the fact that he truly wanted to know more about her. He wanted to dissect her, put her under a microscope and observe her on a cellular level. As it was however, he would settle for simply stopping the car, turning in his seat and staring at her. And, as he looked ahead down the road, he saw that fate might provide him with just such an opportunity.

"Oh, what is this?" said Cat, obviously frustrated. A black-and-yellow sign flashed announcing roadwork being done; expect a delay of ten minutes. "Give me a break!" she sighed, closing her eyes.

"Is it so bad being in my company, Ginger?"

Cat rolled her head back and forth as if to say no, then huffed, and said, "Yes."

Brake lights began changing to parking lights and Ritter shifted the car into a resting state. Cat looked out her window at the backup ahead and when she turned back to face forward, she caught a glimpse of Ritter out of the corner of her eye. He was turned in his seat completely toward her with his right leg tucked under him. His chin was resting on his fists as if his elbows were on a desk that was about chest high.

"What are you doing?" Cat said as she jumped from surprise.

"I just want to know all about you, Cat. Start anywhere you'd like!"

Cat looked in the side mirror and shook her head. "There is nothing to tell. Turn around, traffic is starting to move."

Ritter maintained his impish position looking at her with the same cherubic grin. "Tell me something about yourself, Ginger."

Cat gestured ahead with her face. "Traffic is moving and you look very effeminate sitting like that!" Ritter didn't budge. "I embrace my feminine side. You are accustomed to people submitting to your will, aren't you?"

Cat shifted in her seat then nervously looked at the line of cars behind their car and ahead at the widening gap between them and moving traffic. "What are you doing? GO!" she begged. Ritter simply shook his head.

Cars began honking and Cat heard someone shout profanity. "Okay, okay, I will tell you whatever you want. Just go!" Ritter turned with a smile, shifted the car into drive, and it lunged ahead like a cat after a ball of yarn.

The car caught up with traffic and Cat exhaled hard in a short-lived sense of relief. "So . . . Cat . . . ," Ritter said with a comical, interrogatory inflection. Cat closed her eyes in fear of what questions he would ask.

"Okay, wait," she interrupted. "I reserve the right to not answer any questions that I deem too personal! Agreed?"

Ritter looked at her with counterfeit shock. "Cat, I am a gentleman! Surely you don't think . . ."

"Oh go on with it already!" she interrupted.

"Okay," he said as he glanced over at her and smiled. "For starters, why are you so secretive?"

She huffed in response and shifted in her seat. "I am not secretive. I just don't open up like a Sears catalog to complete strangers. Next question, please."

He laughed at her agitation and asked why she had become a horse doctor.

"I am not a horse doctor."

There was silence as he waited for her to explain further. She didn't.

"Cat, we can do this the easy way or the hard way."

"Is this the hard way now?" she huffed acridly.

He smiled then puckered his lips slightly. "You can be an acidic little thing, can't you? No, this is not the hard way. The hard way would entail me disrobing as I drive."

"Excuse me?"

Ritter took off his left shoe and sock as he spoke. "I can completely undress as I drive and I have found, strangely enough, that there is something about my naked body that causes women to do whatever I ask."

He put his left foot on the gas pedal and removed his right shoe and sock. Cat shook her head and looked out the passenger window.

"Fine with me," he said and unbuttoned his pants. "When I called it the hard way, I didn't mean for me, love."

Cat heard what he was doing, thought about the line of his hip she had seen earlier, and her face became hot. "I have seen you in your underwear twice before if you recall," she said, trying desperately to seem unfazed. "It's not as a big a deal as you seem to think it is."

Ritter paused for a moment. "I will disregard your double entendre there and I assure you this time will be different. I am wearing my Friday-night knickers now! Much sexier. Lots of lace! Besides, if memory serves, you've not seen me in the nib as I wholly intend to be in a few moments. Here, hold the wheel, ginger girl."

"What?"

"Hold the wheel please," he said as he let go. Cat leaned over quickly and gave a painful moan.

"I am sorry it had to come to this. I know you are injured and that must hurt," he said with a grunt as he lifted his shirt and began sliding his arms out. Cat instinctively looked down at his lap and saw a line of dark brown hair leading into the band of his black designer briefs. She swallowed hard and forgot about the road for an instant until she heard a horn honk.

"Okay, okay, put your shirt back on! Please!"

Ritter laughed and pulled his shirt down, taking the wheel from her. "See what I mean! Women just bend to my will somehow once the clothes start coming off!"

"Well maybe it is because they don't want to see you naked! Have you considered that?" she said loudly and, for the first time in his presence, truly angry. He smiled a smile that seemed to remember some of those women who had succumb to his wishes.

"If past actions serve as an answer to that, I will have to say that they absolutely did not behave as if they opposed to my being naked."

Cat looked away from him, hoping he would think her to be disgusted. In truth, she was trying to get a bit in the drooling mouth of her wild thoughts and block out the image of his perfect stomach that she had now seen three times too many.

"So you were saying that you were in fact not a horse doctor." Traffic had come to a standstill again and Cat could see that Ritter was a man who would get his way.

"Okay. Okay." she relented, rubbing her forehead. "I am a large animal veterinarian so I have specialized training in the care of farm animals more or less, minus exotics like emus or alpaca. I deal with cattle but also care for the horses of my godfather when necessary, as they are an important part of the ranching. However, it was a pony that gave me a jolt today not a horse. And no, they are not the same. A pony is smaller than a horse although there are some horse breeds that are smaller than ponies. Ponies have heavier coats and are, as a whole, stronger for their size and in my experience more difficult to deal with. But, for the record and in her defense, the pony from today was young and easily spooked. A bull we have that hates me, so help me he does, lunged forward against a fence and scared her. And, well, you see what happened. I don't blame the pony. I would have thrown me off too."

She finished speaking, laid her head back on the headrest, and closed her eyes. Ritter smiled. "Well, that was a terrific answer, Cat. Well done, you!" Cat rolled her eyes and he continued, "So ponies are small, sturdy, and petulant. Hmmm, this is a natural phenomenon I do believe I have encountered before, quite recently in fact. I don't know about the coat," he said, reaching over and touching her hair.

"So help me, I'll kill you if you don't . . . ," Cat said, moving her head to the side, fighting a laugh. Ritter was amusing and enjoyable to be around as dangerous as he clearly was. She wondered if fish thought the same of cats as they watched the felines dip their paws into their watery home playfully before making use of their claws.

"Do you work out of a clinic somewhere?"

"No, I work out of my home, well, truck more like it and have an office on the ranch but I am affiliated with a clinic in town. I can use their equipment if need be, but they generally use me more than I do them."

"How is that?"

"Vets can't keep wild animals in with the domesticated so if somebody brings in a hurt deer for example, it generally gets handed over to me. I get deer a lot actually."

"So how goes the day of a large animal veterinarian?" Ritter asked genuinely curious. He couldn't remember the last time he wanted to know so much about someone that didn't have something broken.

"My godfather, Cruz, is a cattleman. He has sheep too but mainly he raises organic dairy cows for a Texas-based organic grocer. I head up care for his livestock's medical needs and handle all of the breeding. I also help out with the purchase of new livestock both here and his ranch near Albuquerque. That's in New Mexico, the next state over to the west. He has several ranch managers over there, but they are still learning the ropes. I go all along to check on the health of the herd. But, as for when I am here, I can't say there is a *normal* day. Depends on the season, and even then, no two days are the same. There are some days I am up to my eyes in blood and dung, and some days, I just do grunt work!"

She paused and he looked at her. He loved her accent. It was as comical as it was charming and Ritter hoped he could keep her talking. "And where were you when I arrived two weeks ago? In New Mexico?"

"No, it's the beginning of our calving season and there were a couple dozen heifers calving for the first time so I wanted to be there. It was just easier to stay out on the ranch. It's kind of like going home anyway."

Ritter could see that she was becoming more comfortable with the conversation and he nestled down in his seat like a hen on a warm nest.

"We bred about a hundred heifers this year but there are several dozen more organic ranchers that we stud out to all over the country. We're actually doing that more and more and lightening up the milk load. That bull that lunged at me today is the top stud in Texas with a long list of prized calves. That's the only thing keeping that heinous thing alive: his looks!"

Ritter narrowed his eyes and looked at her flirtatiously. "So you breed livestock?" he said with a smile, feeling himself squeeze through her impenetrable wall.

"Yea," she said nonchalantly as if everyone bred farm animals. "But I care for the cows too."

Ritter held up his hand. "I don't care about that bit. Tell me more about the sex."

"Sorry"—Cat laughed—"no sex involved. We inseminate. You run the risk of getting an animal injured otherwise and you don't want to take that chance with productive cows."

Ritter smirked and looked in the mirrors to change lanes. "Well, if you ask me, the risk of injury is all part of the fun! Seems hardly fair to deny these animals the pleasure."

Cat realized how comfortable she had become when she giggled flirtatiously in response to his comment. She regained her composure and straightened up in her seat. "It's a science and very controlled."

Ritter heard the emphasis she put on the word *control* and saw that he had lost her a little. "Explain it to me, Dr. Douglas."

Cat scratched her nose and looked away from him. "Natural selection produces a calf, but breeding isn't just about getting a healthy calf. It's also about getting a visually pleasing animal that will sell or will turn out more good-looking cattle themselves. You don't just put any bull and cow together. They have to complement one another. You match deficiencies with attributes. If you have a cow with a back that is set a little low, you choose a bull whose back is a little high, and hopefully, you will have a calf whose back is set just right. And if you have a cow that is perfect in every way, you can match her up with a bull that is lacking in several arenas and vice versa." She smiled and paused for a moment in thought. "All a flawed animal needs is the right mate."

Ritter's face fell a little as he pulled into the parking lot of the hospital. "So it's not always the handsome bull that gets the fit cow, eh? What side of the spectrum would you say I fell on, Cat? Which type of bull would I be on your ranch?"

He smiled as he looked for a parking spot, eagerly awaiting her answer. Cat looked away trying to hide her grin. "A castrated one."

"That I don't doubt for a moment," Ritter laughed, "and I will bear that in mind."

"Your girlfriend is beautiful." The words jumped out of Cat's mouth to her own mortification. She had no idea where they had come from and wished desperately they could be called back like a dog to its owner. Ritter shrugged, neither agreeing nor disagreeing. He turned into a spot reserved for physicians and looked over at Cat. "Ashta's not my girlfriend."

Cat paused a second and added, "You seem very comfortable with her." The sentence was well punctuated by the expression on her face and she immediately caught herself from further stating, "And her body." Something about this man was like hard liquor to her brain and she had completely lost control of her mouth.

Ritter looked out his passenger window and smirked, biting the inside of his cheek. He then cleared his throat before saying, "I would say I am."

The car was turned off and Ritter grabbed his ID from the center console. Cat caught a glimpse of the picture and narrowed her eyes as she read. "R. J. Thomas. What's the *J* for?" she asked.

He smiled and looked down at the ID. "Jacob. And, the *R* is for Reed. Ritter is a nickname my dad gave to me. Well, in a roundabout way. I'll tell you about it some time. That is, if you bless me with an audience again, your highness. No, wait, I'll help you out. Stay there."

He walked to her door cavalierly and helped her out. "You okay?" She nodded her head in affirmation and shivered slightly as the warmth of his hand spread out on her lower back. "You shouldn't have to open the door for yourself," he said in a genuinely kind voice. She looked up at him after he said it and he winked at her. Cat felt like a kid next to him even though she knew she was in college before he had barely hit puberty.

The two walked slower than Cat needed but Ritter had set the gait and she was happy to comply since walking was the last thing on her mind. She was distracted by the pain, the company, and the questions that buzzed around in her head like a mad swarm of bees. Of one thing there was no question: she was attracted to him. He was intelligent, charming, and easy to be around. He made her laugh, made her talk, and in doing both of those, he made her feel beautiful as well. That was a task no other man had been able to accomplish since her husband had been killed.

"Are you okay?" Ritter asked and stopped walking. Cat looked up at him and wondered if he could see her thoughts on her face. "Yea, I'm good."

She sniffed, looked down in embarrassment and he tapped the end of her boot with his shoe. "You seem preoccupied. You've nearly stumbled three times since getting out of the car. Are you hurting?"

"Uh-huh. Good," she replied without thinking. Ritter poked her chin playfully and then ran his finger from her chin down the line of her jaw.

"I'm confused," he laughed. "Are you in pain or not?"

"What? Oh, I'm fine," she said, looking up at him wide-eyed as a second shiver ran through her body, jolting her back to the present.

Ritter smiled seeing that an opportunity to kiss her had openly presented itself without restraint from her. In most cases he would have taken it and he surprised himself in not doing so. The kiss would have been an effortless precursor and what would follow would presumably have been an easy feat for him. She seemed willing and he was able. However, there was some unseen force restraining him from his normal seductions and demanding of him what no other woman had: righteousness.

The couple reached the doors of the ER and each successfully suppressed their disappointment with having to share the other with the rest of the world. "Radiology is just down the corridor from here," he said. "But I would just like to take a moment to point out from what I have saved you tonight!"

Through the glass, Cat could see the room full of injured rugby players of all sizes, several children, and two or three people over the age of sixty-five. "Thank you," she said with a sigh that showed her resignation to his being right.

Her phone rang and she looked at the caller ID. "Oh, let me get this."

"Okay," he said, "I will run in and see how busy radiology is."

He walked inside and the phone rang three more times before Cat realized that she had forgotten all about it. She made a quick exclamation of frustration, opened the phone, and watched Ritter glide gracefully like a snake on water to the ER reception desk.

Cat's godfather asked about her injury and Cat spoke to him with a smile, still slightly intoxicated by Ritter's presence. She rubbed her eyes, looked down at her dirty clothes and then back into the ER to see Ritter leaning toward a blond and giggling receptionist. The girl, who was far younger and prettier than Cat, was leaning forward as well. Ritter whispered something to her that caused her to blush. He then playfully poked her chin just as he had Cat's not five minutes earlier.

Cat's heart leapt up into her throat. "Let me call you when I get home. Okay? Yea. Love you too, Papá. What? Yea, yea, estoy bien. Más o menos. Bye."

She closed her phone and felt the muscles of her stomach tighten as if her insides were wincing. Ritter's back was toward Cat, but she could tell by the nature of the wanton look on the blonde's face that he was giving her reason to look at him that way. It was the same reason he gave all women to look at him that way.

Cat's face went pale, and she caught a glimpse of herself in the glass of the ER doors as they opened and closed for patients. She felt like an idiot. She had been effortlessly lured into his den and she was so comfortable there she failed to see the scattering of bones around her.

The blonde giggled again and Ritter leaned far enough to put his weight on the counter. Cat saw the muscles of his shoulders move under his shirt and, for the first time, saw him for what he was: a predator.

Ritter looked back at Cat and an expression of concern washed over his countenance. He turned, without even a parting gesture toward the blonde, and started back toward the door. His gait was as fluid and easy as before. His eyes were still brilliantly blue. The whole of him had not lost any of its seduction but Cat now saw it for the ruse it was.

The flirtatious smirk that seemed to live constantly on his face now struck her as a malevolent snarl despite his wagging tail and down turned ears. She knew he would look at her lovingly and lick her face but only to get a better look at what place would be the most convenient to tear into. He would leave her for scraps without hesitation or remorse. She would become yet another pile among the many bones in his lair.

"Cat? Hey, is something wrong? Was it the call?" He brought his hand up to her face, and she turned her head away. "Cat? Hey. Hey! Look at me."

She obliged his request and he could see that the fire that had kindled in her golden eyes had turned to white ash. "Did something happen?" he questioned with sincere concern. "Cat? Look at me a sec. Are you seeing well? Your pupils are a bit dilated."

Cat sniffed and replied with a pleasant and unemotional tone, "I am seeing clearer now than I have seen all night."

With that, she walked through the open doors of the hospital and her heart pulled itself back into the safety of its shell.

Chapter 5
Prayers for Prey

Within thirty minutes, Cat was standing in a scrub gown, dusty jeans and boots and was being fitted with a lead apron. The x-ray technician, Hank, said from the looks of her a child size would be best. He was right. Even at her most optimistic, Cat was barely five feet tall.

The right shoulder of the apron was left open and the edge tucked under so that the entire right side down to the pelvic bone could be captured. Cat looked down at her chest and was embarrassed at the subtle point of her prepubescent breast pronounced against the thin cloth of the hospital gown. She closed her eyes and slouched, hoping to make the contour less visible and wished she had just stayed home and taken her chances. A collapsed lung and chest tube weren't seeming so bad at the moment.

Hank put a panel in behind Cat and positioned her carefully. He asked if she were able to stand still for a few moments comfortably and when she consented that she could, he and Ritter left the room. Within a matter of moments a click sounded and Hank's voice echoed over the loudspeaker. Although in the necessary paperwork Cat had indicated she was not pregnant, it was hospital policy to ask verbally as well. She looked up at the glass enclosed control area and shook her head. Ritter immediately grabbed the microphone.

"Now, Ginger, he is not asking if you are on birth control or have been *extra careful*," he said making quote gestures with his fingers as he spoke. "He needs to know, and you need to be honest, are you sexually active because if so, you could be pregnant. Unless you are menstruating now? When was your last menses?"

Cat gave Ritter a look that could have left a mark, and Hank reached out to turn off the loudspeaker. "I am just looking out for you, love." Ritter's muted voice yelled from behind the glass.

After a few moments, Cat faintly heard Ritter's voice. "On the count of three take a deep . . ." "Wrong room, Doc!"

Cat heard a click, and the voices echoed above her. "Oh, sorry, can you hear me now?" Cat rolled her eyes at Ritter's voice and he took the gesture as affirmation to his question.

"Give me that!" the tech said, pushing the doctor aside. "Sorry, ma'am, this office controls the MRI in the adjoining room as well. Okay, on the count of three, take a breath and hold it. One, two, three . . . good."

Hank walked back toward Cat with a new panel under his arm. "You okay?" Cat smiled and said that she was fine. Hank returned the expression politely.

"Okay, just relax. It will take me a minute or two to get ready for the next image. Oh, do you mind if I leave the door to the MRI room open? It gets hot in here. If someone comes in over there, I will close it right away. They would enter through the front of the room and never see you so don't worry."

Cat consented without hesitation and Hank nodded appreciatively before returning to the control room. The sound of the door closing behind him echoed strangely from the MRI room and within a matter of seconds, Cat found out why. The speaker to her room was turned off but the speaker in the next room that Ritter had turned on in error had been forgotten. The two men's voices were clearly audible to her through the opened door.

"So, Ritter, I heard about you getting caught in the supply closet with what's-her-name! What is her name?"

Ritter shrugged in response and the two laughed. "Yea, a bloody janitor walked in on us! I can't believe I didn't lock the door!" Ritter ran his fingers through his hair and shook his head thinking about the unsecured door. A "virgin error" he called it. "I gave the bloke a hundred dollars to keep his pie hole shut!"

Hank stopped typing and gawked. "A hundred! Did you offer less to begin with or . . . was it worth it?"

Ritter nodded looking at some paperwork. "Worth it. I wish I had caught her name."

The two men laughed heartily and then Hank looked up at Cat to gesture that it would only be another minute.

"Oh, by the way, good Doctor, I have to thank you for Ashta!" "Work you over, did she?" Ritter laughed. Hank paused from typing and leaned back in his chair, covering his face with his hands and then stretching like a lion after a meal. What followed was a sexually explicit description of an interlude between Ashton and Hank and the two men comparing notes on her.

Cat made a subtle expression of disgust then heard the speaker in her room click. "Okay, Dr. Douglas, hold it," Hank said, still breathless from laughing. "Got it. You can relax."

The speaker above Cat was turned off, but voices continued to ring in the adjoining room. She heard Hank question the *unattractive expression* she had made and then crudely ask Ritter how many women he been with since having moved to the States. Ritter shrugged and said that a gentleman never told such things. Especially if he had lost count.

Hank made a gesture of salute then asked whether the nature of Ritter's relationship with Cat was carnal.

"She is my neighbor. I barely know her, of course, that has never deterred me before."

"How old is she? Forty?" Hank asked with a slight air of disgust. Cat closed her eyes, wishing they would notice the speaker was on. She was in too much pain physically and from embarrassment to point it out herself.

"Forty! She doesn't look forty!" Ritter replied defensively.

"Whoa, Doc, didn't mean to offend you or anything. I just don't know why you would give her the time of day. You've got Ashta!" Hank laughed and then made a gesture of grandeur with his hands. "I mean, come on! That boney chick's basically a boy in comparison! How could you want that?"

Cat's eyes filled with tears and she hunched forward even more hoping just to disappear within the lead apron and over-sized hospital gown.

Ritter paused and thought about Cat's body. He couldn't answer Hank honestly as to why he was attracted to her. It was based on something entirely different than just physicality. What, he didn't know.

He looked up at the small injured woman then back at Hank, smiled, and said wickedly, "Well, I will admit, I prefer a little more flesh between my teeth."

He was being truthful. He liked the feel of Ashton and the countless other well-formed women he had been with and, to the world's standards, Cat was not as attractive physically as they were. Nevertheless, something about her was, to Ritter, alluring to the point of engrossing and didn't seem to originate from this world.

The two men walked out to ready Cat for the x-rays of her ribs. Hank demonstrated how he wanted her to stand. "Inhale real deep and make your chest like a barrel, as much as you can without hurting yourself, and hold it."

Cat thought about her small right breast pushed out and the jokes that would certainly follow. Even if they realized the speaker was on and turned it off leaving her unable to hear them, their previous conversations gave her a legitimate idea of the things that would be said.

"Okay, ma'am, move back here so that this target is on the middle of this right side here . . ." The light from the x-ray machine put crosshairs through the midline of her right pectoral muscle. The line on the vertical axis cut directly through the center of her breast and she could see a slight wave in the fabric of her gown over the small knot. A lump formed in her throat. "That's enough. I'm done," she said quietly and walked away.

The two men exchanged a confused look, and Ritter ran toward her. "Give us a moment, Hank." Hank smiled and shook his head as he walked back to the office.

"Cat?" Ritter said, gently grasping her left arm to stop her. He walked in front of her and saw her wet face. "Mary and Joseph, woman. What is wrong?"

She folded her left arm over her chest and put her head down. "Come here," he said as he put his arm behind her back and rubbed it. "You've had a night, haven't you? I can see you are in pain, but I really need to look at your ribs."

Cat laughed in response and wiped her face. "Oh, I am skinny enough you could just hold a flashlight up to me to see if anything is broken."

Ritter smiled at her curiously and wiped her cheeks. "You're just a small person, love. I don't think you are skinny! You are perfect!"

Cat laughed and wiped her nose. "You sure about that? I could have sworn you preferred a little more flesh between your teeth."

The drive home from the hospital began as quietly as had the drive to it but, for far different reasons. Hank noticed the loudspeaker left on in error and any questions the men had regarding Cat's behavior was immediately answered. A female technician from the ER finished the x-rays.

Ritter chewed his bottom lip as he drove, thinking of the x-ray images. He had seen evidence of massive trauma to Cat's right pectoral girdle and collarbone. Four ribs had required surgical intervention to set, as had the upper portion of her arm. The scapula had been injured in such as way as to suggest, more likely than not, a penetrating trauma like a bullet wound. Her collarbone had been repaired surgically as well and because of the similarities in all of the traumas, it was easy to assume that they had all occurred at once. Ritter had mentioned none of that to Cat as the two looked at the images together, only the small hairline fracture that ran along the last of her true ribs.

Cat sat with her legs drawn to her chest, resting on her left side toward Ritter. A sling was around her neck and immobilized her right arm against her side to protect the shoulder that had been dislocated. She wrapped the uninjured arm around herself as well. Her eyes were closed and her expression denoted peace, but Ritter was certain she was in pain. He appreciated however the position she had taken to ease her discomfort as it afforded him an unobstructed view of her face. He looked at it as often as possible for not only evidence of distress but also any sign that would help him better understand the effect she had on him.

The silence in the car was without hostility but guilt hammered against the walls of Ritter's chest. As he began to speak, Cat interrupted.

"I was what people used to call a crowing baby. I made a funny sound with my exhalation as I slept. My daddy thought it sounded like the mewing of a kitten and started calling me his kitten. That was actually what I was called for almost a week until a name was decided on. Anyway, Kitten became Kitty Cat and then Cat."

Ritter looked over at her and smiled. "I thought it was perhaps your eyes." Cat smiled and nodded. Her almond shaped eyes were slightly upturned and a curious golden color. People often assumed that the nickname was in reference to them. She smiled and opened them slightly to glance out at the highway. The passing lights cast a glow on them and Ritter could see that she had shed a few tears that had escaped his view.

"The eye doctor said they are hazel with a low level of blue pigmentation."

"Does that run in your family?"

Cat was silent for a moment and then quietly replied, "I don't know. My father's eyes were green. Very green."

Ritter noticed that she used the past tense. "And what about your mother?"

Cat shifted slightly and grunted. "I don't know. What about you? Whose eyes do you have?"

Ritter smiled. "My father's. Cat, I'm so sorry about tonight," he interjected with soft desperation.

Cat closed her eyes. She had hoped nothing would be said about it. "Would you have said those things if you had known I could hear you?"

"Of course not," Ritter replied in a serious tone.

"It's okay. I forgive you, Reed. You didn't know what you were doing. I should have spoken up."

Ritter stopped at a traffic light and tapped his thumbs nervously on the steering wheel. He tried to remember the conversation with Hank but couldn't recall specifics other than the phrase Cat had repeated to him. He didn't think he had said anything disparaging about her. There was nothing to say. She was older and far thinner than he preferred but still the only adjective that came to mind as he looked at her was *perfect*.

"I think you are a beautiful girl, Cat."

She sighed and rolled her eyes. "Don't do that. I am not your type and that's fine. You don't have to lie about it."

"I am not lying to you. I may be a salacious piece of work, but I am not a liar."

"I never said you were any such thing, Reed."

Ritter looked over at her and swallowed hard. "I just wish you had not heard those things, Cat."

"Which things?"

Ritter rolled his eyes. "Any of it but especially my . . . abominations," he said sarcastically with an uncomfortable laugh.

"I'm not bothered so much that I heard. I'm sad that you did them."

Ritter ran his tongue along the inside of his cheek and sighed in relief as the car pulled into Cat's driveway. Being with her was akin to how one feels after surfacing the water when all air in the lungs has been depleted: frantically grateful and completely exhausted.

He turned off the engine and noticed Cat looking at Ashton's car that was still parked on the curb. "I am serious about your taking it easy for a while. It is a small fracture but nonetheless needs time to heal. You should stay in bed and not attend your function tomorrow."

"Well, I told you, Doctor Thomas, I can't. I am speaking at a cattleman's breakfast. Not attending, speaking, and before you offer again, thank you but no, I don't want any pain medication. I can't very well speak with a hangover. Does she know how you feel about her?"

Ritter was caught off guard by the change of subject and looked at Cat who had not taken her eyes off the car parked on the curb. "Who, Ashta?" He could see by the look on Cat's face that she was worried for the girl's feelings.

"Yea, you said you two weren't dating and your friend Hank . . . I just wonder if she honestly knows how you feel or how little you feel I guess."

Ritter looked out his window, saw his reflection in his side view mirror and quickly looked away from it. "Look, Cat. I don't mean to discredit your judgment, but I think in this instance you have mistaken the predator for the prey."

Cat continued looking at the car and Ritter saw her eyes drift to Paul's house where they both knew Ashton was waiting for him. "So she is a predator?" Cat questioned in a contemplative tone.

Ritter laughed. "Oh, most certainly and of the most dangerous sort."

Cat's amber eyes went to him and his heart shuddered. "So what are you then? Prey?"

Ritter raised his eyebrows and exhaled hard. "And there it is! Let me help you out," he said, as he opened his door.

He helped Cat from the car and the two made their way toward her door. "Ashta," he said as they walked slowly, "I don't know how else to say it but plainly. She values sex as a gratifying expenditure of time but little more. If a person chooses to worship at the altar of her body, she sees no reason to deny them or herself. She sees whomever she wants for whatever reason she chooses. Love has nothing to do with it. Feelings have nothing to do with it. She doesn't hurt anyone in the process so, no harm no foul, yea?" He shrugged and smiled, hoping to assuage the tension he saw in Cat's forehead.

"But what about you? Is that all sex is for you? Or that girl you had sex with in the closet, did that mean anything to her? Didn't sound like you knew. You might have really hurt her."

Ritter sighed and laughed slightly, putting his hands in his pockets. Cat's front porch was dark and he was thankful. He didn't want to see her face and he certainly did not want her to see his. He hoped her eyes weren't as reflective as they seemed. They looked as if they could cut through the darkness and see him plainly down to his soul.

"You've certainly opened up," he said, changing the subject and leaning against her door facing. Cat shrugged. "I'm too tired to be otherwise."

"So you have kept up your defenses until now?"

Cat laughed and sighed. "I guess so, yea."

Ritter nodded and looked back at Ashton's car. "Well, since you have your guard down, why were you so angry with me after your phone call in front of the hospital? You practically crushed the tiles underneath you to rubbish on our way to Radiology."

Cat rubbed her forehead and sat down on the glider next to her front door. She looked at her feet and shook her head. "I mistook your professional kindness for attraction and, when I saw you flirting with the ER receptionist, I just felt kind of stupid and jealous. I was mad at me more than you."

Ritter raised his eyebrows and folded his arms over his chest. "Well, that was brilliantly honest."

Cat laughed and shrugged her good shoulder. "I always tell the truth. I'm not accustomed to anything else really. There's no lying in the animal kingdom and that's where I spend most of my time."

Ritter traced a line on the cement with the toe of his shoe. "Lying is a frustrating human function," he said wistfully. "I am woefully honest as well, sometimes to my own detriment. My ma calls it my greatest *faultribute.*"

Cat rose and stood opposite Ritter and looked at him with sincere compassion. "Then why are you living like this?"

Ritter coughed in shock. "What?"

"Why are you living this way?"

"What are you talking about? What way?"

Cat reached out and took his hand in hers. "You are worth a whole lot more than the way you live your life."

Ritter took his hand away and paced uncomfortably looking at Ashton's car. "Cat, I haven't a clue as to what you are referring. I live the life most men only dream."

"Then why did you refer to it as an abomination? You said you hated I overheard those things and I said what things and you said any of those things especially your abominations. You called yourself salacious."

"I didn't call my whole life an abomination, and bloody hell, Cat, it was just talk!"

His tone stopped the conversation and he ran his hand through his hair angrily. "I am sorry. I didn't mean to be coarse," he said with a sigh, walking back to her and resuming his original roost opposite her at the door.

"Reed, your head may consider it just talk, but your soul spoke plainly."

"Oh, okay, your holiness . . ." Ritter turned his head away and Cat's hand reached out and touched his chest. The touch startled him slightly and he looked down at her from beneath his veil of feigned confidence.

It was then, seeing the vulnerability in his eyes, she realized that her earlier estimation of him was not correct. He wasn't a predator in a constant, hungry state of chase. He was a wounded beast biting in response to the confusion and fear that only pain can give an animal.

"I am sorry you are hurting. There is nothing that can't be healed, Reed. I'm living proof."

Ritter's hand grasped hers and he pulled it to his nose and smelled her. His chest caved in slightly with emotion and he quickly released her. He then reached into his wallet and pulled out a business card.

"If you don't feel well at all, call me. My work mobile is my personal mobile as well, so you can reach me anytime. I can still get you something for pain . . ." He paused, thumbing the business card, then looked at her seriously. "Cat, how'd you get so bashed up like that? Your arm, ribs, and whatnot? Were you in an accident? What happened? Did some one do that to you?"

She smiled, looked up, and then back to his face. "I'll tell you what left me like that when you tell me what left you like this." She tapped his heart as she said it and Ritter laughed.

"Oh, you are going to be the death of me," he said with a smile as he handed her his card. He looked at his hands, then feet, bid her good night and began to walk away.

"Thank you, by the way, Reed. I don't think I have even said that. I'm sorry. And, I know I was petulant, as you said, and I'm sorry for that as well I guess. I am very grateful to you for going out of your way for me tonight. And I'll pray for you. Prey needs prayers," she said with an uncomfortable smile.

Ritter stopped and saw Ashta walk out on Paul's porch with her greed glossed lips and hungry smile. Ritter looked at her for a moment and then turned and walked back to Cat stopping just inches away. Had he known what life had in store for them and how quickly death would rip Cat from his world, he would have kissed her, gathered her up in his arms, and secreted her away into the night. He would have guarded her the way a wild animal guards its last bit of life sustaining food and hissed murderously at anything with breath that dared to step close. As it was however, he swallowed hard and put his hand on his chest trying to keep his heart within its flesh and bone enclosure.

"You were right and you were wrong, Dr. Douglas. I set your shoulder purely out of professional courtesy. But I drove you to the hospital because I was, am, attracted to you." He shook his head and pushed her hair from her eyes. "You are not my type of woman." She looked down, and he raised her chin back up to him. "But I think you should be."

The light caught Cat's eyes and Ritter could see her looking intently into his. "I'm not ever going to sleep with you, Reed." Ritter closed his eyes and laughed at her. He then pulled her head to his chest and kissed the top of it. "Oh, woman. You'll kill me for certain."

He adjusted her sling, restated his instructions about putting it on and how long to wear it and then took the keys from her hand and opened her door for her. "Call me if you need anything, Ginger. Or if you don't." She nodded and bit her bottom lip to keep from making a smile that would betray her efforts to hide her attraction.

"Thank you again, Reed."

"Thank you, Cat. And hey, nice to meet you, finally."

Ritter smiled, reached out and took a bit of the hem of her shirt and then looked at her, wishing she would invite him in to curl up with her. Instead, she wished him good night, removed his hand from her clothes, gave his palm a last squeeze and shut the door.

He stood there a moment and his smile quickly left him. A part of him wanted to stay there on her porch and bed down for the night hidden in the darkness like a stray dog fleeing from danger. He laid his forehead on her door and caressed the grain of the wood with his fingertips. He knew he was on the threshold of more than a house but of what else, he wasn't certain.

Ashta knew. Anger churned in her hollow chest and she called out to him to shorten her length of leash around his neck. And, with the slight, effortless action of a turn, Ritter left the safety of Cat's porch and went instinctively into the waiting arms of Ashta Roth.

CHAPTER 6

Hope Flies the Coop

Cat started the shower and began the arduous task of taking off her clothes. The pain had steadily increased throughout the night and she found the removal of each piece of clothing more exhausting than the last. She sat naked on the cool edge of the bathtub and closed her eyes to rest momentarily.

The fog from the shower sat like a dreamy mist on the ceiling, and her mind immediately went to Reed. She inhaled deeply trying to find any notes of him that might have clung to her face and skin. She could still feel his heat against her cheek and she imagined that he was there with her holding her face against his bare, warm chest. It had been so long since a man had held her. She gasped uncontrollably with a welling of emotion and a pain shot through the injured muscles in her side.

Her tired body slowly brought itself to standing and Cat looked up at her naked form in the bathroom mirror. She had always been a small woman—small in stature and structure. However, she had not always been as thin as she was now. She had lost fifteen pounds after she and her husband were attacked and, over the years since, she had not been able to reclaim any of those. Grief had left her rawboned as a scar of sorts, a constant reminder of that night. With a single bullet, the fleshiness of her youth had been forever lost.

She thought of Ashta and the girl at the ER desk who also seemed very *familiar* with Reed. Life had not left either of them threadbare. On the contrary, life seemed to boast itself in their fecund curves.

Cat put her hands on her hips and tried to stand as upright as pain would allow, pushing out her chest and pulling in her nonexistent stomach trying to imagine Ashta's full breasts and hips on her small frame. She was suddenly overwhelmed with jealousy and coveted the woman's youth, form, and easy access to Reed Thomas.

After a few moments, she released her pose with a sigh and grimaced at the sharp ache in her side and heart. She was fooling herself. What could a man like him see in an effete form like hers when curvaceous nymphs surrounded him and begged for his attention? Never mind that she was seven years older than he and every month of it showed on her face.

Humidity clouded over the last bit of her reflection in the mirror until all that remained was a flesh colored blur. At that point, her body looked much like anyone else's, threadbare or not. An amused smile crept across her lips as she considered walking to the mirror and drawing in an edited version of herself.

"Forgive me, Lord," she laughed, returning to her senses. "I have more than I could have ever hoped for and am complaining over a handful of inches. Well, maybe more than a handful. Couple yards more like it."

Cat ran her hands over her hips then looked down at herself and the scars on her side, arm, and lower abdomen. She was grateful for being alive although, there were days she wished God had taken her home with her husband instead of leaving her behind. Her fingers traced the caesarian scar, another consequence of that night, and she smiled wondering if her little girl would have had her daddy's unruly dark curls. Her nourishment on many grief-stricken nights had been the knowledge that one day, she would know.

She eased herself down into a sitting position in the shower and let the soothing water run down the line of her back. She closed her eyes and let the warmth spread over her like a blanket. Her toes wiggled and she looked at their polish that shined under the lights. Water swelled in beads on the crimson lacquer like drops of blood and Cat's mind went back to that night. She remembered the ruby spattering of her husband's blood on her ivory feet and how similar in color it was to the polish now on her toes.

It was never a violent image on TV or report of a similar crime in the paper that took her mind back to that evil night. Rather, it was simple, seemingly inconsequential things like colors, shapes and sounds. And, although it was darkness and death that consumed that evening, the few glimpses of light within it were what most often poured through her brain like sunlight through a storm-torn roof. She smiled as she thought of her husband resting his face on her belly and his eyes widening as the baby kicked upward just moments before the back door was kicked down. She remembered vividly the look of peace on his face as he accepted his fate and the hope in his eyes as he spoke his last words: "I love you, wife. Close your eyes." The pistol report cut his third statement short, but she knew him well enough to know what it would have been. "See you soon."

Cat dried herself slowly and then lied down in bed in just her underwear. The cool sheets felt good on the skin of her tired body. Her late husband had hated cold sheets. It was a nightly ritual for him to complain of being chilly until she rolled to his side and snuggled against him. He would then put his arms around her, pinch a bit of her fat, and say she was his hundred-pound hot-water bottle. Her cat, Beau, often slept in that cold portion of the bed now. More than once she had awakened on that side with the cat stretched out completely along her bodyline, wrapped in her arms.

Cat reached out her warm hand to run across her husband's cold, empty pillow and she winced. It suddenly occurred to her that she had not taken anything for the pain. If she didn't take something tonight, she wouldn't be able to sleep and subsequently far worse off in the morning.

She tied the belt of her robe around her loosely, walked into the kitchen and saw the business card Reed had given her before she went inside for the night. She picked it up from the counter, flipped it over without thinking, and noticed he had written on it. "Cat, call if you need anything. Ever.—R." He had also written a personal e-mail address on it. She smiled and rubbed the card between her thumb and index fingers and then tapped it against her lips. She wondered at what point in the night he had written that. He had taken the card from his wallet as if it were an afterthought.

"Hmmm," she said to her massive cat that had launched himself up on the cabinet. "He's a sneaky little weasel." The semiserval feline rubbed his toothy mouth against her chin hard and chattered a reply. Cat grinned, returned the affectionate caress then returned the card to the counter.

She poured herself a glass of milk and as she drank the first sip looked at the back door and remembered how deliciously perfect the night was. She stepped out into the screened patio and looked out at the moon as the temperate evening ran its hands over her skin. Despite the physical and mental pain incurred during the day, it had been a very good day, and she hoped she would see more of her new neighbor.

The thought of Reed caused her to smirk. She giggled to herself, brought the glass of milk to her mouth and froze in mid-gulp. Sounds from the neighboring yard, that neither she nor anyone else should have heard, reverberated in her ears like shattering glass. It was Reed's voice, and it shook as if his body were being rocked.

"Oh! Ow, that's it! Yes, there is it! Marry me! Marry me now, you dark-haired beauty . . ."

Cat choked on her milk and her body immediately froze like a deer's after seeing a flash of hunter's orange. The voice quieted and she heard movement in the grass of the neighboring yard. As quickly as able, she scampered back into her house, shut the door quietly behind her and stood in shock. She didn't know whether to scream in anger or cry with heartbreak. Had she not been so sore, she might have sunk down where she was in a pile of tears and slept until her godfather, cat, or Jesus decided to wake her.

The cold sheets of her bed embraced her sympathetically as Cat pulled them tightly around her. "Give me strength, Lord," she prayed. "Give me strength to stay away from him. Forgive Reed for the thing he has become and forgive me for wanting such a thing in my life!"

She then turned out the light and curled up on her side. The strength that remained in her bones spilled out in tears and with a sigh, the bit of hope that had begin to nest in her heart was flushed out.

CHAPTER 7
From Scratch

Ritter closed the sliding glass door but continued looking over his shoulder at the fence that separated him from Cat. He was certain he had heard a cough but before he was able to look over the fence to speak to her, a door sounded itself closed and Cat was gone. Again.

He tapped the cold, smooth mouth of his beer bottle against his warm lips and thought about the few moments he had spent with Cat on her porch. The incandescence of the yellow streetlight in front of her house had reacted with her eyes like flint against rock. The resulting spark had been like everything else about her: mesmerizing. He was not a man for regrets but having not kissed her would be a decision that would sit on his lips like a stinging welt.

Paul glanced into the den and saw Ritter standing at the sliding glass door, transfixed, with his bottom lip sucked down into the mouth of the amber-colored bottle. He laughed and the sound of a voice broke his housemate's trance. With a soft but deep *shwuck* noise, Ritter quickly pulled his mouth free.

"Why do you suppose she went back inside?" he wondered aloud.

"Because you were carrying on like an idiot, RJ! She probably thought you were having sex," Paul huffed. He then narrowed his eyes and shook his head. "Dude, what are you doing to yourself?" he laughed. Ritter had pulled out his bottleneck-sore bottom lip and was inspecting it like a monkey.

Ritter paused a moment, then continued his simian self-inspection while considering what Paul had said. Cat knew Ashta was at his house when they returned from the hospital. She had also heard him unabashedly admit, albeit inadvertently, to his hyper-carnal nature. How could she not think the noises he was making in response to Paul rubbing his shoulder were anything but sexual?

Ritter put his hand on top of his head and rubbed it down his face. "Well, it would bloody well go along with the night that's for certain." He rolled his eyes, resigning himself to the horrible impression he had given Cat, and threw himself down onto the recliner. "Thank you for popping my shoulder back into place" he said with a grunt. "Just pops herself out now and again. I really should go to hospital and see an orthopedist about this someday. And hey, I meant what I said, Paulette, I would marry you today if you would have me, you raven-haired vixen, you."

Paul shook his head and then looked in the refrigerator. "Oh, that reminds me," he said with a tone that announced impending sarcasm, "thanks for leaving Ashta behind tonight!"

He closed the refrigerator door harshly, went back into the den, stood with his hands on his hips and made it clear in no uncertain terms that Ashta was not to be in the house without Ritter. "If you aren't here, she isn't here! Got that? I don't know how you can get that point across to her but do it! And quit smiling, man, I am serious as a heart attack!"

"You mean a stroke, don't you?"

Paul's eyes narrowed and his fists clenched. "RJ, I, look at me, I did not have a stroke! You may be a doctor, but I am the one that went blind, and I know what I saw while I was blind."

Ritter sat up and raised his hands in surrender. "Fine, fine. Let's not get started on that course. I'll take care of Ashta. Honestly, I had no idea she would wait for me. Why do you dislike her so much anyway? She's been nothing but amiable to you."

"No, she has been *inviting*," Paul said wryly. "That's not the same thing and I don't want any part of her! I don't know why you do. That chick's just dark. Yea, she's hot and all," he said, walking back to the kitchen. "But I'm telling you, RJ, it's the kind of hot that will get you burned!"

Paul returned to the den and threw a bottle of water to Ritter. "Do you not see the way she looks at you? It's like she is hunting you and preparing to tear you to shreds!"

"And that she does, Paulette ole girl. That she does," Ritter replied before taking a long slow drink of water.

Paul grabbed the remote and channel surfed for a moment. "You love her?" he said with a side ways glance to his housemate. Ritter choked in response, beat his chest, and then belched. "I'll take that as a no. So why are you with her? RJ, you can have any girl you want. You get any girl you want for crying out loud. You're a famous doctor."

"Not famous," Ritter interrupted between sips.

"You were featured in the British Journal of Medicine!"

"It's the British Medical Journal."

"Whatever! You were featured in it! Twice! What do you call that?" Ritter rolled his eyes in response and Paul shook his head. "Okay, RJ, fine, take famous out of the equation. You are a rich, single doctor that isn't completely disgusting to look at! I mean, you aren't Greek or anything," Paul said with a smile, pointing to himself, "but still, you're not a total butter face. And, you have that dorky accent that American girls are way into. Any girl! You can get any girl! Why her? And I am willing to bet, no, not bet, I know full well you have a few on the side other than her, so why is she the one that you are always with?"

"Could I get Cat?"

Paul rose up on his elbows and looked at Ritter who was finishing off the dregs of his beer with the edges of his mouth curled up. He was thoroughly appreciating how the question had thrown his friend.

"Ashta is with you all the time. She works at the same hospital, she goes to the rugby pitch and out with you to bars. She's got you on a short leash there, Irish. Man up and be your own dog. Get up and go to temple or to church with me and find a good woman for a change."

"But not Cat, yea? You glossed right over my question there I noticed." Ritter cut his eyes over hard awaiting a response and, with each second of silence, found himself growing angrier. Finally, Paul sighed and said quietly, "No, man. Not Cat."

"But you just said I could have any girl. Oh what, am I not good enough for her—"

"No," Paul interrupted calmly. "No, you're not."

Ritter stuck his finger down hard into his beer bottle, sat up, and pointed at Paul with it. "Oh, but I guess you are since you're Christian and all."

"It's not like that, RJ—"

Ritter got up and his sudden pitch of movement cut Paul off. He walked into the kitchen and opened the refrigerator door hard, causing glass bottles in the door to clang together in terror. "What is wrong with you?" Paul called out in confusion. Ritter didn't have a temper for the most part. Not anymore anyway. He didn't care enough about anything to summon up enough emotion within himself to get angry. This was the most emotion Paul had seen from his friend in years.

"You, you bloody hypocrite," Ritter said in an accusing tone as he reemerged into the room red-faced. "You're what's wrong! You just sat there and said I could have any girl I wanted when what you meant was any girl for whom you deemed me worthy! Well, sod off, mate, all right? Who are you to judge me? You know, you're a whole lot more like me than not! For one: you're just as Jewish as I am! You're parents might have jumped teams but you are still what you are no matter what! Guess you lost that bit of memory with the stroke! And two: I knew you before you *went into the light* and *found Jesus*! You've smoked and shagged your fair share, in case you've forgotten that as well, so don't act like your moral fiber is somehow woven thicker than mine, ya bloody Holy Joe!"

Ritter walked toward the hallway but a sharp blow to the back of the head stopped his storm. He turned and saw the remote on the floor at his feet. "Oh, you've gone mental! If we didn't have a tournament tomorrow, Paul, I would bash your face—"

"I didn't have a stroke, RJ. I know you think I did. Everyone thinks I did, but they never found evidence of one. You know that."

Ritter closed his eyes and growled to let out the welling of angry steam within him. "Paul, we have had this conversation—"

"No. We've had conversations, but we've never had *this* conversation."

Paul sat up. His dark eyes scanned the room as he considered the best way to say the words that were at any moment going to leap on their own from his mouth.

"I was addicted to porn and got myself into debt because of it. I had hundreds, literally hundreds of DVDs, RJ, and tons of magazines but the computer stuff is what really sunk me."

Paul rubbed his fingers over his eyes and exhaled hard. "I got home from work one day and there was a message on the answering machine from the mortgage company saying they were going to contact my cosigner if I didn't call them to discuss missed payments. Well, my cosigner is my dad. You know that. I couldn't get financed for a house like this on a teacher's salary! Anyway, I was four months behind on payments and there was no way I could catch up because I had gone through my savings so, I did what an addict does: I went to get a fix to forget things. I got on the computer and a girl I had been having sex with online had sent me a picture of herself . . ."

Paul rubbed his eyes again and cleared his throat. "It was one of my students, RJ. We had both been using an alias and she looks older than she is but, man, she's a sophomore!" He stopped and wiped his mouth as if sickened.

"I threw up. Then when I didn't have anything else to throw up, I dry heaved until my eyes bruised. You remember that? The doctors tried to attribute that to the so-called stroke.

"So anyway, I cleaned up and went out to the car. I guess I was going to run into a tree somewhere out in the country and kill myself. I don't know. I put my hand on the car door and this light came out of nowhere. So help me, it was as if somebody had physically hit my face with light like a punch. I fell back on the ground stunned from the hit and, after a minute or two, realized I was blind. But, there wasn't blackness or the flashes you see like when you get punched. There was just this light and I heard a voice. It was just as clear as your voice is to me in this room. It said, 'Paulus Anastasios Moysiadis, why do you continue crucifying me?'"

Paul shook his head and looked down at his hands. "RJ, I was in the hospital for three days and in my blindness, I saw my whole life. I saw it for what it really was. I didn't lose consciousness the entire time. They said I wasn't responsive but I heard them and felt them checking me. My brain was just too consumed inwardly to make me react outwardly."

His dark eyes went to Ritter who had moved closer. "They never found anything wrong with me, RJ. Nothing. I didn't have a stroke. You made a joke and have made the same joke several times that my life changed because I *found Jesus*. Well, I didn't find Jesus. He found me. As cliché as that sounds, it's the gospel truth, man."

Ritter sat on the coffee table opposite Paul. "Pauley," he said in the same low voice he used with unstable patients, "you spoke to Jesus as in *Christmas Jesus?*"

Paul shook his head. "No. He spoke to me."

"Why do you suppose he used your whole name? It's kind of a mouthful."

"He was speaking in Greek."

"Jesus was Jewish, Pauley, and He spoke Aramaic. We Jews have a secret club and we get together and talk about this sort of thing. What do you think we are doing on Christmas morning? Club meetings at curry houses."

Paul looked up and saw an expression of bemused pity on his friend's face. "Do you believe me, RJ?" Ritter sighed and let his arms fall limp. "Yes, Pauley, I believe you believe you heard Jesus. I also believe you had a cerebral event of some nature, now wait, wait, listen. Paul, I flew in that last day you were in hospital. I saw your records. I saw you! You had not eaten or slept since you had gotten there and then suddenly, you were completely lucid as if none of it had happened. They may not have found the aneurism but there was evidence of it in your actions. You don't have to see a lion to know one has been about!"

"See," Ritter said, slapping his legs and standing, "this is why we're mates! We're both crazy as hell!"

"It changed me, RJ," Paul said seriously. "You've seen how I've changed! Man, I tell ya, I couldn't go on living my life the way I had been because of that day.

"I'm not saying I am perfect. I'm no *Holy Joe*, like you said. I struggle every day. It's a never-ending battle. The things I know I should do I don't do and what I know I shouldn't, well, I end up doing every now and then. But, I am getting better at it. And part of the reason I am getting better at it is . . ." He stopped talking and pointed with his thumb toward Cat's house. "She is the one that found me in the driveway and called 911. Apparently, before the paramedics got here, I told her everything, gave her my house keys and asked her to help me.

"RJ, she stayed at the hospital until my parents could get there and then she came back to my house got every magazine, book and DVD. She even cleaned my computer. I have no idea how she did that! She saw everything. God forgive me."

Paul chuckled, wiped his face and clicked his tongue a few times. "Then she did my laundry, dishes . . . I mean, she cleaned this place like it had never been cleaned before. RJ, if she hadn't done that, my parents would have seen every bit of that filth when they brought me home from the hospital. I thought they were going to! I started shaking on the way home! You remember? You wanted to take me back to the hospital."

Ritter looked away and cleared his throat. He did remember and had thought his best friend was going to die right there next to him in the car.

"Pauley. Why didn't you tell me? I would have paid your debts off, whatever they were."

Paul nodded his head in affirmation. "I know you would have. But, I would have just gotten back into debt. I didn't need help with the symptoms. I needed a cure for the disease! Listen, the day you left, my first day alone, seven guys from Cat's church showed up. She introduced me to them and then left. Several were church leaders, one was a youth pastor, one a family counselor, another a deacon; they were of all ages. My age on up. They had all been where I was. One had even been addicted to sex and been with prostitutes! They talked with me, prayed with me, which, yea, was kind of awkward but I needed it. They gave me their numbers, called me, their wives brought meals over. Their wives, dude. They let their wives come into my house. Do you know what that meant to me? Porn's not like alcohol or drugs. You tell people you used to be addicted to one of those two and they look at you with respect and pat you on the back. But porn? They look at you like . . ." He stopped and shook his head.

"Anyway, after a week, I got my courage up to call my mortgage company and it had all been taken care of. Same thing with my credit cards. Debt gone. Paid in full." He again pointed next door with his thumb. "Twenty thousand dollars, man. She paid it all off. It's like I got to start over with a clean house, clean computer, clean credit line, and clean slate.

"You and every other doctor say I had a stroke, but I am telling you, God got tired of me nailing his Boy to the cross and knocked me blind until I saw things His way! When I did, He let me start over from scratch. I know you don't believe me. You didn't see what I saw. But, it's like what you said about a lion. Do you have to see the actual animal to know it has been somewhere? Can't you see how I've changed? We've known each other for going on fifteen years now! You know me! Look, the Lion was here, RJ. Look around you. Look at me. He tore me apart but only what needed to be torn away. And the bloody mess He left behind, left me clean."

Ritter looked over at the wall that bore the weight of his house just twenty feet from where Cat slept. "Sounds like she's the one that helped you, Pauley."

"No! No, she's not. She just dressed the wound. It's like what you do. You set bones, but it's God that knits them back together. He could have done alone what He did for me but when He used Cat, and by the way, she had only lived there a couple months when this happened. When God used Cat, He not only brought all those guys into my life, one of which I still see for counseling on occasion, but He set up a physical reminder for me. She's like a pile of rocks you put somewhere to remind you where you buried something. Every time I see her, I remember what of me has been buried. I don't feel shame or anything like that though. Just this, I don't know, this big relief. It's humbling, man.

"You know, she never mentioned any of the stuff she saw in my house to me. The first time she saw me out of the hospital, she hugged me a long time. When I asked her about the money she just said to help somebody else that was hurting. That was all the pay back she wanted."

Ritter smiled. "Who did you help?"

Paul laughed and wiped his nose with his shirt. "I'm still working on that."

The answer caused Ritter's head to snap back toward his friend. The realization of what was being said to him made him narrow his eyes and laugh. "Oh, give me a break, you cheeky bastard," he said before slapping Paul on the side of the head hard but playfully.

"All right, Paulette," he said before stretching, "you say you spoke with Jesus, I believe you. And, as for your pile of rocks over there, I'll spare her my charm. You're right. I'm not good enough for her anyway. However, for the record, neither are you. In fact, it doesn't sound like any bloke is. No wonder she's single."

"She's widowed."

"What?"

Paul smiled and grabbed the remote again before repeating himself. "She is widowed. I don't know why I am smiling. It's so horrible you have to laugh or it will depress you to death. She and her husband were living in Dallas and he was murdered during a home invasion. I kid you not." Ritter's face widened in shock, and Paul held up his hand. "I know, RJ! Crazy stuff."

"What do you mean, *murdered during a home invasion*, that's insane!"

"I didn't ask for any details, she didn't offer. She said three people broke into her house, shot him, and beat her. They might have shot her too, I don't remember, but, I know they left her for dead."

Ritter stood stunned as if he, himself, had been shot. "What do you mean you don't remember if she was shot? How can you not remember if she was shot! That's a bit of a stunning detail!"

"It was kind of a heavy story, RJ! A lot to take in. Get to know her. She'll tell you about it."

Ritter's hands went to his head and he laughed. "Oh yea! That's what I'll do. Hey, Ginger, yea how's your ma and da? I heard your husband got shot and you got left for dead? What's that like? Ace idea, Paulette. Brilliant!"

Paul choked, sat up, and the water he had just tried to swallow came out his nose. The two laughed and Ritter threw a box of tissues like a baseball at his roommate's crotch.

"I think both her parents are dead actually," Paul said and the two doubled over in laughter.

After several moments of tension-relieving gasping, and giggle-induced tears, the two propped themselves up in their respective spots and tried to catch their breath.

"Oh sweet King of England! It's not funny," Ritter whispered in a high-pitched voice trying to contain himself. "Okay. Enough. I'm going out to catch my breath."

"Hey, RJ," Paul said, holding his stomach and stifling his giggles. "Cat told me that there is a difference between regret and shame. *Regret* is rubbing your fingertips across a scar, remembering the wound that put it there and being thankful for the lesson you learned through healing. *Shame* is rubbing your nails across the scar and opening it up repeatedly because you don't feel worthy of being healed.

"What happened with your sister was horrible and then you had the breakdown. But, maybe you had that breakdown to get you here. God himself might have broken you down to break you free of something. And maybe, like me, He put Cat in your life to set those broken parts of you that you refuse to allow Him to heal.

"You have been an open wound for a long time, bro, and infection has set in so bad you have forgotten what it's like to be healthy. That's why you're with Ashta and all those other girls. You don't see them for the disease that they are because you can't feel it anymore. That part of you is necrotic. In fact, you seem a whole lot more dead than alive to me. Nobody else might can see it. But I knew you before you . . . well, got killed I guess."

Paul got up and scratched his stomach. "That being said, being interested in Cat is the first healthy sign of life I have seen in you in a long time so, go on and do whatever. You're not worthy of her. I'm not worthy of her, heck, I don't think anybody is, but that's what makes it feel so good when she does love you. It's probably just what you need. But, don't think healing doesn't hurt or that you are going to make her a part of your sickness. She's not going to sleep with you, I can guarantee you that!"

Ritter laughed and nodded. "She has thus informed me already."

Paul nodded his head on his way to the kitchen then called out to Ritter and asked him to turn off the pool filter.

"Anything else, wife?"

"Yea, RJ, one more thing. No, two things." Paul stopped, took a solid stance squarely toward his roommate and folded his arms over his chest. "I know I am Jewish. Being a Christian doesn't change that any more than it changes me from being Greek. I haven't forgotten what I am and I never will. So, don't say that kind of crap again.

"Secondly, don't hurt her," he said in a serious tone. "So help me, don't hurt her. Just because she's wholesome doesn't mean you can't punch holes in her. She's not superhuman or anything."

Ritter put his hand on the door and looked out at the fence separating him from Cat. He then nodded and rapped his knuckles against the glass. "I won't hurt her, Pauley. If I do, I'll go home. You have my word on it. But hey, what if she hurts me? See, didn't think of that one did you now?"

Paul went into the kitchen and began loading the dishwasher. "Well, RJ," he called out amidst the clatter of plates, "you got to be alive to get hurt. If she breaks your heart, at least you can take comfort in the fact that you aren't dead. Therefore, arise good Lazarus, and walk! Walk I say! And while you're at it, turn off the pool pump!"

Ritter closed the sliding glass door carefully behind him, grabbed a water bottle that had been left on the patio, and flipped the switch controlling the pool filter. He then looked up at the full moon, down at its reflection in Paul's pool, and felt an overwhelming desire to howl. He stretched, inhaled deeply, and imagined the liberation of stretching his neck, opening his mouth, and bellowing a primal scream that would release him from his human form and leave him free to run four-footed into the night.

A soft breeze blew and his nostrils flared following a familiar and soothing aroma that seemed to hang in the air like incense: Cat. The smell of her hair and skin stood like a pillar of smoke in front of him as if she were still there with him, in his hands. It made his pulse slow and the beast within him walk back into the dark recesses of his chest and lie down.

He interlaced his fingers and rested his hands on his head, opening his chest. His breath became rhythmic and his body rocked slightly back and forth like a blissfully occupied hammock. His blue eyes closed and he imagined Cat against him and the two bound together tightly by one another's limbs, sleeping and breathing as one animal.

His muscles relented momentarily and his body stumbled off balance. Ritter caught himself against a lawn chair and realized he had fallen asleep standing. He laughed and his body immediately erupted into a deep yawn. His fingers rubbed over his eyes and his heart stopped at an unexpected discovery. He put his hands to his nose and found the source of the lingering smell of Cat. She was, indeed, still in his hands. Despite the passing of time, despite exposure to Ashta, the scent remained on his fingers as if hanging on of its own will.

A smile suddenly forced his cheeks back aggressively and Ritter inhaled from the bowl of his hands repeatedly until light-headed. A cascade of peace rushed through him and pushed away some of the rocks that covered the sun-starved resting place of his broken spirit. The seeds of darkness that had been strewn about within him were washed away and the fertile, anxious soil of hope, long held captive, found the freedom to turn itself in search of light. Ritter put his hand over his heart and felt both lightness within it and crushing weight upon it. He looked up at the stars, searched the sky, and then felt for the first time, in a long time, something was looking back.

The glass door closed quietly and Ritter went to the bathroom. He splashed cool water on his face, dried it with the shirt he had just taken off, and stood to look at himself. His eyes went immediately to the scratch Ashta had given him on his chest. What had been evidence of passion now felt like a mark of shame and Ritter wanted to be free of it.

The four talon marks glowed brightly against his fair complexion and he rubbed his hand across them in hopes of erasing them from his chest. The longer he stared at them, the redder they became, and the sense of relief the scent of Cat had given him, quickly turned into a sense of urgency to be clean of Ashta.

The shower cried out as hot water and steam spewed from its mouth. Ritter stepped into the downpour and his body recoiled from the refining heat. It left a hateful red trail down his back and he gritted his teeth feeling somehow that he deserved the punishment of the burn. He looked down at his inflamed skin and suddenly felt like a reptile in desperate need of shedding.

His hands grabbed a washcloth, held themselves in prayer-like fashion and moved around the soap. Bleached white suds exploded from the effort and fell down around his feet like clouds. He closed his eyes and deeply inhaled the last bit of cool air in the room. He then exhaled hard, opened his eyes, and began scrubbing with the hopes of not only tearing away all that he had become, but also of reviving the pure flesh of the man he used to be: a man deserving of a woman like Cat.

CHAPTER 8

Tall, Single-Shot Seduction. To Go.

The next morning came quickly. Ritter had fallen asleep as soon as his head hit the pillow and he had slept as if in hibernation. He woke up dangerously rested with an insatiable thirst for sweat, mud, and blood that would only be quenched by one thing: rugby. He was up, dressed and putting the gear bags on the front porch before Paul had even stirred.

Three hours later, Ritter was sitting on the sidelines of the field where his rugby team was playing with the sad look of a dog tied to a tree. After some reasonable thought, brought about by a call from the hospital's chief of surgery earlier that morning, he had reconsidered playing in the tournament. Although his reputation was well-known in the medical community, he was a stranger to the hospital and as much as he loathed to accept it, it wasn't professional to come into work bruised and bloodied so soon after being hired. And, were he to get on the playing field, that would be the outcome. The only thing Ritter craved more than sex was rugby and he didn't feel he had truly played until his body was a mass of sweat-mingled blood, welts, and contusions. He resigned himself to being the team doctor and hoped he would at least be bloodied in that respect.

He looked at his watch anxiously. The game had started at 9:30 and had barely been underway for half an hour. His mind wandered to Cat, as it had sporadically all morning, and he wondered if she were finished speaking and how she felt. He imagined he were in the audience and tried to picture her form, features, and voice. Then suddenly, as if a plug had been pulled from a drain, thoughts of Cat swirled out of his brain and the image of the woman from the coffee shop rose up like Venus from the foam.

Ritter, because of the call from the hospital, had left the house that morning thirty minutes behind Paul and the rest of the team. However, because he had decided to not play, he had time to spare and decided to waste a bit of it by stopping at a coffee shop.

It was a typical Saturday morning and the drive-through was packed tight with caffeine and carb-starved zombies all moving forward hypnotically in a slow crawl.

Steam rolled out of the back of the shop as bagels were boiled by the bushel, giving the entire scene a supernatural quality. Ritter watched the white vapor belch out in amorphous, ghostlike heaps, and he tried to find shapes within it before it evanesced in the morning air.

From the belly of the spectral cloud a dark figure appeared. Its long legs split the billows and brought with them a beautiful blond goddess. The sides of her hair blew up around her ethereal face like horns and the blue heat of her eyes focused ahead intently. Ritter looked over his shoulder to find the object of her attention and, when he turned back around, found that it was him.

The woman took a long drag from her cigarette then leaned down and placed her folded arms on his lowered window. Smoke curled upward from her nostrils as her deep-cut T-shirt fell downward and she smiled as Ritter's brain took her in. She spoke briefly and propositioned him sexually in no uncertain terms. He smirked knowing she was most likely a prostitute, and full well that he didn't care, and then motioned his head toward the passenger door.

The woman stood and began walking around the front of the car, watching Ritter as she did so. The car behind them honked, startling her and nearly causing Ritter to choke on the saliva that was all but dripping from his teeth. He looked in his rearview mirror and, to his surprise, saw his teammate Peter who should have long since been on the road to the tournament. Peter waved, Ritter returned the favor uncomfortably, and then looked back to find the woman gone. All that was left as evidence of her existence was a ribbon of smoke.

A ref's whistle brought him back to the present boredom of the rugby pitch and away from the morning's enigmatic encounter. Ritter laughed to himself and shook his head as if in an effort to roll all the wandering pieces of his brain back into their respective holes. He checked his phone for messages, looked over the team roster and practice schedule, and then sighed in frustration. He began to dig around in his duffle bag for a ball cap and as he did, a dark shadow cut the sunlight over his shoulder.

"Is this seat taken?"

Ritter looked up and his mouth fell open. He sat upright and, as he stared, his look of shock turned into a wickedly flirtatious grin. He cleared off the seat next to him, patted it, and the mystical blonde from the coffee shop sat down. She was even more beautiful than he had remembered her being.

"I, um," she giggled without finishing her sentence. Ritter looked at her with open desire, not saying anything. The girl pushed her blond hair behind her ear. "I don't guess I really know what to say," she said. "I don't suppose you will be so kind as to get the conversation going and take some of the pressure off me?" Ritter continued smiling at her as if she were to be his last meal, and slowly shook his head no.

"Okay," she sighed, fondling her hair nervously. She started to speak again, looked over at Ritter, and broke out into a laugh. It was obvious he was enjoying every second of the awkwardness. She covered her face in embarrassment and Ritter put his arm around her and pulled her to him. When she looked up, their faces were inches apart. She cleared her throat and composed herself, trying not to smile, and failed miserably.

"Okay, okay," she said finally in a cracking voice, "I am sorry for my public display of indecency this morning at the coffee shop. There. I said it."

Ritter pulled her closer and put his lips to her ear. "Was that so difficult?"

She bit her lips and closed her eyes as her face turned pink. "No," she said softly mirroring his look of desire. Ritter brought his mouth close to her again and she closed her eyes, feeling his warm breath on her jaw. "And don't you dare apologize," he said in a purring tone that resonated with lust.

He released her from the half embrace and straightened himself. The girl turned her face away and, after a moment, cut her eyes at Ritter who had not taken his gaze off her. "Well, it was very forward and not like me. I've never done anything like that before, which I know sounds cliché. I am serious! Stop laughing! I have never done anything like that before."

"Really?" Ritter replied sarcastically, feigning a serious look and nodding his head.

"I haven't! Stop it! You are embarrassing me!"

Ritter laughed and closed his duffle bag. "You embarrassed? After what you said to me in the shop take-out line? I can't believe anything embarrasses you. What you said was without a doubt the most fantastic stream of perversion I have ever heard in my life! What do you have to say for yourself, young lady?"

The girl looked away and grinned. She then lit a cigarette, licked her lips, and let the smoke roll out of her mouth with a round, seductive sigh.

"Enjoy your coffee?" she asked coyly, trying to change the subject. "No, I did not," Ritter replied. "Why not?" the girl asked. "Because I had hot tea."

The beautiful blonde glanced furtively at Ritter and saw he was shaking his head. "Tch, tch, tch. Shame on you," he said, pinching the flesh on her side and tickling her slightly. "There I was, a foreigner in a strange land, minding my own business, innocent and vulnerable as a boy, when seemingly from thin air appears this siren who, without regard for law or retribution from the fleet of cars behind me, invites me to partake in a carnal liaison. Naughty goddess."

"And then the car horn," she interrupted. "Yes," Ritter said, pulling away from her, stretching and groaning slightly. "A message from fate no doubt warning me to come back to my senses before your beauty lured me to the rocks, dashed me to bits, and sent me straight to the watery depths of hell with a smile on my face."

"Oh, please! Don't be silly. There's no water in hell," she said with a wink, kicking his foot playfully.

The girl looked around nervously and Ritter pushed a lock of her blond hair from her eyes. She smiled innocently and again blushed.

"I'm Ritter Thomas, by the way," he said, extending a hand to her.

"Madeline Loch," she replied in a twirl of white smoke, grasping his hand in return.

"Lock?" he questioned. "As in, *lock me up and abuse me however you would like?*"

"No!" she laughed. "Loch as in Loch Ness."

"Oh! Are you Scots?"

"My father's family is," she lied convincingly.

"Madeline Loch," Ritter said in a low voice. "That's a romantic name."

"Yes, it is," she laughed. "Unfortunately, my entire family and just about everyone who knows me calls me Mo."

Ritter sniggered. "Mo? Why on earth?"

"Well, my middle name is Olivia so Madeline Olivia, MO, it's stupid but that's what they call me."

"Hmm," Ritter said, looking back out at the field and the mass of dirt-covered boys struggling for the ball. "And apparently," she continued, "when I was little, I cut my own hair and ended up looking like a blond version of Moe Howard from the three stooges!"

Ritter laughed out loud. "There it is, the real truth of it. Well, if it's any consolation, you don't look a thing like him now," he said, tucking strands of her blond hair behind her ear and then rubbing her earlobe. "In fact," he whispered, "you may be one of the most beautiful women I have ever seen."

He released her ear and smirked. The right side of his mouth rose higher than the left and curled around like a ram's horn. "Of course, I have to admit, I always found Moe attractive as well. It's true."

The blonde burst out laughing. "I was a Curly gal myself."

"So," Ritter said, nudging her tan thigh with his knee, "Mo Loch, what brings you here today?"

The girl sighed and leaned back against the bleacher behind her as Ritter had done. "Oh, my cousin is playing on field 2 at 11:30 and asked me to come as team doctor."

"You're a doctor?" Ritter asked, smiling.

"I'm a physician's assistant."

"Well, Mo Loch, PA, where do you work?" he asked with a wide grin.

"I'm in residency and working in a NICU right now," she replied avoiding his question.

Ritter laughed and nudged her perfect leg. They were long and round with muscle and he wanted desperately to sink his teeth into them. "And what hospital was that?"

"Well, at the moment," she said, rubbing her hands down her shins, tempting Ritter all the more, "Cypress Memorial Northwest."

"What? Here in Houston?" Ritter questioned, pulling his head back in shock, "I work there!" Mo smiled and nodded her head. "You knew that!" he said, narrowing his eyes. "Have you seen me there?" he asked, intrigued. The girl smiled, giving away the answer. "Wait, did you know who I was when you came up to me at the take-out line?" Mo bit her thumbnail seductively and looked away. Ritter laughed hard and put his arm around her, drawing her face to his. He put his nose in her ear and whispered, "That's called stalking, mademoiselle, and it's a crime. Add that to your previously mentioned crime of solicitation."

Her shoulder shrugged in response to the tickle his breath had brought to her neck. She turned her face to him, and their noses brushed against each other. "Let's go somewhere," she said. Ritter smiled and looked back out at the field. The team had only a few minutes left before the half. "Okay," he said, taking the smoke from her mouth into his own as if it were a kiss.

The couple took a last surreptitious glance toward the field and quietly climbed off the metal bleachers. They clasped hands and began their clandestine escape looking expectantly at each other until a whistle blew from behind them. Ritter's name was called and he stopped, looked back, and saw Paul motioning for him to return. "Hold that thought," he said to Mo with a wink and jogged back to the sidelines.

Peter began walking toward the bleachers with his hand on his eye as blood streamed down his forearm. Ritter knew less of him than anyone on the team. All he knew was that Peter was as huge as he was gentle of spirit and the strongest prop position player he had ever seen.

Ritter put on gloves and sat down. He looked like a child next to the man's massive form. "Let's get a look at that, Pete."

Peter lowered his hand and Ritter saw a cut on his eyebrow. "Sit down on the ground here facing behind me and let me clean that up, you huge beast. How big are you, mate?"

The angel sat down slowly and in a slightly cumbersome manner like an elephant lowering itself on its knees. Worry knitted his brows and caused the wound to bleed heavier.

"You look upwards of twenty stone at least. That's about three hundred pounds or so," Ritter said in a low voice, trying to calm the man. "And may I add the most formidable prop I have ever seen on a rugby field. Have you ever played another position?" Peter swallowed hard and hummed with a tone that suggested he had not. "You make short work of a defensive line that is for certain." Ritter said as he grabbed an irrigation bottle and gauze and began cleaning the wound.

He glanced down at his patient intermittently and saw that he was looking at Mo. Then, he glanced over his shoulder and saw that the indecipherable stare was being reciprocated. It was as if the huge man and beautiful blonde were having a silent conversation. One that was not amiable and made Ritter entirely uncomfortable.

"What were you doing at the coffee shop this morning, Pete?" Ritter asked, hoping to stop the strange visual exchange.

"I remembered something I needed to take care of."

Ritter expected more and, when nothing followed, raised his brows and simply continued with his work.

"Do you do anything special the night before a game to prepare, Dr. Thomas?" the large celestial asked, hoping to pull Ritter's brain toward a newly and recently trodden righteous terrain.

Ritter eased the pressure he had put on the large man's brow and re-examined it. "Oh no. Nothing much really. I down a bit extra water is all. Yourself?"

"Not really. But, I know people that take long hot showers the night before a game," Peter said. "They say it relaxes the muscles and clears the head. They seem to think better and see things better afterward. Think it's because of the steam?"

Ritter continued putting pressure on the wound and his stillness allowed him to think about the night before. He truly had wanted to be different. Now, here at the pitch, with the beautiful blonde eager for him, it was if none of it had happened. As quickly as his desire for change had come upon him, it had been filed away in the tightly packed portion of his brain that held all evidence of his pain.

The field ref raised some papers to Ritter and Ritter nodded. He put a last butterfly on his patient's cut and then excused himself to fill out the necessary medical paperwork.

Peter held a cold pack against his quickly swelling brow and the seductive, evil angel slid down beside him with the elegance and stealth of the thing she was.

"I had heard the rumor but had to come and see for myself," she said with a whisper. "Our kind isn't exactly known for truthfulness. But, here you are! My, my. I heard the prince of Israel himself recommended you. How is the ole archangel Michael these days by the way? Busy no doubt," she sneered as smoke slid out of her mouth like a reptilian tongue.

Peter said nothing and Mo looked around the field. She saw various holy beings of light reveal themselves to her in warning and she laughed trying to conceal her fear of being outnumbered.

"Tell you what, big boy," the feminine-guised demon said in a comical tone, "take me now, and I will leave the good doctor alone. I won't change forms. I will stay as I am now unless of course you prefer me in my true form." The impeccably cloaked demon leaned over and kissed Peter on the neck. "What do you say? You have all the equipment. Use it." Mo put her hand on Peter's thigh and ran it up toward his hip. "I'll be gentle."

Peter grabbed the hand in a vice grip and calmly moved it away. "Will you steal, murder, commit adultery, swear falsely, and offer sacrifices to Baal and walk after other gods that you have not known then stand before Me as if it is acceptable to do these disgusting things?"

"Yawn!" the demon's pink-glossed lips said rudely in response. "Does your kind not get to use its own words? Besides, I wasn't asking you to steal, murder, or lie blah, blah, blah. I don't know why you even brought those up. And, I'm not Baal, honey. He was busy, and my legs are way better."

Moloch leaned back through ribbons of smoke and looked at Ritter again who was going over the finished paperwork with the referee. "Come on, Pete, let's fight for him. Winner takes all. How does that sound? You, me, a sword?"

Peter looked out at the field at the angelic forces of darkness and light and awaited response from the heavens. When no directive was sent, Peter bowed his head humbly. "The battle belongs to the Lord."

Ritter returned, handed the paperwork to Peter for him to sign, and glanced up at Mo. The thrill she had given him earlier had dissipated slightly and a sensation of fear had crept in amidst what was left.

"What time is it, Dr. Thomas?" Peter asked respectfully, needing to note the time as well as date with his signature. Ritter laughed and shook his head. "It is 10:42, and for the record, I let anybody who can fit my entire head in their hand call me Ritter."

Peter smiled and nodded politely. Ritter liked Peter a lot. There was something serene about him that gave Ritter not only a sense of peace but security, which was exaggerated against the sense of discomfort he now had in the presence of Mo.

"Here you go," said Peter, handing the paperwork to Ritter. He rose to his full height of nearly seven feet and shook Ritter's hand gratefully. "Will you be staying for the entire game, sir?"

Ritter looked at Peter curiously. He was the team doctor. Of course he would stay.

"I just meant, will you be leaving the stands? I would like to get back into the game as soon as possible, Dr. Thomas. I can't do that without your consent to the refs. I just want to know that you will be here. You won't leave, will you? You will stay right here?"

Mo laughed and rolled her eyes at the angel's attempt to thwart her plans.

"I won't go far," Ritter said with a smile.

"You will be here or you won't, Dr. Thomas. Even if somebody doesn't go far, they've still gone. Ma'am," Peter said to the blonde with a nod. Then, before turning to walk away, he looked at Ritter with what Ritter couldn't help but think was an expression of pleading.

Mo drove to a secluded place barely within hearing distance of the field and parked. There was a bridge in front of the vehicle, thinly veiled by trees, which kept them from being seen or approached from the front. A tall layer of rocks reached above the driver's door and on the passenger side was a clearing that looked out over a lake. There was only the back of the car that remained unguarded and both she and Ritter felt it added to the excitement of the scenario.

"We have ten minutes at most," Ritter said, looking at her legs.

"Well, we better not waste time, Dr. Thomas."

Mo climbed over to Ritter's side of the car and the two started pulling at one another's clothing. As she pulled his shirt over his head, she heard the sound of celestial horses and knew her time was short. She needed to kill him now. It would be so easy. Just one bullet. The trees would muffle the sound that the car could not and she would wait among them to laugh as others cried in horror upon finding the body. But, if it were to happen, it needed to happen now. If there was anything a devil knew, it was to stab an opportunity as soon as it was presented.

Mo looked at Ritter and, seeing that he was sufficiently preoccupied, leaned back to open and reach in the glove box. Her hot hand pressed itself firmly around the grip of the pistol and her finger pulled back the hammer slowly. She brought it out behind her back and looked down at Ritter with a smile.

"You ready to die?" she said with a snarl. "What?" Ritter mumbled, completely engrossed in her body.

Suddenly, a form outside the passenger window startled Mo. It was Peter in his angelic, guardian form, blazing sword in hand, body dressed for battle. The demon bared his teeth in response and then saw the bridge behind him in the reflection of Peter's armor. The devil looked back in panic to find a battalion of angelic soldiers on horseback waiting for the call to attack. A rumbling echoed from heaven as the archangel Michael dispatched more soldiers, and in terror, the demon cried out, "Okay! Stop! I'll stop!"

"What! What happened?" Ritter yelled back in horror. He put his hands on the blonde's face. "Are you okay? What's wrong?"

"I just saw a policeman on a bike ride by! I think he saw us. Get dressed!"

Ritter looked at her aghast. He wasn't concerned about being caught as much as he was horrified that he would have to stop. That stupor kept him from noticing Madeline leaning back and returning the .45 to the glove box.

The two returned quickly to the tournament and Mo looked in the rearview mirror at her face and then over at Ritter. "Am I all fixed here?" she said lighting a cigarette. He smiled at her question and replied, "Quite. Am I?" She nodded in reply.

Silence hung heavy in the car. "I am sorry we had to stop, Ritter. Are you mad at me?"

"I'm not angry, love," Ritter sighed. "It's not your fault." They each then looked out at the field and thought briefly of how it might have gone. Ritter imagined himself satisfied and Mo Loch imagined the sound of him strangling on his own blood and his melodic final death rattle.

The two exited the car and met around the front. "Nice running into you again, Mo Loch," Ritter said, smiling and running a finger along her jaw. "Nice running into you again as well, Ritter Thomas. Let's meet for coffee later," she said. "Maybe after the tournament is over?"

Ritter gave her an approving look. "Sounds good. I know a coffee shop not far from here. The tea is good. I can't vouch for the coffee. There is a problem with solicitation in the parking lot though," he said with a wink. He then reached in his wallet and pulled out a business card. "That is my mobile number. Call me."

Mo looked down, laughed, and nodded her head.

"You know," Ritter said taking her cigarette and inhaling deeply from it, "smoking is quite bad for you."

"The best things in life are, aren't they?" she said taking back her cigarette. The end glowed an angry red as she pulled it's burning fumes into her chest.

Ritter turned to walk away but, before he did, looked over his shoulder and gave Mo a last wink.

The female guised demon smirked malevolently in response and watched the mortal walk away, taking in his form and beauty. Reed Jacob Thomas wasn't the best-looking man Mo Loch had had a hand in sending to hell, but he would be among the most enjoyable.

CHAPTER 9

Where the Wild Things Are

The evening sky was red and Cat sat out on her porch enjoying the tranquility. The edges of her hammock curled around her like a cocoon and she held a warmth-filled pillowcase in her arms. The bundle jerked slightly and a long brown leg emerged causing the large, rust-colored dog resting on the floor to raise her head anxiously. Cat grinned, tucked the fawn's leg back into the pillowcase and the baby deer quickly cuddled itself back into a gangling ball.

The dog raised its head again and looked toward the fence. She whimpered, sat up in attention, and wagged her tail with anticipation. "What is it, Mama?" Cat asked, leaning up slightly from the comfort of the hammock, her aching side preventing her from raising herself completely.

"Are you sleeping?" a voice said from the fence. It startled Cat and she gasped. "Good grief! Ugh, Reed! You nearly scared me to death!" The bundle in her arms struggled from fright and Cat soothed it back to stillness.

Ritter laughed and rested his arms on the top of the fence. "Here's another ginger girl! How are you?" he said, patting the fence. The dog stretched to her full length up toward him as her tail wagged her entire body.

"I am not sure how the English are but Americans appreciate privacy!" said Cat with irritation as Ritter continued playing with the dog.

"Well, actually," he said, rubbing the dog's ears and not looking up, "I am Irish. Like this girl here! Yes, I am! Like this beauty here!"

"She's not an Irish setter and what—"

"How are you feeling by the way?" Ritter interrupted. "I'm fine, what are—"

"And your presentation went well?"

"Yes, it went well— You're coming over the fence? It is called a privacy fence for a reason! It's for privacy!" Ritter paused, holding his weight up with his straightened arms. "Are you in a private sort of way at the moment, Cat?" he asked with a smirk. "'Cause I think this girl here is in need of attention! Yes, you are, you beauty!"

Cat sighed, suppressed the urge to smile and watched in irritation as Mama Dog jumped around with excitement in expectation of the new plaything climbing over the fence. In truth, despite the still bleeding wound of hearing what she presumed was Ritter having sex the night before, there was something in Cat that was hopping around expectantly as well.

Ritter deftly brought his lower body over in one movement and without hesitation the dog stood upright, putting her paws on either side of his chest. Ritter rubbed her sides and wrinkled his nose as she licked his face. Cat couldn't help but be a little jealous of the huge mutt but at the same time felt comforted by the dog's behavior. Animals, dogs in particular, smelled kindness on a human in the same manner they smelled fear or depravity and, upon finding it, felt no need in restraining their joy.

Ritter walked through the opened screen door of the porch and sat on the floor. The dog, brazenly infatuated, laid herself across him and he rubbed her belly. "Oh give me a break!" Cat said, rolling her eyes at the display. "Does the female of every specie surrender to you at some point?"

Ritter smiled and looked up. "I don't know, Cat. Do they?" Cat shook her head and looked away, realizing that she had inadvertently included herself, as a female of a specie, in her question.

"How do you know Paul again?" she said taking the attention off her blunder.

"We met through an international youth sports exchange. We roomed together. Been best mates ever since. Haven't we, girl," he said patting the dog's chest with a deep thud.

The bundle in Cat's lap suddenly began to struggle and the dog brought herself away from ecstasy to attention. "She's okay, Mama Dog," Cat said in a soothing tone.

Ritter lied back on his elbows, stretched out his legs and crossed them at the ankles. Cat was a bit embarrassed by how comfortable he seemed around her. It was as if he knew how badly she wanted him around as well as how nervous he made her and was trying to put her at ease with the latter to accomplish the former.

"Mama Dog? Is that her name?"

"Yea," Cat said, petting the dog's face. "She plays mama to anything at the vet that needs one."

"And that bundle there needs a ma?"

The fawn poked its nose out as if curious of the answer. "Oh would you look at that," Ritter whispered with fascination. He crawled toward Cat and put his fingers out for the little nose to smell. Mama Dog licked his hand nervously and pushed it away, not completely comfortable with the baby deer being touched. "I won't hurt her," Ritter said kindly before glancing up at Cat. "I wouldn't dare."

His hand rested on Cat's arm and the fawn ran its nose across it. "Is it a female?" Ritter asked in a playful tone. Cat rolled her eyes then closed them while nodding her head in affirmation. The tiny doe peeked her big brown eyes out from the pillowcase and then pulled her head back in quickly as if shy. "Oh!" Ritter laughed. "Well now. There's a female that can resist me! Or two, I guess I should say," he said wryly, not looking up at Cat but knowing she caught the joke.

"Come on out, love. Come on." Ritter urged as he lifted the edge of the pillowcase. The fawn was curled around in a knot of legs and white spots. Her nose was tucked under a leg, and her eyes looked at him with irresistible purity and innocence.

"That is one of the most beautiful faces I have ever seen," he said with wonder. Cat smiled down at the bundle as it wiggled toward his hand. When she looked back up at Ritter, she saw that he was not looking at the fawn, but her. Just as she caught his eye, Ritter looked back down at the baby deer and quietly cleared his throat.

The fawn edged herself toward the opening of the pillowcase again. "Oh, come on now, don't deny me those lovely doe eyes," Ritter said flirtatiously. Cat looked away feeling that he was again intentionally speaking to her without speaking to her, but her eyes pulled themselves back toward him defiantly.

"There they are!" Ritter said as the fawn put out her entire head. It wiggled completely from the pillowcase and Mama Dog put her paw on the hammock, whimpering with concern.

The fawn jumped down and her weight folded her legs under her. The dog began licking the deer's face and, like any child, the fawn shook off the maternal affection and bounded away. The adoptive mother followed closely behind.

The deer leaped wildly on the soft grass and then stopped suddenly. She wiggled her white stub tail and looked back at it as if surprised by its presence. Ritter and Cat both laughed.

"If not for the obvious differences, I would swear they were meant for one another," Ritter said, sitting back smiling as he watched the animals play. He then asked from where the fawn had come.

"Juan, the kid that brought me home yesterday, found her next to the road last night. A car had hit the doe and the fawn was lying next to the body. I doubt she is much more than a week old."

"Oh," Ritter said, looking at the tiny deer with pity. "And where did Juan come from?"

Cat looked at him curiously, not quite able to translate the tone of his question. "He works at the animal hospital in town that I'm affiliated with."

Ritter nodded his head as if approving of the answer and continued watching the mismatched animals play.

"And so the dog will care of the fawn as her own?"

"Yep. Mama Dog will take good care of her and the deer will be just fine. She'll go to a reserve somewhere when she is old enough."

Ritter's brows knitted at the answer. "What about the dog? Won't she miss her baby?" Cat looked over at Ritter and saw that he seemed genuinely concerned, if not saddened, by the dog's impending loss.

"Yes. She will miss her very much. However, there will be other babies that will need her and she will care for them without hesitation or sadness from the ones she has lost. Animals don't look back," she said in a positive tone. "They just go forward. That's how they stay alive."

Ritter considered the answer for a few moments. "That makes sense, I suppose. And why your house?"

"The vet clinic," Cat said with a yawn, "they can't keep wild animals with the domesticated, so my place ends up being the halfway house for all things wild and in need. I told you that yesterday!"

Ritter smiled, recalling the conversation, then lied back on the warm cement floor, putting his hands behind his head. He was immediately as comfortable as he had ever been in a soft bed and felt completely tranquil. He watched the white explosion of clouds move languidly across the fading light of the sky and felt himself become lighter. A light breeze heavy with the scent of Cat passed over him, and he tried to pull all that he could into his chest. *This is indeed a place for all things wild and in need,* he thought. His eyes closed under the heaviness of his thoughts and he wondered if there was a heaven, and if so, was it anything like this?

Cat looked at Ritter, mystified by his actions. "You're just going to lie down, huh?"

Ritter smiled in response. Cat shook her head and contemplated telling him to get up, but he seemed complacent at a cellular level. His chest rose and fell softly as if on the edge of sleep and his feet, crossed at the ankles, shook slightly, rocking his body. Her mind struggled to pull her back to the hurt from the night before but her heart brought her forward to the peaceful perfection of the moment and she lowered herself back down into the hammock, curling up like a marsupial in a pouch.

The two relaxed silently in the warm placidity of one another's presence until the sun gave itself over to the inevitability of twilight. Mama Dog coaxed the rebellious fawn into a large kennel and they quickly settled themselves after several, well-choreographed turns. The two very different animals suddenly became indistinguishable from each other and formed a single warm mass of stillness. Ritter looked at them and smiled.

"They just curl up together like that, eh?"

"Yep," replied Cat without opening her eyes. Ritter rolled on his side toward the kennel. "I would have never imagined two animals so different would go so perfectly together. They both seem completely satisfied."

"They are," Cat said with a yawn. "Nature can set two beasts at odds. But in the end, the needs of the heart are stronger than the instinct in the blood."

Ritter hummed in consideration of what Cat had said. He looked at her and saw that she had rolled to her side to share his view of the kennel. Her magnetic eyes pulled the breath from his chest and Ritter felt his heart pound in desperation to make up for the loss of oxygen.

He watched as Cat's eyes yielded themselves closed again and he stared at her face. He imagined her nestled securely in the tangle of his limbs like a bird in a nest. The thought cause a deep exhalation to make a wild escape from his chest and Ritter wrapped his arms tightly around his ribs trying to calm the mad, thunderous applause of fluttering within him.

A laugh surprised her and Cat looked down to find Ritter smiling a full smile and chuckling with his eyes closed. "What's so funny?"

"Oh, bloody me," Ritter said while stretching. He chuckled once more, rubbed his chest and looked over at the kennel. "Do you suppose they each genuinely enjoy lying next to the other?" he asked, diverting attention away from his unintentional display of felicity.

Cat smiled over at the kennel. "Well, sure. Who doesn't prefer a warm body next to her at night?" She winced after the words left her mouth, realizing that once again she had inadvertently revealed too much of herself in a poorly thought out remark.

Ritter smiled. "Have a bit of experience behind that opinion there, Cat?" Silence was given in reply.

Ritter raised his head to glance at the still hammock then relaxed back onto his side. His folded arm took the weight of his head again and his heart took the weight of his emptiness. As full as being in Cat's presence made Ritter feel, it also made him very aware of his current very hollow state.

"You're right regardless," he said with a thoughtful exhalation. "Who wouldn't rather curl up next to a warm little thing at night? The only thing better than cold sheets is the weight of someone warm in the middle of them."

"Have a bit of experience behind that opinion there, Reed?"

Ritter laughed out loud at the sarcasm and in thankfulness for Cat's silence being broken. "No, Cat. Despite how I may seem, no, I do not."

He sat up and looked at the hammock. Cat was so deep in its fabric, only the smooth curve of her weight gave evidence of her being there at all. "Cat, I need to say something, and I need you to fight that estrogen-flamed tenacity of yours and not chime in."

"I heard you last night," she quietly interrupted.

"What?"

"I heard you."

Ritter smiled, remembering the noises he had made as Paul had rubbed his shoulder. "And what was it exactly that you heard, cupcake?"

Cat heard the taunting tone in his voice and her eyes watered.

After a too-long pause, Ritter slid himself toward the hammock. "Maybe you should go now, Reed." Her words stopped him momentarily, but the tone of her voice pulled him closer.

"Cat?" He pulled the edge of the hammock down and saw her hands covering her face. "Cat! No, love, no. It was Paulette and me." Ritter touched her arm and felt her emotion travel upward from his fingertips through his veins. "Cat, he was massaging my shoulder. It pops out on occasion. I swear to you on everything I hold sacred. Please! Look at me!"

Cat's hands pulled away from her eyes and Ritter immediately looked away. "Oh bloody hell. Put your hands back up. I can't bear that!"

She laughed at his response and sniffed. "I am sorry. I'm tired and sore. And . . ." She paused, but not nearly long enough to consider her next words. "It just hurt. I know it's none of my business what you do. But . . . after that conversation we had on the porch, you doing that right there under my nose made me feel like you were mocking me, and it really hurt." Her face knotted itself again, and Ritter felt her give over to a small heave.

"Cat, you have to stop crying and you have to stop being so emotionally available as well! I don't know which is more gut wrenching. All is well. Tip-top! Okay? It was me being an arse that you heard."

Cat wiped her face and laughed again as she saw Ritter covering his own to keep himself from looking at hers. "I'll stop, Reed. I'll stop." Ritter looked back at her and shook his head in response to his heart's urging him to hold her.

"So you didn't have sex with Ashta then?" Cat asked with a sniff. Ritter immediately rose to his feet, hid his hands in his pockets, and cleared his throat. "As I was saying earlier, before I was interrupted, I have to tell you something"—he glanced down at his watch—"and I need to get on with it."

Cat didn't miss his not answering her question regarding Ashta and took it as an admission of guilt. "If you need to leave Reed, go," she said in a bitter tone, looking away. Ritter spun on his heels toward her. "No, I don't need to leave. I just need you to look at me and listen."

Cat turned her tear reddened eyes and face toward him and, in that one instant, Ritter suddenly found himself battling between telling her what he had been sent to her house to report or falling to his knees and pouring out all his life at her feet like a drink offering. "Cat, I" was all he was able to say before the phone rang, and he sighed in relief.

He looked at the caller ID and then glanced at Cat before answering. "Dr. Thomas . . . Yes, how are you, sir? . . . She's fine. She's right here, but I haven't told her yet. I apologize . . . Okay, sir. Yes, sir. Keep well. Here she is."

Ritter smiled uncomfortably and extended his hand to Cat, motioning for her to take the phone. Cat moved her head back, knitted her brows and shook her head with refusal, unsure of what was happening. "It's for you!" Ritter said in a manner Cat found suspiciously sweet. She folded her hands and remained steadfast in refusal. "Woman, can you please acquiesce! We have an audience here!" he whispered in a pleading tone.

He finally sat down on the floor next to the hammock, put his hand on hers, and the phone back to his ear. "Give me another minute here, sir. I'm trying," Ritter said laughing. "Yes, she truly is!"

"I truly am what? Who is that?" Ritter shook his head at her and put his finger over his mouth in an attempt to silence her. The gesture angered her just as he thought it would.

"Yes, sir. I know. It's a bit endearing though . . . Yeah, she's making that face now actually . . ."

"Give me the phone!" she demanded.

"Hold on, sir, here she is . . . yea, yea, I know . . . adorably angry."

"Give it!" she said louder, reaching out toward the phone and wincing.

"Okay, hold on. Yes, sir. My pleasure," Ritter said politely while also helping Cat sit upright. He handed the phone to her, not releasing it until she agreed to speak only in English.

"What are you talking about? How do you know I speak Spanish?" Ritter put the phone in her hand, and his fingers under her chin. "All's well, Cat." Cat slapped his hand away and answered the phone. "Hello?" Her face filled with shock. "Papá? Eres tú? Dónde estás? Qué pasó?"

"English please," Ritter said softly, putting a hand on her back to comfort her.

Five minutes later, Cat hung up the phone and handed it back to Ritter without looking at him. He could practically feel the anger radiating off her skin. "Start talking," she said coldly.

Ritter swallowed hard, unsure why he felt like a child being scolded. "Hospital urgent care phoned me today whilst I was still at the rugby pitch and said a man had been brought in from an accident and was asking for me. I didn't recognize the name. Pauley overheard what I was saying, asked the name, and when I told him, he said it was your godfather."

"And you didn't think to call me!"

"Cat! I couldn't because of patient confidentiality. I shouldn't have even told Paul the name! I did so without thinking!"

"And you couldn't break confidentiality just once more to tell me my own family was in the ER? Whose friend are you anyway?"

Ritter looked at her in shock and after several quiet moments responded, "I don't know, Cat. That hasn't been made clear as of yet. However, I do know that I nearly went mad wondering if you were in the accident as well! I didn't ask for fear the answer would keep me from being able to drive with any amount of care! I know you are angry with me and worried for your godfather, but grant me a bit of license here, okay? I spent forty-five minutes today not knowing if the most fantastic —"

Ritter stopped himself. He took a deep breath and rubbed his eyes. "Give me a second. My Irish is showing," he said, laughing slightly with his face in his hands.

"Okay. Where was I? Got the call, went to hospital. Your godmother, Paloma, was there and met me. Cruz wasn't conscious when I got there but came to shortly after. He's had a CT scan and been checked completely. He's got a slight concussion and touch of whiplash but otherwise he's tip-top. I stayed and talked with him a bit and he thought it best for me to tell you about the accident. He didn't want you to know until after visiting hours were over in the case that you cajoled me into taking you up there, which"—he grunted as he stood—"you most certainly would have." Ritter then looked away as his face warmed red. "He said you spoke kindly of me."

"How long were you up there?" Cat asked coldly. Ritter sighed, knowing his answer wouldn't please her. "Up until about an hour before I came over here. Four hours or so I guess. Your godparents are charming, gracious, and they love you absolutely.

They are how I knew you spoke Spanish." He smiled in thought of the things they had said of Cat. "I thoroughly enjoyed meeting them."

The coldness from Cat signaled the end of his welcome and he slapped a rhythm on his legs before heading toward the screen door. "But I've done my job, however poorly, and you ought to get a bit of rest. Cruz said you were sorer than you let on so, I guess I will say good night."

Ritter left the screen porch, his chest aching increasingly in proportion to the distance growing between him and Cat.

"Was that the only reason you came over here?" she questioned sarcastically as he reached for the top of the fence.

Ritter put his hands on his hips and shook his head before huffing disdainfully. "What do you think, Ginger?"

Cat, taken back by the tone of his answer, looked down at her feet and then up to see that Ritter was staring at her with his arms folded. "I mean that literally, Cat. What do you think?"

Cat shrugged and looked away.

"No, no, don't act as if you don't know why I came over here and why I am still here. Yea, I had a job to do, but I could have had that done within a minute and told Cruz to ring you directly. You know what brought me over that fence and you are being coarse to me in return. I have my faults, but cruelty isn't one of them."

Ritter turned back to the fence and brought himself up. "Wait, Reed. Wait." He lowered himself and stood with his hands up on the fence and his back still to her.

"I am sorry . . ." She paused and Ritter turned to look at her. "I lost my real daddy in a car wreck and . . ." Cat stood to walk inside but her emotions left her legs paralyzed. She bit her bottom lip and turned her face away.

Ritter saw that she couldn't finish and walked back to the porch and wrapped his arms around her. "I do understand, Cat. I wish I didn't. But I do."

Cat's arms remained wrapped around herself, but Ritter felt her body relax against his and her lungs lose girth with relief. He kissed the top of her head and she felt his heartbeat against her cheek fall into rhythm with her own. One body ebbed where the other flowed and the couple stood in silence fixed together like two long-separated halves of a complete whole. Ritter rubbed his cheek against her hair and she sank herself deeper into the abyss of his affection. Suddenly, her stomach howled a long ripping complaint of hunger.

"What was that?" Ritter said as Cat covered her face with her hands. "Apparently, I am hungry." "Then we best feed you before whatever that is makes its way out and devours us both. Come on, little warm thing, let's go get a bite somewhere."

Cat put her hands on his chest and pushed herself away slightly. "No, I'm okay. Thank you. I have some food in the fridge I need to eat before I leave, and I haven't even started packing!"

"Packing? Where are you going?"

"Oh, I'm going to New Mexico for two weeks—"

"Two weeks!" Ritter interrupted, surprising the both of them with his tone. Cat stepped back, smoothed her hair and wiped her cheeks.

"Cat, as your doctor—"

"A doctor. Not my doctor."

"Fine! As a doctor, I really think you should stay home."

Cat smiled and put a hand on Ritter's chest, quieting both his mouth and his grumbling spirit. "I have to go and I'll be fine."

Ritter stepped back from her hand and rubbed the back of his neck. "I can't stop this madness then?" Cat smiled and shook her head. "You can a get suitcase down for me though."

Cat flipped a switch, and the lights from the ceiling glowed softly like fireflies. "The lights will get brighter. Just give it minute." Ritter closed the door quietly behind them and inhaled deeply. Cat's house smelled not just clean but of having never been soiled.

He walked slowly with a look of serious inspection as if in a museum. He touched the walls, the table, chairs, fabric of the couch and anything else that would allow. His fingers ran along the edges of pictures and he scanned each for evidence of Cat.

"Is this your father?" he asked holding up a picture. Cat smiled and nodded her head. "He was a vast one!"

"Vast is an understatement," Cat said, leaning on the door of the hall closet. "My daddy was cartoonish big! He said he was wearing his own daddy's shoes to school by the time he was thirteen. And I guess it's a good thing to be a huge man when you have hair that orange!"

Ritter smiled and looked from the picture to Cat, comparing the two. "He was a handsome bloke. You look a bit like him."

"Thank you. I take that as a compliment."

"It was meant as such," Ritter said, replacing the picture on a shelf. "Now where is that weighty suitcase? I feel like I should prove myself a bit after looking at your da's muscles there."

Cat smiled and pointed to the top of the closet. Ritter looked up and rubbed his chin. "Oh, no, I can't lift that. Looks like you'll be staying home after all."

Ritter rolled the suitcase through the kitchen and inhaled a hard gasp. He jumped from fright and instinctively put himself in front of Cat in a protective posture. "What the devil is that?"

Cat laughed and put her head down in Ritter's chest. "It's a cat, Reed."

"It's a puma!"

Cat pushed Ritter to the side and walked over to the cat that sat on the kitchen counter like a gargoyle. "This is Beau."

She leaned down toward the huge cat and the beast ran its cheek along her chin forcefully enough to expose its teeth. Ritter couldn't tell if it was an act of ardent affection or an attempt to establish dominance.

"He's a serval. An F2 we think. That's a second generation domestic. He was found and dropped off at the vet and you know the rest of the story."

Ritter and the cat continued looking at one another intently. "It's a male then?"

Cat hummed affirmatively in response and stroked down the feline's long mottled back.

"He won't stop looking at me."

"Well, probably because you won't stop looking at him, Reed! Come pick him up."

Ritter shook his head. "I don't think so."

"Oh for heaven's sake," Cat said, hoisting up the animal and putting it in Ritter's arms.

The feline pushed its heavy paws against Ritter's chest and looked him in the face. "He wants to kill me, Cat."

"He doesn't want to kill you! Just because something doesn't surrender in the way you are accustomed doesn't mean it isn't yielding to you."

"But it's pushing against me!"

The animal's nose quivered and it vocalized a chirp. "Cat . . ."

"Reed, just relax and let the animal be what it is." Cat put her hand on Ritter's back just before the serval rubbed its face against his chin. The animal then pushed his nose against the stubble on Ritter's neck and licked him with its equally course tongue. "See. He likes you," Cat said, looking up at Ritter's face. He smiled and looked down at her with a sigh of relief. She reached up, stroked the animal's chin, and then Ritter's. Ritter look down toward her hand and then, with obvious apprehension, held the animal close. It extended its long arms around his neck and rubbed its face forcefully against his throat.

"He's found my jugular, Cat. Has he slashed me open yet? Am I dead?"

"You're ridiculous is what you are."

Ritter loosened his hold and once again, the animal pushed itself back and looked the human square in the eyes before bounding down to the floor with a thud.

"What was that look?" Ritter asked with a slightly relieved tone. Cat laughed and said that the animal wanted to take Ritter in before taking him too close.

"He likes you, Reed, but he won't just love up on you all at once! He'll take you in a bit at the time but keep up his guard all the same. He's a smart little fella," Cat said, tossing a toy for the animal to retrieve.

Ritter nodded and then grinned. "So is that something all cats do or just that one?"

Chapter 10

The Devil Takes a Break from DC

The final boarding call was given for Cat's flight and the two stood. She looked at Ritter and raised her eyebrows. "Thank you again for giving me a ride. I could have driven myself or gotten a taxi."

"I wanted to bring you," he replied with a smile, handing Cat her backpack. "Yea, but you got called in early and all," she said, motioning toward his scrubs that, in her opinion, looked amazing on him. She felt herself blush and looked down at her shoes and wiggled her toes.

After she felt the heat leave her face she scratched her nose and narrowed her eyes at him. "And you won't tell me how you got a gate pass, huh?"

"I have told you already, Cat," Ritter said, smirking and stretching. "I asked for a gate pass and got one."

Cat sighed and began to walk away. "Wait! Come back," Ritter said in a loud whisper, and Cat turned with a smile. "Come here, woman."

Cat stood an arm's distance from Ritter and he reached out and pulled her closer by the collar. "I have something for you." He reached into the waistband of his underwear and pulled out a small drawstring bag.

"I don't have reliable pockets in my scrub suit here but fear not, good lady. There was no contact with my bits and pieces." Ritter opened the bag and took out a flat river rock about two inches long. "This is what they questioned me about in security."

He took Cat's hand, put the warm stone in her palm, and folded her fingers around it. "This stone means a great deal to me, and I want the both of you home safely in no more than two weeks time."

"What if I decide to not come back?"

"Don't say that," Ritter said with quiet seriousness and a tender smile.

The two stood before one another awkwardly in silence for a moment as Cat looked at the stone. "RJT. Are these your initials on here?"

Ritter smiled knowing that the answer was both yes and no. They were his initials but those on the rock were inscribed in memory of his twin. Cat smiled at him awaiting his response. "What is the *J* for again?" Ritter cleared his throat before answering, "Jacob." Cat nodded. "Reed Jacob. That is a beautiful name."

Ritter smiled in gratitude at the compliment. "And your name?"

Cat looked at him inquisitively and then laughed, realizing that she had not told him such a basic thing as her name. "Rachel Emmanuelle. They called me Emma in school."

Ritter smiled and pushed a strand of hair from her eyes. He then leaned over and kissed her on the head. "I took the liberty of putting my mobile number in your phone when you went to the toilet. Call if you like. Oh, and I wrote down your return flight information. I will be here to pick you up."

"You went through my backpack!" Cat protested. "And my phone!"

Ritter shrugged in response. "Boundaries, Reed. Boundaries," Cat said, emphasizing each syllable. Ritter winked and Cat rolled her eyes before turning toward the gate.

"Oh, when is your birthday?" she suddenly asked, recalling that he had said on Friday night that his birthday was in two weeks. Ritter put his hand in his pocket, looked away, and rubbed his chin. "Thursday of next week, but I don't really celebrate it so . . ."

Cat knitted her brows. "Oh. But you won't mind if I celebrate it though, right?"

"Boundaries, Emma . . . Boundaries." Ritter sighed and rolled his eyes, mocking the manner in which Cat so often rolled hers.

The flight attendant at the gate desk announced final boarding and Cat gave a final nod of good-bye. Just as she began her walk down the tunnel to the plane, Ritter called out, "I gave her my number." Cat walked back in sight of him. "What?" she mouthed. "The gate pass!" Ritter said loudly. The woman at the desk hushed him, and he winced in apology.

"I gave the woman at the ticket counter my number," he mouthed while motioning the action of writing and the holding of a phone with his hand. He then put his hands in his pockets, rolled back on his heels, and wiggled his eyebrows. Cat threw her hands up and backed away, shaking her head until the two lost sight of each other.

Ritter laughed, apologized again to the gate attendant, and then walked to the window to watch Cat's plane. He did not notice the dark woman walk to his side until her Caribbean accent drifted over his shoulder like mist.

"Your sister, she is very cute. Impish." Ritter was caught off guard and when he turned to look at the source of the voice, he was pleasantly surprised.

The woman's dark skin shined against the light coming in from the window and her mocha eyes narrowed as her cheeks rose into a smile.

"She's not my sister," Ritter said, looking back out of the window with a wry smile.

"Oh! I apologize."

"We're friends. Why did you think she was my sister?" he asked, furtively cutting his eyes down at the body of the beautiful, shining stranger.

The woman crossed her arms and shifted her hips. The thin lines on her pinstriped skirt rounded out against her backside. "I could tell there was an affection between the two of you. However, she is much older. Far too old to keep with the likes of you."

Ritter turned away from Cat and her plane, leaned against the glass of the window, and offered his hand. "I'm Ritter Thomas." The woman accepted his hand and, as the two touched, Ritter felt electricity travel up his arm.

"I am Lucy. Lucy Ferguson. And, your sprightly friend? What is her name?"

Ritter gave a confused look and glanced over his shoulder at the plane that was pulling away. He turned toward it completely, trying to see something from inside any of its windows.

"I heard you call her Cat," the stranger said, jealously pulling Ritter's attention back. "I would assume it to be a familiar version of Catherine. The name is Greek in origin. It means pure. Is that what attracts you so to her? Her so-called *purity*. Yes, it must be." The woman huffed a sardonic giggle from her nose. "Your friend was quite attractive at one time, that's easy to see. But alas, beauty like purity never stays intact with the passing of time, does it? I suppose it is true what they say. The lady that remains both beautiful and chaste does so only on canvas."

The woman ran her long finger down the crease of Ritter's scrub sleeve. Ritter looked down at the hand and then the woman's lips. He wanted to protest the disparagement of Cat, but something about the woman charmed his thoughts the way a glimmering object bewitches an animal.

"Rachel. Her first name is Rachel . . ."

"Aaaah," the beguiling woman interrupted as she sat on an adjacent seat. She hummed in thought as she crossed her long black legs that poured like steaming, hot coffee into her red high heels.

"A Hebrew name. It means, female sheep." Her dark eyes looked back at Ritter who was taking in her legs. "Ironic, wouldn't you say?"

Lucy's enchantment was temporarily broken as he glanced over his shoulder to watch Cat's plane taxi down the runway. But as soon as the plane ascended into the heavens, out of sight, her hold on him was quickly regained. Ritter went from standing in front of her to sitting down next to her.

"And just why would that name be ironic?" he said flirtatiously.

The woman laughed and the edges of her full red lips curved like licks of flame. "Well, one would think such a name would inspire peace and security. And yet, she conjures up such turmoil and vulnerability in you. Doesn't she, Dr. Thomas?" His name undulated within her accent and he found himself preoccupied with the movement of her tongue that flashed crimson between her perfect ivory teeth.

Her smooth hand reached down to his hip and fondled the hospital ID hanging on it that Ritter had neglected to remove. She rubbed her thumb across his name as well as the nickname, Ritter, he had written on the bottom of the badge that morning. Her touch rattled his senses further and he shook his head as if trying to awaken himself.

"She doesn't evoke any such thing from me . . . ," he said as bile churned in his stomach. The image of the ewe he had destroyed with his car a year earlier flashed in his brain followed by the image of his mangled sister. He rubbed his hands over his eyes trying to erase both.

"Oh, now, Doctor," Lucy purred as she put her hand under his chin. "Appraising one's appearance is vital to your job, is it not? Well, good doctor," she said slowly as she brought her hand down, tapped her finger on his badge, and then stroked it lightly down his thigh, "one has no need of a degree to diagnose what is seen on your face. Such turmoil within you and she, this *Rachel,* knows it as well as you and I. She knows what her presence does to you. It gives her power and leaves you settling for what she will give rather than what you want. You wanted to kiss her lips before she left, but you settled for only a kiss on her head. You wanted to give to her your heart but settled for a rock. Tch, tch, tch. As chivalrous as your name denotes. Ritter, from the German meaning knight. A lesser man would not tolerate a woman who treated his heart so thoughtlessly and left him feeling so emasculated. He would soon become bitter, resentful perhaps. But not you, Dr. Thomas, *le chevalier.*"

Ritter ran his tongue up and down the inside of his cheek and he squinted trying to focus his eyes. A silken ribbon of fog had wrapped itself around the cogent portion of his brain and he struggled to think clearly. The woman saw the evidence of internal struggle on his face and laughed.

"More turmoil, Dr. Thomas? Come." Lucy stood and held her long obsidian fingers out to him. Ritter looked at the lithe extensions of her flowing hand that beckoned him. They looked completely untouched by work or the sun. It was as if they had been created and taken from their smooth mold just before reaching out to him.

Ritter took the perfect hand in his. It was hot and soft: the type of hand he wanted all over him. The type of hand that made him forget what he relived in the back of his mind daily.

"So, Miss Ferguson. To what iniquitous place are you taking me?"

She giggled and the sound was like soft bells in Ritter's ear. "Ah, mon chevalier. Let's not be so formal." She ran a pyretic finger down the side of his face. "Lucy will suffice although," she brought her lips to his ear and whispered, "my friends call me, Lucifer."

Ritter froze and unclasped his hand. Lucy held fast and laughed. "Oh come now, Dr. Thomas! It is a play on the sound of my name! You are a man of Science. Surely you don't believe in such nonsense. Look at me. I have neither horns nor trident and honestly, could I conceal a tail in this skirt?"

Ritter looked down at her tight skirt and laughed uncomfortably. He swallowed hard and the two walked away hand in hand as the din of the airport whirled around them.

Lucy looked up at Ritter's worried twisted face and smiled. "Ah, hell. 'Whatever the tortures of it, I would think the boredom of heaven to be worse.'" She laughed and pulled Ritter's hand around her waist. "Isaac Asimov said that. He was a Jew as well."

Ritter stopped, pushed the woman out of the crowd, and pinned her against the wall with his anger and proximity. His face looked down at her hatefully. "What are you? I never told you I was Jewish and that is far more appropriate term than *Jew*!"

Lucy smiled and pulled his hand to her lips and kissed it. "I certainly meant no offense, Dr. Thomas. It was a lucky guess. The surname Thomas is Semitic in origin, Aramaic to be precise. And you have the bone structure so common among the western European Jewish population." She raised her face up toward his. "I find it most attractive."

Ritter backed away, put his hands on his hips, and looked down. Lucy could see he was trying to control his breathing. She walked to him and placed her hand over his racing heart.

"Your blood has quite a low smoke point. Let's have some refreshment. Oh, come now, Dr. Thomas. Don't be a petulant boy."

She tugged on his hand and he submitted to her wishes. He was both titillated and terrified like a condemned man readying for his last carnal liaison.

The restaurant was dark and Lucy chose a table in the corner that was most distant from the door. As requested, the waiter brought a cup of hot tea for Ritter and red wine for the lady. "You wouldn't prefer something stronger perhaps, Dr. Thomas?"

Ritter smiled as his tea steeped. "I am not much of a drinker. I don't have the blood for it."

Lucy took a long sip, licked her lips and smiled before saying, "An Irishman that can't drink? I have never heard of such."

Ritter pushed back from the table. "Okay, what are you? A bloody witch? A clairvoyant? How did you know that I am Irish and don't tell me luck."

Lucy threw her head back and laughed. After a cleansing sigh, she took another long sip of wine then replied, "No, no! I am an anthropologist. I study people. It is my life's work. I hear the brogue under your British accent especially in words containing an *r*. But it does so happen that I know several very good witches and clairvoyants if you are interested. Their guidance would suit you."

Ritter sipped his tea and sat quietly. Lucy could see he was uncomfortable and tried to ease him. "I am just finishing up a book on the psychological effects a name has on its bearer. I am seeking to find if a rose by another name would indeed smell as sweet."

Ritter looked at his reflection in his cup. "That is how you knew the meaning of the names?"

Lucy nodded and propped her chin on her hand. "It is. What is your middle name?"
"Jacob."

"Oh," the dark woman said, shaking her head. "That is not as lovely as Ritter. Again, Hebrew in origin: to supplant or take over by force or treachery. Very different than a *chevalier* and not in keeping with the surname Thomas which means twin."

Ritter coughed and put down his tea. "Twin?"

Lucy extended her hand to soothe him and he drew back.

"My studies have shown that someone bearing such a dichotomous name may subconsciously struggle to find a connection. To which name do you aspire and by which do you live? Are you the virtuous knight or deceitful Judas? You cannot be both as one negates the other and yet perhaps you are. But if so, how can the two be products from a single source, as are twins, when they are so contradictory? My guess is you battle with who you really are. Perhaps the two names pull at you as two dogs over a single bit of flesh?"

Ritter's eyes watered and he looked toward the restaurant's double doors that were open wide, feeling as if he should run.

"It is only a theory, my handsome Israelite. Don't be troubled. My study did not investigate the significance of surnames anyway. Enough of that look, now! Let's have some dessert! Shall we, Dr. Thomas? You look as if your blood needs a bit of thickening," Lucy said as she motioned for the waiter.

"What do you have in the manner of sweets, young man?" The waiter opened a menu and described the various desserts. "Hmmm, do you have a preference, Doctor? No? Well, what do you suggest"—she leaned over and looked at the waiter's nametag—"Manny?" The man pointed to the last item. "The caramel apple pecan pie. It doesn't look as good as the others, but all the girls say it is sinful."

"Mmmm," Lucy hummed, raising her eyebrows. "Let's try that," she said with a wink.

Ritter watched the waiter walk away and then looked across the table at Lucy who was looking back at him wantonly. "What does Manny mean?" he asked, motioning with his head toward the waiter. Lucy rolled her eyes, and the wine in her mouth, as if thinking.

"Most likely his name is Manuel which," she laughed, "yet again is Hebrew in origin. So many Hebrew names today! It is a form of Immanuel or Emmanuel, with an e, the feminine being pronounced the same, which means, of all things," she laughed and shook her head, "God with us. Bit of an overly ambitious name for a child. The very presence of God, the Hebrew God, among men. Hmm. Too great a burden to place on a child and such a foolish notion besides. *God among men,* indeed. Now, my question is, does the young Manny live up to such an expectation? Does he strive to be an example of the great Yahweh among men?" she asked sarcastically. "Or does he live as he chooses and expect others to treat him as a deity on earth, free and above condemnation. Does he oppress those around him with notions of sin and eternal damnation while he himself partakes of every iniquitous act he so quickly condemns with others?"

She extended her long leg, rubbed the pointed toe of her shoe against Ritter's leg, and then looked up. "Oh, thank you so much, Manny."

The waiter placed the pie between them. It was steaming and, as Lucy placed a fork in it, it oozed caramel. "Here, you have the honor of first taste," she said holding the fork out to Ritter.

"No, thank you. I am mildly allergic to pecans."

"Oh, come now, sir. There are no pecans in this bite! Only apple!"

Ritter smiled and held his hand up politely in refusal.

"Come, Adam, take a bite of the apple. You won't die," she laughed and nervously, Ritter took another drink of tea.

"My given name is Reed. Ritter is a nickname."

The woman rolled her eyes back in ecstasy as she took a bite of the pie. "Oh, you don't know what you are missing." She wiped the edges of her glossy lips and smiled. "Hmm, let's see. Reed is English, I believe. It means literally *reed*, which is interesting. Reeds are rather fragile plants. Once bent, even in the slightest, it breaks. Are you such a man?"

Ritter looked away sheepishly. "Oh my!" the woman said, changing the cross of her legs. "What a blush! How appropriate. Reed also means red, a color that throughout time has been associated with evil. You are a damned mess, aren't you! Yes, Reed is a name that fits you. I should have included you in my study!"

Ritter forced a laugh and looked away.

"Oh now! Don't worry. You don't have to live up to your name or stoop down, as the case may be. Others have held up under worse, Dr. Thomas." "Like what?" he said, swirling the dregs of tea in his cup.

"Well, in my experience, in the Western culture, the most burdensome of names is Christian. Far worse than Immanuel even. The weight of the cross on the shoulders robs one of the lightness of life all together! Now, its derivatives such as Christopher do not seem to have such an impact. But *Christian*? Honestly, who could live under such a weight of impossible expectations, sinful beings that we are! Some more than others," she said, seductively licking a bit of caramel from her lips.

"Speaking of sin, I will be damned to hell if I miss my flight. Although, I think you might be worth the condemnation."

Ritter paid for the meal, as any gentleman would, and the two made their way back to Lucy's gate. "To where are you flying?" Ritter asked, looking down at Lucy's arm that was entwined under his.

"Well, you think I am the devil, don't you? Obviously, I am going to Washington DC."

Ritter laughed in earnest and wiped away a bead of sweat from his forehead.

The two stopped at her gate that was beginning to board. Lucy stepped forward, dangerously near Ritter, her breasts touching his chest. "Aaah, finally, a smile from your lips, and here it is time for me to leave," she said as she tapped his bottom lip with her finger. She then looked deeply into his eyes.

"So, I suppose this is good-bye, Dr. Thomas. At least for now."

"For now?" he questioned.

"Yes, I will be back. You can count on it. I believe you would be worth the effort."

The wine on her breath smelled sweet and Ritter felt himself edging closer toward her. "You know, you never said what Lucy meant."

Lucy put her arms around his waist. "From Latin. It means light. Do you feel enlightened, Dr. Thomas?" He put his arms around her waist in return and slid his hands down to the sides of her full hips without regard to the crowd around them. "I definitely feel something," he said fearfully.

Lucy laughed. "Aaah, I am your *Angel of Light* in disguise then. However, I do not think that the meaning of my name is the question of the day. There are others more pressing." "Such as?" Ritter said as his eyes traveled down her neck.

She brought her face so close to his that he could feel the heat radiating from it. "Well, Dr. Thomas, the crucial question here is, will you settle for kissing me only on the head?"

Ritter took Lucy by the hand and pulled her into a corner away from the crowd boarding the plane. He put his cool hands on either side of her warm jaws and kissed her deeply. A feeling of faintness washed over him and he began to pull away to steady himself against the wall. Just before he did, she bit his bottom lip. Ritter gasped and put his hand to his mouth.

"That is just in case later you wonder if all this was a dream," she said with a smile. Her tongue rolled across her lips and licked a bit of his blood from her mouth. She then turned, as if none of it had happened, to walk away.

"Why me, Lucy? Of all the men in that room, why me?" Ritter asked. The dark woman stopped abruptly, turned with a flourish, and walked back toward him looking him up and down. "There were plenty of better-looking lads at that gate. Why did you choose to speak to me?" Ritter questioned with a breaking voice.

Lucy reached up and traced the line of his brow. "You are right. There were better-looking men, but you, Ritter, you looked, what was it that the waiter said? Oh, yes," she laughed and leaned forward letting her breath fall on his jaw, "deliciously sinful."

Lucy gave her ticket to the boarding agent and looked over her shoulder at Ritter once more before disappearing down the tunnel. Ritter slid his back down the wall and sat on the floor with his head in his hands. Sweat had dampened his forehead and he wiped it as well as the blood from his mouth. He felt bile rise up and he ran to the restroom barely making it to a trashcan before the scant contents of his stomach erupted.

He walked to a sink, closed his eyes and tried to steady himself as he pulled in cool air through his nose. He splashed frigid water on his face and then looked at his reflection in the mirror. It had a bloodless pallor and, had he seen it in a photo, Ritter would have thought it to be an image of himself in death.

CHAPTER 11

Babylonian Habits Are Hard to Break

By 4:00 p.m. Ritter was at Ashta's apartment and the two were lying naked on her floor sharing a joint. Ritter's head was resting on Ashta's stomach and his eyes stared at the ceiling as she ran her long fingers through his thick hair. The things Lucy had said to him at the airport sat heavy on his brain but the pot and the numbing presence of Ashta was steadily lifting the weight.

He began looking around at the decor of the apartment and the photos on the walls. There were several of friends and a few of Ashta in different picturesque places but none seem to be of family. He almost asked about her parents and then stopped himself realizing he didn't care enough about the answer to take the effort to ask the question. Ashta was as much a stranger to him as he was to her and he liked it that way. They knew each other well enough on a carnal level and that was all he wanted.

Ashta grabbed a handful of his hair and turned his face toward her. "Why are you so quiet? Pot do this to you?"

Ritter smiled and looked back up at the ceiling as he took another drag.

"Rit? Honey, you know if something is bothering you," she said in a syrupy tone, "you can always pretend it's not."

Ritter laughed and she followed suit, her stomach bouncing his head. He continued scanning the room realizing that as many times as he had been there, in that exact spot, it was all foreign to him. Ashta continued pressing him for an explanation of his silence and, to assuage her, he commented on the decor.

"You've a lot of Middle Eastern items. What does that engraving there say?"

Ritter pointed to a ceramic vase with Arabic calligraphy and Ashta smiled.

"*In the name of Allah.* My mom gave it to me. You want it? Take it. I just have it up to cover a hole in the wall," she laughed.

Ritter turned on his side and propped himself up on his elbow. "You Muslim?"

"Ha!" Ashta laughed. "I have way too good a body to be Muslim. It would be more of a sin to cover all this up than show it like I do!"

Ritter laughed and pinched her on the side. "Sin, eh? Would you say that I look sinful as in sinfully delicious?" he questioned, remembering how Lucy had described him.

"That's kind of random," Ashta replied with a laugh as she traced her finger down the line of his nose to his lips. "What happened to your lip here, Rit?"

Ritter grabbed her hand and bit her fingers playfully. "The devil bit me. Answer me, you. Do I have a look of sinfulness about me?"

Ashta sat up and looked him over. "You are a temptation. I will give you that. You have a great body despite being so short. How tall are you?"

Ritter laughed at her frankness and rubbed his bloodshot eyes. "I'm about 5'10". How tall are you, Circe?"

"I'm 5'11". Who's Circe?"

Ritter laughed and shook his head, holding his breath as long as possible to achieve the full mind-dulling effect of the pot.

"She was a beautiful witch," he hissed before exhaling, "in Greek literature that lived on an island. She lured hapless sailors in, Odysseus for one, and turned them into beasts with her potions. Is that what's in this fag here, Ash? Some magical herb? You planning on turning me into a pig?"

Ashta stood and slapped him on the chest on her way up. "You're a pig already, Rit. Trust me!" she said as she walked into the kitchen.

"So you don't think I look sinful so much as tempting, is that what you're saying?"

"I don't know, Rit," Ashta replied with slight irritation as she returned from the kitchen. "Look, you are gorgeous and, like I said, despite your shortness, you're built like a god. You seem much taller for some reason. Must be your build. Maybe that Roman nose."

Ritter smiled and gave her a sideways look. "Are you suggesting I have a large proboscis."

"I think you could smell what's cooking on the moon! But anyway, you're smart, rich, and nauseatingly pleasant. You're always smiling and without a care in the world. Until now of course. No more pot for you!"

She poured a few chips in her hand and then tossed Ritter the bag. "Thanks, love," he said before turning on his back and proceeding to finish off the entire contents.

"Oh yea, there's that accent! It's as good as a poison dart. Add that to all that other stuff. And, you are deceptively strong. Really! You pick me up like I weigh nothing!"

"What do you weigh?" Ritter questioned playfully. "That's not important!" Ashta said quickly with a smirk. "As I was saying, you throw around guys twice your size on the rugby field and run like a cheetah. And, you're surprisingly violent if I may add. I love watching you get into fights! It's such a wild side of you." Ritter grunted in response and hit his chest with his fist like an ape.

"Oh, and you're funny, and above all"—she moved toward him and kissed his neck—"totally fine with meaningless relationships, which consist of nothing but sex! Were it not for that and your heartlessness, I would be repulsed by you completely!"

"Just how am I heartless?"

Ashta rolled her eyes at his question. "You're kidding, right? You feel nothing or maybe just enough. I can't tell. And did I mention you are gorgeous? Love that nose!"

"You know, Ash, you don't have to keep chatting me up. I am a sure bet," he said, moving himself beside her. "Well you asked!" she said, pushing him away. "Perfect Rit the Brit. No worries," she continued while looking intensely into his cloudless sky blue eyes. "No complications, no dark and depressed side lurking in the background. You would need a heart for all that. You are tempting. I will give you that! And yea, if there were such a thing as sin, I would say you look sinful. I'd happily be damned over you that's for sure. If there were such a thing as hell."

Ritter kissed Ashta and pushed her head back with his face. "You don't believe in hell, Lucifer, and whatnot?" Ashta grabbed his face and pulled him back toward her. "I'm Jewish, we don't have a hell," she whispered.

"You said you were Muslim!" Ritter said, rising up suddenly. Ashta shook her head and continued pulling him toward her, reminding him that she had said that her mother was Muslim. She herself, however, was not due to her unwillingness to cover her "blessing of a body."

"I'm Jewish!" he exclaimed, laughing.

The demon sighed and lifted herself up on her elbows in a very human-like fashion. "Well, my dad is Jewish, but the only thing that confuses people more around here than telling them you are Jewish is that you are Jewish and Muslim! I just go with Jewish. Christians don't seem to mind it as much and this state is crawling with Christians! Speaking of, one Jew to another, don't tell anybody you're Jewish. In Texas, honey, Jews ain't nothin' but *Jesus Killers*!" she said with a mocking, heavy, Southern drawl.

Ritter smiled obligingly at Ashta's crude attempt at humor as she continued.

"But anyway, my dad liked my mom more than he liked being Jewish, so he gave it up. He couldn't very well have them both. So my dad is only Jewish by blood and, like I said, I can't be Muslim! It's just as well because I don't believe in any of it anyway. Which is lucky for you, you sinner! You're not a very good little Jewish boy, are you? What's that holiday that Jews are supposed to call people and apologize for all the ways they've wronged them? I will be expecting a lengthy call from you! You've wronged me all kinds of ways!"

Ritter smiled wickedly and looked Ashta over. She was, without exception, the most beautiful woman he had ever been with. Her black hair shined and poured out around her fair skin like gleaming hot tar. Green eyes sat like emeralds fixed in the settings of her long, dark lashes beneath her perfectly groomed black, Persian brows. The center of her full flushed lips were flattened like a doll's and always tasted of something sweet as did her skin.

He ran his finger down the side of her alabaster neck, over her heaping mound of breast, along her ribs to the chasm of her waste, and smiled as a wave of gooseflesh overtook the perfection of her. Her bodyline flowed and curved like the lateral, undulating pattern of a snake track in the sand and there didn't seem to be a square inch of her that did not speak of fertility.

"I should have known you were Babylonian," he whispered with sexy hatefulness. "Why is that?" she laughed.

Ritter explained that what began as captivity for his people became a culture. Even in exile, the men of Israel, his forefathers, had trouble remaining faithful to their wives and their God because of the inexplicable allure of the women of Babylon. With the Babylonian women came pregnancies, half-caste children, a new culture, and gods. Modern day Iraq was the epicenter of the Babylonian empire.

"You should have listened to your history professors, Ash!"

"I was too busy bedding them!" she joked in response.

"Oh," Ritter said as he ran his hand along Ashta's skin, "what is it about you Babylonian women that draw us Israelite men from our righteousness?"

"What is it about you Israelite men that makes it so easy for us?"

He rested his hand on Ashta's thigh considered her response and thought. After a moment, he asked, "How will you raise your children?"

"I'm not gonna have kids!" she snapped. "Are you kidding? Gag. I'm an L&D nurse if you've forgotten! I have seen what kids do to your body just in pregnancy! And childbirth? Have you seen what it does to a woman? Because let me assure you, it ain't pretty!"

"You don't plan to marry?"

"What? Who are you? Where are these insane questions coming from!" Ashta exclaimed. "Rit, I have no interest in what lurks in that hole in your chest where a heart ought to be! But for the record, no, I will never marry, you won't ever marry, and since when do you have to be married to have kids or have kids because you're married!"

Ritter laughed at her animation and pinched her stomach. "I plan to have children, and I will do so with my wife."

"Ha!" Ashta guffawed. "You want to be my baby-daddy, Ritz? Is that what all this is getting around to? I am not marrying you!"

Ritter grabbed a lock of Ashta's hair as she rolled away from him. She playfully slapped his hand away saying that she was going for more food and to escape his marriage net.

"I don't want to marry you, Ash!" Ritter called out. "Don't worry. I will never attempt to make an honest woman of you. But I will marry one day, despite what you think." Ritter could hear her laughing from the kitchen and talking as she opened the refrigerator. Neither of them would ever marry, according to her, as they were both incapable of fidelity.

"Your people, case in point, Rit," she said as she re-entered the room with a bag of cookies. "You said yourself that Israelite men weren't able to hold on to their faith for too long without wandering off like dumb sheep! I am a half-breed, prime example of that! Seems infidelity is in ya'lls DNA! *There is no good in me*," she said in a deepened, accented voice. "Know who said that? Your King David! It's in Psalms. Look it up. And by the way, didn't he have an affair with someone's wife, get her pregnant and then murder the husband? Yea, I think I remember that from somewhere. Hmmm.

"Maybe," she said softly with a smile, "you should stop trying to be what your king couldn't even be and embrace what you are: a sinful and lost dirty, dirty boy." Ashta wrapped herself around Ritter passionately and he laughed as the bag of cookies was crushed beneath them.

Ritter's phone sounded from near the door and he struggled to pull himself free of Ashta's embrace. His strength made short work of the battle and he jumped up from her side victoriously to run for the phone. She swore and threw a pillow at him.

"Ah, shut your pie hole, Ash! No one would call but hospital. You would deprive them of me, their god?"

"Dr. R. J. Thomas," he said, holding the phone with his chin while searching for underwear.

"How many names do you have?" the voice on the phone said with a laugh.

"Cat! Oh, Cat!" His face ached with the enormity of his smile and the phone fell. He grabbed it before it hit the floor and then stood dumbfounded for several moments, absorbing the visceral effect her voice had on him.

"Reed? You there? Or should I say, what is it now, RJ?"

"Yea!" he said excitedly, walking in circles. "I'm here. I just can't believe it's you! I miss you!"

"Oh please, Reed! You don't even know me!"

He stopped and tried to control his breathing and the wellspring of pure joy in his chest. "Well, you know me, Cat. You know me better than anyone quite honestly!" he said, feeling as if a yoke around his neck had been lifted.

"Cat?" Ashta said from behind him.

Ritter jumped and turned, putting the phone to his chest. "Just give me a minute, Ash," he mouthed. He could hear that Cat had said something and brought the phone back to his ear. "Say again, love?"

"'Love'!" Ashta exclaimed. Ritter waved his hand, motioning for Ashta to be quiet and laughed nervously. "Cat, you still there? Emmanuelle, mon petite femme . . ."

Ashta's hands slid around Ritter's waist, and he put his hand on her wrist to free himself. The more forceful his grasp became, the harder she pulled him toward her. He found himself in a tug-of-war between the woman who nourished him from beyond his reach and the woman he had in his hands who would love nothing more than to devour him.

"Can I call you later?" he asked. Cat could hear the evidence of struggle in his voice and a woman's laugh in the background. "I want to talk to you, love. Can I please call you later?" Before Cat could respond, she heard the phone being muffled as if a hand had been placed over it, Ritter's voice speaking in a harsh tone, and finally, the sound of a closing door.

"Rachel Emmanuelle," he said, walking into the guest bedroom, "come on now. I'm beggin' ya, lassy," he said jokingly in what he assured her was his finest *Oirish*.

"Reed, you don't have to—"

"Cat, I want to call you. Let me give you a ring in a bit. It's only fair. You got my heart. A body ought to be able to talk to its heart, yea?"

"Look, it's not big deal. I left you some messages on your phone and wanted to know if you got them. And Reed, I know you're with Ashta, so I have a feeling there are other things your body would rather do than talk to me!"

Ritter laughed and rubbed his chest. "Come on now, bird," he said, continuing with his childhood accent. "Ya know I wish I was wid ya! Seriously—"

Cat interrupted him with a hard sigh and breathy sardonic laugh. Ritter made a dramatic gasp, feigning shock and then assured her that he was being completely honest regardless of his present company.

"That's not what I am laughing at, Reed. If you would rather be with someone else then you are not completely happy where you are and yet, you are still there. You really have no concept of your worth, do you?" Ritter's face lost its smile, and he ran his tongue along the inside of his cheek. He was starting to feel angry, not at Cat but the truth of what she said.

"Not everyone is as wholesome as you, Ginger," he said in an amusing, melodic tone. "I'm like King David. *There's no good in me.*"

Cat was silent as if waiting for something and then replied sympathetically. "Reed, that's only part of the verse. David said, 'You are my God, I have no goodness apart from You.' It's not that he wasn't good, he just knew that any goodness he had was because of God's presence in his life. What is it with you accepting a half measure of things! Good grief, have you had the whole of anything beyond self-contempt? Reed, you are so worth much more than that!"

She said the final statement emphatically yet with the gentle forcefulness of a shepherd guiding with the curved end up his staff. Ritter slowly paced the room, feeling a bit disoriented, and wondered how he had managed to wander his way to the place he now found himself. He wished there were some way to turn back the clock if not eight years then at least eighty minutes. He should have gone straight home and not taken the slight merge eastward toward Ashta's house.

Cat read into the silence and apologized. "I am sorry. I have mouth issues. Things just come out on their own, and you need to go . . ."

"It's okay, love. I am glad you called me, and I would very much like to ring you later. That is, if my face is not too swollen to speak! Do you slap as hard with your hand as you do your words? Sod all, I may be permanently altered! I think, wait, yea, I can feel it swelling already. I'll look like the elephant man by nightfall."

Cat laughed and apologized again. "I am sorry. Really, I did not mean to hurt you. You need to go."

"What time should I phone you, Cat? Say a time! Say it or I will go straight way to your house, break in, and put on every pair of knickers you own!"

"Okay! 8:01! How's that? We're an hour ahead here though."

"8:01 it is then. And, Cat, thank you. I need a good knock on the head now and again."

Ritter went to the den and began putting on his scrubs.

"Oh, so we're done now?"

He looked behind him and saw Ashta standing in the kitchen with a glass of wine. She wore a short crimson-and-purple satin robe and when she walked toward Ritter, it fluttered like water, making her seem as if she were rising up from amidst the ocean during a red sunset.

"Who's Cat?" Ashta asked intrusively. "Oh, wait. Is that the . . . No! You are sleeping with that skinny little neighbor woman! Oh, I bet that's a sight!"

"What does that mean?" Ritter said acridly, turning toward Ashta with his hands on his hips.

"Oh, Rit, I know you, as you say, fancy a man on occasion but—"

"And what does that mean!" Ritter interrupted with eyes narrowed and nostrils flared. Ashta looked at him with incredulity and laughed.

"Because she hardly has a woman's body! Are you getting mad about this? Well, she must be better than she looks!"

"Stop talking about her like that!" he said in a low, slightly wild tone. "We are not sleeping together! She's not like that. She's a good girl."

"Oh!" Ashta said with a laugh, putting her glass down hard on the coffee table. "So what does that make me?"

Ritter closed his eyes and put his hand up to silence her. "I best be off," he said calmly as he tied the strings on his scrub pants and headed for the door.

"When she finds out who you are, she won't want anything to do with you, Rit."

Ritter froze with his hand on the door handle and Ashta continued.

"I have seen her kind. I have been judged and condemned by her kind for most of my adult life. She will rule over you with guilt! Count on it! And she sure won't share you! If you think you can sleep with anyone else while you are seeing her, you are sadly mistaken! Not that she will sleep with you! You are wasting her time, your time . . . my time."

She untied the sash on her robe and smiled as he looked up at her exposed body. "She doesn't know you like I do, Ritter. She never will."

Ashta walked to Ritter and took him by the hand. "Look at me, Rit." Ritter's jaw clenched and he pulled his hand away.

"No, you look! Ash, I know we have a bit of a regular thing going here but that doesn't mean we are a thing. You have known from the start that this relationship began and ended in the carnal realm. We're not even mates, you and I, okay? This is it. This is all there is between us. So keep your unsolicited opinions to yourself, yea? I don't want ill to befall you in any manner but Ashta, I have no intention of pretending to have affection for you that I do not. I'm heartless, remember? Now if you want a bit of a shag, then I am more than happy to oblige. However, if you want anything more meaningful than what we had on the floor there, then you need to set your sights elsewhere. Do you understand?"

An insidious smile crept across Ashta's face. "I understand, Ritter." She straightened the shoulders of his scrub shirt and ran a finger along his jaw. "But do you understand? You will have to give me up. There's no question about it. Are you really ready to give me up?"

Ritter sighed and looked at the beautiful girl coldly. "You are not the last sexual oasis in the desert, my good woman."

Ashta laughed, raised her brows, and swirled her wine in the glass. "Oh, yea. I know. But I am the only oasis that won't require you to pay for the water you drink!"

She took a sip of wine, rolled it around in her mouth and narrowed her eyes at him. "Every other woman is going to want something a titch more meaningful and, as we've agreed, you don't have the heart for that. They won't say it outright. It will be more subtle. She'll ask about your plans for the weekend or when your birthday is so that she can send you a little card or"—she paused and fluttered her lashes dramatically—"a picture of herself! The next thing you know, she'll want to know how you feel about something and what your family's like and then she'll want you to meet hers blah, blah, blah."

Ashta rolled her eyes, put down her wine and opened her robe completely to put her hand on her hip. "In the real world, it takes a long time to find somebody as shallow as me, Rit. You have to break a lot of hearts to do it, and that's nothing but a source of irritation. Speaking of, that girl you had in the hospital supply closet, you seen her again? I mention her because you pass her every day and I have seen her look at you. You broke her heart!" Ashta poked her lips out and sniffed like a crying child. "Pathetic. Ritter, you've been with half a dozen girls at the hospital and five I know of from bars, oh, and I know about Mo too! Shame that didn't work out. She's gorgeous. All those lovers, and yet, you keep calling me. Why is that? Is it that hard to leave Babylon?"

Ashta reached out and pulled Ritter's arms to either side of her waist. "I don't want anything from you except what you enjoy giving. I don't care to own you nor want you to declare you belong to me!" she joked with a wink. "And I never get jealous because I'm not selfish. However, your little friend on the phone, well, I assure you she is another story! She will have at least a dozen rules carved in stone from the get-go and will just add to it daily."

She reached down, untied his scrub pants, and pulled him closer by the strings. "Sweetie, I don't have rules to impose. I will not ask for devotion, burnt offerings, or self-sacrifice. All I am asking for is a little physical worship on occasion. Basically, I want a prostitute that I don't have to solicit or pay. That would be quite a Want Ad, wouldn't it? I bet I would get plenty of résumés!"

Ritter laughed and Ashta poked him in the chest playfully. She then pulled him close and whispered in his ear. "The job is all yours if you want it. You are highly qualified! The dress is casual, optional even! You can just leave your clothes at the door right beside your soul! I couldn't care less where your heart is. Just give me your treasure. Deal?" she questioned, looking him in the face. Ritter looked her over, and she could see the tension in his eyes had lessened.

"Don't mention Cat again," he said in a low, decisive voice. "Oh gladly!" Ashta replied with a laugh. "And how about you not mention me to her as well, Dr. Thomas?"

Ritter nodded in agreement.

"Great! You're hired!" Ashta said loudly, startling Ritter, causing him to drop his keys and the phone that he still held in his hands. "Now, Rit, as your boss, I am telling you to take off your clothes right now and get in my office."

Ritter sighed hard and started kicking off his shoes. "Well, I've not been sacked from a job yet. Be a shame to ruin such a spotless record."

The two traveled familiar territory with each other, and despite the lingering effects of the marijuana and the goddess-like beauty of Ashta, Ritter couldn't take his mind off Cat. His body tried to imagine it was her against him but instead of bringing passion to the liaison, his entire being filled with shame and with each breath he found himself feeling more vulnerable.

He opened his eyes briefly and felt as if the body beneath him had miraculously grown up around him like a dark, imposing forest. Suddenly, nothing in the room seemed familiar and he felt completely assailable. In response, he widened his back and lengthened his reach around Ashta. His chest filled itself with air, his body extended to its full length, and he still found her seeming to grow taller, more substantial and stronger in comparison to him. His heart began to race and he felt as if at any moment Ashta, her body, and all she represented in his life could send out its acidic vines and overtake him completely.

Some small thing inside him cried out for help and his heart tightened its grip on the one thing that seemed to provide a bit of light and refuge in his dark forest of self-imposed captivity: Cat.

Chapter 12

While the Cat's Away, the Rats and Cheese Prey

Reed swung slowly in the hammock on Cat's porch. Both Mama Dog and the fawn had managed to maneuver themselves to either side of him, and the three nestled in the fabric cocoon like peas in the proverbial pod. Ritter had set the alarm on his phone to sound at 7:59 p.m. and, until then, vacillated between the worlds of coherency and dream.

After leaving Ashta's apartment, he had pulled into the first parking lot available and listened to the messages Cat had left. She had given him permission to care for her animals and Ritter could barely contain himself on the drive home. Greater still was his effort to feign ambivalence as he got the key to her house from Paul who saw straight through the ruse. He kidded Ritter, as any self-respecting male friend would, mercilessly about it.

Both of Cat's messages dealt mainly with the care of the animals but the end of the second took, to Ritter's relief, a more personal tone. Unfortunately, at about that same time, the connection became weak and intermittently disrupted with static. Ritter had narrowed his eyes, held the phone close to his ear, and concentrated as if listening for a life-altering arrhythmia in a heartbeat. Three phrases he discerned completely: he was to kindly leave closed doors closed, not let the cat out under any circumstances, and finish off the raw milk in the 'fridge.'"

Ritter had laughed and wrinkled his nose in both mild frustration and confusion. Cat knew little of him but enough to know he would snoop and also that her simply asking him to not do so was probably sufficient to keep him from it. He had had no idea however what "raw milk" was or in what way he was to "finish it off." Paul had needed to translate that bit for him.

The final moments of the message had been the least comprehensible and, to Ritter, the most precious. From what he could piece together, Cat had said she was thankful to God for their new friendship and that she "would pray . . . and might actually miss . . ."

The connection seemed temporarily lost and Ritter had growled and shaken the small phone in frustrated desperation as if somehow the jostling would cause the missing words to fall into place. Strangely enough, the final phrases had rung clearly and they caused Ritter to listen to the message a half a dozen more times. Each time he did, he felt his chest tighten as if something inside him was swelling and pushing outward with the tenacity of Manifest Destiny.

You have a good heart, Reed. My daddy would have liked you a lot.

After the final playing of the message, Ritter had closed his eyes and held the phone against his lips for a moment. Good heart? He didn't understand why she would have said that but, as one who had lost someone dear to him, he understood completely the weight of her saying that her father would have liked him. Relating the feelings of someone dear to you that was no longer among the living was a brief resurrection for the deceased. It wasn't simply a matter of remembering them but remembering who they were. If Cat's attachment to her father was anything like Ritter's for his sister, she cherished and made careful use of those momentary miracles of his resuscitation.

The alarm on the phone sounded and the three sleeping animals were startled. The hammock shook wildly as the dog and doe quitted Ritter in favor of the quiet in their kennel, nearly knocking him to the floor. He laughed, sat up and checked his watch.

Cat's phone rang at exactly 8:01, Houston time, and the sound caused Ritter to sweat. The ring was answered and Ritter smiled and held his breath in anticipation. However, instead of Cat's, it was a man's voice that spoke. Ritter's jaw immediately dropped and silence overtook his ability to speak.

The greeting was rude and Ritter's voice faltered several times in an effort to respond. After clearing his throat and composing himself, he asked if he had reached Cat's *mobile*. The man on the other end had laughed mockingly at him, affirmed that it was, and questioned his reasons for calling it. Ritter's body immediately raised itself to standing in a defensive posture. His top lip quivered slightly and he rubbed the points of his canine teeth with his tongue.

Summoning all of his propriety, he asked politely to speak to Cat. There was a muffling sound on the phone as if it were being covered, but Ritter could clearly hear a woman laughing in the background. After a moment, the male rival on the other end of the line replied, in a mocking English accent, that Cat was busy. However, he assured Ritter, whom he called *Guvnah*, that Cat would return the call as soon as she found her panties. A swelling of laughter was heard in the background as the call ended.

Ritter was in complete bewilderment and confusion was a place he avoided like plague. He preferred standing on the firm concrete of experience and scientific fact. There had been no choice in this particular instance though and like a feral animal in an iron-barred enclosure, he was terrified. And, as a means of defense, that terror quickly turned to rage.

He leaped over the fence, stormed through his house, and grabbed his running shoes like a gorilla grabbing limbs of trees to beat against the ground. "You going running now?" Paul asked in confusion. Ritter wielded his eyes toward his roommate as if they were swords and left in a tornado of testosterone.

He began running as soon as the front door shut behind him and, with each step, felt his instinct to fight pour its energy into flight. He loved to run and, like every other thing at which he excelled, it came naturally to him. His body moved fluidly, efficiently, and quickly. He loved the initial ache in his legs as they rebelled against the movement and how they gave themselves over to instinct within minutes. He loved how his breath came rhythmically like a metronome in time with his heart, the primal drumming of his paws against the earth and, above all, the freedom that it all afforded him.

This run, however, was not about rejoicing in liberation. It was about unleashing rage and Ritter's legs bore the tyranny of his anger. His mouth filled with the bloody taste of lactic acid from muscles commanded to full throttle without mercy and his teeth began to feel loose in their sockets. He spit repeatedly and followed each with a hateful hiss of inhalation. The cry for oxygen in his legs caused a sudden deprivation of blood in his stomach and, in self-defense, it began pushing out its scant contents. Ritter swallowed back the jealous-green bile and focused his eyes ahead like a falcon. His brain thought of nothing except *forward* as the wind of his own furious speed rushed through his hair.

His feet maintained a hummingbird cadence until the felled oak that he had first seen the night he took Cat to the hospital came into view. As he closed in on it his paced slowed and, as soon as his muscles resigned some of the blood they had hoarded, his stomach triumphed in its effort.

Ritter stumbled toward a pine tree, braced himself, and vomited hard. His eyes swelled and small vessels in the skin under them engorged from the strain. After three heaves, there was silence. Ritter wiped his mouth on his arm and then rested his forehead against the rough tree. He glanced down at the ground and hoped any emotion he had in his heart for Cat had been purged as well.

The uprooted oak was smaller than he had originally estimated. His arms could easily encompass it with room to spare. Still, Ritter could not imagine why this tree, rather than the myriad of others, had given way. The roots were long and reached farther out than he would have imagined. However, from what he could tell, despite the expanse of the root network, there had been no depth to it. It was as if the tree had put all its effort into what would be seen and forgotten the necessity of what would not.

Ritter walked to the end where the tendrils of root hung heavy with earth. He ran his fingers along several and rubbed the cool damp grit between them. The roots all bent toward the ground, bearing witness to their last attempt to hold fast, and he wondered how long it had taken them to let go. Had they released strand by strand or all at once like a hand losing its grip? Above all, Ritter wondered if at the moment of their being torn away if there had been some measure of relief in having ceased their fight, having given themselves over to the will of the wind.

"Pretty awesome, huh?" a voice said from behind him. Ritter jumped and a figure appeared from the darkness to his left.

"Oh, man, I am sorry! I thought you heard me walk up."

The streetlights cast a glow on the man's bare chest as he came forward. He was about Ritter's height and build, and his features were similar as well.

"It's cool, isn't it? Looks like somebody just came up and pushed it over. And look down here," the man said as he pointed to a freshly dug hole under the bottom-most roots. "Somebody's set up tent down there."

Ritter asked what type of animal it might be and the handsome stranger shook his head. "I have no idea. Maybe an armadillo. Want to stick something down in there and find out?" he said with a wink and elbow to Ritter's side. Ritter laughed and a grin of conspiracy found its way to his muzzle.

"I'm Baylor. Call me Bayle." Ritter took the man's hand and returned the introduction. The two then walked around the oak kicking, pushing, and prodding it like boys.

Ritter broke an exposed root in half, noticed it was still green, and commented on the tree's impressive will to live. While talking, he glanced over at Bayle and saw the stranger's blue eyes looking him over and not in the way one male creature instinctively sizes up another. Ritter smiled to himself. As often as he had seen that look from men and women, it had never gotten old. It gave him a rush every time. The beautiful have a certain power over those that find them so.

He held up a stick then motioned for Bayle. The two squatted down in front of the mysterious hole at the root bed and giggled in the way only trouble-seeking boys do.

Ritter put the stick in the hole slowly and prodded around. After a tense moment of silence, Bayle grabbed Ritter and pushed him down into the small, damp pit. A hiss rose up from the ground followed by a movement in the dirt, and the two men/ children jumped and ran.

When they slowed, Ritter bent over with laughter. "Oh, I needed that!" he said in a breathless voice before pushing Bayle hard.

"Why? You got woman troubles?" Bayle said with a laugh before pushing his prey hard in return. "Don't tell me it's not a woman! Every man knows the look you got on your face. What, she cheat on you or something?"

Ritter stopped laughing, exhaled hard, and rubbed sweat from his forehead. "She's not even my girlfriend."

"Good! Keep it that way! That deep ache in your chest that's all over your face? Man, that's her gnawing on you like a rat does cheese! And she knows it! Girls try to accuse us of being the rodent in the relationship, but they know that's not how it is! They're the one with the teeth.

"I don't care how great this chick seems, she's not any different from any other gal! They all chew on you until you don't have anything left to defend yourself with. And then you know what they trick you into?" Bayle held up his left hand and displayed his wedding band as if it were a shackle. "It gets tighter every day!"

Ritter looked confused. "Was it tight the day you married?"

Bayle shrugged. "I don't know. A little maybe. She's a nice girl and all. She's just not the girl I want to sleep with for the rest of my life! Good thing too 'cause we never do!" An obligatory laugh followed and then Ritter asked why.

"Oh, you know," Bayle said, raising his eyebrows. "It's the same person every single time! You can't get away from that. You just get bored and lose interest. I mean, Mexican food is good, but it's not what I want for dinner for the rest of my life. I like variety myself and lots of it."

Ritter stopped. He had no respect for the sanctity of sex but a great deal for marriage. "So you just cheat on her?"

"I do what it takes to keep us together. Simple as that. I actually do love the girl, man! I'm not heartless. Divorcing would kill her, and I do like Mexican food every now and then!" he laughed.

"Look, she's away working as much as she's home! When she's here, she's got her cheese! She leaves, the cheese gets a meal of his own! She's never suspected and won't.

"Hey, I live right over there. Come have a drink with me. The *missus* is out of town on business. We can do whatever you want to do."

Ritter contemplated the invitation and all that he suspected it might imply. "You're thinking too much. Come on!" Bayle laughed as he grabbed Ritter's arm and tugged on him.

The road home was just ahead but, just as he had earlier that day, Ritter took a detour. And, he spent the next several hours drinking, laughing, and being both rat and cheese.

CHAPTER 13

Prison, Prophecy, and Texas Hold 'em

Later that night, the moon poured like an interrogator's lamp through Cat's blinds onto her couch where Ritter was lying. It was just past midnight and he couldn't believe it had not even been a day since she had gone. It felt like more. He had certainly been lecherous enough for it to have counted as several.

Ritter thought about the man who had answered Cat's phone and found himself ferociously jealous, a feeling he had never before experienced. Now he knew why it was a sentiment associated with green. It made your guts churn and feed on themselves with the body's own alkaline, grass-colored bile.

He turned on his side and looked around at her walls. The only picture of her on them was the one Ritter had seen of her and her father. She had changed very little since childhood, as beautiful then as she was now. Beautiful in a way Ritter couldn't describe as it had little to do with her appearance. It was just a magnificence that she gave off like a scent and being near her made a person feel as lovely as they found her to be.

Captivating, he thought finally and rubbed his eyes with his fingers. That was definitely the best description. However, not in a way that held him captive, bound, or burdened. On the contrary, around Cat, even thinking of Cat, he felt lighter. He felt liberated. He felt *forgiven*. And, for the first time since his sister's death, had not a bit of guilt about it.

Ritter was, as he had boasted, allergic to remorse. Outside of his family and Paul, he refused to feel culpable for his selfish or thoughtless treatment of others. Any kindness he showed was generally self-serving and, combined with his beauty, always seemed a grander display than it truly was.

In truth, Ritter wanted to hurt people. It made him feel more deserving of the prison term to which he had sentenced himself. He was a criminal, blood-guilty, and neither the law nor his family would convict him. Somebody had to make him pay his debt to the world. If no one else would lock him up and throw away the key, then he would lock himself away and hold on to the key so that no one else could set him free.

That was the only thing for which Ritter Thomas would allow himself to feel guilty: feeling absolved. And yet, at that moment on Cat's couch, with sleep seducing his brain and body, his past and present crimes seemed to belong to someone else entirely. Cat's home was like an impenetrable womb where he could let go of all that came before and be reborn innocent, washed clean and rubbed with salt. It was the one place where he didn't hear the constant, clattering drip of blood from his hands.

Just before surrendering to exhaustion, Ritter clicked his tongue and Beau bounded out of nowhere toward him. The semiserval feline walked onto his chest and lied down. Its purr rolled through Ritter's ribs and shook away the feelings of jealousy that had affixed loosely to his heart, leaving only faith behind. Faith that Cat was somehow better than the night's events had bore witness to her being and that he, himself, was as well.

Ritter scratched behind the cat's firm, tall triangular ears and kissed its nose. "You want to break out of here, mate? Yea, I know. You miss the wild, don't ya? It's overrated there, lad. Trust me. It'll tear ya to bits, and, if it doesn't, you will wish it would. You just keep yourself here. Yea, just stay here."

The cat reached out its long arm and buried its paw in Ritter's hair that was still damp from Cat's outdoor shower. Then, it laid its head down on his chest and slowly blinked its shimmering eyes. The two males looked at one another, each fighting the heaviness in their lids, until an instinct greater than curiosity interceded, and the two semiwild creatures succumbed to sleep.

The next week went by much as the weeks before meeting Cat. Ritter went to work earlier and stayed later than necessary. He ran, worked out, practiced with the rugby team, and had lovers both old and new. Come nightfall however, Ritter's world changed as he went next door to his refuge.

He fed the animals, played with them, kissed them all, without hesitation, on the mouth before tucking them in and then curled himself up on the couch with his feline soul mate. There was no word from Cat but being in her home, surrounded by her clean smell, was an analgesic to the wound caused by her silence.

He voluntarily took a shift at the hospital the Sunday before his birthday. By 6:00 p.m., he was driving home and contemplating what to do to keep his mind off Cat. As he pulled into the driveway, he saw Paul coming out of the house with a bag of poker chips in one hand and a bag of tortilla chips in the other.

"Where are you going, Paulette?"

Paul motioned across the street with his head. "Texas Hold 'em. It's the fifth Sunday of the month. We always play when there's a fifth Sunday. Come on."

Ritter put his keys in his pocket and took the bag of chips. "I have no idea what you are talking about, but I'll go wherever it is you're—"

"Oy!" an elderly voice called out. Ritter stopped with shock and looked up at Isaiah. "That's what you Brits say, ain't it? *Oy?*"

Ritter laughed and nodded.

"Well, come on then. We ain't fixin' to wait all night, know what I'm sayin'?"

Ezekiel walked out and yelled at his buddy. "Get ya old tail in this house and quit yellin' like a loon out here! Oh, howdy there! You the *tea drinker* I take it. I don't think I have introduced myself formally. I'm Ezekiel Washington, but folks just call me Eazy."

The elderly black man extended an aged but strong hand, and Ritter returned the introduction. "All right then! Ya ready to lose your britches in poker, Earl Grey?"

Ritter had never played poker but understood the concept quickly. Over the next several hours he managed to win almost every game and pull out quickly from the games he knew he wouldn't. The men kept a tally of the winnings on a piece of paper and, according to it, they all owed Ritter a total of over four hundred thousand dollars. The money wouldn't actually be given of course. In fact, the winner was to donate twenty dollars of their own money to the charity decided upon by the biggest loser. However, pride was at stake and, in that respect, Ritter was stripping the three other players mercilessly and walking away rich as a true king of England.

"I'm 'bout to tump this h'yer table over!" Izzy said, throwing down another losing hand. "I'd have to help ya but the idea is striking me as a good one," Eazy said, throwing down his cards as well followed closely behind by Paul.

"Good grief, RJ! You've never played poker?"

Ritter laughed at his friend's frustration. "I told you I haven't, Pauley, but it's not so difficult a concept! It's all about probability. You determine the number of possible outcomes that satisfy the condition being evaluated and then divide that by the total number of possible outcomes. There are only fifty-two cards in the deck, mate! Look at the cards we saw on the table this round—"

"Whoa! Hold up! Yur countin'!" Izzy yelled.

"What's *countin'*?" Ritter questioned, laughing at Izzy's face that was quickly reddening with anger.

"Cheatin'! 'At's what it is, tea drinker! That's all I'm sayin'! I got to get up outta this hyer room 'for I kill somebody," the elderly white man said as he stormed out of the room, continuing his rant as he went.

"I don't know if that's considered card counting, Izzy."

"Don't bother, Paul," Eazy said in frustration while cleaning the table. "That ole' mule's just mad he lost is all. Sore loser! Always has been!"

The elderly black man looked over his shoulder toward the kitchen and then leaned toward Ritter. "I saw an unidentified flying holy object once—"

"I hear you in there! Don't you say it were an alien," Izzy yelled.

"I ain't said nothin' of the kind! What kind of hearin' aid has the Veteran's Admin done give ya?" Eazy yelled back before leaning over and continuing in a whisper. "It come at me like a whirlwind from the north and inside was a creature with four faces—"

"You say alien again and I'll blow you up out the water like a German U-boat, Eazy!"

"Ya, listen here, Isaiah, I know what I said and I didn't say nothin' 'bout it bein' no alien! I know what it was! Only reason you know anything's 'cause I went and told ya! I'll add that to my list of thangs I done wrong right after taking a bullet for ya in Iwo Jeemer!"

"I never asked you ta put yur baggy britches in the way! That's on you and yur butt!"

Paul stood and stretched. "I'm getting out of here before the crazy train makes a stop. You comin'?"

Ritter rubbed the laughter-induced tears from his eyes. "No. I'll stay and have another drink or two. Somebody will need to be able to testify as to what went on between these lads tonight!"

"Oh, you leavin', son?" Ezekiel said, immediately changing in demeanor and tone. "Don't let that old goat run you off, Paul!" Isaiah said coming back into the room with a bottle of prune juice, a bag of dried fruit, and a bowl of peanuts on a tray.

"No, I better go fellas. Hey, two drinks is his limit, which he has had already," Paul warned, pointing to Ritter. "He gets awfully precious after three and after four he will tell every secret he's ever heard and then want you to play with his hair until he falls sleep!"

"I have no idea what you are talking about, Pauley! You have confused me with someone else," Ritter said, shaking his head and then pouring another glass of scotch from the bottle he had run home to get when his winnings were still in the ten thousands.

An hour and three more glasses later, Ritter's head was on the table. He was laughing, twirling a lock of his hair, and telling every embarrassing story he knew about Paul. He followed each with a plea not to tell anybody. They were secrets no one was supposed to know.

Isaiah and Ezekiel laughed and then looked at one another. Their demeanors took a more serious tone as they considered what needed to be said and looked with pity at the man before them. He had told so many secrets, none of which were his own. Even inebriated Ritter held tight to the concealed hurt within him.

"Ya love her, boy?" Ezekiel asked.

Ritter glanced up and smiled before again laying his head down. "Paulette? No, no. Not my type!"

A silence caused him to look up at the two men, and he rolled his eyes. He knew the men were referring to Cat but simply shrugged and mumbled something unintelligible.

"Listen to yourself babble. Don't go denyin' it, Reed Jacob. You dream yur with her and then wake up with yur soul unquenched. And so what do you do?"

Ritter looked up and tried to focus his eyes and remember when he had told Izzy his name. He didn't recall that he had.

"You go an' quench yur thirst with adulteries. You turn yur eyes from her and play the harlot with those who are nothing next to her in comparison!"

"Tell him the Word, Izzy! Ya standin' tall in your iniquities, boy, but on the inside, ya loathe yaself! Ya whole head is sick and ya whole heart faint."

Ritter put his hands on either side of his face and tried to keep the room and his mind still. The men's voices had become indistinguishable from one another and were flying wildly around his head like birds. In his drunken state, Ritter couldn't decide whether to let the words light upon his ears and nest in his brain or to bat them away.

"Okay, lads. I am totally pissed drunk. I can't tell which of who you're spanking! Wait . . . speenk, speaking . . ."

Ezekiel reached out and put his hand on Ritter's head. "Ya, speakin' nonsense like a baby, livin' like a rebellious child and have dishonored the name of ya Father, the god of Jacob in the way only a man can. Ya got no shame and have lost the ability to blush!"

"But God ain't forgotten you, young feller! Can a mama ferget the child she nursed? Boy, yur inscribed on the palm of His hand."

Ritter's head moved slowly as if floating in water and he laughed. "Wait, who are we talking about again? I thought this was about Cat."

"You just a remnant of who you used to be, Reed Jacob. Yur a temple whose bricks have just fallen all down."

"But He gon' rebuild ya with smooth stones."

"Jehovah's got wisdom and understandin' and judges not with only what He sees and hears."

"He know ya heart, child of Jacob! It ain't nuthin' but a heart of stone, but He gon' replace it with a heart of flesh!"

"He'll be yur God and you gonna be His people!"

"I should have known," Ritter said in a corroded tone. His pride sobered up his brain enough for him to think clearer and he raised himself to standing. His body swayed slightly and he sniffed hard before haphazardly pushing his hair back from his eyes. Nothing on him seemed steady except the condescending smirk on his lips.

"Don't you two bloody pensioners talk to me about God!"

"In repentance and rest ya gon' be saved, but oh, ya ain't willin', are ya?"

"Ha!" Ritter laughed. "Why should I be willing? Huh? What do I have to repent of and to whom should I spill out my heart? Who, God? HaShem? Where is He? Huh? Where was the *God of Jacob*, as you said, the day her body was bashed to bits? Huh? Where? And, where has He been every day since? Tell me that! Ask Him! What answer has God got for that one?"

"Son," Ezekiel said in a quiet, calming voice, "God ain't gonna be inquired of by man."

Ritter shook his head and sniggered. "Of course not. What is He going to do exactly if not *be inquired of* by me?"

"He'll refine you like silver. That's why you been put to the fire. He's put you through judgments to gain you righteousness."

"And why is it I need righteousness? For what should I be judged, aye? For an accident? It wasn't my fault!" he yelled with a nod, pointing an accusing finger at himself. "I was tired! I had been up all night helping others with their studies. Charity! I was being charitable, and where did it get me? It got me a scarlet letter to wear 'round me neck!"

The sarcastic tone and mocking accent fell away with a piece of his armor and, for a moment, he spoke as the broken human that he was.

"I was tired," he whispered hatefully. His eyes welled with tears and he wiped his nose quickly before reaching out to steady himself against the wall.

"It wasn't my fault! I fell asleep at the wheel." Ritter put the heel of a hand over an eye and his back quivered slightly with emotion. "Why was she there? Huh? Why was she out so early? Why so close to the road? Do you know what it sounds like when a body hits the bonnet of your car? Do you? It sounds like death! Just, hollow. Heavy. Dead."

He leaned against the wall and inhaled deeply to compose himself. "I should have died, you know. Should have been me. I am the best of doctors, but she, she was the best of people. I deserved to die and if it weren't for my parents I would have done myself in long ago."

"Don't go sayin' that boy," Eazy said, walking cautiously toward Ritter. "Ya in a dark place now, but God's gon' guide ya into the light. From rugged paths to open plains! He is ya Creator and has called ya Himself by ya name."

Isaiah pulled a chair over. Ritter looked at the offer and rolled his eyes. He was a man that could handle his liquor and life and didn't need to sit down on anything an account of either. Izzy shook his head and sat in it himself.

"I ain't too proud to sit, young feller. I might be old but yur weak! Weak from the work of yur own hands. But, God's gonna make you strong. He's gonna uphold you with His right hand and He ain't gonna reject you no matter how much you go a' rejectin' Him or yurself.

"He gon' wipe out ya transgressions like a heavy mist," Eazy said with a raised hand. "The Lord has declared a new thang for ya. Ya got to let go of what has been."

Ritter looked at the men standing before him and smiled. He then counted off on his fingers as he spoke. "One, I am abso-bloodly-lutely, in-the-bag drunk. You're good men albeit a bit forward. You are my elders and finally," he said, holding up a fourth finger, "I like you. Not sure why but I do but, it is those four reasons that are keeping me from thumping you both squarely on the head."

The three laughed. Both Izzy and Eazy told him that they loved him and, for some reason, despite the alcohol and air of cynicism, they were believed.

Ritter turned his head toward the window and, through the sheer curtains, he saw the outline of Cat's porch just beyond the glow of the streetlight.

"Hey, lads, that new thing you say God's got planned for me. Is it . . . ?" Ritter motioned with his head toward the window and the two elderly men smiled. They walked forward and each put a hand to his cheek the way a grandfather would his grandchild.

"Hear the words of the prophets, young feller. Cat's been sent to you and she gon' find you."

"Ya gonna be strugglin' on ya own blood. Then she gon' cover ya with her robe, sprinkle water on ya, and cleanse ya flesh of its filth."

"She'll heal yur wounds and strengthen yur heart. She will be yurs, but you won't settle for being hers."

"Ya gon' follow the road back to Chaldea, back to the Babylonian ways, and ya sin gon' take root in that fertile ground."

"Yur gonna break Kitty's heart. She'll weep bitterly and be bathed in her own blood."

"Her presence will leave ya, and ya gon' know what it's like to walk through this world without her."

"But she'll come back. She will hold you as her own and willingly take yur part of the oath you gonna make with death."

"Three days she'll be in the still tomb of her own body. Then she will come back to ya, young fella. And you will be with her when she is delivered back to her Father."

Ritter looked at the men's faces with fear. "Wait, what? Bathed in blood? A tomb? Are you saying she is going to die? What are you saying?"

"Then God's gon' lead ya into the land He's promised ya, back to ya true home."

"You'll see yur children, yur son and yur daughter, and yur gonna know they are the work of God's hands!"

"Then you gon' sanctify the Holy One of Jacob! Ya gon' be filled with joy and gladness!"

"Yur sorrow and sighin', they're gonna flee! Yur gonna be restored, Reed Jacob!"

"In Zion ya gon' be blessed with a double portion!"

"God has, in His love, delivered you and cast all yur sins behind you! Rejoice exiled one!"

"And hold tight to the servant He has chosen to lead ya! Through the broken, ya gon' find wholeness."

CHAPTER 14
Pictures Speak And Old Habits Scream

The days after the poker night began passing quickly as if the planet itself was eager for Cat's return. Ritter plundered his mind on several occasions trying to remember what all had transpired at Isaiah's house that night, but it was to no avail. The memory had been mentally digested and expelled as waste, never to be reclaimed in its entirety.

There were, however, tiny glimpses of the night with its emotional regurgitation and prophetic words that bubbled up in Ritter's brain unexpectedly and intermittently like belches. What he saw in those brief recollections caused him also to see something new in the smiles of both Isaiah and Ezekiel: clarity of knowing. Their elderly faces looked at him as if he were a book they had read more than once. And, some aspect of their visages made Ritter feel, and he could not explain why, as if they knew the entirety of his biography to include the chapters Ritter had not yet lived.

Thursday afternoon Ritter left work on time for a change and came straight home. It would be his last night at Cat's house before her return and he wanted to spend all the time there that he could.

He went to his house to grab more clothes before heading to Cat's and, as he walked into the kitchen, he saw a package on the counter. The light above the sink cast a halo down on it in the dimly lit room.

"It's yours," Paul said, walking to the refrigerator. "Got here yesterday. I think it's from Cat. It's been sitting right there. You not see it?"

"I thought it was yours," Ritter said, tearing into the box ferociously and quickly unwrapping the present inside. It was a framed pictured with a note taped over the glass, obscuring the image. Ritter read the note, looked at the picture, and burst into laughter. He then handed the picture over to Paul whose head immediately went back in revulsion.

It was a photo of, without question, the most hideous-looking bovine to have ever walked the earth. The cow's back was swayed, her hind legs were much longer than the front, and an udder seemed to be MIA. She had one horn and one stub, a lazy eye, and the picture was taken at just the moment her tongue had begun investigating a nostril. There was a garland of flowers around the cow's neck and what looked to be lipstick on her bottom lip. Standing behind the beast was Cat, laughing heartily.

"What is that about?" Paul asked, handing the gift back. Ritter wiped a laughter, and relief, induced tear from his eye and read the note aloud.

Reed,

If you were a bull on my ranch, this would most certainly be your mate! Don't let the looks fool you. She's a catch. You two were made for each other. Moo.

Happy Birthday,
Cat & "Bonita"

Ritter briefly explained the conversation he had had with Cat concerning the mating of cows and the criteria for their pairing: attributes were matched with shortcomings and the perfect with the most imperfect.

Paul laughed and scratched his head. "Well, I am glad to see your birthday being acknowledged for a change. And it sounds to me like Cat is acknowledging a whole lot more than that."

Ritter felt heat wash over his face and he tried to contain his smile. If ugly animals were matched up with beautiful, what type of specimen did Cat consider him to be if that hideous conglomeration of a cow were chosen to be his mate?

He examined the picture again and ran his finger over Cat's image. Paul smiled and pushed his friend's shoulder as he passed by him.

"Another guy answered her phone."

Paul looked over his shoulder having hardly heard what his friend had said to him.

"I said, another guy answered her phone when I called her. And Paulette, old girl," Ritter said before putting the picture on the counter and rubbing his hand through his hair, "it sounded as if Cat was rather keenly occupied."

Paul gave a look that showed he had not understood and Ritter sighed. It was hard enough to say it the first time without having to explain the implications. "What don't you get, Pauley? She was *with* a man," he said, making quote gestures with his fingers.

The entire scenario was painted for Paul and he immediately giggled. Cat's phone had been stolen in the airport not long after Ritter had spoken to her from Ashta's apartment on Sunday. Whoever answered any calls she received that night was the thief and apparently considered himself a bit of a comedian as well.

Cruz had called later that night to let the boys know about Cat's phone and that they should call him if there were any problem with her house or animals. He said he would call the boys when Cat had a new phone but, as it turned out, she herself had called and left a message the following Tuesday telling them her new number and to ask if all was well.

Paul told Ritter he had left two notes on his bed telling him as much and Ritter went quickly to his room without regard of how desperate his speed made him seem.

The notes were lying on his pillow undisturbed just as they had been for days. Ritter's only reason for going to his room since Cat had gone was to grab clothing and, because he had no intention of lying in his own bed, never looked at it.

He put his face in his hands and although he wanted to be angry with Paul for having not made sure he had gotten the messages, found he was too overwhelmed with a fresh excitement to be so. Not only would Cat be home the next day, she had thought about him while she was gone.

As soon as he had showered himself then toileted, fed, and tucked in the dog and deer, Ritter decided to call Cat. In truth, he had decided it as soon as her number was in his possession, but he was trying to remain collected although he wasn't sure for whom. Maybe for that part of him that giggled at just the thought of hearing her voice.

He paced for several minutes chewing his lip and finally sat down on her couch to dial. His right foot shook nervously as he listened to the rings, counting them with painful expectation. To both his dismay and relief, she didn't answer. Instead, he heard a familiar, thickly accented voice.

Cat's calls had been forwarded to Cruz. She was spending the last two days of her trip at a silent spa retreat that did not allow media nor communication devices. If there were an emergency, he was to call the spa itself that would in turn contact Cat.

Cruz said she that was going to call on her way to the airport and mentioned that she seemed disappointed at having not heard from Ritter. Ritter sighed, wiped his forehead, and explained the mix-up to Cruz who laughed heartily.

After several minutes of small talk, Ritter assured Cruz he would pick Cat up from the airport. And, immediately upon ending the call, he wiggled excitedly in his seat as if he were a dog being wagged by its own frantically jubilant tail. His excitement was unfortunately as brief as it was genuine however, docked cruelly close to its base by a text that reminded Ritter of the dog he truly was.

Do u want 2 go eat b4 the party 2mrow nite?—Ash

A few days after Ritter had met Ashta, she had invited him to an event that she said she didn't want to attend alone. It was, in short, an orgy. She told Ritter what she knew about it and Ritter had said he had attended several before that sounded much the same.

They generally took place outside of town at a house large enough to accommodate a crowd and private enough not to attract attention. Spots on the guest list were given only after a notary-signed clean bill of health was submitted along with a signed agreement of confidentiality, copy of photo ID, and a hefty fee. Ritter said that the money assured partygoers of a certain caliber of guests, provided drugs, alcohol, prophylactics, bouncers, and funds for after-party cleanup. He assured Ashta that he had never been to one that he considered a waste of money.

Now, several weeks later, Ritter didn't want to go. He wanted to pick up Cat and spend the evening with her. There would be other parties and lovers. And, although $600 was a hefty bit to go to waste, it was a price Ritter would have paid outright just to be with Cat for the time it took them to drive home from the airport.

Ritter went limp and slithered down to the floor with the exaggerated flair of a horrible actor and stretched out on his back. He laughed at himself, rubbed his face, and the groan of irritation that began to immerge from his chest found itself born as a shriek of terror.

Beau flew through the air as if ejected from a cannon in a sprawling, thirty-pound blur of fur! The animal landed dangerously close to Ritter's head with a thud and immediately attacked his hair as if settling an ancient score. It rolled around wildly, kicked with its hind legs, and chewed on wet locks as Ritter laughed and tried to free himself from the vicious fray.

Wrestling commenced between the two and Beau, being the more agile beast, quickly escaped. He jumped five feet or more up in the air, repelled himself off a wall, and then skidded out of the room on the slippery wooden floor.

Ritter began looking around for his assailant and preparing for a secondary attack when a rattle sounded from the hall. A click and the clatter of a bell being shaken followed it. Ritter followed the noise and found the cat sitting regally with a toy in his mouth next to a wide open door. "Leave all closed doors closed," Cat had said emphatically and, like a dutiful servant, Ritter had obeyed.

His blue eyes looked back and forth from Beau to the open, darkened room, and he put his hands on his hips. Respectfully, he denied temptation and closed the door with a grimace as if it pained him greatly. The cat dropped its toy, walked to the door, raised up its long body to grasp the French handle with its paws, and once again, the room was opened like Ali Baba's treasure-laden cave. Ritter stood shocked for a fraction of a second and then darted in the darkened room for fear an unknown voice would shout, *close sesame* and the opportunity be lost.

The walls of the study were painted maroon and bookcases lined three of the four. Ritter smiled. *Little reader,* he thought and began perusing the titles that spanned every interest and age group. He laughed when he saw the entire collection of Jane Austin. *Cat would be the type,* he thought. Just like his sister had been.

The books ended with a selection of various veterinary publications and were followed by what looked to be photo albums. *Jackpot,* his brain whispered with a grin and Ritter sat down to plunder his booty.

He watched her grow from infancy to adulthood through the small lens of someone else's perspective. She grew up on her father's hip around farm animals, the latter of which had obviously taught her to crawl in a curious hand-toe fashion. Strangely, there were no pictures of Cat as a newborn or of anyone who could be assumed her mother.

Cruz had been there since her beginnings. Although much thinner and younger, it was obviously him, and he seemed to take as much pride in Cat as if he were her father. Even in his wedding pictures to Paloma, he was holding a toddler version of Cat as if she were his own child.

Her life moved under Ritter's fingers, and he watched Cat grow into a beautiful young woman. Pictures of her father disappeared about the time Cat seemed to be in high school and pictures of her began lessening as well, replaced by ribbons from livestock shows.

There were very few pictures of her college years, and Ritter soon found himself nearing the end of the albums. Only a white, leather-bound volume remained.

Ritter opened it and his heart gasped into a moment of stillness. It was Cat in a white wedding gown standing in a field that seemed infinitely filled with blue flowers. She was much younger in both form and expression. Her body was plumper and curvier, her hair longer. She looked then to be the form of which her current body now seemed a shadow.

Her husband was handsome. He was taller than Ritter, a fact Ritter noticed immediately. He had olive skin, dark hair, hazel eyes, and Ritter would have thought him to be of Middle Eastern decent. However, on none of the pages could he find a name. It was not until he turned the final page that the ethnicity and, sadly, ending of the man were known.

A clear plastic bag was taped to the interior of the back cover of the album. Inside, there were several newspaper clippings folded in half regarding his attack, subsequent death, as well as that of his unborn child.

Ritter looked up at Cat's desk at a framed sonogram he had noticed upon entering. He looked closely and compared the date with the newspaper clipping. On September 10, 2001, the sonogram estimated the baby to be thirty-two weeks. The burial had been about two weeks later.

The deaths were the result of a home invasion that happened in what a newspaper reporter described as a "feverish post-9/11 wake."

> *The family of Dr. Emma Douglas, still comatose, has stated the couple had received*
> *threatening phone messages in regards to her husband's Middle Eastern surname.*

An obituary was the last of the articles and was laminated. Her husband's name had been Daniyyel Yoel Ben Laban and, like Cat, he too was a veterinarian. The baby was given only the name Baby Girl Ben Laban, and the two had been buried together in his hometown of Tel Aviv in Israel.

The articles were followed by a picture of Cat and her husband standing together proudly displaying Cat's very expectant stomach. Ritter immediately turned his face away out of not only the pain he felt for the couple pictured, but also the jealousy he felt for the scenario as a whole.

He put the album back on the shelf then sat in silence for several moments before Beau dropped a toy at his side. Ritter kneeled down, scratched the animal's ears and tossed the toy in the air, which, by accident, landed on top of Cat's desk. The massive cat bounded up and Ritter could foresee the destruction that would follow. He immediately hopped up to retrieve the toy and took hold of it before the cat was able to dishevel any paperwork that was lying out.

The bell rattled in the shiny ball and Beau's eyes locked in on it. Seeing that the animal's attention was fixed, the toy was thrown. In the cat's propelling its weight from the desk, a leather-bound book was pushed off and onto the floor at Ritter's feet. He picked it up, glanced at the blank cover, and thumbed through the pages. It was a sketchbook and in it were renderings of animal anatomy to rival any scientific manual. Then, there were several very much out-of-place drawings.

A male right hand and forearm were sketched from three different angles. The drawings were not as precise and deliberate in appearance as those of the animals. It seemed that the hand in question would not stay at rest for the artist or the artist was recalling them from only a brief observation.

Pity welled up within Ritter with the sudden assumption of what he was seeing. Cat had been the artist, he decided, and these sketches were of her late husband's hand. She had drawn from memory the hand that had touched her in an effort not to lose sensation of its touch. But then, just before his twisting of emotion caused him to close the book, Ritter saw something in the drawing that was vaguely familiar.

He walked with the sketchbook to a mirror and held his arm up, mimicking the angle of the limb on the page. The scar in question was on the underside of his forearm near the elbow and had been acquired falling down the cement steps of his childhood home in Ireland.

Ritter bit the inside of his lips as he smiled. He ran his hand through his hair and looked over his shoulders, wishing that there was someone else present to confirm what he knew he was seeing. It was unmistakable. Cat had drawn his right hand and forearm. The vein patterns, the half moons on the thumbnails, fine dark hair, and random spray of freckles had been replicated perfectly although it seemed from the pencil pressure that Cat had not been sure of herself.

He thumbed through several more pages of bovine anatomy and once again found himself among the vivisection diagrams. Like the animal subjects, he had not been drawn in his entirety but rather in parts as if she had been trying to analyze different pieces of him as they related to the whole. The curve of his jaw, his chin and lips, his profile with only eye and brow, his neck and collarbones framed by a T-shirt: all these Cat had mapped without his knowing.

A page immediately following was torn free from the binding. Ritter shook the book in the case the curiously absent page was wedged amidst the others and, when gleaning nothing, he returned to the study. Finding the trash can empty, he scanned the floor.

Under the desk, near the corner, was the crumpled page in question that had obviously fallen, or perhaps escaped, from the trash can. On it was his profile complete in form and detail all the way down his throat. His eyes were closed, his face relaxed minus the tiniest expression of bliss that seemed to lay over his image like a transparent film. A small hand was on his neck, its thumb on his jaw and fingers hidden in his rebellious hair. The owner of the hand was drawn with as much accuracy as he had been. The profile was concise and unmistakable. And, her lips were pressed against his forehead.

An hour later, Ritter was lying on the couch as still as death despite the furious, electrical impulses of thought in his brain. Cat had kissed him. It was only a drawing, but he had felt it nonetheless and in that fictitious depiction, he had found a very real truth: he was falling in love with her.

There had always been a looming shadow of doubt in his mind that he would ever know love for the simple fact that he was not sure if he would recognize it. Pain had distorted his vision and dulled his perception. However, the phantom of uncertainty had quickly disappeared in the brilliant burning light of his ardor.

He turned on his side and decided he would pick her up from the airport, take her out to eat and then, at an opportune time, tell her how he felt. Premature though it seemed, it was not something that he could contain. Cat's reciprocation wasn't necessary and wouldn't change what was violently nailed down in his heart although, it would be more than welcome. Then, Ritter remembered the party.

A shout of profanity shot from his mouth and his hand hit the couch. His foot began shaking nervously and he chewed the inside of his cheek. Old urges surfaced and dark, denied desires reached out their parasitic tendrils in search of nourishment.

Ritter pressed his hand down hard on his chest, thought of Cat's lips against his forehead, and wondered if that would be enough for him. The new man born from his newfound love knew without question that it would, but he needed a burial of his old self. There had to be an end in order to begin and the party would provide the nails needed for the coffin.

He closed his eyes, rubbed his hands down his face and made a decision that satisfied both his old passions and fresh hope. The heat of his last night of erotic indulgence would be the spark to light the pyre of his funeral bier. "One last night of defilement," he said aloud. "Just one more." Then, he would rise from its ashes the next morning, purged, reborn, and ready to give himself completely to the woman in whose hands his parts became whole.

CHAPTER 15

Wild Oats for the Price of Rubies

As she neared the exit from the terminal, Cat saw Ritter. Even in the midst of a crowd, his presence was easily marked by not only his aesthetics but also lack thereof. He had on a blue plaid, button-up shirt that fit the lines of his athletic form perfectly yet slightly askew, as it had been mis-buttoned. The collar was open slightly to the side because of the error, but the angle of it further accentuated his jaw line and thick neck.

The sleeves were pushed up past the elbows without the effort of being rolled, leaving the round muscles of his forearms to keep them in place. His jeans were worn and, like his shirt, looked to have been slept in. She couldn't see his feet but wouldn't have been surprised to see that his shoes, although most assuredly expensive, were untied, mismatched, or both. He looked to have not shaven in days and his thick, dark hair, that had probably seen no other comb than his own fingers, was tucked behind one ear and seemed slightly damp.

Cat smiled. Every time she had seen Ritter he looked the way he did now and she had chalked it up to timing. Now, she saw that was the way he always looked, and it was strangely romantic. He should have looked disheveled, tousled, and unkempt. However, against the canvas of his painful beauty, his haphazard appearance seemed more of an expression of abstract art rather than carelessness.

A young woman approached Ritter from the side and to say that she gawked, as had over a dozen others, was an understatement. After the woman composed herself, she tapped him on the shoulder and looked to have asked for the time. Ritter had glanced at his watch and responded to her with a smile only he was capable of giving. As the two chatted, the girl's posture opened up flirtatiously and Ritter's stance shifted approvingly. Then, his entire demeanor became, ever so slightly, seductively predatory.

"And there it is!" Cat mumbled to herself as she rolled her eyes and looked away. She and Ritter were incongruous in many ways, the greatest of which was morally. That was, for her, the end of any possibility of a beginning. But, there was also the little inconvenience of their disparities of age, beauty, and many, many more things Cat had a hard time thinking of but was sure she would remember later when she was trying desperately to not think about them. This was why she had thrown away the drawing she had created of the two of them together. It was a wonderful dream to be sure. But dreams were things to be indulged only when they enhanced one's reality, not made a disappointment of it.

Cat straightened the straps of her backpack on her shoulders, blew a heavy sigh through closed lips, and looked back at Ritter who was, as it turned out, looking right back at her. His arms were folded and his head was cocked to the side. His blue eyes were narrowed in mocked scrutiny and he was grinning despite the fact he was biting his bottom lip. Cat laughed, closed her eyes, and nodded as if admitting that she had been caught. Then, because she knew moments like this were priceless and anomalous to the mundane, constantly turning cogs of common life, she looked back at him. There was no roll of her eyes, hint of sarcasm, or expectation. There was just a subtle smile and a look that said everything her brain refused to concede but her heart was unable to contain.

Ritter was caught off guard. His handsomeness was something of which he was graciously aware and he was well accustomed to being undressed with people's eyes. However, this indefinable look was different. He wasn't just being stripped. He was being flayed, uncased completely without the courtesy of the violence or pain to divert his attention from his own excruciating vulnerability. All that the world praised him for and he cowered behind, was suddenly lying at his feet as a freshly removed pelt. He was now simply a man: frightened, fallible, frail, and still somehow worthy of a look like this from a woman like that.

He swallowed hard and crawled out from behind his smirk and looked back at her without pretense. After several moments, he shrugged as if to say, *this is it, this is all there is,* apologetically. Cat's smile deepened and without words she replied, *it's more than enough.*

The two headed for the luggage area. They walked happily, each looking at the other as often as possible, completely oblivious to the surrounding crowd until a reflection in a window caught Ritter's eye. He saw her. He stopped suddenly and looked over his shoulder at the passing faces but failed to find the one that had stopped him in his tracks. His chest filled with an inexplicable sense of warning and he put his arm around Cat, pulled her close, and walked faster.

The baggage claim belt for Cat's flight was broken. Passengers grumbled, fidgeted in irritation, and groaned collectively as the belt started and stopped teasingly. Neither Cat nor Ritter minded the wait and he, unable to contain himself any longer and feeling somehow hidden in the thicket of the crowd, pulled her to him. Cat smiled and bid farewell to common sense. This embrace was far better. Ritter's chest was warm and solid against her cheek and the smell of him drained all the energy from her muscles. Had he not been holding onto her, she might have fallen into a flaccid heap in front of him.

Ritter rested his chin on her head and ran his hand through her newly cut, short hair. "I like your haircut. You look like a like pixie! Should I drive you back to your house or have you quitted it for a mushroom some where."

Cat laughed and cuddled herself closer to him. He ran his lips over her hair and let several coppery blond strands slide between his lips. Then, after a couple courage-inducing breaths, he leaned down to her ear. Ritter had never told a woman he loved her and although this was not the right place, it was the right time. His heart was ripe and heavy with affection.

"Cat," he said before swallowing hard, "I—"

The belt started with a loud jerk and the crowd applauded. "What?" Cat yelled above the riotous din. Ritter laughed and said loudly, "I said that I—"

And then, he saw her. The shine of her caught his eye. He ran his tongue over the healed yet still tender bite mark on his lip and knew this too was not a dream.

"I'll get your bag," he said loudly to Cat. "I'll go up there. You stay back here in the case that I miss it. What does it look like?" She described the suitcase and the two parted: one in search, one on a hunt.

"Hello, good Doctor. I was wondering if you would come speak to me."

"Hello, Lucy. What brings you here?"

The woman smiled and looked him up and down. "You of course," she purred. Ritter shook his head and looked over his shoulder for Cat. A hot hand went to his face and pulled it back.

"Still looking for your little ewe? Your Rachel? Oh, Jacob, there are others for whom you need not work so hard. Seven years is far too long."

"What did you say? What do you mean seven years?"

Lucy laughed, seeing her words hit their sticking place. "Silly boy. You remember nothing of the Torah? Jacob labored seven years for the hand of Rachel."

"It was fourteen. Jacob worked fourteen years for Rachel."

"Ah, yes," Lucy said, running her hand down his chest. "And you, Dr. Thomas?" She lifted the edge of his shirt and stroked her red-nailed fingertip along his body at the top of his jeans. "Can you wait fourteen years? Fourteen days perhaps? My guess is that you won't be able to deny yourself fourteen whole hours, especially in light of the fact that everything you ever wanted can be yours before day's end."

"What does that mean?" Ritter said, feeling the sexually carnivorous part of him beginning to bare its hungry teeth. Lucy grabbed a belt loop, pulled him close, and her free hand glided from the center of his stomach around his hip to his lower back.

"My, but your muscles are strong. The body is a house, a temple of sorts, and yours, my handsome Israelite, feels hewn from solid stone." Her lips went to his, and she whispered with wine-soaked breath into his mouth, "Oh, how I look forward to plundering it!"

Cat found her suitcase and looked around at the crowd that towered over her. She shouldered her way free from the melee and made for to the top of the conveyer belt area where a wall of backs and shoulders stood in front of her like a bulwark. Seeing no alternative, nor possibility of finding Ritter until the crowd thinned, she sat on a bench and waited patiently, smiling like a fool in love.

Then, as if on cue, several people moved away from the belt. Cat's golden eyes looked through the newly opened door and ahead of her was an unobstructed view of Ritter's back and the hand that encircled his waist. His head lowered as if to receive a kiss and slowly, another hand reached up and hid itself in his hair.

Ritter struggled to drive. It was hard to continually look at Cat and keep his eyes on the road at the same time. She had completely changed. The flame that had begun to ignite between them seemed to have never sparked. Her presence was cold and she was silent as she stared out of the window. He wasn't sure but thought he had heard her sniff once as if crying and could have sworn she had changed her shirt.

Ritter finally pulled into the parking lot of a restaurant, turned off the ignition, and refused to go further without Cat telling him what was wrong. She had seen him, she confessed, and told him that he need not explain himself to her. She also asked that he not create some type of lie in defense as lying was beneath him as well as a sin and any person that cared about him wouldn't want him to sin.

Ritter knew there was nothing he could say. He turned his head, looked out the window and rubbed his chin. His breathing became harder, his nostrils flared, his jaw clenched, and everything within him wanted to tear at his own flesh. He had everything he wanted and had lost it over a kiss from woman who claimed he didn't.

"I am sorry, Cat."

"Sorry you hurt me or sorry you got caught?"

Ritter sighed hard and rapped his knuckles on the steering wheel in frustration. He then looked over at Cat and smiled. She occupied so little space yet crowded him completely. He couldn't deceive, dissuade, or distract her with anything with which the world around him so easily fell victim. So, he didn't even try.

"Both, love. But more so for the former."

Then, after several moments of silent, self-flagellation, he asked, "Can we still be mates at least?"

Hesitantly Cat nodded and Ritter was grateful. Friendship, after all, was fertile ground in which love often grew. If it never did, it was at least something, and to Ritter, something from Cat was worth more than everything from anyone else.

His hand went to the ignition and, just before turning it, Cat's stomach growled. Her eyes widened with surprise, and they both laughed.

"Can I buy you dinner? Where are we? Solomon's Kosher Deli? Oh, this I have to see! Come on, Ginger, let's have a pickle and some corned beef! Friends have dinner together in the States, yea? Yea? Come on, look at me . . . Cat, did you have a nosebleed?"

The two were shown to a table and, after ordering, Cat excused herself to the restroom to clean the remnants of blood from her nose. An older gentleman who was walking regally around the floor with an air of authority approached their table and introduced himself as the owner of Solomon's Mediterranean: Solomon himself. He asked what Ritter and his wife had ordered. Ritter answered and then corrected the man's use of the word *wife*.

Then, perhaps with a desperate hope that the man's name was a portent of wisdom, Ritter vomited out the events of the past hour. He confessed how he felt for Cat and that he hoped to redeem himself and make her his own someday.

Solomon sat down and rubbed his chin in thought. He then nodded and absentmindedly wiped his shirt as if he had in fact been regurgitated on. It was a great deal to take in so quickly, he said with a long, drawn out sigh and hum. However, it took only a moment for him to tell Ritter that one didn't have to work in a kitchen to know the best time to start cleaning up a mess is right after it happened. Messes left unattended tend to be harder to clean up. Either that, or they become so much a part of the scenery you forget they are there and then they haunt you with a stink.

"Oy vey! You're af tsores, bubbee! In deep doo-doo! Ok, ok, here is what you do: first, you apologize to that girl. And look her in the eye when you do it! Then, you buy her dinner, dessert, and spend the rest of the evening telling her that you are not worthy of her and what steps you plan to take in order to become a man that is. Then, feed her chocolate until she goes into a stupor!"

Ritter giggled, looked down and explained that he couldn't. He had a party he needed to attend. It was sure to purge him of whatever had driven him to foul things up as badly as he had.

Solomon nodded. "So, what you're saying young man, is that you need just one more night to *sow your wild oats*? Is that right?" Solomon stopped a waiter, handed him his cell phone, and asked him to look up wild oats on the Internet.

"I have no idea how to work that phone! Don't know why I even have it, but, eh, I digress. Son, have you ever seen a wild oat? Know what one is? Then how do you know that's what you want to sow? My mother, aleha ha sholem, may she rest, told me once that a good woman's price is above rubies. What? Oh, thank you! Okay, here we are. I need my glasses! That's better! Okay, wild oats: a type of grass, yadda, yadda, yadda . . . nuisance weeds in cereal crops, they cannot be chemically removed, any herbicide that would kill them would also damage the crop.

Now son, you don't have to be a farmer to see the problem there! You want weeds? Or do you want a flower whose price is above rubies? Choose the latter. It's just good business!"

Cat returned to the table and the two men immediately stopped their discussion. Solomon stood, put the phone in his pocket and, after introducing himself, pulled Cat's chair out for her.

"Ai, ai, ai, what type of earrings do you have on there, young lady? They are stunning." Cat thanked him and said that they were rubies.

"Oh, are they?" Solomon said with great animation. "Must have cost a fortune! Rubies are priceless things. Better than weeds, wouldn't you say, young man?" Solomon winked, patted Ritter on the arm, and excused himself. Cat gave a questioning look to which Ritter grinned and said, "Don't ask!"

The two talked effortlessly as if old friends. Ritter spoke fondly of home, his parents, and explained that his father had, indirectly, given him the nickname Ritter. It began as Little Reader as Ritter began reading while still a toddler. Little Reader became Reader, and when he began school, his classmates mistook the name as Ritter.

Cat narrowed her eyes at him and smiled. "So how old were you when you began reading?"

Ritter shrugged. "I don't know. I didn't have all my milk teeth yet. About three, I guess."

Cat raised her brows. "About three as in two or close to four." Ritter smiled and took a drink without answering. He then asked her about her family and quickly found out why he had not seen a picture of her mother in the photo albums. There were none. Cat said she was a product of a *brief relationship*. About a year after, the biological grandfather had driven up on the ranch where Cat's daddy worked and lived and handed him some legal documents, a four-month-old baby, and a feedbag of diapers and bottles. The man said nothing to Cat's daddy except that if he saw him or the *little red-headed bastard* in Austin ever again, he'd have them both killed. Cat's daddy had been just seventeen.

"I'm the little red-headed bastard in case you didn't get that from the story," she said with a wry smile.

"What did your grandparents say?"

Cat shook her head. Her daddy was orphaned at fourteen. He had been taken in by a local family and lived on their ranch as a hired hand, but they considered him a son. They offered to take Cat in and raise her but her daddy had refused.

"He said God gave me to him to take care of and he did. I slept next to him at night and, during the day, went to work right alongside of him, literally. He fashioned a sling and tucked me in it like a joey.

"When Daddy couldn't hold me for whatever reason, he handed me off to a gangly, no-English-speaking ranch hand named Manuel Cruz de las Colinas who had helped raise his six younger sisters that were still back in Mexico. That would be Cruz. I'm named after him, incidentally. He really was like a brother to my daddy and his people are all the family I have now.

"Daddy was killed in a car wreck when I was fourteen. But, like I said, Cruz was there from the beginning so he was a father to me as well. God provided two for me from the get-go to make up for the one He planned on taking home early, I guess. What about you, do you have any brothers or sisters?"

Ritter's face had been lit with interest but quickly fell. He moved food around on his plate with a fork and then said quietly, but with a smile, that he was a twin.

"There is another one of you? Heaven help us all!" Cat said with a cough.

Ritter laughed and said that he was a fraternal twin to his sister, Reece. She was, as Ritter described, wonderful and perfect in every way. "She was a lot like you actually."

Cat looked up, saw that the comment was genuine, and thanked him. She asked if they looked alike and Ritter laughed. He and his sister shared the same initials but that was it. Reece was beautiful, like his mother while he, on the other hand, was the spitting image of their father.

"Wow, your dad must be hideous!" Cat said, rolling her eyes. "I would love to meet your sister if she ever comes to visit. I am curious as to what the beautiful half of your family looks like!"

Ritter smiled, shook around the dregs of hot tea in his cup and, just before taking a last sip, said, "She's dead."

Cat stopped chewing and looked at him not knowing what to say except that she was sorry. After a few awkward moments and Ritter clearing his throat several times, he explained that a car had hit his sister a little over seven years earlier. The driver had been up all night working and, while coming home early the next morning, had fallen asleep at the wheel. The car had driven up onto the sidewalk and struck Reece who was out jogging.

Cat reached over immediately and took his hand. "I am so sorry. Did they catch the man?"

"Oh, it was an accident. He wasn't prosecuted. Not so much as a driving ban," he said with a shake of his head. "My parents forgave him. He was as devastated as they."

Cat rubbed his arm sympathetically and after a moment asked, "What about you? You forgiven him?"

Ritter looked at her hatefully then moved his arm away to take a drink. He shifted in his chair and sniffed several times before looking up and saying under his breath, "Oh you have got to be bloody kidding me."

Cat looked up and toward them walked Ashta, a gorgeous blonde, and a handsome man that, strangely enough, looked enough like Ritter to make him a triplet rather than twin.

"Well, there you are! You standing me up tonight? Hi, I'm Ashta. You must be Rit's neighbor. Heard soooo much about you! This is, Melissa."

"Call me, Mo."

"And this is Baylor."

"Hi, call me Bayle."

Cat smiled and returned the introduction.

The three spoke to Ritter and Cat watched the four of them interact. The man she knew as Reed quickly became the Ritter the rest of the world knew him to be. He moved slightly away from her and looked at the three in front of him as if they were co-conspirators to something of which they were all wickedly proud. Ashta looked at Ritter with a hungriness that fit the relationship he himself had described them having. Then, Cat looked at Mo and Bayle and found they were looking at Ritter in the exact same way. The three of them seemed to be creating an invisible storm of sexual violence and Ritter was in its eye, panting with anticipation.

It engulfed Cat's soul with godly fury. Reed was not hers but nor was he theirs and she was not about to allow the three of them to run off with him in their muzzles regardless of how much he liked it. She wanted to throw the table on its end and drive them away with the righteous violence of a herdsman protecting his herd.

"Cat, did you eat all of that food?" Ashta said with feigned shock. She could see the anger in Cat's soul rise up like incense and knew that energy needed to be diverted before it summoned holy warriors.

"You are so tiny. You must exercise a lot. I think I saw you out running. I wish I could run, but I have to wear so many sports bras! You are so lucky to be flat-chested."

Cat's nostrils flared and she smiled. There are certain weapons that women only wield on other women, and Cat saw that Ashta meant to use her decidedly larger weapons as a means of intimidation. The attempt had failed.

"Oh, it's not luck. It's a blessing! I'm sorry, what was your name again? Oh, yea, Ashta. I don't wear a bra half the time, and sometimes, if I comb my chest hair just right, I don't even wear a shirt!"

"Oh! You are so funny!" Mo laughed. "Really, you look great. I hope when I'm as old as you I look that good!"

"Oh honey," Cat said after laughing in earnest, "don't worry. Science will have made great strides by then."

Ritter looked down and rubbed his forehead trying to not laugh. He looked over at Cat and saw that she was looking the three of them squarely in the eyes without a hint of anything but miraculously grandiose and aggressive confidence.

Bayle looked Cat up and down. If a woman couldn't intimidate her away from the protective posture she had taken over Ritter, perhaps a man and his sex could.

"You really are a gorgeous little thing," Bayle said, moving slightly toward Cat. "You should come tonight!"

Ritter's hair stood on end and he looked at Bayle murderously, willing him to shut his mouth.

"You've got that fiery redhead spirit. Men love it! Yea," he said as he reached out and rubbed a bit of her sleeve, "they'd be lined up for you."

Ritter hooked his foot around the leg of Cat's chair and jerked her quickly toward him. Cat grabbed the table to keep herself from falling and looked at Ritter in shock. His eyes seemed to have darkened, and for the first time since the three beautiful strangers arrived, she felt afraid. She didn't know where it was the four were going that night but even the slightest mention of it bore a heaviness of evil.

Cat's heart began to race, and the Spirit of God cried out within her to flee, not in fear, but wisdom.

"Ritter could get you in to the party tonight," Ashta said, and Cat could hear her heart begin to quiver and quicken, pushing blood into her muscles with an echoing percussion. *Glub nub, glub nub, glub nub.*

"Yea, Ritter wants you to come tonight, I can tell." *Glub nub, glub nub, glub nub.* Lucy wouldn't mind at all!" *Glub now, glub now, glub now.* "Lucy?" Ritter asked hesitantly. "Yea, Lucy Ferguson, the hostess tonight. You know her, Rit." *Go now, go now, go now.* "She said she, um, kind of bumped into you today, among other things, at the airport baggage claim. Do you know what she told me her friends call her? You know, since her name is Lucy Ferguson. They call her Lucif—" *GO NOW, GO NOW, GO NOW!*

Cat put her hand over her face and ran for the door as if the room had been set ablaze. Ritter immediately jumped up and hissed through his teeth, "Go! I will see you at the door at ten!" The three smiled triumphantly and watched as Ritter gave Solomon a hundred-dollar bill then ran in search of Cat.

The blood streamed from Cat's nose, ran into her hands, down her forearms, and dripped onto her pants and shoes like flung paint as she ran. It had been years since the dam between her eyes had burst. Thankfully, this episode wasn't terribly bad. Maybe the lesser bleed she had gotten at the airport after seeing Ritter tangled with another woman had quelled the pressure that had obviously been building.

She stopped in front of Ritter's car on a grassy area and leaned forward. Two sanguineous streams ran from her nostrils, came together as one, and dripped quickly in fat drops from the top of her lip. Cat breathed deeply and prayed to calm herself.

The irritation from Ritter was palpable on the ride home. He was unable to convince Cat to go to the hospital or even contact her physician. He wanted assurance that she was not in any danger and resented what seemed to be a lack of respect on her part for his medical expertise.

It wasn't a typical nosebleed in his highly educated opinion. There was a ruby red spot outside of the restaurant where more than a cup of blood seemed to have burst explosively from her face. Cat assured him that it was normal, at least for her, and a matter of which her doctor was well aware. All that seemed to really concern her was the possible soiling of Ritter's car. And, although she never would explain the reason for her nosebleed, Ritter assumed it was the result of allergies. It wasn't.

He opened the door of the house for her and carried in her suitcase so that she could avoid touching anything. Cat went straight to the hallway bathroom to wash her face and hands and assess the damage.

"Ugh! I look like I have been hit with a water balloon of red paint! Gross. Thank you for dinner and taking care of the animals. And the airport . . . shouldn't you be going?" she said uncomfortably, walking back into the foyer.

Ritter put his hands in his pockets and shrugged. He wanted to apologize for the airport scene as well as the actions of his friends. However, pride had managed to build up within him like artery clogging plaque.

"I am not even sure where I am going. Chaldea or something." "Wow," Cat said, raising her eyebrows. "It's big time out there, buddy. There is more money per capita in Chaldea than anywhere in the US. Gorgeous houses, gorgeous cars, gorgeous people. Everything is gorgeous! It's almost unsettling. It's about an hour east of here off county road 616. It's pretty dark and winding, but the road is wide and has a big shoulder. You can't miss it. The road dead-ends into a subdivision, Abby Dawn something."

Ritter scratched his nail on a stray bit of plaster on the wall and chewed the inside of his bottom lip. After an awkward silence, he began to speak, but Cat stopped him.

"If it's about the airport thing, let's just not go there, okay? It's done," Cat said, nodding. "We're just friends and it's your life. So good ni—"

"I want to ask you one last time," Ritter interrupted, "let me take you to hospital to get checked out."

"I am fine."

"You need an MRI, Cat."

"It's fine!"

"It's not bloody fine! Sod all, you are not a cow! If you were, I would say, 'Physician, heal thyself.' I am the people doctor here! And a good one too! No, you know what, to the devil with propriety! Cat, I am the best doctor you will probably have ever have the luxury of seeing personally and I say you need medical attention! Is that not enough? Am I not enough?" he said before swearing loudly and hitting the wall with the side of his fist.

Cat's golden eyes narrowed. She leaned against the door of the bathroom nonchalantly and spoke deliberately and quietly.

"Three things, Reed. One: You will not curse God under the roof He has provided for me. Do it again, and you will not be welcome here. Two: Don't you ever rise up on your hind legs at me again! I won't tolerate it from a half-ton horse and I sure won't stand for it from you. Three: You, Reed, as you are without all the things you seem to think are so great about you, are enough for me. However, I am obviously not enough for you and I will never change so I can be. I will never lay down in the mud for you nor will I ever stop believing that you are more than the filth you roll around in. That being said, this soiree, or whatever it is you are doing tonight, what little I know about it frightens me for you and makes my soul hurt. So, I will say this, and be done. Reed, please look at me."

Ritter looked up at her with resentment brimming in his liquid blue eyes. "Reed, if you find yourself in a situation tonight that you don't want to be in or can't get out of, call on Jesus Christ. Then call me. We'll both come for you. No questions asked."

Ritter laughed acridly, shook his head, and turned toward the door. "What are you?" he asked with angry sarcasm. "My champion that I shall call upon to slay the dragon and save me from a fiery death? Pathetic. I'm no Christian, Cat! I don't believe in all that."

"You don't have to. I do. And the faith of one has spared the lives of others more than once before. And besides, His name alone has power," she said as her heart shook in her chest.

"Why? Is it magical?" Ritter said, wiggling his fingers in the air. "No, Reed. It's miraculous."

Ritter sighed and opened the door. "That's perfect, Cat. You believe in fairy tales but give no credence to my medical opinion that is based in scientific fact. You know, maybe if you didn't have your head in children's books you wouldn't be alone," he hissed before closing the door. Cat startled at the sound and then stood with her hand on her chest feeling the gaping wound that had just been inflicted.

Ritter walked to his car, thrusting his legs hard through the mire of his own anger. Just before opening the door, he was startled by a voice that drifted over his shoulder like a mist.

"*Don't go, Reed Jacob. Please.*"

Ritter straightened up. His neck stiffened, and he refused to look back.

"Why? Why not go?"

"*Because it won't go well. Please, trust me.*"

He huffed like a rebellious child, put his hands on his hips, and his nostrils flared in irritation. "You don't know anything."

"*I know I love you, Reed, and I would give my life to save yours. Knowing that is the beginning of all knowledge. Please don't go! Stay here with Me!*"

"Bloody hell, Cat," he said as he raked his hands through his hair like pitchforks. His jaw clenched and he turned around to look her in the face. Instead, he found himself looking into the darkness, completely alone.

Chapter 16

The Road to Hell Is Paved and the Path to God Is Steep

The road out to Chaldea was just as Cat had described: dark, winding, and wide. And, although it was more than an hour away, Ritter had not felt alone. His anger was seated beside him and kept him comfortably distracted from and disaffected toward anything that would pull him off course from his destination, namely Cat. She was a cross he wouldn't bear in Chaldea.

The highway led straight through a subdivision and finally dead-ended in front of a white mansion that was impressive in size and structure. Ritter had never seen the likes of its architecture. He couldn't imagine how it would appear during the day but at night, with the shadows created by the lighting of the landscape, there seemed to be jutting teeth around the top balcony that, with the line of the roof, gave the appearance of an open, hungry mouth.

He gave his keys to a valet and watched his car disappear into the dark. A beautiful escort showed him through a side gate and Ritter's eyes gaped open with wonder. The entire back patio area was larger than the house. There was a stream that ran through the middle, rock formations all around, plants of every nature, exotic birds, luxuriant reclining areas, wine that seemed to never run out of anyone's glass and the grandeur of it all culminated above his head in a hanging garden filled with lights.

Ritter scanned the crowd for his cohorts and, in the dimness of night, found Peter. A halo of light from the garden above shined down on him and the two made eye contact. Ritter walked toward him, shaking his head, and told Peter that this was no place for him.

"Go home, lad. You shouldn't be here."

"I am working security here tonight, Dr. Thomas. Why are you here? Do you know what is waiting for you in there?"

Ritter looked away and took another sip of wine. "Well, I know it's not a sermon, Pete. I won't stay long, and I would appreciate this not being broadcast amongst the rugby team."

"Does Paul know you are here?"

Ritter looked behind him and saw Ashta, Mo, and Bayle enter. "I've got to go, Pete."

"Dr. Thomas, if you need any help . . ."

Ritter laughed and patted the angel on the arm. "If I need help, my big friend, it won't be the kind you provide."

The identities of the four were verified and they were led though a back door. It opened into a great room that had been decorated to resemble an opium den and appropriately so. Opium was available as well as any other drug anyone could want. Guests mingled amongst the cascades of sequined scarves and floor pillows that seemed to hang and sit weightlessly below the full-bellied, gray cloud of smoke above them. People drank, petted and paired or grouped off with one another to different areas of the house.

As soon as Ritter entered all eyes went to him and he saw immediately that he could have his pick of the room. And, although each guest seemed more beautiful than the next, Ritter only had eyes for the one standing in the middle of them all: the one who had brought him there and was looking back at him.

He walked toward her and, without speaking, pushed her toward the outer edges of the erotic throng. As soon as they neared a darkened portion of a hallway, Ritter grabbed Lucy's neck, pinned her to the wall, and kissed her voraciously. After a moment, she gasped for air and growled, "Come with me."

The room she chose was filled with men and women entangled around one another like piles of snakes. Lucy closed the door, locked it, and then, to Ritter's shock, swallowed the key.

"That was not smart there, Angel of Light. You are going to need some medical attention for that."

"Are you not a doctor?" she said, smiling, unbuttoning his shirt and pushing him to a sitting position on a bed. "Besides, what use is a key when there is no door?"

Ritter laughed, helped Lucy in her effort to undress him and, by chance, glanced to the place on the wall where a door had been but was no longer. Confused, Ritter looked around and found there was no exit except a window draped with scarlet curtains. His eyes filled with fear and he looked back at Lucy. She stroked the side of his face, smiled, and from the corner of his eye, Ritter saw a dark object swing toward him.

He awoke some time later. How much later, he didn't know. His watch was gone as was every bit of his clothing. He opened his one eye that swelling had not rendered useless and looked at himself. He was lying alone in the corner on the floor like refuse. His body was covered in welts, quickly darkening contusions, cuts, bite marks, and every manner of human filth. There was blood under his nails, his hair was matted, and his limbs were lying haphazardly as if broken. Hesitantly, he put weight on his arms, pushed himself upright and gnashed his teeth to keep himself from crying out in pain.

He looked around the doorless room and saw that the events of the evening carried on as if he weren't there and he hoped the writhing mass of flesh wouldn't notice him. Perhaps he could make it to the window. What he would do then, he didn't know.

He maneuvered himself into a crawling position and moved as quickly and quietly as physically able.

"Oh, our good friend has awakened."

Ritter froze as the island-flower accent cut through him like a knife and then, he looked up.

Lucy stood over him as a brutal master would a dog and laughed. "The night has just begun. On your feet!"

Ritter shook his head and his lip quivered as fat drops of tears fell from his good eye. "I don't want to be here," he said softly as a whimper burst uncontrollably from his chest.

"Oh, silly boy! Là où est mon chevalier? Where is my brave knight? Stop this crying!"

She crouched down beside him and smiled. "You do want to be here. In fact, you went to some trouble to be here. There were several forms to fill out, sign, and have notarized, blood tests, six hundred dollars, and a long drive into the night. Yes, you want to be here. No, no. Don't shake your head. I don't know what you were thinking, but I heard clearly what you wanted. What was it you said? Ah, yes, *one last night of defilement. Just one more.*"

Ritter's heart stopped. Her voice had taken on an accent and tone so much like his own, he would have sworn it was. "Ask and ye shall receive, young man. Defiled you were. However, don't thank me. Thank them."

Quiet filled the room, and Ritter looked over to see that the human snake pit had risen up to standing. Their eyes were fixed on him: waiting, watching, wanting.

There was not a square inch of his being that didn't ache from violence. And, after one look at their faces, hew knew that it was not over. He curled tightly into the fetal position and began weeping.

"Stop crying!" Lucy yelled, kicking him hard in the ribs. The blow caused him to cough and spit out blood. "Oh no, save that blood, man! The night is far from over, and you will need it. You have yet to have me!" Lucy leaned down, grabbed his hair, and pulled his face up toward her. "And I plan to rip apart this temple," she said, running the sharp side her nail down his back, "this house of Jacob!"

Ritter's lips trembled as blood-mingled spit dripped in long strings from his chin. His entire life flashed before his eyes and he knew he was about to die. But before he did, he looked into Lucy's death-dark eyes, pulled in as much air as his bruised ribs allowed, and said, "Jesus Christ, save me."

The room began shaking, and the sound of a thousand feet jarred Ritter to his teeth. Lucy dropped his head, opened her mouth, and a beast emerged, pushing flesh behind it as if turning her inside out.

The leathery thing inhaled and, before releasing its breath, an explosion of light burst through the wall of the doorless room. A stream of armor-clad men poured in quickly in a bright metallic blur. Their swords were brandished and blades were put to use against Ritter's assailants who, like Lucy, had burst from their skins into putrid indefinable, nightmarish creatures.

Lucy exhaled a gush of lava and one of the Warriors of Light stepped forward. He wielded his shield to protect his fellow soldiers and turned the boiling bile into steam and stone.

Ritter began scrambling away and from the midst of the hellish combat stepped Peter. His armor rang as he moved and he grabbed Ritter up as if he were a child, told him to cover his face and threw him through the window. No sooner did he hit the ground that he felt himself being picked up again. "Up you go," another angel said as he put Ritter's violence-wearied body over his shoulders in a fireman's carry and ran toward a car that was parked on the street.

An explosion of shattering glass and falling brick thundered from the house. Peter jumped from it with a beast hanging on to his back. It hissed and sank its teeth into a place on his neck that was exposed.

"Stay here!" the soldier said, shoving Ritter's body into the car. Ritter shut and locked the door quickly then curled around and watched as the angel went to his fellow warrior's aid.

Free of the attacker, Peter moved with a bolt of light to the car and before Ritter could turn to look at the driver's door, the car was started and the two had driven away. Ritter clung to his seat, looked out the back window, and saw a dozen of the devilish beasts running after the car like dogs. He cried for Peter to go faster. In response, Peter calmly released the wheel, closed his eyes, raised his hands, and spoke in a strange, melodic language. Ritter looked forward and screamed out as the car accelerated to full speed, broke through a guardrail, and sailed off the edge of a bridge.

The car stopped and Ritter's body was thrown into the floorboard. After a quiet moment, he opened his eyes and saw that the sun streamed in above him from all around.

Peter offered his hand and helped the frightened man back into his seat. The human looked out of the windows and saw that they were in a clearing filled with flowers. Animals began walking out of the surrounding trees in curiosity and Ritter was startled as a fox and her pups jumped up on the hood and lied down to enjoy the warmth from the motor.

"Am I dead?"

"Oh, no, Brother." Peter laughed kindly as he unfastened the bracers around his forearms. "Hell is infinitely worse and heaven infinitely better. Just relax. The Prince and the Counselor be here shortly. I am early for once!"

Ritter trembled and looked around himself for signs of anything that would help his mind grasp where he was and what had happened. "I'm dreaming?"

Peter shook his head in response. "No, not a dream," he said nonchalantly, completely disregarding Ritter's increasingly nervous state. "You are completely awake and all you see is real. You are alive as you ever were, if not more so after a brush with doom."

Peter smiled but Ritter's already anxious state and most recent experiences made him assume the worse. "What are you? Are you going to kill me?"

"Kill you? Why would I fight to save you if I was just going to kill you? Do you think I was just letting those devils tenderize you so you would be easier to eat?"

Ritter pressed himself against the door and his chin trembled. "You're going to eat me?"

"What? No! Gross! Look, I am an angel and more like you than not! I was created, I have a soul, free will, a language of my own, ten fingers, ten toes," he laughed.

He held out his hand for inspection and Ritter winced, expecting a hit. The angel shook his head slightly and then continued removing his armor. "I am simply much stronger physically. I have emotions, I eat, have a job, and wow, I stink! Obviously, that is another thing stronger about me!"

"You have no wings," Ritter said with a still-quivering voice.

"It's a common misconception. Only the cherubim and seraphim have wings. What appears to be flying or hovering on our part is just a result of the Holy King allowing us to be stronger than gravity."

Peter's head turned quickly and from outside the passenger window a deep, soothing voice said, "You're early!"

Ritter jumped and his body moved violently away as if being shoved by the voice itself. He was pitched through the suddenly empty driver's seat and fell out of the car door with a hard thud on the ground below. Upon impact, his body became heavy and immobile as if dead.

His good eye glassed-over and remained open. From under the car, he could see Peter lying prostrate at the man's feet under a strobe light of what appeared to be lightning. The man put his hand on Peter's head, said something in Hebrew, and then lowered himself to kiss Peter on the cheek. The soldier raised himself to stand and once again prostrated himself in front of what seemed to be nothing. Then, the *nothing* moved and Ritter saw a distortion in the landscape that had the shape of human feet and legs. The optical aberration leaned down, as had the previous man, and kissed Peter. The three then spoke briefly in a melodic language and exchanged embraces that seemed contrary to the previous formal display.

Suddenly, the first being's feet disappeared. And although Ritter could not move his head to look around, he knew the man was standing over him. It felt as if his whole body knew.

"It's okay. Everything is okay. Let me take care of this for you." The Man kneeled and touched Ritter on the arm. There was a sensation of warmth and his body seemed to awaken obediently without a hint of pain.

Ritter's eye widened. He rolled to his side hesitantly and touched his right shoulder. It had been out of its socket since leaving Chaldea. He moved the joint around and, as he bent the arm to further test the mobility, noticed every wound on his right arm had vanished. The left arm was brought beside the right for comparison, and it was only then that Ritter realized the extent of his injuries. His right arm was completely clean and appeared stronger than it had before. The veins running across the top of his right hand from his wrist to forearm were fat and lay across the underlying, sinewy musculature like engorged blue worms. The rest of him looked like something on which worms would feast.

Lost in mute marvel, Ritter unwittingly accepted the liquid form's hand, came to standing and took in the metamorphosis of the landscape. Every plant that reproduced by flowering had bloomed and the verdure of every plant and tree had deepened. Butterflies, bees, birds, and every manner of beast was roaming and interacting with one another as if in the Garden of Eden.

He looked down at the smooth, untainted flesh of his hand and saw the transparent being's hand holding it. The grip was firm and gave Ritter a strange sense of security. He looked up at the blur, the man, Peter, the world around him, and found that all the fear and questions that had been churning in him like a tempest had settled themselves placidly.

"Come on," the Man said with a smile. "We have a walk ahead of us. I know you have many questions you want to ask. I imagine most will be answered on the walk."

Ritter pulled his hand away from the liquid form and covered himself with embarrassment. For a moment, he had forgotten he was completely naked.

The Man laughed and walked past Ritter, slapping him amiably on the back as He went. "Come on! If you can walk with your destroyer naked, certainly you can walk with your Creator. Don't worry. I won't let the trees laugh at you."

The forest canopied the three as they walked the steep path. The Man led and Ritter and the liquid being followed a few paces behind side by side. Flowers sprang up from the Leader's footprints and the trees seemed to lean toward Him as he passed. At one point, He stumbled slightly, and a branch reached out to steady Him.

"What are you?" Ritter said to them both. The being at his side spoke in a wind-chime voice.

"He says, that He is the Counselor, or the Advocate, if you will," the Man ahead translated as He walked. "And He's not made of water like you are thinking. Although, admittedly, He comes with it." The being beside Ritter laughed at what seemed to be an inside joke.

"The better you get to know Me, the more you will see Him and understand Him. And, don't let the apparition He is now fool you! He arrives with just a small bit of water but hangs around like a hurricane!"

"And who are you?" Ritter questioned.

"Oh, I have a lot of names. Yeshua Ben Yosef is the name my parents gave me." The Man looked over his shoulder at the two following and smiled. "Of course, the name that matters most is the one you give Me, Reed Jacob. Who do you say that I am?"

Ritter shrugged. "Peter said you were a Prince. You don't look like a Prince." He was surprised at his bluntness and apologized. The two with him laughed and said no apology was needed. Nothing but the truth could be spoken in Their presence.

"If you were to describe Me in your medical reports, how would you? Again, don't think your honesty will offend Me. We three are big fans of honesty, the Counselor, King, and I that is."

Ritter looked around himself and laughed. "Okay, well, you are about my size in stature and build although the tunic you are wearing makes that hard to ascertain. You seem to eat well. Your hair, skin, and eyes are healthy. Ethnically, you look Middle Eastern. Considering your name and, I don't mean to be stereotypical or offensive but, appearance, I would say you are Jewish."

The Man and Counselor laughed hard and both nodded. "Why would that offend me? I think we Jewish folk are a handsome lot! What else?"

"Your shoulders are rounded and the back of your neck is quite brown. You don't even seem winded by this climb, so, I would assume you work out of doors or participate in outdoor athletics. But that hair must make you hot!"

The Counselor chimed with an agreeing tone and the Man smoothed his tight curls back away from His eyes. "I know, I know!" He said, seeming frustrated. "I have a head full of it, but My mom doesn't like it cut very short. It ends up looking like a ball of wool. Oh! Hey! Here we are!"

The three exited the woods out onto an area that ended at a cliff. There was a deep chasm and cliff on the other side that again led into a wooded area. Yeshua stepped off the solid ground toward the gorge and Ritter lunged and pulled Him back violently. "Oh!" Yeshua laughed. "Look who is saving who now."

The Counselor spoke as He took Ritter's hand and Yeshua translated. "The King is on the other side. I will go first. I am the bridge. The Counselor will walk beside you and keep your steps solid. Do not look down and do not look back. If you feel as if you are going to fall, let the Counselor steady you. You can't make the walk by yourself. Got all that?"

The Man again stepped off into nothingness and with each step, a wooden plank appeared under his feet. Ritter clung to the Counselor who held tightly in return, burying Ritter completely in a liquid embrace.

Their steps were steady and sure until a cry screamed out from below and, instinctively, the human's eyes went down. There was darkness and a stench that caused Ritter to grow faint. The Counselor pulled him back tightly and pointed ahead toward Yeshua who had stopped and was waiting for the pair to catch up.

When they reached the other side, the Man paused and gestured Ritter forward. "Go ahead of Me. I am first and last."

Ritter stepped out onto solid ground with the Counselor and, as Yeshua followed, the bridge behind the three disappeared. Ritter then leaned out and looked down into the dark chasm.

"What is down there?"

"Death," Yeshua said matter-of-factly. "Now then, the King is just through here—"

"Are you leaving me?" Ritter interrupted anxiously.

"Oh no. In fact, I am the only way you can get to Him. Come on! I can hear Him wringing His hands with excitement!"

Ritter hesitated and the Prince and Counselor stopped. They both felt his pain and were moved. "It's okay, Reed Jacob. When standing before the great King of Kings, everyone is stripped naked. That is the only way one can be with Him. I know you're embarrassed and that is good. I was starting to think you had lost the ability to blush. Your sins are what are causing shame to sit in your belly like a millstone. And there is nothing the Liar would love more than for that weight to cause you to drown in your own self-loathing."

Yeshua took Ritter's hands in his own. "You are by birth an heir to the King and His holy kingdom. Everything He has was created just for you, His chosen, and I would sell my title as Prince for thirty pieces of silver to see that you have it. How can you hang your head when you are worth all that?"

The three journeyed a little farther then stepped from another gathering of trees out onto the highest point of a bright green landscape. Emerald hills rolled all around in pregnant mounds and sheep grazed in the valley. "It looks like Ireland," Ritter said softly, and the Counselor patted him on the back.

The clouds began to move into a stair-like pattern, and there was a sound like rushing water. "Okay now, you are still human and your sins couldn't bear the magnitude of His presence. So, the Counselor is going to put a veil over your eyes. Now, don't worry! Come on! Hey, we have taken care of you so far, haven't We? Enhance your shalom! Your sight will be restored afterward. Have faith. Let it be your eyes! And here, you can put this on."

Yeshua began taking off His own tunic and Ritter tried to stop Him. He didn't want the Man to be naked in his stead.

"I won't be naked!" the Man laughed. He smoothed His wild locks back and handed Ritter the garment. "I am wearing underpants! What kind of place do you think this is?"

The Counselor helped Ritter maneuver his sore body into the tunic. It fit perfectly. Ritter looked down at its length and the fit on his shoulders and laughed, "Hey, it fi—"

Words left him as he looked at Yeshua who was covered with bruises, cuts, and swelling to include a very swollen eye. Ritter felt his own eye and noticed that not only it but also his entire body was free of wounds.

"Don't say a word, Reed Jacob! You take My garment. I take yours. That's how it works. Now straighten yourself up here. We will see you after. Counselor?" The Advocate stepped forward and Ritter stopped him.

"Wait! Thank you," he said to Yeshua.

"No, thank you, Reed Jacob."

The Counselor stepped forward, touched Ritter's eyes, and they darkened in submission.

The ground shook and Yeshua and the Counselor held Ritter's hands. Thunder clapped, there was a sound of waves crashing and the wind became tornadic. Then as suddenly as the frenzy had begun, there was peace.

"Look at him!" said a still, quiet voice. "He is so beautiful! Oh, Reed Jacob, my Beloved, my Beloved."

Chapter 17

Divorce, a Decision and Dessert

When a child is lifted, there is no heaviness of the body, or within the brain, dangling below to burden them. Their smallness in both size and sense of self allows them to readily accept the comforting weightlessness of someone else assuming responsibility for their life. That was how Ritter felt as his feet left the ground up toward the heavens into an all-consuming embrace.

The Presence was beyond human words. Everything both within and without responded to it. There was an electrical charge in the air and Ritter could feel his body give itself over to gooseflesh as his hair responded to the static. The swirling, tactile mazes on his fingertips swelled against the softness of the King's clothes and his nervous system happily relented control of his entire being knowing the Presence would provide its life.

There was a pleasing aroma of incense in the air and Ritter's ears lifted at the sound of immense wings beating against the air. Voices cried out, "Holy, holy," from above his head. Every animal gave its cry in a single, harmonious chord and Ritter was suddenly very thankful to be blind. He had thought the vulnerability of it would frighten him. But, his remaining active senses were so overwhelmed by the King, he thought the addition of sight might have caused him to explode.

"Look at him!" the King said. "What a beautiful heart! Oh! I have to hug you again!" Ritter was embraced again, but this time, he was shaken playfully side to side. "Okay! I have to stop or I will hug you all day and we have a great deal to talk about. Oh, just once more!"

The two walked hand in hand in silence for quite sometime until the King laughed. "Yes, it is far too quiet," He said in response to Ritter's thoughts. "And, think of it like this, Beloved. I am somewhat like the sun I created. I am warm and provide life but a Consuming Fire nonetheless. Human eyes can't look at Me without being mortally injured. Here, have a seat!"

Ritter sat down on a smooth wooden bench and his hands searched it curiously. "This is the perfect spot for the surprise that I have planned for you. Do you think you can handle another surprise today?"

"Well," Ritter said with a laugh, "you would know better than me, Father."

The King smiled and rubbed Ritter's head with an ancient, paternal affection. "You know who I Am. You called Me Father."

Ritter nodded and smiled. "Everything knows who You are! How could they not!"

"Ah, that's true, Beloved, but you said it out loud. Now, even the devils are aware that you know. The spoken word is a very powerful thing. The belief within a man's heart leads him to righteousness, but his words are what save his soul."

Ritter smiled and thought about what the King said as his fingers traced the dark whirling patterns in the wood grain of the bench. "This is a brilliant bench! I have never seen the likes . . . wait! I can see!"

Ritter looked at his hands and the jade landscape. He then looked at the King and the confusion in his heart caused the Father to giggle.

"Your faith has given you sight, Beloved, and you are now able to see clearly. You are still human however, and the sight of Me would still be the end of you. But rest assured, I am here on my throne. I AM. Were you to go to the depths of the ocean or highest of mountain peaks, you could not escape Me."

Ritter felt a hand pinch his chin playfully. "Oh yes, the darkness heard what you said," the King said in response to the question in Ritter's chest. "They are angels, Beloved, nothing more. They cannot read your mind but your words, ah yes, they can hear your words. That is one of the many reasons the tongue can be such a source of corruption. Not only does it cause injury to yourself and others with its actual words, it also gives Darkness an ample opportunity to study you and look into the recesses of your heart. It allows them to fine-tune their strategy to take you from Me."

"Why would they care to have me?" Ritter asked, shaking his head. "I am just a man."

"Oh, no, Reed Jacob, you are not *just* a man. No human is *merely* anything. Look at our shadows there on the ground." Ritter looked ahead and saw the shadow of the invisible God beside his own.

"Despite a few subtleties, son, they are obviously of the same design. You are cut from My pattern. That alone makes you far more than *merely* and is enough cause for the Darkness to want you. They like to take what is Mine not only out of treachery toward their Creator but anger for all they have lost. They hurt you to hurt Me and their stratagems are brilliant. For example, they know that if they can corrupt something that looks like Me," He paused and the shadow of his hand pointed toward Ritter, "they might be able to convince one that the defilement is Me. Once they do that, they strip Me of my holiness in the eyes of the one they have deceived. I then am made to seem limited and instead of the God with Whom nothing is impossible, I become a byword, the what-kind-of-god-would-let-this-happen god. I believe that is a name you have used more than once."

Ritter looked down at the shadows and thought of the years he had lived in anger against his Creator. He wondered if the King knew the pain He had caused him.

"I am always amazed that My own creations think I don't understand how they feel. Beloved, you were created by My pattern. Not I, yours. Happiness, sorrow, fear, surprise, anger, disgust, these are all things I Myself have experienced which is the only reason you are able to feel them. I also know amusement, contentment, excitement, regret—What? You think I have never regretted something? On more than one occasion I, because of his actions, regretted making man! I wanted to destroy him completely and begin again. Noah didn't try to talk me out of it but Moses did and was successful more than once, obviously.

"That's a good question, Beloved. Your brain is talkative today! How could man disappoint Me? If I am perfect, then shouldn't My creation be as well? He was, originally. Adam and Eve were sinless, and I walked among them in the garden. I loved them absolutely as any parent does their child. And, because I loved them, I gave them a choice. Every created thing has the option not to love Me in return. Yes, even angels. From where do you think the darkness came? They lived with Me. The pride of one of them made him believe that he was greater than I was. He left and some went with Him. I would never allow loving Me to be a forced or passive action. Love is a choice and love gives a choice. Evil is what it is by its own choosing not by My assignation!

"And that, My precious one, brings Me to you. You are here to make a choice not to find out the *meaning of life* or *why we are all here*. I know those are things you wish to know, but I cannot suffer questions I have answered already time and time again!

"You were put on the earth, young man, to love Me completely and absolutely above all other things. That is the meaning of life and the whole duty of man. Humankind may try to pervert that into selfishness but it is not. Loving Me completely saves you from a world of hurt and makes existence as it was meant to be. It makes you as you were meant to be which among other things is, at peace.

"Yes, yes, I know. You are not at peace and say in your soul that I am the reason. You are angry with Me for the loss of your sister. I understand that and I have let you continue in that anger because it bound you to me. As long as you hated Me, there was still a *Me* in your heart. However, there comes a time when a father tells his child that it is time to set aside childish things. If you are to be bound to Me, it will be out of love. And, that love will be based on who I am not what you perceive that I do or do not do for you.

"Man is fragile, son, by his own choosing. Wounds and sickness can be fatal but not because of My design. The created sought to rise above the Creator and that rebellion brought with it the consequence of mortality. Could I have aborted natural law, suspended that inherited consequence, for a moment? Could I have sent an angel to rescue your sister or put My hand down to save her? Could I have made you leave five minutes earlier or later?" Ritter felt two strong, warm hands on his shoulders and his body was turned to face the direction of the infinite voice.

"Did I let Reece Johanna Thomas die? Yes, son. I did. I did in that I had the power to stop her death and chose to not exercise it. Beloved, I AM. Do you understand? I am not *a* being. I *am* being. There is nothing I cannot do. All that exists is Mine because I am existence and without Me, there is nothing. But, let's be clear about something. Reed Jacob, I didn't allow her death in order to turn you toward Me. My nature is one of generosity and justice not cruelty.

"So, why did she die? You know that answer. Oh, you have buried it beneath the heaping mound of culpability you have put My face on, but the answer is there. Reed Jacob Thomas, you put yourself behind the wheel that morning. You knew you were far too tired to drive and yet you did for the very same reason you were tired in the first place: pride. You believed you knew more than a professor that had been teaching medicine longer than you had even been alive! And, because of that, you conducted your very own weekly study groups in order to *properly teach*, those were your words if you recall, what had already been taught sufficiently.

"The night in question there were one hundred and forty-four in attendance to hear you *clear up* several lectures. And oh, my Beloved, you were on fire in more ways than one. You covered the week's assignments and then commenced to go ahead in the syllabus. The whispers from the audience fed your flame: *brilliant, prodigious, god of medicine*. Oh, my Beloved," the King sighed. There was a pause and Ritter saw the divine shadow slowly shake its head.

"When the custodian entered at 4:30 a.m.," He continued, "and asked who was the professor in charge, what was your answer? Oh yes, you do remember! You remember the roar of laughter from the room as well. Say to Me, the One Who Sees, what you said that morning!"

Ritter closed his eyes and exhaled. He had never felt shame about those words until this moment. "I said, 'I am and there is no other.'"

The hills in the distance burst into flame and the earth around the precipice on which Ritter sat fell away in a mass of thick, molten lava. He closed his eyes in fear and trembled as a mighty voice shook him to the marrow of his bones.

"I AM! I am the Creator, the Almighty, the Everlasting, the Hope and Holy One of Israel, Lord of Hosts, your Rock, Provider, Refuge, Most High, Battle Standard, Shepherd, Healer, Strength, and a Consuming Fire. I Am and there is no other! Do you understand? Say it to Me out loud, for all to hear!"

Air trembled past Ritter's vocal chords as he said that he understood. And, for the first time, he truly did.

The fire disappeared as quickly as it had combusted and Ritter once again saw the two shadows side by side.

"I am also your Father, Reed Jacob. Not only your Father, but your *abba*, your *da* as you say. And, on occasion, a da has to do what it takes to get his child's attention. I see now that I have yours and I will not apologize for commandeering it any more than your father did the night he walked out onto the rugby field in the middle of a game and grabbed you out of a scrum!"

Ritter wiped his face and laughed. He had been twelve, and his father had heard him curse at an official.

"You truly thought he was going to kill you! And hey, just between you and Me, he wanted to seriously injure you!"

Ritter nodded in agreement and the two laughed.

"My precious creation, you are a genius because I created you as such and those whom I exalt, I am able to humble. However, on the morning of your sister's death, your humbling was not My doing. Beloved, you exalted yourself even above your own body. You were far too tired to drive, and yet, you did. You fell asleep, ran off the road, and your sister was struck dead. Every day since you have beaten Me over the head for it mercilessly, not only in word, but in the deeds you have committed against yourself. With your body you have cursed Me for taking her from you. Son, she was not yours to keep. And, she wasn't taken. She was brought home."

Ritter hung his head and his soul mourned for the time he had lost with his God.

"Do you see those hawks there?" the LORD said, putting a finger under Ritter's chin. The man looked out toward the valley and saw two birds circling and flying by one another. On a final pass, the two crashed and tangled together in a mass of beating wings, falling headlong toward the ground. Just before crashing to their deaths, the male released the female, and they flew away together.

"They are mates, those two," the King said, "and will be for life. Just as you and I were to be. I made a covenant with your fathers that I would be your God, and you would be My own possession, My Beloved Israel. I would love you and care for you as a husband should a wife. Just like those birds, we would cling to one another, and you would have faith that I would keep you safe from harm and cause you to prosper.

"But the world called, and you left me for it and went on to behave far worse than even a prostitute. A prostitute stands and waits but you, ah, you went out in search of those who would defile you and were not even paid in return!

"Beloved, you do not know the pain of infidelity. It rips at your heart like death! Just as any husband would be, I was brokenhearted, angry and jealous as well. Not jealous *of* but jealous *for*. If your mother left your father, would you think his anger, hurt and jealousy to be righteous or selfish?

"My people did come back. I was eager to forgive them and love them, as I am you. And, they left again and again and again. Each time, I searched for them and brought them back with hopes they would stay and be the faithful wife I had planned for them to be. However, they refused to let go of their foreign gods. Oh, they tried to love Me as well but, just as your father would not share your mother, I too refuse to share my Beloved.

Therefore, as a loving spouse, I let them leave Me. If they wanted to be with another, I would never force them to stay. They would always be my Beloved, and I would always wait for them to come back to Me. However, I would not let them wear the crown of My holy name and worship other gods with acts of sex, sorcery and human sacrifice. A divorce decree was written, and I took my presence from them.

"That is by no means the end of the story. They lost the right to be sheltered from the rain under the umbrella of their Husband, their *Ish*. However, they did not lose My love or the promises I made to their fathers. I will return to reclaim My holy possession.

"And that brings us to you. Reed Jacob, I love you and because I love you, I had planned to let you go. You made it clear that you love another and I had a writ of divorce awaiting your signature. But then, you said the Name Above All Names, the name of the promised Messiah. Your words caused the rush of angelic soldiers and brought you salvation from your moment of death, and it changed the matter here between us."

Ritter looked down at his lap as a scroll and pen materialized. "Normally, Reed Jacob, I take actions as signatures on this document, but because of your cry for salvation, I will dismiss protocol. Instead, I will give you the choice to sign. In doing so, you will give up all that a righteous husband provides a wife. My hand will not rest on your shoulder, and therefore, you will not feel the burden of shame that comes with sin. In fact, I will give you over to sin completely. You may have all that you would like and roam freely without the irritation of My voice calling you home."

Ritter shook his head. He had no idea what he had said that had caused him to be saved that night. He wasn't exactly sure what had even happened that night. All he knew for certain was that he felt as if he were being doomed eternally right then and there.

"I don't understand, Father. You are sending me to hell? Is there a hell?"

"If you mean to ask if I am killing you now, no, I am not. You will be alive until the One who holds the keys to life and death calls for you. And, after the events of tonight, I think you know the answer to your final question."

Ritter rubbed his hands through his hair in frustration and fear. "The One who holds the keys? Isn't that You?"

The King smiled. "You mentioned this bench earlier. You are correct; you have never seen the likes of it. There is only this one. It is made of one solid piece of wood. See the imperfections here, wormholes and such? This particular line in the grain came during a year of drought, this one here from torrential rain. The knothole by your right hand was an injury caused by an animal. I love those imperfections. It shows the brilliance of the artisan to leave them and still be able to create such a thing of beauty. And all the hardships that put the imperfections there make for a stronger wood and, thus, stronger place to sit!

"The Counselor put on the clear lacquer. And, because of that, this bench is completely sealed. Regardless of the storms that come or heat that bears down relentlessly, the wood will survive and this lovely seat will always be My very own. Nothing can take it from My hands. The Man who made it is the best carpenter I know. He is the One who holds the keys to life and death. I am surprised you did not hear them jingling together earlier tonight!

"Now, back to the matter at hand! Again, Beloved, this will not be the end of My love for you. It will release you from loving Me."

Ritter took the pen in hand and opened the scroll. "And it doesn't mean I die now? I will continue living just like before?"

"Yes and no, Beloved. To be given over to sin is to be made numb to its presence. You will see it as natural and your right as a human so, in some ways, your life will be very different. But in the earthly sense, as you mean, yes, you will remain vitally functioning."

Ritter's foot shook nervously as he read the document. "Don't you know what my answer will be?"

The shadow nodded. "Yes, I know what you will do. I see straight through to your soul. You need to declare it however for all those that don't have My strength of sight, which includes you."

Ritter looked around and began trying to stall the resolution. He asked about historical mysteries, the science of how the Earth came to be, the fate of different people, the King's opinion on world events, and finally, as many questions as he could imagine regarding the bench. All were met with silence.

"This is not about any of those things, Beloved. This is about you and Me. The last question however, I will answer, and then you will declare your intentions.

"This bench was made by Yeshua. Why? Does a son need a reason to make his abba a bench? Now then, take up the pen, Reed Jacob, the world awaits your decision."

"But what about the surprise you said you had for me? Is this document my surprise?"

The King laughed. "Spoken like a true child," He said and then promised the surprise would happen after Ritter had made his decision, regardless of what it was.

Ritter sat quietly several moments in contemplation. The decision was made, publicly declared, and the document was sealed and filed accordingly for the Day of Judgment.

"All right then, I am a God of My words and a surprise you will have."

Suddenly to Ritter's left, a glass of milk and a plate of cookies appeared. He smiled and picked up the cookies, trying very hard not to be disappointed. He truly thought the Creator of all that is created would have had something a bit flashier than a plate of cookies, ugly cookies at that.

Ritter picked up a cookie and prepared to take a bite. "Oh, dunk it in the milk, son!"

Ritter laughed, dunked, and took a bite. His mind worked as his teethed chewed and he smiled. "These are Ugly Cookies! That's what they are called! Reece used to make these all the time! They were my favorite!"

"She still makes them, Reed Jacob. And those she made today, just for you."

CHAPTER 18

It's Alive!

Cat was startled into a waking state by a light bursting through her bedroom window. The motion-sensitive lamps on the back of her house had been triggered and she knew it was most likely Mama Dog taking a midnight potty break. After several seconds of Cat's brain yelling at her to wake up, she remembered that the dog and doe had left her house that afternoon. The realization caused her to sit up and listen for any hints of an intruder.

The screened door of the back porch whined, and within a matter of seconds, Cat's hand had warmed the grip of her pistol that lay in wait in a strong box under her bed. Her feet moved silently across the kitchen floor and her eyes watched for passing shadows by the window. She grabbed her cell phone and prepared to call 911, not to report an intruder, but to request an ambulance for one that had been shot.

A strange gagging sound echoed from the porch followed by coughing and dry heaving. Beau ran to the back door, stuck his softball-sized head through the blinds and immediately began chattering. He ran back and forth between Cat and the door, prompting her to open it, but instead, she turned on the porch light hoping to frighten whatever was out there away or to improve her aim.

The coughing and gagging suddenly changed to sounds of hissing and then, there was quiet. Cat lifted a blind and saw a naked man lying on the floor of her screened porch. His back was toward her and his head was lying in a pool of blood-mingled spit and vomit. The body was still pink but limp with death.

Her thumb dialed her cell phone but before hitting Send, her eyes looked closely at the dead man's arm and hand that was draped over his head. She gasped, flew out the door and pushed the body onto its back. A pulse was located but no air escaped his chest. Her fingers swept the inside of his mouth, pulling out stringy saliva and congealed blood, and she immediately began giving chest compressions. "Live! So help me, you better live!" she said in a low angry voice through teeth gritted with effort.

With the third thrust his throat and jaw moved and she turned him on his side. His face swelled with the strain of heaving until a mass of blood was vomited out. Ritter then heaved wildly for air.

Cat grabbed a robe she kept hanging on a hook on the porch, wiped his face and cleaned out his mouth. When he seemed to be breathing freely, she put the robe over his naked body and rubbed his back aggressively as he were a newborn puppy hesitant to draw in a full breath.

His blue eye, not rendered useless by swelling, opened. After a moment of focusing, Cat saw a look of terrified confusion pour over his face. Ritter looked up at her, his surroundings, and quickly pushed himself away spastically as if his vigor had come back to him with a massive jolt. Cat held her hands up and spoke in a soothing voice as she would to a frightened animal. She assured him that he was safe and that she would call him an ambulance. As she raised the phone, Ritter lunged like a dog toward her hand and knocked it across the porch.

"I'm okay," he said with a raspy voice. "Don't call anyone!"

Cat pleaded with him and the more wounds she saw on his exposed skin, the more insistent she became. Ritter shook his head and then rubbed his forehead to gather his senses. His head turned quickly toward the movement of her hand and he retreated against the screened enclosure. "Don't touch me, Cat!" he threatened.

"Reed, it's okay."

"Where am I?"

"You're on my porch."

"What day is it?"

Cat shook her head at his confusion and replied that is was 1:00 a.m., early Saturday morning. Her eyes welled with tears and she wiped her cheek with the back of her hand. "Reed, you have a concussion, please, let's go to the hospital!"

Ritter refused and Cat hung her head. "Come on then," she sighed, "let's get inside."

"Cat, I said don't touch me! I am serious as death now, don't bleedin' touch me! I am filthy beyond what you can imagine!"

Cat spoke kindly and reminded Ritter of the outdoor shower. He looked over his shoulder at it and, although it was less than ten yards away, it seemed like ten miles. He shook his head and again gave a sharp look to Cat who moved too quickly for his comfort.

She went inside and, after several minutes in the house, returned to the porch dressed in full scrub gear including exam gloves that reached her shoulders. She sat down, pulled her mask from over her mouth and smiled as a mother does to coax a child. Her voice was calm, and her words were purposeful.

"You seem to have forgotten that I make a very good living up the backsides of cows. I have had every type of animal fluid on me and in my mouth at one point or another."

"This is human filth, Cat. Look at me! Human filth! Do you understand what I am saying to you?"

"Yes, Reed. I get it. What I do not get is your insistence in staying in it! Look, there is water! What's keeping you from it?"

"I am too bloody dirty to—"

"To what? Be clean? Reed, you are never too dirty to be clean."

Ritter looked at the shower then down at his fingernails that were lined with dark blood. "I don't think I can walk that far, Cat."

"I'll help you."

"You can't help me! I am twice your size."

"Well, let's give it a shot."

Ritter hummed in negation and held his hand up to stop her from moving closer. He didn't have it in him he said, and even if he did, he certainly didn't have the strength to raise his arms to wash himself. There was also the little matter of him being naked.

Cat held up a black towel and smiled. Ritter looked at it in confusion and then understood. He pulled the robe she had put over him tighter around himself and sighed knowing her tenacity had more vigor than he did at the moment.

"Reed, the biggest thing between you and that water is your pile of excuses. You're right, you can't get yourself clean, and I doubt you can make the walk alone. But, you won't have to. I will walk with you. I will wash you. I will dress your wounds and lay you down to rest. All you have to do is have enough faith in me to let me."

Cat stood and held her hand out. Ritter looked at it, the shower, and then himself. "You can do this, Reed. Getting over there with me is going to be a lot easier than whatever got you here like this in the first place." She walked to his side, put her arm around him, and the two struggled the short distance together as a single shadow.

Cat helped Ritter into the large wooden box of a shower stall and then exited. He slowly wrapped the dark towel around his waist and then sat down heavily on a wooden stool. Cat rejoined him and put a bucket of washcloths on the floor at his feet and an oversized white towel over the door. To Ritter, it looked more like a burial shroud than towel, and he thought that was appropriate in more ways than one.

The temperature of the water was warm and it gently cascaded over his tired shoulders and down his torn back. After a moment, Ritter pulled away and grimaced at the stinging on his skin. Cat inspected him and ran her fingers lightly over the wounds.

"It looks like you have glass in your back. It's okay. I'll take care of it. Just relax." Her tone made him feel completely guarded and safe and his body slumped over gratefully. He breathed slowly and watched as dirty water cascaded off him in sheets, swirled around his feet, and disappeared down the drain.

Cat bathed him with maternal care. Her fingers pushed the shampoo gently against his scalp and combed the filthy tangles from his hair. She then kneeled beside him, took off her gloves, and washed him in sections to not miss even an inch. When he needed to straighten his spine for her to reach his chest, she kept one hand behind his back to support him. And, when cleaning his limbs, she bore their full, dead weight. Just as she had said, there was no effort needed on his part except to accept the effort on hers.

When all that was not covered by the dark towel was clean, Cat left the water running and stepped toward the door to give Ritter privacy to finish bathing. Fearing the loss of her, his hand jumped forward and grabbed her soaked pants leg with such force she fell out of the door. She looked back with surprise and saw Ritter still sitting limp with his head down. The only sign of vitality was the one arm reaching out desperately like a lone branch on a stripped tree.

Cat put her hand on his and he released his grip from her. She kneeled down in front of him, pushed his hair back from his eyes tenderly, and smiled. "I'm not leaving you, I promise. I'll be right outside."

"I killed her," he said quietly. Cat's eyes narrowed in confusion and Ritter repeated and clarified himself. He had been the one to hit and kill his sister. Her body had flown up onto the hood of his car and come to rest on the windshield. And, before she died, he could see in her eyes that she had known the face of her killer.

Ritter's chest heaved, and he covered his head with his hands. His heart and body sobbed, and between heaves, he cried out, "I'm sorry, God! I'm so sorry!"

Cat put his face in her hands and kissed his forehead. He moved forward, put his arms around her, and she held him against her chest until the tide of emotion within him ebbed.

Ritter slowly slid on a pair of jogging pants that had been hung over the shower door. Cat then helped him to the house and into her bed. As he lied down on his stomach, his skin sighed with relief as it surrendered itself to the icy bliss of the cold sheets. He inhaled the smell of her from the pillow and knew from the small indention in the mattress, that was the side on which she slept. He rubbed the top of his feet against the bed and put as much of his own form as possible within the small hollow place beneath him.

Cat changed out of her wet clothes and then went to work on her bipedal patient. As best as she could, with what little light and equipment she had, she began removing the shards from his back. One by one the pieces of glass dropped into a metal pan, the sound of each denoting its size. The crystal percussion rang in Ritter's ears as he looked at the clean, freshly scrubbed skin on his hands.

"You're not going to ask what happened to me tonight?"

Cat smiled and replied that it wasn't relevant. All that mattered was that he was safe and for that, she was thankful.

"I'm sorry for the things I said to you earlier this evening, Cat. I was cruel. If you are alone, I know with certainty it is not for lack of willing company. You are wonderful, infinitely kind, and—." He paused and smiled. Beautiful was what he wanted to say, but he felt certain the setting would dull the luster of its truth. Instead, he simply remained quiet, hoping that somehow she could read his mind.

When she had finished bandaging his back, Cat pulled the sheet up around his shoulders and tucked in the edges. Her hand ran across his hair once more and she whispered, "Good night, Reed. Are you okay?" He nodded and she turned out the light.

"I wasn't always this way," he said before she closed the door. "I used to be a good man if you can believe that." A sardonic laugh escaped him and then he sighed. "I was a virgin until I was twenty. I fully intended to wait until marriage. Then she died and everything changed."

The lamp beside Ritter clicked and the room glowed once again. Cat walked to the opposite side of the bed, climbed up, and laid on her side facing him. She stretched her arm out, moved the sheet down away from his face, and patted his arm before drawing her hand back to rest under her head. Ritter was so lost in thought he did not seem to notice.

"Have you read *The Odyssey*?" he asked. Cat smiled in affirmation that she had. "It was my favorite book as a lad. Even at such a young age, I felt such sadness for Odysseus. His life was perfect. His wife, Penelope, loved him, they had a newborn son and then, the war he wanted no part of pulled him away from his home, his beloved Ithaca. I could not imagine being so far from my family for so long. I was eight years old and, although I couldn't grasp such a massive amount of time, I was cognizant of the fact that I couldn't.

"Now ironically, here I am twenty years later, the same amount of time Odysseus was away from home, feeling like the man himself, trying every day to get back home wherever home is. They say it's where the heart is, but what if you don't have a heart?

"I don't know. I feel lost and adrift, and it's made worse by the fact that I know how it feels to be happy and secure. I know what Ithaca feels like! I know what feeling feels like! But . . . every day, I just drift and get more and more lost in this numb state."

Cat brushed a lock of hair from Ritter's swollen eye and sighed. Her mind considered what he said and Ritter took her silent contemplation for lack of understanding. He closed his good eye disappointedly. No one understood.

"We buried Reece the next morning after she died," he digressed. "I had seen her just two days before. She was smiling, we had lunch and then, she was in a pine box in the ground. Just like that," he said with a snap of his fingers. "And I changed just as quickly.

Our house was open after the funeral service to visitors, and I couldn't bear to be in it. I went home with her best friend and, for the first time since the accident, cried. She cried as well and we held each other. Consolation turned to intimacy and that was that," he said with a shrug.

"I realized afterward that for that brief amount of time, I had neither one thought of Reece nor a pang of guilt. My brain was consumed with instinct rather than emotion and my chest seemed to appreciate the relief. I guess those two pieces of me came to an agreement to accept the consolation and not question the manner in which it was provided. Sex was a crude anesthetic but effective nonetheless. And thus, in those few moments of intimacy, the monster was made. Let the lightning commence!"

Ritter laughed and picked at the flowered print on the sheets. Cat's heart ached for him. She reached out and put her hand on his arm and his smile retreated. He bit the inside of his bottom lip then cleared his throat to reset his emotional switch.

"The last time I cried for Reece was the afternoon I lost my virginity. I didn't shed a tear afterward. I ceased to sleep and ceased to feel which, ironically, worked to my favor. I was able to bear heavy class loads without complication. I worked while others slept and, if I felt stressed, sex proved an excellent purgative. Oh, bloody hell," he said, rubbing his healthy eye and, again, pushing an uncomfortable laugh though his nose. "I have passed through life these past eight years without living for a moment. I've just existed. Nothing more."

Cat turned her head up toward the ceiling and scanned it in thought wondering how someone so crippled could survive in the wild of life without being consumed. She felt a touch on her ear and, by turning her head toward the sensation, laid her face in Ritter's hand.

"Until you, Cat. Something about you has resurrected the bit of me that died." He rubbed his thumb across her cheek and then pulled his hand away.

"It's fantastically frustrating actually!" he said with a grimace and Cat laughed. "Honestly, when I'm with you"—he paused in thought—"it's what I imagine a paralyzed person would experience if they were suddenly able to feel again. It's overwhelming. I feel happiness, sadness, guilt, remorse, and worst of all, hope. Hope! Oh, woman! It is the view through the hangman's noose! Closer you come to the scene on the other side of the rope, the tighter the noose about your neck! I hate *hope*. However, I am glad you crept into my life although I do resent the tardiness of your arrival. Perhaps if you had come round a bit earlier, I wouldn't have had to take a holiday in mental hospital."

Ritter realized what he had said and looked at Cat. "That's a story for another time, Ginger. I don't think I have it in me just now."

She smiled and got up from the bed to make a cool compress for his eye. Upon returning, she asked if he wanted a hand mirror to look at it and he said that he didn't. Knowing how bad it was wouldn't make it any better.

Cat folded the washcloth to fit his eye and Ritter thanked her. She sat back on the bed and looked at him as if in appraisal. "I wish you would see a doctor."

"Aren't you a physician, Dr. Douglas?"

"A people doctor, Reed!"

"Well, I don't feel much like a *people* at the moment, so you're actually more suitable. Treat me as you would any of your patients. What would you do if one of your animals turned up in this state?"

"Shoot it," she said without hesitation and the two laughed.

The neck hole of Cat's sweatshirt fell to the side and Ritter could see a lump on her collarbone and a scar on the skin above. He thought of her x-rays, the newspaper articles, what Paul had said, and wondered out loud, "Do you miss him?"

144

Cat looked at him inquisitively and then an expression of knowing washed over her face. She looked down and nodded.

"Who told you? Paul or the lawn-chair prophets across the street?"

Ritter smiled and placed the culpability on Paul.

"It's okay. I don't mind if you know. It is public record after all! You may not feel like *people*, but you're still *public*!"

"Oh me," she said, scratching her nose and looking around as if viewing the story in the air. "Danny was a good man and, yes, of course, I miss him. You and me, we made a little agreement about this didn't we, on the front porch? Quid pro quo. You tell me, I tell you."

Ritter assured her that she wasn't obligated to tell him anything. He had not told her about his sister with the expectation of knowing about her attack.

"Ah, it's okay. Well, let's see," she said as she laid back and interlaced her fingers on her chest. "We met in college in the veterinary program; he was a small-animal vet. We married the day after graduating and moved just outside Dallas. We both had jobs there and lived in a tiny house we rented from one of my clients. It was in the middle of his land and we, no joke, had cows looking in our windows all the time! Very surreal! Nothing like putting in a video and looking over your shoulder to see a bull watching a movie with you!"

She laughed and smiled from the memory and then, after a silent pause, the light in her eyes dimmed.

"Then, September eleventh happened and this cloud of fear toward Middle Easterners just blanketed the whole country. Well, Danny was Israeli and his name in the phone book attracted some attention. We started getting threatening calls but our address wasn't listed so we felt pretty safe. There was also this cow that, for whatever reason, meant she was going to bed down on our front porch right in front of the door! We called her our *security system*. She wouldn't do anything, but somebody would have to have a whole lot of hubris to wake a half-ton sleeping cow in the middle of the night!

"But, we also had a back door," she said after a hard sigh. "And, one night, three people broke it down and accused Danny of working for al-Qaeda. He told them he was Israeli and Israel and America had long been allies, but they didn't care. Danny's last name was Ben Laban and that was about as bad a surname as anyone could have had at the time! *Bin* is Arabic, but *Ben* is a Hebrew prefix. They both mean son of like *Mac* does. We tried to explain to them and I told them that in all likelihood Jesus' last name was Ben Yosef, meaning son of Joseph—'"

"What did you say?" Ritter interrupted.

"It's a Hebrew prefix," Cat continued.

"No, no, you said Ben Yosef."

"Well, yea, that's most likely what Jesus was called. 'Yeshua Ben Yosef—"

Ritter held up his hand to stop her and a deluge of memories poured into his brain.

"Yeshua Ben Yosef?"

"Yea, Reed, are you okay?"

He thought for another moment. "Yea, I'm sorry, I just, that reminded me of a dream. I'm so sorry. Keep going. What did they say to that?"

Cat shook her head. "Nothing. They didn't care. And so then, they shot us: him for being a terrorist and me for being a traitor. Then apparently, after shooting us, they beat us. Killing us wasn't enough I suppose."

Ritter removed the compress from his eye and raised his head. "They killed you?"

"That's what the paramedics said. I had lost so much blood I was gray and cold. I had been shot through the chest here. The bullet just missed my heart and exited through my shoulder, thus, the shoulder break you saw on the x-ray."

Ritter asked who called 999 and Cat smiled. "It's 911 here. That's why they chose September eleventh. You know, 9 is September . . . never mind. Anyway, the emergency dispatch didn't get the recording. The operator's voice was there but no other voice and there were no prints on the phone other than ours and we couldn't have called."

"Could your husband have?"

Cat sighed and said no. Danny had been shot in the back of the head.

She was in a coma for three weeks afterward. And, when she woke up, Danny's parents had come and taken them to be buried in Israel. Ritter caught her use of the word *them* and remembered the sonogram. That was the only hint Cat gave of there being a child.

"It was so strange. I woke up in the hospital, didn't know why I was there, and my whole world had changed. When I did get back home, it had been cleaned and Danny and all his clothes were gone. There was just this empty place in the closet and an echo in the house."

"Did they ever catch the three who attacked you?"

"No. The only physical evidence was a big ole bloody glove print on the *security system's* head! The police said they went to the back door and there was a cow standing there just chewing grass with a handprint on her forehead! Now that's like something out of a B mystery movie!"

After waking from the coma, she had required therapy and all together spent nine weeks in the hospital. Ritter nodded. It was the same amount of time he had been a patient after his breakdown. If his swollen eye could have taken the pain, he would have rolled both of them at the strange and gruesome commonalities in their lives. They each bore the scars of tragedy and loss, and ultimately, they had both been killed: one literally, one figuratively. However, it was the one who had actually been dead that seemed to have gone on to live her life. Something about that made Ritter jealous and left feeling slightly emasculated.

"And you're fine now, yea? Wounded, rehabilitated, and set free. Completely at peace with it all."

146

"Oh woe, now, I never said that!" she replied, giving Ritter a serious look. She could hear the bitterness in his voice.

"God carried me through it. And, you know, from the beginning, people have wanted me to examine the whole thing and come to terms with how the tragedy worked toward a divine plan as if that's proof that God is really there and was there that night. Well, I don't see the plan! I don't. I don't know why it happened."

Cat paused as her bottom lip quivered. She wiped her eyes, cleared her throat, and smiled at Ritter.

"I don't get it. I see families with little kids and it makes my heart hurt and I get angry and yea, I feel cheated. I don't understand it. But, I don't need to understand it. I don't need an explanation and I don't need to find proof of God's existence in the midst of it. The proof is here," she said, putting her hand on her chest.

"I know that no matter how rough the storm is, how much I get pulled around or under, I will never be pulled away. God is my anchor and no man or bullet can or will ever take me out of His hand. His Son made that possible and His Spirit reminds me of it and comforts me through the storm every day. I know that I will see my husband, my daddy, my little girl, everybody again in heaven." Cat shrugged and smiled, not realizing what she had said about her unborn baby.

"Reed, my life is not up to me. I am not in control. Someone far wiser than me is and I am thankful for that and find it comforting. There was not a moment during or after the attack that I didn't know everything would be okay if not in this life then the next. I was terrified that night but still knew come hell or high water, I had an anchor that I could count on and I was not just going to be shipwrecked and left behind.

"But do not think," she said in a suddenly very stern tone, "for one second, I am at peace with what happened that night. I am not! But, I don't need to be at peace with something to be at peace. I am sorry I can't dazzle you with insight or show you a divine link between tragedy and heaven. I can't and I don't even try because I don't need a connection. And searching would just leave me reliving the night and I would rather live than relive. I know all I need to know and what I don't, God will tell me Himself when I meet Him. And until then brother, I am going to hold on to my anchor."

"Just like that, eh?" Ritter said softly with a nod of his head.

"Yea," she laughed through tears. "Just like that. I am simple! What can I say?"

Ritter huffed in disagreement and said that he couldn't just accept something. His mind had to tear things apart and look at its guts to see how the cogs all fit together.

"Well, I guess that's the torment of a genius! Your brain gets in the way of your thinking! By the way, how did you get here tonight? Did you drive?"

Ritter shrugged and said he had no idea.

"Oh, I see. Who put you on my porch naked and left your clothes, wallet, and cell phone all in a tidy pile beside my door. Your stuff is on the kitchen table by the way.

And why did they put you here? Why not your porch? How did they know I would find you before you strangled to death on your own blood? Don't know, do you? Well, I see it hasn't kept you from finding a comfortable place to lie down! I don't know Reed, you seem pretty peaceful despite the unanswered questions!"

Ritter laughed and nodded. She was completely right.

"Well, Mr. Genius, I can see I have blown your mind. Why don't you get some sleep?" Cat moved from the bed and Ritter begged her to stay. His intentions were not sexual. He just wanted her beside him. She laughed and said that he wouldn't get any sleep with her anywhere near him. Cat was a self-described aggressive cuddler and crude bedmate.

"I sleep very hard, snore, drool, talk, steal covers, invade personal space, and on occasion, walk around." She then apologized in advance if she woke him using the master bathroom.

"If you want to know if I'm asleep, just ask. I'll say if I am! Just tell me to go back to the guest bedroom. I'll go."

Ritter smiled. "Not a chance, Ginger."

Cat huffed, bid him good night, and turned out the light. Just before the door shut, she heard him say quietly, "Hope to see you soon."

CHAPTER 19

Tea of Three for Two

His eyes opened, and again, Ritter found himself seated on the beautiful wooden bench. He felt no strangeness about his sudden reappearance there. It all was very familiar and serene and he smiled as he looked around at the emerald landscape. The sun was at its peak and its light gave the fecund hills and foliage an almost more real than real aspect.

Ritter took a deep inhalation and, to his surprise, smelled hot tea. He looked to his left and saw a tray set up with a small teapot and two cups.

"I thought you might like some," a voice said, startling him. The two laughed and Yeshua apologized. He then asked Ritter for a cup.

"You like tea?" he asked and Yeshua gave him a strange look. Of course He liked hot tea. Why wouldn't He? He also liked three lumps of sugar.

"I just wouldn't imagine you drinking tea."

"Well, imagine it! And imagine some cream too, please."

Ritter laughed, handed over the cream, and said he just never pictured Jesus, if He in fact was what the Christians claimed Him to be, drinking anything. Yeshua blew over the top of the steaming liquid and nodded His head. "Common mistake. Heaven is full of great food, which includes tea!"

The two sipped quietly for several moments until Yeshua laughed out loud. "Why don't you just ask Me!" He finally said, nudging Ritter.

"Are you a god or human or some type of strange demigod-prophet?"

Yeshua took a sip, nodded, and cocked his head to the side as if thinking. "Yes slash no, not anymore, not sure about the strange part, no and yes. That clears things up for you, doesn't it?" He said with a wink. "Reed Jacob, I am not a god. I am God. Do not confuse the two. Yes, I was human for a while as well as prophet, priest, and king. I understand the temporal realm of man as a mortal man and the infinite glory of heaven as the Eternal God. As a prophet, I spoke of what will be. As a priest, I atoned for what was. And as a King, will reign over all that is."

"I'm sorry," Ritter said narrowing his eyes in frustration. "I just cannot comprehend how something can be both human and deity." Of course, he couldn't, Yeshua agreed. There was no standard of reference.

"You don't need to comprehend everything, Reed Jacob. I know I created you with a desire to understand but you are the one that turned it into a need."

Ritter shook his head and held up his hand. "It didn't compute," he said. Yeshua had claimed to be human yet divine and now his Creator. To him, the whole suggestion of it seemed blasphemous. Was it not YHWH who had said, "Here O Israel, the LORD our God, the LORD is One"?

"Well, look who is quoting scripture! I am glad you remember that verse and have so much respect for My Father as to not want to blaspheme Him. God is One. You are correct. He is both singular and one as in complete. Look back at the very first verse of Genesis. *In the beginning, God . . .* The Hebrew word used there for God is *El Elohim.* That's the plural form of *El Elohe.* So, from the start, you were told there was more than One of Us. Yes, I know that doesn't make sense to you. Again, not everything can to make sense to you yet. Leave something for heaven why don't you!

"There are three of Us: the Father, the Son," Yeshua said, gesturing to Himself, "and the Spirit or Counselor as He was introduced to you. We each have many different names. We are three distinctly different Beings with different personalities and areas of work.

"However, we are also corporate in a way you can't grasp just yet. Here, look at your tea. You have water, sugar and tea. Point out to Me which is which. You can't. They are infused. All distinctly different yet, when one refers to it, they simply call it tea. We are God, completely separate yet components of a single tea.

"And while I was on earth, I alone was an infusion. I was the Mighty God yet, a man all the same, not half and half but whole and whole. My being both of those things completely was vital. You know Israel's worship to the LORD was centered on the sacrificial system. It was not designed out of cruelty but to remind them daily of the value of life and to prepare them to recognize the Ultimate Sacrifice: Me.

"Man in and of himself was sinful therefore he couldn't be a pure offering and it would be against My Father's nature to ask for murder anyway. The blood of animals, although completely innocent and therefore pure, was not as valuable as the blood of man. Until I came along, the sin offering of animals was a means of atonement for the sins of that year. My offering was an atonement for all sin, past, present, and future. And yes, I died a willing sacrifice. But, I had to be a man to die.

"Another reason I lived as a man, and I think people forget this, is because I wanted you to know that I have been where you have been. The best king is the one that walks among his people. I would not rule over creation as One who only knew it from a distance. No. You deserve more than that.

"I know temptation. I know hunger, heartache and humiliation. I know what its like to lose someone you love and to be, in the truest sense, alone. I know what its like to carry a secret that sits on your heart like a brick. I know how it feels to know that no one understands what you are going through. And, Reed Jacob," Yeshua paused until Ritter looked at Him, "I know what its like to see the anguish of loss on your mother's face because of the death of her child and know you are responsible for every tear."

Ritter glanced down at Yeshua's hands and Yeshua held them up. The brown scars shined on his olive skin. "And you know what else I know?" He said, putting His arm around Ritter. "I know what it's like to laugh so hard you think you might throw up! I know how good honey is on warm bread and that sour taste you get in your mouth when you start out running too fast. I know how hard it is to stop your teeth from chattering after a cold bath and how warm a sleeping baby on your chest makes your whole body. I know how soft my mom's hair is against my cheek and the roughness of my dad, Yosef's, hands on my shoulders. I know what it's like to be a son, big brother, nephew, uncle, and above all Father," He said, tapping Ritter lightly.

Silence then fell between them. Ritter put his cup down, and Yeshua could see the storm of emotions and questions beating against his skull.

"Because I want to be here, Reed Jacob. Draw near to Me and I will draw near to you. And yes, you have been coming closer to Me. Closer all the time. How?" Yeshua smiled at Ritter's silent question. The Son of Man rubbed His chin and grinned.

"Let's just say this: sometimes We put people in your life to lead you to Us when you are too stubborn to answer Our call. If you a have a mule and a master that are separated by a narrow bridge, the master may call and coax all day and the animal not cross over to him. The mule may not even realize it is being called. The rushing water under the bridge or even the quiet lush greenery under its hooves may distract it too much. When that happens, the master may call a worker from the field to lead the mule over. And you, Beloved, are being led over the bridge to the Master, and you don't even know it. You're the mule by the way if you didn't catch that."

The Sinless pulled the sinful one closer and kissed the side of his head. "You, Reed Jacob Thomas, are worth, listen to your Father, worth the effort it takes to call in a worker from the field to lead you to Me. You are worth My time and patience. And above all, worth the price for which you were redeemed!

"And as for that other thing floating around in your brain, well," Yeshua shrugged and Ritter gave him a sheepish look.

"Oh, it's okay. Most people think that which was part of the problem then and is now and I get that. I am not as tall as King Saul was. Not as handsome as King David, although my mom and dad think so, thank you very much. I don't appear to have the wealth of King Solomon. I don't look royal, I admit that! Our people were looking for a man that would restore Jerusalem to its former glory, sit on its throne, and punish all those who had hurt us, and I absolutely agree I don't look like that kind of guy. However, neither did David when he was chosen to be king and he is the one whose throne I am supposed to take.

"Those who have hurt our people, yours and Mine, will be judged. I will come back with the wrath of the Almighty God for them. I will stand on the Mount of Olives, it will split in two under My feet and I will watch as those people rot from the inside out. My eyes will be of fire and My voice alone will cut like a sword. There will be and there is no limit to My authority, strength and the glory I have prepared for those who love Me.

"Now, you tell me, what type of king do you want? A man like Saul that stands a head higher than the crowd? Or the Man whose hands can reach from heaven through the very gates of hell? You want Solomon's temple rebuilt? Or an eternal temple not made with hands in which you are royal? You want a king like David, a man after God's own heart? Or the Man that is God Himself?

"Trust me! I am all that I have said and more. However, I am not going to be what my people have wanted Me to be because what My people need Me to be is what matters. If you doubt and want to test Me, please do! Look at prophecy, look at history and by all means, ask Me to show you I am who I say!

"Yes, it's going to be hard. Since My sacrifice, My people, My own family, have defined themselves not only by believing in the One true God but also by not believing I am His Son! You are going to struggle with it and feel that you are turning your back on your people but Reed Jacob, I am your people!

"Don't dismiss me! Let's fight it out hand to hand in the dirt! *Bring it* as they say! I would love that, and do you know why? Because you will have to hold on to Me to do it! And when the dust settles and you realize I have won, you will never be more thankful to have lost a fight!"

The sound of children floated in from the distance, and Yeshua looked over his shoulder. "And on a different note, who do we have here?" He said as the two children emerged over the hill. They looked to each be about four years old and had dark, curly hair. Their eye colors were not the same but the shape of their eyes, as well as all their other facial features, made it obvious they were closely related.

Giggling like monkeys, they jumped in Yeshua's lap and He grunted at the impact. They pulled at both His and Ritter's hands and Yeshua laughed. "Let's go or they will never stop pulling at us! Trust Me, they are as stubborn as their father!"

The children led them to a tree, and the boy and Yeshua began climbing. Ritter stood hesitantly at the bottom until he felt a tug at his hand. He kneeled down and looked at the little girl. Her brown eyes were big and eyelashes thick and dark. Her skin was fair and her cheeks were fat and pink with youth. The thought suddenly struck him that, in some strange way, she looked like some one he had seen before.

"What's da matter? Can't ya not climb up?" Ritter smiled at the little girl's voice and accent. He kneeled, grabbed a flower from the ground beside him, and tucked it behind her ear along with one of her long dark curls. He then tugged playfully at the lock and thought that if he were to let his hair grow as long, it would look much the same.

"Well now, aren't you a fine Irish lass? Where might ya be from, love?"

The little girl scratched her nose and shrugged. "I live at home."

"And where might that be?"

"Ummmm," the little girl hummed as her big brown eyes rolled in thought. "Next ta me swing."

Ritter laughed at the simplistic and genuine answers then straightened the hem of the girl's pink dress.

"Let's start over. What's ya name, flower?"

The girl laughed at what seemed an inside joke and said that her name was Christian. Ritter nodded. "And is that your brother up there?"

The girl nodded. "That's Cohen. But, I'm older. Ma says I am a cartoon older."

Ritter laughed and after more questions realized the mother had meant the girl had been born a short time before her brother. About the same amount of time it took the girl to watch a cartoon. They were in fact, twins.

"So your parents named you Christian and the littler chiseller up there Cohen? That's an odd pairing of names."

The little girl gave him a strange look and he could see that what he had said made no sense to her. The combination of names was interesting however, and he wanted to know how they came to be. If in fact, one of her parents was Christian and the other Jewish, perhaps there was a hope for him and Cat.

"Okay, tell me this, do you celebrate Christmas?"

The girl laughed and said that of course she did. "And this year," she continued excitedly, "Ma says it's the same as Hanukah so we can see everybody at the same time! But," she whispered, "I don't think Pop Pop Levi likes you, Grandpa Jack, or Nan Juda very much because of the bat eyes you gave Ma!"

Ritter asked what she meant and the girl shrugged. She said all she knew was that Pop Pop said he had "bat eyed" her mother.

"Wait, why did you say Grandpa Jack and Nan—"

"Da!" the little boy yelled suddenly. "I see a lizard an' she's a fat one!"

The little girl started screaming and jumping on Ritter. "Pick me up, Da, pick me up!"

Ritter lifted the little girl, and she clung to him tightly.

"Cohen put a lizard in my bed, Da!" she whispered with a shiver as she buried her face in his neck and her hands in his hair.

The crush of emotion grabbed Ritter's throat, and he swallowed hard. He looked up at the little boy in the tree and it suddenly occurred to him that the child looked much like he had at that age.

The little girl pulled away from him slightly to look him in the face and he asked her why she had called him Da. The girl didn't reply. She simply gave him a look that said she thought his question ridiculous and then laid her head on his shoulder.

After a moment of stillness, the girl kicked her feet slightly and asked her father to dance with her. Ritter smiled put his hand on her back and began to sway slowly. He then turned his head, put his face in his daughter's hair, and inhaled the perfume of his future.

CHAPTER 20

Death Comes after a Dirty Goat

Ritter's eyes opened and he knew from the halo surrounding the curtains that it was late in the morning. He looked around and smiled at the comfort given to him by his dream and the realization that he was still at Cat's house. He put his nose in her hair, filled his lungs with the scent and moved his head slightly, letting his lips drag along the silkiness of it.

Her stomach was warm and soft against his fingers. He pinched a bit of skin lightly and then pulled her closer. His little finger rested in the small dimple of her navel and he stroked the hollow between her ribs with his thumb.

Reality suddenly hit him like a belt and he gasped with a small snort. His hand that was under the edge of Cat's sweatshirt shot up and he held his breath. Stillness poured into him like cement and his wide eyes looked around as if he were hugging a live bomb.

Ritter rounded his back out and prepared to move away from her. As he did, the arm that rested under Cat's head like a pillow moved and caused her to stir. She sniffed several times, turned over, slung her leg over his hip, her arm around his ribs and rested her nose in the crook of where his neck and chin met. As soon as she was settled, her mouth fell open and she snored like a fat and happy sow.

Irrepressible giggles caused Ritter's chest to shake and Cat shifted in dissatisfaction. She smacked her lips and mumbled, "Stop it," with irritation. The leg she had tossed over him pulled him closer and she nuzzled herself aggressively against him. Within seconds, her rhythmic snoring resumed.

Feeling safe, Ritter let his top arm fold over her back and kissed her. His body ached from the previous night and his head whirled with confusion. But, if all that was the price for his current state, it was a price he was willing to pay.

He closed his eyes and inhaled, hoping the air would cool the hot but vague memories of being beaten and thrown through a window. Amidst the cerebral humidity were also flashes of meeting God, Jesus, some other strange being and children. Being thrown out of a window seemed completely plausible but everything else, Ritter dismissed as a dream although doing so gave him an inexplicable sense of uneasiness. It seemed too real to have been a dream. As real as the warm little thing in his arms.

An expression of satisfaction stretched itself over Ritter's face, and he suddenly understood what Cat had meant by being at peace amidst a storm. With her in his arms, he felt completely anchored.

An hour later, Cat's cell phone rang from the kitchen. Ritter felt her body twitch and then quicken. Her eyelashes tickled his neck as she opened them and he could feel her whole body smile. She sighed, rubbed her nose along his collarbone and kissed his Adam's apple. "Good morning, Reed," she said with a sigh.

The sound of his name slipped easily from her tongue and echoed beautifully in her head like wind chimes. However, that blissful melody in her brain was immediately followed by the cacophony of screeching breaks and Cat's eyes opened wide in unison with the metallic, mental squeal.

Her head moved back and she looked at her location that was far too close with comfort. "What the! Oh no!" she whispered as she absorbed the full shock of the fact she had walked in her sleep and where she had ended up. After a heavy sigh, she began unlacing herself from Ritter's limbs. He in turn, pretending to be asleep, sniffed hard and pulled her back to his chest and cuddled her like a wild animal does its young: gently, yet with a full display of strength.

"Oh you have got to be kidding me!" she grumbled in response and felt movement on the bed behind her. Beau had catapulted himself up and was standing in place, kneading the quilt. He stretched long and then threw himself down behind Cat's back and commenced to give himself a morning bath.

After a good while of Cat struggling between the two lazy and stubborn males, she freed herself from their wedge. Ritter opened his eyes just slightly and saw her standing by the bed rubbing her head and face as if hung over and finding herself with a one-night stand she didn't remember. Beau walked to the edge of the bed and Cat huffed at him. "Traitor," she said and stormed from the room. The animal, in turn, looked over his shoulder at Ritter and chirped.

She went to the kitchen and, through the closed bedroom door, Ritter heard her talking on her phone in Spanish. After ending the call, she crept back into the bedroom, through the bathroom and into the closet. Several minutes later, she began to tiptoe out just as quietly as she had come in.

"You off then?"

The sound of Ritter's voice startled her like a cattle prod. She jumped, gasped and dropped the boots she held in her hand. After composing herself, she lowered her head in a culpable sort of way and quietly responded, "They need me at the ranch."

"Can I come as well?"

Cat closed her eyes and chewed the inside of her bottom lip. She heard Ritter stir, grunt and grow still again. "I could be ready in no time at all," he said. She grimaced hard, feigned a calm smile, and then turned to respond. The sight of him, however, left her dumb.

He had healed a great deal, almost to a miraculous extent, overnight. His wounded eye was still swollen but appeared to be functioning and no worse for the wear. There were dozens upon dozens of bruises, scrapes and cuts scattered over him but the smile on his face made them all seem to vanish.

Cat immediately looked down at the floor. Him sitting on the edge of her bed, bare-chested with sleep-ravaged hair, made her flush and the task of thinking clearly almost impossible. Her brain had turned to mush and was pressing against the back of her eyes to get a better look at him for itself.

She swallowed hard and told him that it wasn't a good idea. It was a dangerous environment and she didn't want to risk him being injured further. In addition, she could almost guarantee she would end up hurt for looking at him rather than at her surroundings. That bit she kept to herself however.

He could stay at her home and relax she said, but she would not under any circumstances let him accompany her. It just wasn't a good idea and a decision on which she simply would not budge, not even a little. No. Absolutely not.

Thirty minutes later, the two were twenty minutes into the drive out to the ranch. Cat held the steering wheel fiercely and tapped her thumbs on it in irritation at her inability to stand her ground and keep Ritter from coming with her. She was also highly agitated at his obvious satisfaction with it all. He glanced at her repeatedly and fidgeted anxiously in his seat. Excitement whirled around in his chest like a dog chasing its tale and he was smiling so hard his cheeks were beginning to ache

At a four-way stop, Cat looked for traffic on her right and found Ritter's eyes beaming at her like headlights. "What!" she said caustically.

"You put on makeup whilst I was home getting dressed, didn't you? Why did you do that?"

"Oh, it's, um, got sunscreen in it so . . . it's not really . . . ," she stammered with embarrassment. "Ooooh," Ritter said in a melodic and provoking tone. "I had no idea the eyelashes were so vulnerable to UV rays."

"Oh, just shut it!" she said angrily as she downshifted and passed a horse trailer.

The rest of the drive was silent minus Ritter's occasional interjections assuring Cat that nothing had happened between them the night before. The only thing that had transpired was a blissful night's sleep for him and for that, he thanked Cat. She said nothing in response and concentrated on the road.

"I know nothing happened!" Cat said finally as she slammed the truck into park. "That's not the point, Reed! I should have taken you home. I know I have sleepwalking issues and should have seen this coming! And it was inappropriate for you to stay over anyway."

"What? Why? Cat, nothing happened!"

"Because, as a Christian, I should stay away from even the appearance of evil, okay?"

Silence consumed the inside of the vehicle and Cat glanced over at Ritter, who, looked very hurt.

"You think I'm evil?" he asked quietly.

"No! Mercy! That's not what I meant! Look, it was giving temptation an undo opportunity okay? That's what I'm saying! Sinning, especially sexually, is easy enough without our helping it along!"

"Cat, I wouldn't have tried anything even if I weren't incapacitated! I am not some type of compulsive molester! So don't feel guilt for tempting me!"

"I wasn't worried about *you*!" she burst out unintentionally.

Cat winced immediately and turned scarlet red. She looked ahead and saw her godfather and several workers walking toward the truck to meet them. She leaned over to bang her head on the steering wheel and said, "Just, don't say anything about it to mi papá, okay? In fact Reed, do not say anything at all today! Say nothing at all! Nada, ni un pito!"

"Can I say just one thing now?"

"What, Reed! For heaven's sake what!"

"You passed gas whilst asleep this morning."

Cat slammed the truck door so hard the glass trembled. Ritter smiled and got out as well, closing his door with much more care. Cruz began to speak as Cat approached, but her expression stopped him. She stormed past without making eye contact saying only, "No toque su espalda." Cruz looked at her curiously and held his hands up. "¿De qué habla? ¡Oye, Tocaya! ¿La espalda de quién?" He then looked over his shoulder and saw Ritter walking toward him. "Oh, I see *quién*!"

Cruz laughed a knowing laugh and greeted Ritter with a hug around the head. "What happen to you back, mi'jo?"

Ritter shifted his baseball cap up and Cruz saw his face. "What happen to the res' of you? Did Cat do this?" he asked with a laugh.

Ritter fought a smile and said that he had been to a party the night before and gotten the hell kicked out of him. Cruz nodded and smiled. "Looks like you had a lot of hell to kick out! I'm glad i's all gone! Vamos, mi'jo, le's go watch."

The two men walked into the large warehouse-style barn. Cruz led Ritter back to a corner section where there were several wood-fenced stalls laden heavily with straw.

"These are the birthing stalls. This one here, she having trouble and need a pull, but she won't let us near her."

Ritter looked over at the cow that was pacing slowly and lowing. The calf's nose and front feet were exposed from the birth canal, but the rest seemed stuck inside the mother.

"And this animal will let Cat pull out the calf?" Ritter asked with a doubtful tone.

"Well, this is that cow's first calving, but I got twenty that say she let Cat help!"

Cat pulled something from her pocket and the cow walked to her. It licked out the contents of her hand and Cat began rubbing her hand along the animal's neck, shoulder, stomach, and finally back flank. She pulled at the calf's tongue. It wiggled in response and Cruz gave an approving grunt.

"The calf is still alive," Cruz said looking up and making the sign of the cross over himself. Several workers looked over at him and began shaking their heads, grumbling at their imminent loss of money.

Cat led the cow closer to the fence. Her small, gloved hands had been dipped into an oily substance, and she slid them up into the cow to get a better hold on the calf's legs. She then put her boot on the lowest fence railing and began pulling lightly. The cow lowed and Cat whistled hard to startle the animal into moving. Within a matter of seconds, the rubbery, yellow-tinged calf was lying in the hay.

Cruz clapped and held his hand out to several workers who put money in it. He then glanced down at Ritter and smiled. Ritter's blue eyes were fixed on Cat in a way that Cruz knew all too well.

The big man adjusted his belt and cowboy hat, counted the money and started singing a mariachi love song quietly. Ritter didn't seem to notice anything except the object of his affection who was looking over the calf.

"What is she doing?" Ritter asked.

"What are you doing, mi'jo?" Cruz giggled in reply. "You should tell her you love her, Doctor. Either that or get a prescription for you' love sickness face!"

Ritter flushed and he shook his head claiming he had no idea what Cruz was talking about.

"Oh, you don' know? Oh, okay. My apology, Doctor."

Ritter chewed the inside of his lip and then reiterated his question hoping to take the attention off himself and his obvious affection for the man's goddaughter.

"Oh, the baby spen' too much time in the canal and have too much stress. Tha's why i's all yellow. So, Cat is jus' looking it over. She also assuring the mama cow that this thing that jus' fall out is okay!"

The mother cow had walked slowly to Cat and nudged her hard, knocking her over. Having not even seemed to notice, Cat continued checking the calf until the mother began licking it. Cat then looked up at Cruz with a smile and backed away.

Ritter laughed with pride and asked why the animal allowed Cat to help but not the workers. Cruz shrugged before explaining.

"These animals here, they know they can trus' her because she been out there with them in all kinds of weather and all hours of the night going through what they do as bes' she can. That and she always carry sugar cubes in her pockets!" he said with a wink.

"She don' try to be in charge of them. If she wen' out there walking big like some kind of king, the animals, they would not like her. But, she don'. She put her head down and walk with them like she is one of them and they follow her like she is.

"Yea," he continued with a sigh, "she is the queen of El Rancho Paraíso! Everybody love her. The cows love her, the sheep love her, the dogs, horses, everybody love her.

Well, Mort the bull, he hate her, but other than that, everybody love her. Don' they?" he said, kicking Ritter's shoe again. Ritter, in turn, put his hands in his pockets and looked away.

"You think *un anciano* like me don' understand. Is that it? I not so old that I forget that feeling! Oh, mi'jo, the first time I see mi Paloma," Cruz paused and put his hand on his chest and grimaced as if it hurt, "you know wha' she was doing? Cleaning up the caca at a rodeo. But when I see her, I thought, *I wan' to do to her what spring does to the cherry trees.*"

Ritter grinned widely and cut his eyes toward Paloma who was helping Cat take off her gloves. "Tha's not me," Cruz said, putting hands up in surrender. "Tha's not my words! Pablo Neruda say that. I never knew wha' he meant until I saw mi Paloma. I made that little brown gordita my wife and you know wha'? She did to me what spring does to the cherry trees!"

The two men laughed and Ritter looked back at Cat. She was making him bloom all right. Bloom in a way he thought wasn't possible with his lack of innocence.

A call sounded over Cruz's radio. The man on the other end spoke and a communal groan sounded from all the workers. Cat shook her head and politely asked one of the men to get her horse and gun for her.

"Oye, dos caballos," Cruz called out, holding up two fingers. "You know how to ride a horse?" he asked Ritter, who nodded hesitantly in response. Ritter had been to polo camp once and hoped that amount of experience would suffice.

Cat gave an angry look to Cruz who winked to her and told her to *calle*. Her face widened with shock. "Qué me acabó de . . . I am a grown woman, he can't tell me to hush," she whispered harshly to Paloma as the horses arrived.

Cruz adjusted Ritter's saddle and gave him a few pointers. They were *cutting horses* Cruz said, and gave Ritter a few riding pointers telling him to lead with *feet and faith.* He then assured him that no matter what he did, the horse would likely follow Cat's.

Ritter rode behind Cat and admired her from the back. Cat, feeling his eyes, looked over her shoulder and told him to get up beside her.

"Where are we going?" he asked. Cat pointed out to a far away pasture where a small clump of white animals was grazing.

Cruz had been raising sheep for the last year, she said. A neighboring farmer had goats and one of those goats insisted on making its way through the barbed wire to their land and mixing in with the sheep. Cat had called the goat farmer and taken the goat back in person several times, but it soon became evident that the goat had quitted his master's land altogether.

"He lives out in the woods there and about every couple weeks tries to sneak in here," she said, adjusting the strap of her rifle. "So you're going to kill it?" Ritter said anxiously. "Why not just care for it and make it your own? What's the harm?"

Cat shook her head and shrugged. "I tried! I don't want to kill it, for heaven's sake! But, it won't let me get near it anymore and if I can't get near it then I can't check its health. We have rules on this ranch. If the goat wants to live here, he has to live by those rules."

The sheep were grazing in the late day sun and picked their heads up as Cat approached. Seeing their shepherd, they began trotting toward her as she dismounted. Left alone behind them was the goat. He had completely blended in with the flock but now, out in the open, Ritter could see that the animal looked wild. Its hair was matted and filthy.

Cat pulled the rifle from off her back and took aim. The goat looked up, and Ritter begged her not to shoot.

"No, wait!" he said, jumping off the horse.

"Reed," she sighed. "I don't want to kill the goat. I don't ever want to kill an animal . . ."

"Give him another chance, Cat! Look at the poor dumb thing!" Ritter seemed genuinely upset and Cat lowered the gun down in frustration. "I've been looking at a poor dumb thing since last night!" she mumbled to herself.

"Reed, it's not that I dislike the goat. I just have a responsibility to my sheep. That animal is sick. There are a few bald patches on its back end and more ticks than you could count. If it would behave itself and let me tend to it, I would. But it won't and every day that it walks among my sheep is another day they are at risk of sickness."

Ritter looked around at the several dozen sheep standing around them and then back out at the goat that stood alone and helpless.

"Okay," Cat said, putting the gun around her back. "One more chance. But this is it."

Cat left the flock. They began to follow her and she held her hand up and made a strange call that stopped their hooves in their tracks. The goat looked at her and, for a moment, seemed content with her approaching. But, at the last second, began jumping around wildly and lowering its head as if preparing to butt her. It then turned and ran at its full speed toward the forest. As it made its last jump toward safety, a shot rang out and it fell dead.

The flock around Ritter jumped and bolted away from the gun report. His weakness from the night before left him without his full balance and Ritter fell backward onto a lamb. The little animal cried out and tried to run away but only limped.

"Oh no!" he said and rolled toward the lamb that was bleating at top volume. He tried to comfort it but his touch seemed to increase its panic.

Cat walked up with a smile on her face. "Oh, goodness *mi ovejita*! Did this big lunk fall on you? Let me see." She picked up the lamb and held it like a baby. "Oh, I think you'll live."

Cat's head snapped toward the sound of an air horn. The horses rose up slightly on their back legs and then ran back toward the barn. Cat grabbed Ritter by the arm and told him to run toward the trees!

"What's wrong?" he said, breaking into a run.

"Mort's out! Go! There he is! Go! Go!"

Ritter looked over his shoulder and saw a bull barreling toward them.

An ancient magnolia was the closest tree, and its branches spread out wildly not far from the trunk. Cat began climbing quickly, but the lamb in her arms slowed her down.

"Put it down!" Ritter yelled but Cat refused. Mort would be sure to trample it. Ritter reached down, took the lamb under one arm, and helped Cat with the other just in time to let go of her and brace himself for the impact of the beast against the tree.

The animal snorted and pawed its huge hooves into the base of the trunk. It then let out a snort and began banging its head against the big magnolia shaking it from root to tip. Ritter, amidst the juddering, tried to climb higher as the animal was little more than a yard from his feet. Cat told him to just stay still and steady himself where he was. She then looked up and saw the workers riding out on four-wheelers and prayed the tree could bear the beating for just another few minutes.

The animal backed away several feet, charged, and made a violent thrust into the tree. Ritter, having not listened to Cat, was still trying to climb and lost his grip. He fell backward toward Cat and she quickly wrapped her legs around his waist and her free arm around his chest.

"They're almost here, hold on," Cat said in his ear, and Ritter did his best to push the two of them against the tree in an effort to brace them both for another jolt. He then reached behind himself and wrapped his free arm around Cat's back out of sheer terror.

"Almost, almost," she continued saying calmly as the workers dismounted, kneeled, and took aim. Eight tranquilizer darts later, the bull's front legs buckled, and it fell to its side.

Ritter turned his face to the side and looked back at Cat whose nose was against his cheek. They let out a single sigh of relief and both began laughing.

"What in hell was that?" Ritter said, leaning his head against Cat's in exhaustion. "How about you get off of me and give me and that poor lamb some relief and then I'll tell you all about it!" she said in response, and Ritter looked down at the lamb. He was gripping it in a stranglehold and the animal was nearly unconscious.

Ritter climbed down slowly, released the dazed lamb, and then turned to help Cat. They both then stood over the massive 2,500-pound bovine and could tell it was still coherent. "That's Mort!" Cat said with disgust.

"As in Morton?"

"No, as in death," she replied and then stomped out to where she had dropped her rifle.

Ritter kneeled down next to the animal and put his hand on its side. Its heart thundered, and its eyes rolled slightly toward Ritter.

"Mort," he whispered, "if you touch a hair on that woman's head, or even come close to it, I will slaughter you myself! You want a fight? Fight me! I'm game!"

The beast's drunken eyes made contact with Ritter's. Its shoulders quivered slightly, and its head suddenly lurched upward. Ritter fell backward, moved away quickly, and touched the end of his nose that had been grazed by the animal's long horn.

"Hey! What are you doing? Are you okay? Good grief, how many times am I going to have to save you from that thing!" Cat said, helping him up and pulling a magnolia leaf from his hair. "Death comes for each of us soon enough, Reed! Don't go tempting it."

Ritter laughed and, before walking away, took a last glance over his shoulder at the heaving black beast that would indeed come one day for his life.

CHAPTER 21

Going Back in Tears,
Moving Ahead in Stillness

Ritter had begged to take the lamb home with him since leaving the pasture. It was hard for Cat to deny him the request especially since the lamb had insisted on following Ritter and bouncing around his heels the way most women did. And, although ovine creatures lack the physical structure necessary to create a smile, Cat could have sworn she had seen the little bundle of wool grin at him.

"It's not a dog, Reed! Don't give me that sad look! It will get you nowhere," Cat said, holding her hand up to him. "And besides, it's still nursing! You take the lamb, and you'll have to take the ewe with it! Where are you planning on putting them?"

Ritter reminded her that he had a *back garden*. Cat laughed and quickly reminded him in turn that his entire *back garden* was a pool. She then assured him that were he to let the animals spend the night out there, he would wake to find a bucket full of droppings on the cement patio. There was also the distinct possibility he would find two drowned sheep in the pool and there are just not many things worse than a dead farm animal in a pool filter!

The playful argument became more serious as Ritter stood beside Cat's truck with the lamb in arms and the ewe on a rope.

"Can they not stay in your garage? You've a little hay laden area in there! I've seen it! Got a fence and everything!"

"No. Absolutely not," she said. "Under no circumstances!"

She was serious, and it was a decision on which she would not relent.

Thirty minutes later, they were twenty minutes into the drive home: all four of them. The lamb slept in Ritter's arms and the ewe was in a large dog kennel in the back of the Jeep wagon with a less-than-pleased expression on its face.

Cat held the steering wheel fiercely and tapped her thumbs on it in irritation at her inability to stand her ground with Ritter for the second time that day. Her agitation abated with every glance toward him however, as she watched him smile down at the filthy little bundle he held like a baby. It was just a matter of minutes she thought before he put the animal over his shoulder and attempted to burp it.

She sniggered, imagining the spectacle, and the thought of Ritter as a father popped into her mind as quickly as a sheet snapping in the wind. Her heart suddenly became heavy, its sinking down pulled her cheeks up, and she smiled. Ritter saw the far-off look in her eyes and the bliss on her face and asked what she was thinking about. *How lovely you would look lying in bed asleep with a little copper-haired baby on your chest* was her thought.

However, "they can carry Chlamydia you know!" was what she said. "As well as salmonella, bacterial meningitis, tetanus, parasites, shall I continue?"

Ritter said she needed not and asked if her sheep carried any of those things. "Irrelevant," she replied flatly.

The sun began its final descent into the scarlet horizon. Cat smiled and looked out at the dark pines whose thin bodies swayed in the breeze like men who were falling asleep on their feet. She loved the drive out to the ranch. It was an hour well spent for her. She never begrudged it and this evening, she loved it even more. For once, the scenery inside the truck was as peaceful and lovely as that on the outside.

"I hit a sheep about a year ago," Ritter said quietly. He glanced back at the ewe in the kennel and raised his eyebrows. "It was about the size of that one in the back there. I was driving out to a mate's house in the country. It was dark and the animal just appeared out of nowhere like a four-legged phantom in the headlamps."

Ritter let out a sigh as if having finally been released from a constricting garment and smiled at the relief. "The sound was, it was, I don't know. It was a deep, dead thud. Then the thing flew up onto the car bonnet and cracked the windscreen. Blood sprayed from its nose."

Ritter paused and Cat asked if he had been hurt in the accident. He looked down at the lamb and then out of the window. "I woke up in mental hospital. Does that count?" he laughed with a cruel edge.

"Apparently, a local farmer found me the next morning lying beside the road with the mangled animal in my arms. When he tried to relieve me of it . . ." Ritter paused and cleared his throat several times in an effort to keep the bindings around his emotions tied firmly.

Cat pulled off the road, put the Wagoneer in Park and turned toward him giving her full attention. He looked at her and grinned. It had seemed from the day's events that Ritter was the one with the power to get his way despite opposition. However, if Cat could have read his thoughts at that moment, she would have known she had the same power over him. They were each so twisted around the other's finger, they were completely ignorant of the other being wound around their own.

"I apparently," Ritter continued after a deep inhalation, "had a flashback of my sister's death and wouldn't release the animal. I had to be sedated for the police to get it off me. Then, I woke up in mental hospital and didn't speak for weeks, if you can imagine that."

Cat shook her head and said, no, she couldn't imagine him silent for that long. But, she was willing to pay him to give it another try. Ritter laughed and added that he knew several others that might be willing to pitch in on the pot, chief among them, Paul.

"It was Paulette that snapped me out of it. My parents flew him up, hoping it would pull me out of whatever dark pit I had thrown myself into. He walked into the room, threw a rugby ball at my head, and knocked me off the chair I was in! I suppose it knocked loose whatever had wound around my brain because I rushed at him and we commenced to beating each other senseless. I started talking and was released about a month later. He asked me to be his housemate and, well, here I am. You know the rest. Ha! You know more than the rest! You know the preface, the story, and all the blooming encrypted bit in between!"

He sighed and bounced the lamb in his arms. "Oh, Ginger. I have said it once, but it bears repeating: if you were to disguise me and happen upon me at a party somewhere, you wouldn't know me. I am completely different around other people. Rubbish basically. I have been told to my face that I am a cold, narcissistic, womanizing, noxiously confident bastard. But with you, there's just no need for all that."

"Don't sell yourself short," Cat interrupted. "You're all that around me too." She had seen a sampling of that side of him at the restaurant the night before and said she didn't care for it at all. There seemed no good reason for it and asked why he couldn't just be the person he was around her all the time.

"Because, Cat," he said, laughing at what he saw as naïveté, "people don't care to see the truth of a man. Frailty is as natural a part of the human condition as it is the human frame, but the sight of either in a broken state causes people to recoil! It produces a visceral response in them and makes them physically ill! Seriously, the sight of even the simplest fracture will make some people honk their guts out! And I am not just speaking of bones here!"

"Yea, but, Reed," Cat said laughing, "if you just go ahead and lay the wound out in front of everybody, they get used to it, no matter how gnarly it is! They might *honk* at first, but after a while, it just becomes part of the scenery. Seriously, if you tell a person they will be misshapen the rest of their life, they learn to deal with the sight of it and so does everybody else! Being skinny is one of my *fractures*, but nobody thinks anything of it because I have been this way for so long. That's how most people here know me! I was fifteen or twenty pounds heavier before. But, can you even imagine me like that now? No."

Ritter looked her over and smiled. He had liked the fullness of her face and body in the pictures he had seen but, truthfully, could not imagine her any other way than she was now. He also couldn't imagine how she remained so waiflike. Cat ate more than he did, he pointed out.

"Well, that eating is a recent development," she said. "I have kind of gotten my appetite back all at once. Oh, and that nosebleed the other night, or those nosebleeds I guess I should say," she said with sudden recollection, "that's leftover from the attack too. I started getting them after I got out of the hospital and used to have them all the time but way worse! Ugh! You have no idea! The doctors said it was a stress response.

"And here's another fracture: I have only been on two dates in the last five years! Both of the guys were handsome and nice and asked me out again but, I just, I don't know," she said with a shrug. "So see, you aren't the only one walking around all banged up." Ritter nodded in thought and ran his finger along the bony structure of lamb's face.

"Here's the difference between you and me though, Reed. My breaks are healed. The bones may still be lumpy and shaped funky but they are whole! Your fractures aren't even set! I mean, you have broken bones dangling all over the place. You've put a sling on them to cover them up, but they're still broken even if nobody can see them! You won't heal that way! You'll just lose mobility or break them even more! Ewww," Cat said with a shudder. "I hate that crackling, crunching noise!" She then pretended to gag, and Ritter threw an accusing finger at her. She had validated his point and more. People were sickened by every aspect of brokenness, even the thought of its sound.

The two laughed and a pregnant pause followed. Ritter had set bones, reattached limbs, and given mobility to the frozen; but for himself, he could do nothing. "What does one do to mend a broken spirit, Dr. Douglas? It's a rather cliché question, but I don't reckon I have ever heard a proper answer."

"'Let me hear joy and gladness; let the bones you have crushed rejoice,'" Cat said with a hand on her chest. "That's from Psalms, and it was on a bookmark someone gave to me while I was in the hospital. I thought it was a kind gesture you know and meant to remind me that God would heal me. Well, I lost the bookmark and found it about a year later and, when I read it again, I realized that the verse said nothing about healing. In the psalm, King David acknowledged that God had crushed his bones but not once asked for healing. Instead, he asked for the broken parts of him to rejoice in their broken state. A verse or two later he asked to be cleansed and to be made a more pleasing man for God, but he never asked to be healed.

"Now, I know there was poetic license. God hadn't literally crushed his bones but the point remains true. He acknowledged that God had destroyed something in him and it caused him pain but, again, he didn't ask to be relieved of that suffering. There had to be a reason for that.

"I thought about that for a long time and, I am no genius but, maybe we are to rejoice in our broken state for the simple fact that He is God. Whether I am broken or whole, He is on His throne and bigger than my human frailty. Maybe that's why He let us remain as perishable goods: to be a constant reminder to us that He's not.

"All that kind of brought me comfort. And, I realized that I had been looking down at my wounds more than I had been looking up to Him. For me, that was the beginning of healing. Now, was I supposed to ask for literal physical healing and relief from suffering? Of course. But none of that will heal the spirit any more than the healing of a broken bone will cure somebody from getting sick at the sight of one."

Cat looked over at Ritter and smiled. "I'm probably not making much sense. As I have said before, we can't all be geniuses like you, although, you look pretty stupid right now!"

Ritter looked down at the lamb and scratched behind its ears. "It makes sense, Cat," he said almost begrudgingly. "The only thing about it that doesn't make sense to me is the simplicity of it."

"Well, I can't help you there. Perhaps one day you will trade your complicated intelligence for some simple wisdom! But, it doesn't take wisdom to see that what you have done thus far hasn't done anything for you, Reed. Genius or not, you get that! Maybe try a different course of care for a while. What have you got to lose except that crappy alter ego and the sound of cracking bones?"

She was right, and he knew it. What had he to lose except a choking sling that he had worn since Reece's death? Burdensome as it was, however, it had served him well and had become as much a part of him as the mangled, broken mess beneath it. The sling seemed to have become gilded with time and even Ritter ceased to see it for what it was. All anyone had to do was pull back its thin veil to see the crushed man lying beneath, but until now, he had not allowed anyone to come close enough to do it.

"Wow," she said, looking at his face. "You are so busy in your head. Do you know how to be still?"

Ritter froze for a moment, asked if that was sufficient, and Cat laughed. "I said be still not *freeze*, wait . . ."

She looked over his shoulder to the pasture across the road. A clump of cows had stopped grazing and was looking up at them. "Come on," she said. "Put your filthy baby back there in the pen with its mama."

The two walked out to the fence and Cat rested her arms on it. "Go walk out there to those cows and just be still," she said and Ritter laughed. Was she trying to get him killed, he asked. "They are cows not the Hydra, Odysseus!"

"Actually, Cat, it was Hercules that battled the Hydra—"

"Whatever, nerd! Trust me! Just walk out to them. They will scatter a bit but, if you stand still, they will come back to you. They are very placid animals and don't look for trouble. Well, bulls are a bit shifty, but there are no bulls out here. I promise they are more frightened of you than you are of them."

Ritter gave her a look that said he doubted that statement.

"Do these animals not belong to someone?"

"It's okay. I know this farmer. If he tries to shoot us, he will have to use a scope. And, if he does that, he will see my truck. Better hurry though. We are running out of daylight."

Ritter hesitantly climbed through the fence. "Look at me, Cat! I am all bashed up and look a bit of a fright!"

"They don't know that! Go! Trust me, Reed."

"There is cow dung everywhere."

"I've seen you in worse! Get to steppin'!"

With a roll of his eyes and a sigh, Ritter began walking toward the animals. Just as Cat said, they scattered with heavy thuds and Ritter hesitated. He was scared to death.

"Now just stay still!" she yelled and Ritter threw his hands up. The cows jumped in response, which in turn caused Ritter to startle, which in turn caused the cows to jump yet again. After several moments of anxiety on the parts of both the man and beasts, Cat walked out to meet Ritter.

She stood behind him, took his hands that were on his hips, and put them at his side. "Quit taking up so much room in the world, Reed. Be still."

After five long minutes, the cows began coming closer one by one. Soon, Ritter found himself in the midst of a dozen happily grazing animals.

Cat took his hand and put in on a cow's back. "See," she said. Ritter smiled and rubbed his hand along the huge animal's long backbone. "They are curious, but you didn't make them feel comfortable enough for them to investigate things. You were nervous and they figured there was a reason. They didn't know *they* were the reason!"

"They only came up because you came out here," Ritter whispered. Cat said that wasn't the case. They had come to Ritter because Ritter had become *still.*

"Now let's walk a little," she said. The two humans moved slowly and deliberately, and the cows gave them a berth as needed.

"God said we are to *be still and know* that He is God," she said as she held Ritter's waist and weaved him amongst the milk-heavy brood.

"He didn't say freeze or become paralyzed. He said to *be*, to *exist* still. Doesn't matter what's going on around. Exist in stillness inside yet don't stop going forward on the outside. Have faith that God will come close. He is always there but, sometimes, we are too busy fidgeting, yapping, and taking up too much space in the world to let Him get as close as He wants."

Cat ran her fingers along a cow's ear. The ear fluttered slightly and she and Ritter laughed. They then stroked the animal's neck and laughed more when it leaned into them showing an appreciation for their gesture.

"I've been thinking about what you said about feeling like Odysseus." She paused and Ritter looked over his shoulder at her. He would have turned but, in truth, he was still not convinced he wouldn't be trampled.

"I think you are wrong. I mean, I get what you are saying. You feel like you are drifting and lost but Odysseus was not lost. He knew where he was going. He just got hung up by the gods. Wasn't his fault! *You* are the reason you are hung up. You create your own obstacles. What happened with your sister was an awful accident and the guilt from that has become a god to you. You worship that sick feeling and feed it stuff like sex to try to appease it. But, you never will because I think maybe you are afraid to. If you aren't guilty, then what do you feel?

"And Odysseus didn't want to go back to Ithaca because it was his home. I mean, it was his home, but that wasn't the whole reason he wanted to go back! He wanted to go back because he was its king and a part of who he was. It wasn't just where he and his family had a house. Odysseus was who he was in part because of Ithaca. That is why he had to get back there and that is why he never ceased to set his sails in that direction. Yes, the thought of his wife and son drove him as well, but I bet if he knew they were dead, he would have still gone back.

"Reed, you don't know who you are! A home isn't where somebody just lives, it's a part of their identity. I am a Texan and not just because I live here. Put me anywhere and, honey, I'm a Texan!

"I just think maybe you need to figure out who you are again, apart from the hurt and apart from your sister as a whole. And, don't try to associate yourself with a land mass either. Just figure out who you are as you are right now. The land thing will pop up when you figure out who you are.

"You never will be the same man you were! Stop thinking about being that guy again. Time has passed, lessons have been learned, and bones have been broken. All that will make you a different man but that isn't a bad thing. Bones are stronger after healing from a break.

"So, quit trying to go somewhere to find a sense of peace or thinking that once you get to a certain place literally or in life that everything will fall into place. Peace isn't about *going*, it's about *being*. You need to figure out what you are now in order to be anything ever.

"And you do have a heart by the way. I know you said you didn't but you do. If you know you aren't feeling anything, then you have enough of a heart to see there is something missing.

"Your heart may be a little rock in your chest but, it doesn't have to stay that way. God can give you a new heart of flesh. Then all the things you have been missing, all that you have needed, you will have. And you will love them all the more because you know what it is to not have them."

Reed smiled and waited for more pearls of wisdom to be tossed before him. When there was nothing but silence, he said, "Are you quite finished?" Cat laughed and said that she was.

The two then began moving slowly again in stillness amidst the cattle that were now beginning to lie down or head back for the barn one by one. After a moment, Reed snickered to himself and Cat asked what was so funny.

"Oh, Ginger," he said. "I was just wondering how you became so wise in so few years."

"I don't know," she hummed in reply. "Probably the same way you got so dumb in so many."

CHAPTER 22

Leave Him Alone and He's Sure to Come Home, Wagging His Tail Behind Him

The next morning, Cat sat at her kitchen table sipping coffee and nervously tapping the end of her pencil on a pad of paper. She had begun writing out a list of reasons for why she should not be romantically involved with Ritter:

1. *He's not a Christian. No need for any more reasons actually.*
2-5. *I am too old for him. Does he know any songs from the* Footloose *soundtrack? I doubt it!*
6-100. *He is way better looking than me, and yes, I am that shallow!*

But, it had quickly turned into a sketch of his face. She looked at the picture in frustration, rubbed her forehead, and then the artist in her disregarded the list and gave itself over to refining the eyes in the sketch. She could never get them quite right and she had at least a dozen scraps of paper testifying to that fact. Obviously, she thought, number 101 on the list would have to be her disturbing preoccupation with drawing him.

There was a soft tap at her kitchen door and she looked up. Beau bounded across the room and stuck his huge head under the blinds and every question Cat might have had regarding the noise was immediately answered. The only person that would be bold enough to hop the privacy fence, enter her screen porch and knock on her kitchen door was the one person she knew she shouldn't be so excited to see. She exhaled and leaned over to bang her head lightly on the table. He was going to cause her to have a head injury first and last among other things!

The door was opened and there Ritter stood holding a white deli bag. He was wearing an untucked white button up that was, for him, unusually tidy. His tie was loosened several inches below his neck where the buttoning of the shirt began (or ended) and the hem of his khaki pants sat with a slouch on his expensive shoes. His hair was almost dry from the shower and he smelled as if he had slept between two huge bars of soap.

Cat sighed and rubbed her forehead. How could he have known she was going to church so early? "Paul told you I had to play with the band this morning, didn't he?"

"That he did. Good morning, by the way! Might I attend religious services with you, perhaps? You won't get a bloody bite of this here otherwise!" he laughed.

"Reed, I have to stay for both services," Cat said with frustration. Ritter smiled and said that was why he had bought so many muffins. It was, "out of concern for the parishioners that would most certainly be in desperate peril," if she went so long without eating.

They then both stood in silence: him at the door like a tail-wagging stray and her like a woman who couldn't help but feed him. What choice did she have? What was she going to do, tell a man who desperately needed the Lord that he couldn't go to church with her because he was just simply too easy on the eyes?

"Come on!" she said with a sigh. He walked in, breathed deeply and thought for a split second that he had caught a glimpse of his image on a pad of paper. Unfortunately, Cat's hand was quicker than his eyes. She snatched it from the table, threw it in her room, and the two headed for the front door.

Ritter sat near the front of the church auditorium fidgeting, albeit internally, like the proverbial prostitute in church. He had been to Christian services with his friends all through his life. But he had never been to one like this. There was no formality, formula, nor feigned display of piety. People seemed genuinely happy and completely at home in the presence of God and it made Ritter feel all the more like a foreigner, an exile, among them.

Cat, although sitting in front of what looked to be more than five hundred people, holding a guitar nearly as big as her, seemed, as usual, completely at ease. That was what he liked most about her: her complete lack of inner turmoil. It was heartsease that was ironically as voracious as it was generous. It leapt from her and infested her surroundings like flowering weeds. From the moment he had first touched her, as he had examined her shoulder, she had infected him. And the more he looked at her, as she smiled and played, the less he felt like an exile in a supplanted land and more like a like a prodigal son welcomed home.

The band exited as the sermon began. As Ritter waited expectantly for Cat to come sit beside him, his phone vibrated with a text message. He was on call with the hospital and, because he assumed it to be a message from them, did not check the sender's name.

Fancy seeing you here, Israelite. Lost? it read, and the sender's name squeezed the air from his lungs. He began cutting his eyes around nervously and a second text quickly followed. *I'm behind you, foolish boy. I am always right behind you.*

Ritter swallowed hard, glanced over his left shoulder and saw Lucy sitting behind him, just as she had said. He still did not remember all that had happened at the party.

The few things that were clear in his mind however, all involved Lucy's cruelty. Flashes of recollection that were previously absent from his memory surfaced and brought with them feelings of vulnerability, fear, and a crushing sense of worthlessness.

Cat quietly entered the auditorium from a side door and sat down beside Ritter. She looked at him surreptitiously and saw that he was pale.

"Are you okay?" she whispered kindly. He closed his eyes and nodded his head as sweat burst into beads on his face. To comfort him, Cat touched his arm. Immediately his hand covered hers desperately and feverishly like a destitute minor claiming a chunk of shimmering coal for his own. The gesture caused Cat to recoil slightly but, seeing that it was needed, she left her hand in his.

As the sermon came to a close, Cat excused herself to again join the band. Ritter watched her leave and, as soon as the door shut quietly behind her, his phone again vibrated.

Until we meet again, son of Jacob. And I assure you, we will.— Your Angel of Light

Ritter's obvious uneasiness from that point lasted through the second service and made Cat feel sorry for him. It also made the job of convincing her to let him drive her truck home even easier than it normally would have been. She complained a little but, in truth, she was happy to hand over the keys. It made her feel as if the two were a couple: something she knew she would never feel otherwise.

Ritter asked if anyone had inquired about why he was so beaten up and Cat said that they hadn't. The pastor of the youth group was also in a rugby league and bruises, far worse than Ritter's, were something everyone was accustomed to seeing. They were not a group easily sickened by the sight of injury.

"How long have you played the guitar?" Cat asked and Ritter, to her surprise, seemed embarrassed. She had excused herself to the restroom as the rest of the band warmed up before services and, upon returning, had seen Ritter with her guitar. He played it as if his hands were the ones for which the instrument had been made.

He said he had taken lessons as a boy and had played for most of his life. "What else do you play?" she asked in an accusing tone. Ritter laughed and confessed he played the piano as well. And the cello. And violin. And drums.

"Of course," she said with slight irritation and then under her breath muttered, "what can you not do?"

Ritter parked the truck in Cat's driveway and looked at her. "Draw," he said and tossed her the keys. "You asked what I could not do and I am telling you. I haven't an artistic bone in my body. You are quiet superior in that aspect. And I also can't ovulate so you've got me there as well."

"Wait a minute! What makes you think I can draw?" she said after a small gasp. Then, because her brain was anxious for a response, Cat hit the garage door opener without thinking.

172

Before Ritter could reply to the question, a bundle of wool bounced by his window, down the driveway, and stopped in the middle of the street. Cat jumped out of the car and called to the lamb. It stopped momentarily, flicked its tail in a taunting manner, and belligerently trotted down the road.

Cat and Ritter both began running after the young sheep. A major road was nearby and if the animal were lucky enough to get out of the subdivision, it was sure to not make it much farther. Ritter glanced back toward the house as they rounded the corner and pointed back to the ewe grazing in the grass of Paul's yard. "I'll get the lamb," he yelled. "You get the ma!"

The lamb was faster than it looked, but so was its pursuer. Despite the aching body, wounds on his back, oppressive heat, humidity, and his long sleeves and pants, Ritter was closing in on the little renegade. He finally boxed the diminutive beast in at the end of a cul-de-sac and both animals stopped and panted. They stared at one another and their eyes dueled for who would make the first move.

Ritter quickly glanced at a soccer ball in a yard next to him and then looked back at the lamb. The animal seemed to suspect a plan afoot and darted to Ritter's right, hoping its legs were faster than the obviously tired human's arms. It would have eluded him easily were it not for the soccer ball. Ritter picked it up and with all his might hurled it at the lamb's head. The spinning orb hit its mark and the animal was knocked off its feet to near unconsciousness.

Cat stood at the end of their street biting her thumbnail and looking for Ritter. When she saw him turn the corner with the lamb on his shoulders, she let out a growl of relief. She hurried to meet the two and the limp movement in the lamb's neck made her certain that it had not been reached in time. She stopped and put her hands on either side of her head and the look on her face made Ritter call out that the thing wasn't dead.

"It might be a bit mentally impaired," Ritter groaned as he lifted the thirty pounds of wooly rebellion off his shoulders, "but it's not dead. And it's going to have a brilliant headache!"

Cat took the small animal into the dim garage and shined a flashlight in his eyes. Its pupils reacted, and it bobbed its head slightly. She yelled over her shoulder and asked Ritter what exactly he had done to it. He laughed caustically and said that he had saved its life, and she was quite welcome.

His tone caused Cat to stop what she was doing and look at him. He was sitting on the driveway wrestling angrily with his tie. He tossed it in frustration between his feet, unbuttoned his shirt, and wiped the sweat off his face with his sleeve. Cat closed her eyes and suddenly realized how ungracious she was being.

She walked out, stood in front of him, and couldn't help but laugh. It was obvious he had taken great effort to look nice, and now, his shirt and pants were wet with sweat and dirty with dust. His face was red and dripping, there were grass clippings in his hair, but the pièce de résistance was the left side of his shirt that was soaked from the shoulder to the hem in sheep urine.

Ritter cut his eyes up at her and fought the urge to smile. He winced as he tried to take off his shirt, and Cat kneeled down to help him. As he brought it around to wipe his face, they both saw the watery blood stains. His cuts had opened up, and Cat sucked air in through her teeth as she looked at his back.

"Oh, good heavens, Reed! Look, why don't you go jump in the shower and then come back over and let me cook you some lunch. And I'll tend to your back too. It's the least I can do. Okay? I am so sorry and thank you so much. Really," she said with a grunt as she helped him up. "Thank you."

As the spaghetti boiled on the stove, Cat dressed Ritter's back. After this, she thought, there needed to be some type of rule instituted about him appearing shirtless in front of her. And as much as she wanted the rule to be that he not have a shirt on, it had to be otherwise.

"You're going to have to start keeping your shirt on, you know. It's unbecoming for a shepherd to walk around like that."

Ritter laughed. He was certainly no shepherd. If he were, he would have been able to call the sheep back.

"No, that lamb still hasn't learned what a shepherd is." Cat laughed. "I thought it knew, but apparently, it's just been submitting to peer pressure. The ewe knows me, knows my voice, trusts me, and obeys immediately, and generally, the little rascal does the same. But like I said, it's young, away from the influence of the herd, and sheep aren't super intelligent creatures anyway. They will graze themselves off the edge of a cliff, I kid you not.

"But I'll tell you, I had to lead a sheep all over campus one time in vet school for one of my courses, and as unintelligent as those animals are, they are obedient. If they trust you, they will let you do the thinking for them, which is actually quite smart if think about it. Anyway, to me, an obedient animal is far more intelligent than one that can do tricks regardless of what an IQ standard says.

"Pigs? Now pigs are smarter than most dogs and, by the way, can do tricks. But they are a real pain to herd, and boy, they complain about it the whole time! I'll take a sheep over a genius trick pig anytime. Except at dinner! There are few things that aren't improved by the presence of bacon! Maybe high intelligence lends itself to better flavor. I bet you are delicious!"

Ritter slowly turned his head in shock. "I am so sorry," Cat said in a mortified whisper. "I have no idea where that came from, but it certainly wasn't intended the way it came across! Good grief!" she sighed and turned Ritter's head away from her. "No wonder God calls us sheep," she said with a laugh.

"Are we dumb animals?" Ritter asked with a grin. "Are we so stupid as to graze ourselves off the edge of a cliff?"

"Like I just did?" Cat mumbled.

"We are easily distracted," she said, thankful for the attention being taken from her earlier comment, "and like sheep, can wander off without even realizing it. God created us intelligent, reasoning beings but that doesn't keep us from nibbling our way away from the herd or off the edge of a mountain! In fact, I think that is very reason we do it sometimes! Why do I always end up talking about God with you!"

Ritter laughed and shrugged. "No, no. Don't move your shoulder! Aw crud, I'll have to start this one again! Anyhow," she continued while re-applying the last bandage, "that's what the curved end of the shepherd's staff is for. God reaches down and hooks our little waggly tails out of danger. And if the staff isn't long enough—here is your shirt—He climbs out on the ledge to get us. He'll get beat up and bloodied to keep us out of harm's way. You're a prime example of that! Look at what you put yourself through to get that lamb, and it's not even your property."

Ritter said it was his fault that the lamb was in danger. If he hadn't taken it from the farm, there wouldn't have been an issue. The animal's life was his responsibility.

"Well, God sees us as His responsibility! He loves us. We are his children. And children, like sheep, sometimes just waggle their tales and bound down their own path straight toward danger. Do you want parmesan for your spaghetti? I do! I think there is some in the fridge.

"Anyway," she said, returning to the table, "we run away, and He calls out to us just like I did that lamb. When that doesn't work, He runs after us and unfortunately, sometimes, to save us from our own undoing, He has to give us a soccer ball to the head! I have had my fair share of those!"

Ritter nodded and said that perhaps his adventure Friday night was his divine soccer ball to the head. Cat smiled and looked at Ritter's black eye. "But it got you here, didn't it?"

Ritter paused chewing and looked down at his plate. He had never considered that.

He asked why she hadn't made him tell her what happened to him that night. She said that it didn't matter, and anything he said would be his to say voluntarily anyway. Cat had also never asked what religion he was which he told her he found strange, considering how important religion seemed to be to her.

"My actions toward you aren't dependant upon your beliefs. They aren't even dependant on your actions really. I am who I am regardless."

Ritter stopped chewing and looked at her. "So, are you being friendly to me because you are a friendly person or because we are in fact mates?"

"Both," Cat said nonchalantly before getting up to refill her glass.

Ritter moved his food around on his plate and smiled. "So we are mates then?" Cat set the pitcher of tea down and held up her hands. "Aren't we?"

Ritter laughed and said he didn't know.

"Well, my goodness, Reed, you turned up naked on my porch and we had a near death experience together! I would think all that would kind of nail down a friendship!"

Ritter had never been friends with a girl. For him, women had been nothing but a means to an end and a depository for his hurt and anger. If he were to have a first friend that was a girl, Cat would be the one. He also couldn't think of a better person to be his first girlfriend.

"Did you date a lot at university?" he asked, hoping to lead the conversation toward a specific end.

"The normal amount I guess. I didn't always keep a boyfriend if that's what you mean. What about you? Dare I ask?"

Ritter shook his head. He had, in fact, never had a girlfriend nor been on an official date. Cat rolled her eyes and threw her napkin at him.

"Don't even tell me you didn't go out with every girl in high school and college!"

"I didn't Cat, I swear to you. Okay, for one, I never went to college or whatever you call it here! High school! I started at university when I was thirteen. Who was I going to ask out? I'm serious! Look, you asked how one becomes an osteopath by twenty-eight, and I am telling you. I started university when I was thirteen. I knew girls my age through my sister but had nothing in common with them outside the age. And I couldn't very well ask out my classmates at university now, could I?"

Cat looked at him with shock. What he was saying was completely plausible. "You've never even asked out anybody you have worked with? What about Ashta? How are you having sex with all these people if you aren't going on dates with them?"

Ritter ran his hand through his hair in embarrassment. One was not dependant upon the other he assured her and then watched as she ruminated on the concept.

"Would you go out with me?" he asked. Cat laughed and put another bite of spaghetti in her mouth. Paul could walk him through it, she said. He didn't need her to show him the ropes. Ritter sat up in his chair and inhaled deeply. It was hard enough to ask her the first time and it was obvious he would have to do it again.

"I am not asking you to show me the ropes, Emma. I am asking if you would do me the honor of a proper date."

Cat narrowed her eyes and Ritter looked back at her with a subtle, pleading look. The realization of what was being asked hit her and she began choking on her food. Ritter tried to help her, but she held up her hand and assured him that she was fine although she would have given anything to have choked and passed out right then. She would have wanted to be revived of course but much later in a hospital without this question looming in the air.

When she composed herself, she continued eating as if her response wasn't required. "Do you want some more tea?" she asked, rising from her chair. Ritter grabbed her hand and she sat back down heavily like a pouting child.

"I want to know if you would go out with me. You can say no. It's okay. We're friends either way, yea?"

"Nope," Cat said. "No, that's not how it works." Were she to say no, he would be hurt and that hurt would permeate the friendship on some level. And were they to go out on a date, the friendship would still suffer from being stretched beyond normal boundaries.

"Well, as I said, I am ill-equipped in this arena," he said with a disappointed tone. "I truly will be your friend regardless of your answer. It would be nice to have an answer though. I hate to start a thing and not see it out."

Cat sat back in her chair, puffed out her cheeks, and blew the air out slowly as she rubbed her eyes.

"I'm Jewish by the way. I'm not sure if knowing my religious affiliation is what's keeping you from answering. Or maybe it will be the deciding factor of your response," he said with a roll of his eyes.

"I haven't hidden it intentionally from you. I am not ashamed; I just don't talk about it normally. And, I thought if I did, the conversation would turn toward my beliefs which are a bit up in the air at the moment. I rather like the focus being on yours."

Cat shifted in her seat. Had she not sat in that exact spot just a few hours earlier and listed all the reasons why this very thing was a bad idea? Where was that list? And what did he want from her anyway?

"I just want a chance, Emma. That's all," he said as if responding to her thoughts.

"Have you seen my pores?" she said, looking down at her plate as if it were the one speaking to her. Ritter didn't understand. "I am old, Reed! Way older than you!"

"Fine! Then I will order prune juice instead of wine for you!"

"I will be thirty-five soon! That's seven years older than you!"

Ritter laughed and shook his head. "And they say girls aren't good at math! Ginger, don't penalize me for the year in which I was born. I had nothing to do with that!"

"Oh, trust me, that's not the only issue," Cat said, rising from the table and picking up her plate.

"What is the other issue then? Is it because I am Jewish? You know, we are a moral lot despite the behavior I have displayed!"

Cat put her dish down on the counter, turned, and looked at Ritter seriously. "You are more than a *moral lot*! You are a holy nation! I am saved because of the promises made to you! My faith is the child of yours, and no child has an inheritance that did not first belong to his father!"

She sat back down in her chair and looked at Ritter. "The problem is how you live. I wonder if you even see it," she said, rubbing her forehead.

"The way you look now, all beat to high heaven, is the way you treat yourself! Really, your appearance couldn't be more fitting!

"Look, my home is more blessed because one of God's chosen, that's you, Reed, is in it. But my fear is what you bring in with you, which is nothing, God would have chosen for you! The lifestyle that put you in this brutally beaten state is infectious. I am not saying you deserved whatever happened to you, but I am willing to bet it was a scenario that started out dangerous and you knew it. Good grief, that might have been what drew you to it!

"As your friend, I can maintain a certain distance and keep my defenses up. But a date? It's hard enough to resist temptation without sharing popcorn with it at the movies!"

Ritter sighed and leaned back in his chair. He saw her point as much as he didn't want to admit it. She was infecting him, and it only stood to reason he could do the same to her. The difference was that her sickness wasn't a sickness at all. Hers was a healing bacteria while his was one of destruction.

"How about I promise to not share my popcorn? No, no, okay, okay, sit down! I do get it, Cat, and as much as I want to be offended, I am not. I know that a moral life like yours doesn't come by accident. You have worked hard for it and it would be irresponsible of you to bring somebody like me in that might perhaps compromise it, although, I think you underestimate your fortitude.

"But for me," he said, sitting forward, "it is the first morally responsible decision I have made in many years. I told you from the start you weren't my type of bird. That wasn't because of your age or your looks, like you seem inclined to think. It was because of your completely off-putting odor of righteousness, which quite honestly, I have grown to not only appreciate but—"

He paused, ran his hand through his hair and shook his head as if he were being forced to say something that hurt him to verbalize. "I'm besotted with it, Cat. You've gotten stuck in my nose, among other places. Do I want to bed you? Of course. I am a man. But I wouldn't for the same reasons that I am drawn to you."

Ritter reached out, took her hand and put it against his chest. "Emma, you are an absolutely breathtaking woman. Especially considering your sizable pores!"

Cat laughed and tried to pull her hand from him.

"But, love, that is not what draws me to you. Stop struggling! If you pull your hand off, I will simply reattach it and you know I can!"

He put his hand on her forearm, and she stopped pulling. He asked her to look at him and, as much as she didn't want to, she did. "What draws me to you, Rachel Emmanuelle, is the fact that you have somehow managed to turn me back into a man that wants to be the man I had always hoped to be. That and your legs. You've got brilliant legs!"

Cat blushed and pulled her hand free. She looked at it curiously, turning it over, and inspecting it. Away from his, it seemed to be missing something.

"I respect you, Cat. And I would not do anything that would cause you to compromise or even consider compromising the very thing about you which I so esteem. So, come on. What do you say, Ginger? Can you just this once make a completely irresponsible decision and give a lad the same chance to right himself as you would a stupid lamb?"

Cat looked back up at Ritter's blue eyes, sighed, and looked back at her empty, incomplete seeming hand. This wasn't a good idea, she thought to herself. No. Absolutely not. And that was a decision on which she simply would not budge.

178

CHAPTER 23

A Roll of the Dice

The doorbell rang, and Cat jumped up and down in place with excitement. She looked at herself once more in the mirror and then took a long calming breath. The anticipation of just seeing him was enough to make her giddy but that she would actually be on a date with him put her close to hysteria.

She tugged at her dress one last time, took a moment to compose herself, and then opened the door. Their eyes struck together like flint and a spark flew up between them. Quickly, the flash became a flame that heaved itself into an impassioned incandescence. They each found themselves transfixed like moths to a flame and fluttering just as wildly on the inside.

Ritter's eyes broke free of their hypnotic state and traveled over Cat's body with regard. She never wore anything formfitting because she had very little form to fit. Lately however, that seemed to have changed and the dress she had bought just for that night bore witness.

The brown silk sundress moved over Cat's curves like warm wind does a field of wheat. The gilded tone brought out the copper in her hair and gold of her eyes and the cut showed just enough of her to skin to make Ritter's toes curl up in his shoes. Not that Cat would have noticed his feet. Her eyes remained fixed on his.

On more than one occasion, she had drawn Ritter's eyes from memory. The result however never failed to be a weak interpretation. Now she knew why. Ritter's hair had always cast a shadow over them. But now, with a short haircut as well as a freshly shaven face, the color was completely unveiled. Deep blue lines ran like webbing through the lighter pigmentation and gave his eyes a crushed glass effect. *That's what was missing*, she thought, *the cracks*.

Ritter coughed and held flowers out to her. "For you, my lady." Cat took them quietly, never taking her eyes from his face. "You look beautiful," he said, looking down nervously at his feet. "So do you," Cat replied from her dreamlike state. Ritter laughed in response, and Cat's composure resumed its post, causing her to shake her head slightly.

She looked down at the fresh, violet blue bouquet and her smile quickly became a wrinkled smirk of amusement. "I thought you might like them. I spotted them just off the road whilst driving home."

"Oh, I love them, Reed. Bluebonnets are my favorite. Unfortunately, they are illegal to pick in the state of Texas. It's the state flower. Kind of a sacred thing here."

Ritter grimaced and scratched his head. "That explains the car horns. And I thought they were just appreciating my bum! Well, by all means, let's get them in a vase and leg it before the authorities arrive!"

He opened the car door and, as Cat sat down, she saw a present on the center console. She looked at Ritter curiously who assured her it was not contraband as the last gift had been. As they pulled away, she admired the small golden bag in her hands. Emerald-, ruby-, and sapphire-colored tissue paper sprang from the top like jewels from a treasure chest, and Cat looked at it as if the packaging was itself the prize.

"Come on then," Ritter prodded. "Open her up."

Cat smiled, reached in the shiny bag, and pulled out a small square book. She turned it over, smiled at the cover photo, and hugged it.

"I love *Cows on Parade*! I have always wanted to see it, but it's never been close," she said as she opened the book. Photos of decorated, life-sized, fiberglass cows marched proudly under her fingers. She giggled at several and read the names out loud: *Pi-cow-so, Marilyn Moo-nroe, Moo-na Lisa.*

"The exhibition is supposed to come to Houston at some point," she said, finishing the book and beginning it again. Ritter nodded and said that it had opened in downtown that day. Cat clapped her hands with excitement and, in her joy, forgot herself for a moment, pulled Ritter by the collar toward her and kissed him. He gasped slightly and she blushed realizing what she had done. She then wiped her lip gloss off his smooth, square jaw. His freshly shaven skin slid warm and soft under her fingertips and she continued wiping long after the lip gloss was gone.

"My father made me do it," he said, referring to the shave. "I don't reckon I've had a proper shave or cut since before the funeral. I talked to them yesterday and my da said, 'Make an effort there cupcake!' and then my ma chimed in, 'Oh yes, RJ, please do tidy up a bit!'"

Cat laughed and asked if they had any other suggestions. Ritter nodded and counted off on his fingers as he listed them.

"They told me to shower, which honestly, I found offensive! I do bathe!" he grumbled before raising the second finger. "I was to get a proper shave and cut from an actual barber. I had to button my shirt correctly as well which, something I had no idea I did so seldom. I was also to carry a handkerchief which, I didn't quite understand. But Izzy, who provided the thing, said Kleenex had turned ladies into women and gentlemen into 'beatniks,' and I had a responsibility to behave in a manner befitting my company."

Cat asked how Isaiah, and no doubt Ezekiel who was never too far away, became involved and Ritter rubbed his hand through his short hair. "This was a community effort, Cat! You haven't the slightest idea. Paulette ironed everything. These are his socks. Or one of them is anyway.

"What else? I am also to open all doors which, I do that anyway, bring flowers, a gift, oh, and take a photo at some point. This is my first date you remember. Bit of an important thing for my parents. And, my ma said, above all, I am not to enter your house afterward nor kiss you on the lips."

Cat agreed and said that his mother was a smart woman.

"So I am prohibited from kissing you on the lips!" he said with wide eyes. "Oh, I strenuously disagree with that, my dear Emma! That's rubbish is what that is! Unless of course you are offering some other part of you in lieu of your lips." Ritter cast a flirtatious glance at Cat who did not seem amused. "Or not," he said with a sigh.

The park downtown was filled with people, vendors, and music. The painted cows were scattered over the green and Cat and Ritter weaved themselves among the herd admiring, laughing, and taking photos with them. Somewhere between *Udder Romance* and *French Moodle*, Cat's arm intertwined itself with Ritter's. Their gestures became more affectionate and soon, they were moving together like a predestined pair.

As the sun began to sink, they walked toward a tent that displayed small cow figurines. Ritter gave the vendor his name who, in turn, gave him a box. He turned away from Cat, opened it, and then with a smile handed the lady a check.

They continued toward the amphitheater and an area of the green that had been sectioned off with rope fastened to the ground. A grid of 8 × 8 boxes were numbered and people sat inside each box enjoying food, music, and the unseasonably comfortable weather of the evening.

Ritter stopped by a second tent and showed a reservation number. He was given a white blanket, two small throw pillows, and was told his waitress would come shortly. Cat smiled as she looked around at the perfection of the scene and the two made their way to an assigned plot of ground.

After Cat finished her dessert, and the last of Ritter's, he asked her to open her third gift. She thanked him in advance for whatever it was and for all that he had done so far. She then opened the box and her eyes widened.

The cow figurine was porcelain and ten inches long. It was wearing maroon cowboy boots with the letters of her college alma mater painted on their sides. A pink stethoscope hung around the animal's neck and its body was painted with various Texas wildflowers. The hair on its tail was a clownish red as was the wisp of hair on its head that was gathered in a bow. There were gold hoop earrings in its ears and its face was in full makeup complete with long black eyelashes. Its lips were painted bright pink and between them was the handle of a stroller. In the stroller were two calves: one with a blue blanket, the other with a pink.

Ritter turned the figurine over and on its stomach was the Biblical address: Psalm 50:10. He took a slip of paper out of the box and read it. *For every beast of the forest belongs to God, and the cattle on a thousand hills.*

Cat's chin quivered slightly, and she covered her mouth with her hand. The cow was a perfect representation of her, her job, and her personality. And although its workmanship was incredible, it was that Ritter had noticed so much about her and had expressed it to someone else that moved her.

"What's this now?" he said, putting his arm around her and pulling her close. "Come on now, love! My parents will kill me if I tell them I made you cry! Oh wait! Never mind. I've got a handkerchief! Weep away!"

Cat leaned back against one of the few trees on the green that just so happened to be in their plot and continued looking at her gift. Ritter, without asking permission, threw a pillow in her lap and laid his head down on it. She laughed at his presumptuousness and said that because they were in public she would not embarrass him by making him sit up.

She ran her fingers through his hair, over the line of his brows, and down his nose. He drowsily closed his eyes and tried to take in every sensation of the moment, hoping the scene would burn into his brain like a daguerreotype.

"Tell me more about your father," he said after several quiet moments. Cat sighed and thought. "Big. Very big. He said puberty kind of crept up on him all at once in the middle of the night and took hold with a vengeance. At thirteen, he was as big and broad as most full-grown men."

"I assume that is where you inherited your vastness!" Ritter laughed. "You are *diminutively immense* if there is such a thing. And of course, your hair." Ritter paused and opened his eyes. Cat's hair was neither orange nor red. In fact, the more he looked at her and recollected the picture he had seen of her father, the less he thought they looked alike. Her build, the shape and color of her eyes; none of it was like any of the images he had seen of her father. Above all, her skin was a striking antithesis. Her father's was mottled with freckles while hers was completely spotless. Nature had placed neither a freckle nor imperfection on her.

He took her had in his and ran his fingers up from her wrist to the blue lined crease of her elbow. Gooseflesh was left in the wake of his touch and Cat blushed. She looked away and cleared her throat and Ritter saw immediately that he had embarrassed her. He smiled wide. All the sexual adventures he had experienced and yet, this moment, running his fingertips across the perfect flesh of a women's arm was the most sincere, most passionate moment of intimacy he had every shared with another human.

"Do you think you look much like your da?" he asked before kissing her wrist.

Cat pulled her hand away and playfully slapped Ritter's cheek. "He was a good listener, my daddy," she said avoiding the question. Her skin remained tingling from the warmth of Ritter's lips and she scratched her arm to bury the former sensation with another.

"Very observant and a very smart man. His name was David Randal, which he always signed as DR, and a lot of cattleman on the rodeo circuit thought he was a veterinarian. He never claimed to be, they just assumed it because of how he signed his name and because he knew so much. No one would have ever known he never made it past eighth grade. He met the medical needs of whatever cattle he oversaw and taught me to do the same. At ten, I was practicing sutures on soft leather and could talk a person through the anatomy of a cow from pout to pooper!"

Ritter asked if her father had ever married. She said that he hadn't. Her father had claimed his life was full enough. To Cat's knowledge, he had never even had a girlfriend.

"Cruz claimed he married Paloma in part because I needed a mom and my daddy was too preoccupied with cows to see cowgirls! What about your parents? What are they like?"

"Aah, *The Jays*," Ritter said with a sigh and a smile. "They are quite a pair. So much so, one name suffices for the two. My da is Jacob, or Jack everyone calls him, and my ma is Juda. But among their mates, they are just *The Jays*. They are the best of friends and as in love as the day they married. Wonderful parents and incredible people. A child couldn't ask for better. We were all very close."

Ritter became quiet and Cat could see his mind drift to a heavier place. She thumped him playfully on the chin and asked what his parents did for a living. He smiled sheepishly and said his father was a barrister and mother a professor at King's College, Cambridge. Cat nodded. *That would explain your IQ and distinct odor of wealth,* she thought.

"Come on, Ginger," Ritter said, sitting up suddenly. "Let's have us a dance." Cat was hesitant but as usual Ritter got his way.

He was a wonderful dancer, not to Cat's surprise. His body moved gracefully and rather than feeling as if she were being led, she felt as if she were relaxing and simply floating with the current.

They continued talking on the dance floor and laughed so loud they drew attention from people around them. Ritter then whispered something to her but her laughing, and the music, kept her from hearing. He leaned down and she lifted her chin. His lips rubbed against her ear and their dancing slowed. The warmth and sound of his breath moved around her brain and down her spine. Cat closed her eyes and rubbed her nose along his smooth cheek, and his breaths became shallow and quick. He kissed her jaw and smiled at the ache that ran through him.

The couple soon stilled to a subtle sway despite the tempo of the band. Cat rested her cheek over his heart then turned her face and pressed her nose and mouth against him. As she inhaled his scent, a shiver ran through him. He wrapped his arms completely around her and embraced her tightly. "Quit sniffing me, woman. You're killing me," he giggled. His lips then moved across her hair to her ear and whispered, "You'll be the death of me. I swear it."

He remembered suddenly what his father had said once as he had watched his mother wash the dishes. Ritter had thought the comment ridiculous at the time but now understood completely. Jack Thomas was smiling a satisfied smile, looking at his wife in a way Ritter couldn't quite translate and had said, "Reader, my son, sex is an incidental of sex." He had then taken a long, slow drink of scotch and winked at his son.

Ritter had dismissed the comment as a by-product of the flaccid excitement of age and the faint sedating properties of alcohol. But now, twelve years later, with the warmth of Cat against his chest and the searing heat of her burning straight through it, he understood. As practiced and skilled as he was at the act of sex, Ritter knew nothing of the true nature of it. What he had taken for flying, was little more than falling.

At midnight, Ritter walked Cat to her door. She had left the porch light on and he was sure she had done so to more than simply illuminate her door.

She thanked him for the evening and they both stood for a moment in silence. Ritter looked up at the light and back at the road over his shoulder. He took a small step toward Cat and she looked down. His hand reached out, brushed her short hair away from her forehead and his fingers trailed down the side of her face to her chin. In shyness, she turned away and he stepped closer, lifted her face slightly and ran his lips along her forehead.

"I have to say, mon cher, this may in fact be the best date I have ever been on."

Cat laughed and he assured her that he wasn't saying that simply because he had been on no other dates in his life. After a moment of silence, she nodded and said that it was the best date she had ever been on as well.

Ritter moved back slightly and looked at her face. He smiled and winced as if in pain and rubbed his eyes. "Oh, woman, you got me besotted. So help me, you do."

He took her hand, kissed it, and happened to look at his watch. "You know," he said in a decidedly seductive whisper, "it's one minute after midnight and technically tomorrow. Does that make this our second date? And if so"—he leaned forward and rubbed his lips along her cheek to her ear—"can I have a kiss?"

"Who said you'd get a kiss on the second date?" she said, mustering all the resoluteness she could from the sea of desire in which she was blissfully on the edge of drowning. Ritter leaned back and laughed until he saw that she seemed serious. "No kiss on the second date!"

"No. And I don't recall saying I would go on a second date anyway."

Ritter put his hands on his hips and shook his head. He should have known this seduction wouldn't be so easy. "Cat," he said with hands clasped at his chest, "would you please go out with me on a second date and kiss me rotten afterward?"

She said she would go out with him but that there most likely would be no kiss. He asked if not the second then when. Cat smiled, excused herself inside, and returned with dice. The two sat on her glider and she said that whatever number was thrown that would be the date.

"Wait, wait, wait just a minute, Cat! There's a possibility of a twelve there!" Cat narrowed her eyes at him and asked if that would be a problem. He put his face in his hands and then rubbed them through his hair. "Well, yea! I have a problem with that! But oh, bloody hell, fine. I can wait until the twelfth although my jaw may drop off from weariness of anticipation!"

"Thirteenth," she said. "Whatever I roll, then we have to wait that many more."

Ritter snapped his face toward her and she couldn't help but laugh. "You think you're funny, don't you? Roll the dice before I stuff 'em up your adorable little snout!"

The dice were thrown and the decision made. Ritter huffed and rolled his eyes. It could have been worse, he admitted.

They both rose and Ritter wished her good night. "Oh! Wait!" he said, reaching into his pocket. He took out a rock and handed it to Cat.

"I got this from the park. If you would, write *first date* on it and today's date. Flowers, even those illegal to pick, die but rocks remain. I thought that we could get a stone from somewhere on every date and set up a pile somewhere. Maybe one day our children will ask what they mean and you can tell them about how you fell madly in love with me and forced me into marriage."

Cat pushed him playfully and then looked at the rock. "And be warned, ma petite femme," he said with a grin, "when the seventh stone is put down, you better have a lion's share of Chap Stick in your pocket!"

He leaned over, kissed her head, and said he would be happy to drive them to church the next morning. Cat smiled and bid him good night. She then walked inside, closed the door behind herself, leaned back against it, and the fullness of her heart caused a tear to run down her cheek.

CHAPTER 24

And It All Comes Tumbling Down

One rock soon became two, which soon became four, eight, and then sixteen. They had ceased to symbolize dates and instead anything deemed *rock worthy*. "Cat sneezed on me—Apr 10," "Ritter cooked for me, fire dept came—Apr 17," "Vomited on Cat, marriage imminent—Apr 19."

Several days before the seventh date, or as Ritter called it, *The Spit Festival*, the couple relaxed on Cat's screened-in porch after a long day at work. Ritter lied on a blanket face down on the floor and Cat in a hammock just above him. Her arm hung from the edge and her fingertips grazed across Ritter's back. He had pulled his shirt up, as she had forbidden him to remove it, and the sensation of her caress rendered him, *udderly* useless.

"See what I did there? I used the word udder. You know, because you are a —"

"Yes, yes, I know. You are terribly clever, Reed. Terribly clever."

Beau walked to the kitchen door and frowned at them from the other side of the glass. He let out a mournful wail and Ritter looked up at him.

"Let that poor animal out here with us. It's suffering!"

"No, Reed. I have told you. He can't come out on the porch. I don't want him to even think he can."

"And why is that again?"

"If he comes out on the porch, then there is a possibility of him getting out the door into the yard and, if he does that and runs away, he can't come back. And before you suggest that I keep the door locked, that is a simple hook lock that he would quickly master."

Ritter propped up on his elbows and looked at Cat with surprise. Why could it not go out? Was she afraid the beast would wreak havoc on the neighboring villages?

"Blind me, Cat, what would it do? Stalk a bird? What harm is there in that?" Cat sighed and shook her head. Beau was not any ordinary house cat. He was the direct offspring of one completely feral parent and, from the looks of him, Cat suspected the other parent was at least half wild as well. Were the animal to escape, it would likely revert quickly to its undomesticated roots.

"He can't live in both worlds, Reed. The two don't have reciprocity! One will win and make him vulnerable in the other. If he runs away, I won't let him return because he will need to learn to live without me. If he is constantly looking over his tail to find me, he will be left open for attack. And if I allow him back in, it will only be a matter of time before he gets bored and wants another taste of forest life, which would make him dash for the door every time it opens. As it is now, he just looks out the windows not knowing exactly what it is that is so fascinating out there!

"He may not like the rules I've made for him, you may not agree with them, but I made them because I love him and I want him to be healthy and safe. Even though he has clawed up five comforters and two pillows in search of toys!" she said loudly, looking back accusingly at the animal through the glass. Beau returned her gaze and chirped in his own defense.

"After he dies, I am sure God will have a lap so big for him that he won't look back at any of his nine lives with regret or resentment! Until then, I won't allow him to live with a foot in each world. It would cost him both feet!"

Ritter looked up at the cat again. He wiggled his fingers playfully and saw Beau's pupils dilate wildly. The animal crouched and the muscles of his hind quarters quivered in readiness. Ritter could see that the animal could almost taste the freedom beyond the screened-in porch.

"Let me put him on a leash. Come on, Emma!"

Cat huffed a laugh in response. Emma was the name Ritter used when he begged. It had gotten him a pass to sit on her couch past midnight more than once, but it wouldn't succeed in its current purpose.

"How is your stomach?" Cat asked with a laugh, changing the subject. Ritter swallowed hard and laid his head back down. Guilt caused his throat to ache, and he was thankful she could not see his face. Fine, he said, and no, he had not been to a doctor as she had requested. He assured her that his regular bouts of vomiting were stress induced, which was why he never regurgitated when he spent the entire day with her. It was generally only after work on nights he stayed late. Although, he had vomited at lunch that day without telling her.

"I can't believe I honked on you!" he said with embarrassment. "Don't worry about it!" she laughed. "Good grief, that was weeks ago! Can you believe that! It's been over a month now since our first date. Doesn't seem that long, does it?"

Ritter propped himself up on his elbows again and looked up at her seriously. "It's been five weeks and three days, Cat, and yes, it seems nearly a decade!" She flicked his nose and asked if she had been worth the wait. "I'll tell you after we kiss," he joked and then bit her fingers playfully.

"I know it's been hard for you, Reed. Please don't think I ever forget that. I'm not stupid. I know there are a lot of other much younger and prettier girls out there that would have done a lot of things I won't. Thank you for being satisfied with purity."

Ritter turned his head away and lied back down. He would do anything for her, he said. "Yea, but I've asked a lot and you've done all that plus things I never even asked! I never asked you to go to church with me or clean up your language or tell me good night every single night even if you had to walk out of the operating room to do it. And you've hopped over to see me off to work in the morning when you should have been sleeping. You've practically worn a hole in the fence over there!" They both laughed and Ritter looked at the places where he put his hands and feet on the boards to bound over almost daily.

"I got you something a couple weeks ago. Hold on." Cat went inside and returned with a box. She handed it to Ritter who read the attached card, *To Odysseus*, and opened it quickly like a child. He held up the beautiful brass compass that was inside and let it dangle from its chain.

"I was going to wait and give it to you on our seventh date but, oh well. I saw it in a store window and immediately thought of you. Now, no matter where you are in the world, you will always be able to look in the direction of the place you feel is home and set your sails, if only just in your mind. And, if at that point you still aren't sure who you are, or where home is, just trust that it's most likely the place you always want to look toward."

Ritter smiled and looked at the compass closely. On the back was inscribed: *For Your name's sake, Lord, lead me and guide me. Ps 31:3.*

Warmth spread through his chest and he kissed the compass. "Thank you, love," he said. "I hope to never be so far away that I need this to find you." Cat put her hand on his jaw and caressed her fingers over the stubble of his beard that had been groomed with less regard more and more since their first date.

"Reed, I've got something to say to you and I don't want you to speak during or after. When I'm done, just lie right back on down because nothing I am going to say is dependent upon or in anticipation of any words or actions of yours."

Ritter's face became serious and he sat up straight, readying his heart for a blow. Cat lied back down, smiled, and pinched his chin. "I love you, Reed Jacob Thomas. I love you bruises, breaks, and all, and I can't tell you the number of times I have thanked God for you. You have watered something in me that was hesitant to grow. Literally in some ways," she laughed. "I've put on ten pounds in case you haven't noticed.

"I wake in the morning with cheeks sore from smiling in my sleep. Everything I see reminds me of you or is something I want to see through your eyes. I love the feel of your hair between my fingers and the smell it leaves behind on my hand. And next to your voice and that accent, my favorite sound is how the grass on the ground crunches under your feet when you jump over that fence.

"I hate when you perch on top of it and talk to me. Oh, I hate that! I don't even hear half of what you say because my brain is so busy screaming for you to jump over to my side and stay there. And I don't want you on my side of the fence because of anything about you that I can see or the world can measure. It's because of that soft little heart that beats like a drum against me when we hug." She laid her hand on his chest and when its fleshly cadence reached her palm, she smiled.

"Now," she said, pulling her hand away, "I don't want you to feel as if you owe me anything because of how I feel. You don't. As I said, it doesn't matter what you say or do. My love for you is carved in stone and based on who I am. It's not a love to be earned or maintained by you. It's a love that just requires you, well, to be."

Cat sat up and kissed Ritter on the cheek. "Thank you for letting me in your life and giving me the opportunity to love you."

Ritter looked down, rubbed his hands together, and then tucked them out of sight under his shirt.

"Now, about that kiss . . ."

As she said it, Ritter's chin snapped up toward her. His pupils dilated wildly, and his muscles quivered in readiness. He could almost taste the freedom of her mouth.

"Wait, wait, now," she said with a laugh as she sat up. "I want you to understand something, Reed. A kiss will be my telling you that I am yours in a way that everything I just said can't. I hope that you feel the same but, it's ok if you don't.

"Reed, look at me. Don't just say what you think I want to hear and lead me to believe you feel something you don't. If you need time, I understand. But, until you know, we'll remain as we are now: dear friends that will have shared a single kiss. Sweetie, I won't share you while you are figuring things out. That's all there is to it. I won't kiss your lips daily and wonder who I'm tasting. Do you understand?"

Ritter eyes widened in shock at her frankness. He nodded slowly to affirm that he understood, then cleared his throat as he buried his hands deeper out of sight.

"I am a woman of my word and the kiss will happen anyway if that's what you choose. But please go into it knowing completely what it means to me. If you don't feel the same, let me go and please, not with the taste of you left on my lips."

A subtle expression of pleading washed over his face and he laughed a breathy, uncomfortable laugh as he looked away. Cat smiled compassionately, took his face gently, and brought his eyes back to hers. She kissed each of them and then his nose.

"If you get up and walk out now, I will still love you, and there will still be a pile of stones at my front door. And, I will always be grateful for the time I have spent with you, what it brought out in me, and that you cared enough about me to be honest with me."

Ritter looked at her severely and his breath quickened as if in anger. "Would you call me your boyfriend?" he asked. Cat smiled and said of course she would. She also said he could call her his girlfriend to which he replied with a smirk, "I already do. Just to my patients though! Which is a bit awkward because not even one has asked if I have a girlfriend."

Cat laughed and Ritter moved close to the hammock. "Come here my fat little *agneau précieux*," he said, rising up on his knees and gathering up his precious lamb strongly in an embrace. She put her arms around his neck and he kissed her cheek passionately.

"There's nobody else, mon amour," he whispered in her ear. "I've been yours since the night you brought me back from the dead."

Cat turned her head, their lips passed close enough for each to savor the other and she looked deep into his eyes. She then reached around her back, grabbed his hand that had remained out of sight despite being removed from its hiding place in his shirt, and put it against her cheek.

"There is nothing you can't tell me. Do you understand? Nothing. Love rejoices in truth, Reed. And it keeps no record of wrongs." Ritter looked into her eyes wondering if they had seen what he was trying so desperately to hide. He then kissed her nose and closed his eyes, wishing away all his deceptions.

"You know," she said with a humorous tone, "I could totally count this as a date. We had some oatmeal cookies. That counts as a meal I would think. I eat oatmeal for breakfast, and it's a meal then." Ritter smiled widely and agreed. He then put his hand behind her neck. "Wait," she said, moving her face back. "Don't be lukewarm. Please? Hot or cold but not lukewarm."

Ritter smiled, caressed his lips along her jaw, kissed her chin, and then assured her that he was quite hot on the matter. They both giggled like young adolescents and she rubbed her nose against his affectionately. His nostrils flared, and his mouth reached out toward hers.

"Echem!" a voice said loudly behind them. The invisible bubble around them burst and they laughed. "Paulette," Ritter said with clenched jaws and paws, "so help me, if this is not a matter of life and death, you will be the matter of death!"

"You've got guests, man. They're out front. Cat, why don't you just hang out back here with me?" Paul's tone said all Ritter needed to know, and Ritter excused himself.

The unholy trinity stood around Bayle's car laughing. When they saw Ritter, they all began clapping. "There he is!" Bayle laughed. "The man no prophylactic could contain!" Ritter cut his eyes toward the prophets sitting in the garage across the street and then, with feigned cordiality, asked the three what they wanted.

"You hotshot!" Mo laughed, stamping out a cigarette on Paul's driveway. "Oh wait, don't come any closer! You look sickly again! Which actually, to be honest, I am kind of glad to see. I thought it was just sex with me that made you green!"

"Nope, it's with me too," Ashta interjected.

"You would think you were the one with morning sickness!" Bayle laughed. Ritter looked at them with confusion and Ashta raised her hand. "I'm late! How can you not understand that! You are a doctor!" Ritter's face remained unchanged and Ashta shook her head. "You got me pregnant, you dope!" Ritter gasped with comprehension of what had been said and he looked over his shoulder toward Cat's door.

"What!" Ashta said with a defensive tone. "You afraid to tell your little pal? Are you are sleeping with her?" she whispered. Her eyes then looked around, as if to an unseen crowd, and she bellowed dramatically, "Well, truly, Alexander, there are no worlds left to conquer!"

Ritter took a violent step forward and through gritted teeth told Ashta to keep her voice down and that no, he wasn't sleeping with Cat. "You keeping a little virgin girlfriend on the side now? Kind of a goal to shoot for?" Bayle said with a wink.

"She's not my girlfriend!" Ritter hissed back.

Mo looked at Ritter curiously. "Ya, sure there, buddy, because you're acting like you got yourself a girlfriend. You're spending so much time with her your accent is starting to even sound like hers."

"I said no!"

Bayle rubbed his chin and smiled. "So just to be clear, the skinny chick is not now, nor has been, nor ever will be your girlfriend? Is that what the defense is saying?"

"That's what I said," Ritter growled. As he did, he saw Bayle smile and look toward Cat's door. Ritter looked over his shoulder and saw Cat standing there. Her face showed all the hurt her heart held.

Ritter dropped his head and his eyelids and teeth both gnashed. Cat walked forward and took his hand. "Do you three have anything else to say before you leave?" she asked.

Ashta walked around the car, hopped up on the hood and crossed her legs. Her miniskirt slid up and revealed all it did a poor job of hiding even at its full length.

"Well, I know you heard most of that," she said with a smirk. "Here's what you didn't hear but ought to know. He is still sleeping with me."

Ritter stepped forward and spit curses out like venom toward Ashta. Cat held his arm tightly and something about the manner of her touch silenced him. "It's okay," she whispered to him. "This needs to happen."

Ashta looked from Cat's face to Ritter's and she smiled. "As I was saying, we are still sleeping together and, in fact, were together today! Like, four hours ago. Have you washed those hands since then, Rit? Oh, and he's sleeping with Mo and Bayle too by the way. Think your little ultraconservative, buttoned-up-to-the-neck brain can wrap around that? And he ain't just sleeping with us! There's plenty more at the hospital. He doesn't care who, doesn't care where. Hell, he was with a girl in a broom closet the first week he was here! And not a terribly nice one! There are tons cleaner, and I am referring to both the closet and the girl!"

Cat held strongly to Ritter's hand and she pulled him closer with the same ferocity with which her heart was tearing in two.

"Do you understand what is being said, *little one*?" Bayle asked with a condescending tone.

"I understand and I knew already," she said calmly. Ritter looked down at her in disbelief. Her face turned up toward him and she smiled a subtle grin that dammed up her hurt.

"I was downtown last week and stopped by the hospital to surprise you. I saw Ashta leave your office and, by the way you looked at her as she walked away, I knew.

And I knew by the way you two looked at him at the restaurant that night what the nature of your relationship with him probably was," she said looking at Mo and Bayle, "at least at that point anyway."

Ritter turned toward her, held her shoulders, and asked with a trembling whisper why she had not said anything to him about Ashta. She rubbed her cheek on his hand and said the truth was his to tell.

"Did you know he does drugs?" Mo said, interrupting the moment between them. "And he goes to orgies—"

Cat held up her hand to the blonde and nodded. She knew what sin was. She didn't need specifics. And none of that changed how she felt for Reed, she said. There was nothing any of them could say that would make her not love the man.

"Oh, sweetie!" Ashta said, hopping off the car. She walked forward to the edge of Paul's driveway and leaned over slightly as if talking to a child.

"It's wasted emotion. He won't ever love you back. It's just not in his nature! You think you're just going to fly in and save this man from his own self with your undying love? Please! Love does die by the way. Everything dies. Some things sooner than others," she said with a knowing smile and wink to Mo and Bayle.

"Kitty, can I call you Kitty? Kitty, you may have his hand, but we have the rest of him and some of us," she said, patting her inhabited pelvis and standing to her full stature, "have more than others. It's a good thing too because he said he wants kids. And from the looks of his current prospects"—Ashta paused and looked Cat up and down—"I might be his best hope for that."

Ritter's top lip trembled and the throbbing of his heart echoed in the undomesticated portion of his brain. He lunged forward and hit Bayle on the jaw. The force of the strike threw Bayle's head sideways into the corner of the open car door, tearing part of his ear away from his head. He fell to the ground in an seemingly semiconscious state and blood streamed out liberally.

"Why did you do that!" Mo spit out wildly.

"Because you were too far away and she's pregnant!" Ritter responded, pointing to Ashta as if his finger were a dagger. Cat ran into the house and quickly returned with a towel.

She put pressure on Bayle's wound and cradled his head. The sight of her compassion further heightened Ritter's hate for himself and his accomplices. He wanted to tear Bayle's head out of her lap and off his shoulders altogether.

The two feminine cloaked demons were pleased and smiled at one another. They could feel the bloodlust running through Ritter and wanted nothing more than to feed it. Mo, hoping to do just that, walked toward him slowly, watching his desire to hit her increase as the distance between them lessened.

"Hey, guys. What's going on here?"

Ashta and Mo's heads whipped toward Peter who had jogged up without their noticing. "Rit, this is Michael."

Ritter glanced over at the scarred man with Peter and a vague feeling of recognition swept over him. A memory of an armor-clad man battling a dragon flashed quickly through his head with a static pop.

Michael stepped toward Ritter, pulling Ritter from his recollection, and again asked if everything was okay. He responded that everything was fine and that Ashta, Mo, and Bayle were just leaving.

Peter walked over and kneeled down next to Bayle whose head still rested in Cat's lap. "I think he's right," Peter agreed. "You three were just leaving."

Bayle's eyes opened completely as if his wounding had been nothing more than a farce. He sat up and Cat followed him with the towel to catch the blood from his ear. Peter put his hand on top of hers and smiled. He said he and Michael would see to it that Bayle was sufficiently taken care of and suggested that she and Ritter go inside.

Ashta called out as Cat turned to go and restated that she was about seven weeks pregnant. "That means the deed happened about five weeks ago, Cat. A Saturday morning if I remember correctly. That day ring a bell for you? Why do you think he had so much restraint on your first date?"

Ritter closed the door behind them and watched the five for a moment from a window. When he turned and looked ahead, every word he had ever known vanished from his brain. Cat stood looking at him from across the room just as she had the night he had made the drive out to Chaldea and nearly sealed his fate.

She said nothing, and nothing needed to be said. Her eyes expressed their hurt so vividly that the emotion became a third entity in the room. Ritter closed his eyes and plundered his mind wildly for words.

After nearly a full minute of gut-wrenching silence, several prodigal phrases returned to him and he shook his head. "I won't insult you with excuses or lies for that matter. I can only say that I am sorry. What I said in the back garden was true. My heart is yours and has been."

She asked why he didn't tell her about his ongoing relationships when she gave him the opportunity and he shrugged. He said he knew it would hurt her. He never intended for her to find out and as typical as it sounded, he had planned to stop. That afternoon with Ashta was to be the last.

Cat lowered her head, sniffed hard, and put her hands on her hips. "This life you're living, it nearly killed you. I mean, how many soccer balls to the head do you need? Do you think God is just going to run out because, let me assure you, He won't. The day He quits busting you up side your head is the day He finally lets you have the thing you want more than Him. And that, Ritter, will be a joyful day of horror for you."

Ritter looked down and had no response. For the first time since they had met, she had not called him Reed. On her lips, he had become what he was to everyone else.

CHAPTER 25

Love Doesn't Let a Cat Pee
All Over the House

Ten minutes later, Ritter was sitting on the edge of his bed hitting his forehead again and again with his fist, asking himself what he had done. He knew for certain that he had deeply wounded Cat and destroyed whatever possibility there was for a future with her. He didn't know however what that future might have been. What lay ahead for them was more than anything he had ever known. How could he ever estimate the loss of it? It was like trying to understand the value of a lost jewel when one has no concept of money.

Ritter went to the restroom, washed his face, and looked at himself in the mirror. He wished he could have turned back the clock and been honest with her when she had given the opportunity. His deceptions being made known in the manner they had been revealed was as devastating as a flash flood from which he felt he would likely never surface.

As he stood looking at his wet face, he thought about his first date with Cat. After shaving, he had splashed his cheeks and then stood in amazement at his appearance in the mirror. In conjunction with the fresh haircut, his entire countenance had looked so clean that he had had a hard time accepting it. It wasn't until his beard had begun to solidly resurface that he had been able to bear his own reflection.

His hand ran over the bristled terrain of his cheeks and surveyed the land. Fresh, warm water rewet the overgrowth and a thick coat of shaving cream followed. The new, clean blade of his razor glided mercifully through the foamy thicket with enough pressure to leave a clean wake behind it yet light enough to not leave blood in the trail. He extended his neck and contorted his face as needed and leaned over closer to the mirror to give greater attention to the process.

As he rinsed his blade, he looked down into the sink at the wild portion of his face that had been cleared. The shaving cream rested in peppered, cloudlike heaps around the drain. The running water thinned out portions of the foam and it easily disappeared into the silver-circled, black hole never to be seen again.

He looked up at his new face and back down again at the vestiges of his almost-beard. Just minutes earlier, it had been blood fed, alive and tickling Cat's nose. And now, with a sharp swipe, it was gone, and his skin looked as if it had never existed.

It was then he realized that perhaps the scene on the driveway wasn't a flood that he was meant to survive. Not completely. Maybe there was a part of him that was supposed to die and nothing less than the day's catastrophic sharp swipe would have ever killed it. And it would have had to have been a sudden deluge. Only its merciless force could have torn way the necrotic flesh from the new and left him clean. And only its speed could have left him no time to escape. Now the only question was whether he planned to remain swimming in his own filth or forgive himself and let the graceful current carry it away into the abyss of wherever filthy, flesh-soaked water flows.

Cat deserved better than him, he thought as he wiped his face, and the likelihood of reclaiming her was as slim as his indiscretions were fat. But he was going to try and he would wait for as long as it took for the floodwaters to subside. And if they never did, just the hope of being with her again made breathing under water seem possible.

Ritter rinsed the metal gleam back to his razor and, as he set it down, saw the compass Cat had given him. It was lying on the bathroom counter as if this had been the spot he had first received it. He didn't remember putting it there and looked around himself for an unseen hand to explain its appearance.

He held it up, tapped its crystal, and sighed. Somehow, he had managed to break that as well. The needle was not pointing north.

After a moment's contemplation, he smiled. No. Not broken. It was doing more than the task for which it was designed and if that were a result of a malfunction, he hoped it never righted itself. The shining instrument was not displaying the cardinal direction he was facing. Rather, it was showing him the way he should go, which was a force that pulled stronger than any magnetic pole.

The arrow of the brass compass pointed directly, and without shivering, toward the direction of the sunrise and Cat's house: east. He nodded and then turned on the water a last time to wash away what was left of his old self in the sink.

His knock on Cat's front door was fearful and soft. When it was not answered, he rapped a bit louder and then, after a few moments, went to the back patio. He closed the screen door behind him quietly, and as he stepped to the glass door of the house to knock on it, he saw through it to a pool of blood in her kitchen.

Ritter's heart leaped into his hand, throwing it on the door handle. He ran inside and called out for Cat. A bloody knife lay on the kitchen counter beside an apple and he began shaking and running wildly room to room opening doors and calling her name.

When he opened her bathroom door, he gasped. Cat was lying in the bathtub, bathed in her own blood. Before she could speak, Ritter was on top of her, tearing at her clothing in search of a wound.

She screamed for him to stop and as he looked at her face, he realized the blood had come, and was still coming, from her nose. His panic diluted to a purposeful urgency as the physician in his brain took the helm. He ran to the kitchen and quickly returned to her with an ice pack in hand. He kneeled down on the floor, helped her sit up, and placed the cold compress lightly over her nose.

Cat's blue encircled eyes looked up at Ritter's mouth as words slipped around in it, calming, and coaching her into controlled breathing. Her sense of calm increased enough that the physician's portion of him became satisfied. It then respectfully stepped aside and allowed the man in love to return. And as it did, Ritter began to sob.

He climbed into the bathtub behind Cat, pulled her close, and clung tightly to her as if she were the rope keeping him from a fall to his death. She turned on her side and buried her sanguineous face into his chest and held him with the same ferocity.

When her breathing slowed and became indistinguishable from his own, he pulled the ice pack away. The bleeding seemed to have stopped, and he lifted her chin toward him to verify the assumption. He then sighed, kissed her forehead, and again held her face against his chest. He ran his fingers through her hair with a quiet recklessness of despair, and his face fell in upon itself with grief.

He wrapped his arms around her again and pulled her up higher and closer to his chin. As he did, his hands caught his eye. The fingers of his right hand lifted and pulled the palm up behind them. Ritter turned the appendage as if it were a foreign entity and felt a faint sense of horror as he looked at it. Cat's blood had painted it completely to the wrist.

Cat sat up and breathed deeply before putting her hand on the edge of bathtub. Ritter could see that she was preparing to stand and begged her not to go. After the day's events, he knew most likely that this would be the only bath the two would ever share and said as much to her. He grabbed a washcloth, wet it with warm water, and then asked Cat to sit with him a little while longer.

He cradled her in his arms and wiped the blood from her face with the damp cloth. Her eyes closed drowsily, exhausted from emotion, and Ritter told her to sleep. He rested his lips against her head, kissed her, and rocked her gently.

Cat closed her eyes and tried to clear her head but thoughts of Ashta and Ritter together molested all her sense of calm. He had had sex with her before he and Cat's first date, and then shown up at Cat's door not unlike the bluebonnets in his hand: beautiful with a false pretense of life that obscured the fact he had been recently plucked.

Cat bit the inside of her lips to hold tears at bay and said quietly, "I think your focus needs to be on your child and its mother for now. A baby is a gift regardless of the packaging." Her hand laid itself on her stomach, and her body mourned silently for her daughter.

Ritter shook his head. He assured her Ashta would be sending him a medical bill in the mail shortly. Cat looked at him, and he read her face.

"Cat, that's not even an option," he began and then stopped when he realized that Cat herself had probably once been seen as an impossible option. He rubbed his hand through his hair and pulled on it in frustration.

"I know what you are thinking, Ginger. But not everyone shares your morals or your life story. Your father was a massively good man, and I am in awe of the decision he made—"

"No, he wasn't. My daddy was a good man. I never met my biological father. My daddy never slept with my mother. As I said, to my knowledge, he never had a girlfriend. He had no idea why a girl he only knew as a friend would lie to her parents and let him take custody of me. But, he saw my arrival as a gift from God and never questioned it.

"To my own blood, I was nothing more than a swaddled embarrassment. So God put me in the hands of people He knew would look beyond the packaging and method of delivery and just accept the gift. And, Reed, you come from a long line of people that have been richly blessed by strangely wrapped presents."

Cat sighed in obvious frustration and sat up. She rubbed her nose and looked at her fingers for signs of bright red then laughed sardonically. "I mean, come on, Reed! You think Jonah was thrilled to see a big fish bearing down on him? I really doubt it! Now, the both of you were and are the cause of your own circumstances. But the difference between the two of you is that you just see the storm, the fish, and all you stand you to lose because of them! Jonah, he saw what everybody else had to lose! He took responsibility for the storm, jumped off the boat to save innocent people from having to pay for his mistake, and accepted the fish as his fate. That animal didn't just happen to be there! It was sent specifically to Jonah, in the midst of a storm, with a divine purpose. What makes you think your little fish is any different?"

Ritter put his hand on her jaw and rubbed his thumb across her cheek. "Don't leave me, Cat. I can't lose you. You're everything to me."

Cat sighed and looked at Ritter's face. He could see that it wasn't until that moment she noticed he had shaved. The blood in her fingers pulsated and, to keep them from touching his chin, she rubbed her own.

"I don't want that job, Reed. I wasn't meant to be anybody's *everything*. It would wear me down to nothing and then what would you do? People aren't meant for that type of burden. Just Jesus. And despite what you have made me out to be in your head, I ain't Him!

"And besides, it's not true anyway. I am not everything to you. You are everything to you. Your job might serve humanity but you are more than happy to be recognized for it. I've heard how you talk about the surgeries you are preparing for and have done. Makes me wonder if you keep a mirror on the patient so you can watch yourself help them.

"The way you dress and groom yourself makes it look like you don't care about how you look but your clothes are expensive. And the scruff you normally carry never quite becomes a full beard. I doubt that it just stops at that length on its own.

"You love you. Yea, you hate yourself some too. I know that's part of the reason you sleep around. But the other part of that is you enjoy it and you surround yourself with lovers that don't expect you to love. No rules, no expectations. You just satisfy you and then cuddle up beside somebody like me for a little security. You want to be an outdoor cat that gets to live indoors! You want to scratch things up, leave your scent everywhere, relieve yourself wherever you want, and then have somebody pat their lap for you to come sit on it! Well, I am not going to be that person! Love doesn't let a cat pee all over the house!"

After a moment, she sat up and told Ritter that she had meant what she had said on the porch. She would always love him. But he needed to decide what it was he truly wanted, and she didn't think he could make that decision with her in the landscape. If he were constantly glancing over his tail for her, he wouldn't clearly see the reality of the forest around him. If the wild was what he chose, she would still love him. But she would love him the way she did all wild creatures: from a safe distance.

Cat walked Ritter to the back door and the two froze seeing it had been left open. Beyond the haze of the screened-in porch, they saw Beau sitting on a fence post looking out at all the animal had wondered about from behind glass. The cat turned and looked behind himself one last time at the woman who had loved him so much. But the world called louder than his memories, and he bounded off the fence and out of sight.

CHAPTER 26

The Jungle Doesn't Love Back

Cat left before sunup the next morning. A note was waiting for Ritter on her back porch, reading that she would be gone for several weeks. To where, she didn't say. She made one request: that he not look for Beau nor lure him home with food. She then wrote that she forgave him for everything and that she had meant what she had said: she would always love him.

Ritter smiled and inhaled. *There it is,* he thought: *hope.* What had once been seen by him as a means of execution had become an agent of survival. Where there was hope, there was possibility. And, where there was possibility, there was a reason to keep going forward. Maybe he would yet find out the mystery of what the future held for him and the blessed Emmanuelle.

He sat down at his computer to e-mail her before work, but as had been the case recently, he found himself at a loss for words. His hands rubbed down his face, pulling and comically distorting his appearance as they went. He drummed his fingers, made various noises with his mouth, and threw several wadded pieces of paper into his trash can. One paper ball went wildly off course and landed on his bookshelves. He got up to retrieve it and found it resting next to the rock from his sister's grave that he had once entrusted to Cat.

He held the smooth, cold stone in his hand until it became warm and wondered what advice Reece would give him. She had been good at love.

For several moments he stood in thought only to find exactly what he had previously found in his brain: nothing. In frustration, he growled and put the stone back on the shelf. He glanced at the clock and knew he needed to leave shortly for work but wanted to write Cat before he left.

The minutes clicked by, and just before he would be late leaving, he kicked the edge of his bed and grumbled, "Come on HaShem! Where are You? I need You! I really need You!"

And miraculously, a lock in his mind opened with a click and words filled his head with basket loads of excess.

Carla C. Hoch

My dearest Emma,

I have not been a man of faith for quite some time. But it seems that I will again have to become one. I can imagine nothing short of divine intervention repairing the damage I have done.

All that you said yesterday was correct. I have been besotted with my own self. I have been arrogant and conveniently hidden behind my own hurt in a manner that served me best. And yes, you are not meant to be my everything. Reece meant everything to me and I have reduced her to nothing by letting the loss of her become an excuse for my salaciousness. Perhaps if I had simply allowed her to be my sister, my best friend, her memory would be a source of comfort rather than a painful reminder of her death, and constant source of choking guilt.

They say that dogs know when their beloved human is returning home. For that, I am jealous of them. I haven't a clue when you will come back, but I will always assume it is today. And I will always be ready, with tail wagging, as if my assumption is true. But rest assured, you will not return to find me as the dog you left. When you come back, I will be the man that would have never given you cause to leave.

Yours,
Reed Jacob Thomas

The days that followed trudged by, and Ritter went through each with the anxious anticipation of seeing Cat's truck in her driveway when he returned home. When he found it as empty as he had left it, he smiled and knew that surely tomorrow would be the day.

Smiles don't sprout wings however and despite Ritter's optimism, the pacing of each days passing did not quicken. And, after two weeks, *tomorrow* ceased to be the thing of anticipation that clung like a child to its mother, Morning. Rather, it became a lumbering fat parasite that fed off the faith in Ritter's heart and provided nourishment to all his doubts. The sun's rising no longer was a symbol of hope. It was simply a circle of buzzards waiting for him to stop struggling and give in to the hunger of unrighteousness.

His mind pondered all this one evening as his body ran. It was the last moments of dusk when he set out: his favorite time to run. It was when the viper rattle of automatic sprinklers began to shake in foreboding rhythms and the night changed the neighborhood into a dark and wild land. By the time he was less than a quarter mile from the house, the streets would lay ahead like long, slippery black snakes with yellow streetlight-mottled backs.

The moonless sky had cloaked him in darkness completely by the time he reached his turnaround point: the felled oak. A streetlight that normally illuminated the

200

three-way stop was out, and Ritter could barely make out the wooden corpse until he was a few yards away. When he could discern its shape completely, he slowed to a walk.

He had seen this tree in its broken state for the first time with Cat. It had been soon after the plant's demise caused by, as she had said, *a steady push.* Ritter had wondered then if he would fall prey to such a fate and felt certain now that he had.

Falling in love had always seemed to Ritter a poor word choice to describe the process of becoming affectionately intertwined with someone. He couldn't say that he had *fallen* in love with Cat. That made his feelings for her seem to be the result of a clumsy misstep or act of carelessness. But he could say for certain he was *felled* by love with her—struck suddenly, sharply, and mercilessly away from his root bed.

He let his fingers drag along the tree's bark flesh and smiled. In its current state of repose, it was the picture of peace. Because it's full length was now solidly bound to the earth by its own state of decay, the wind could do nothing more to it. And, that was exactly how he felt in regard to Cat. Without question, she excited Ritter both physically and emotionally. But at his core, he was solidly tethered to her as an anchor to a ship. Perhaps that was why he had been better able to sleep. He didn't fear drifting. His eyes would awaken to the same viridian water that had lulled him to sleep. This Douglas, *dubh glas, dark water,* woman that his body had ached to sleep with, had granted sleep to his aching body. Love was nothing if not ironic, he thought as he rapped his knuckles against the still trunk.

Ritter walked to the mangled roots of the oak and saw that the sprout that had begun growing from the soft earth beneath it had doubled in size. The small animal hole that he had first seen with Bayle was still there as well. Perhaps its turning the earth made the seed's roots better able to reach nourishment.

He wondered if Bayle had seen the new growth. Bayle. Beautiful blue-eyed Baylor that had captivated Ritter like the reflection in Narcissus's pool.

Ritter rubbed his eyes and then sat back against the tree. His eyes scanned the darkness and settled on shades of pale that lingered between the trees around him. He wondered if there was a human among the pale figures looking back at him thinking that he too looked like a figment of fading light. And he wondered if that human was Bayle who had first come into his life from among those shadows in this exact spot.

He missed Bayle above all his other lovers. Bayle with whom his bellicose nature was welcomed and encouraged and with whom he didn't need to speak. Bayle whose fair skin had seemed at times indistinguishable from his own in both complexion and complicity, whose hands were equal to his own in size, shape, and strength, whose build and beauty rivaled his own, and whose shadow could lie on his congruently. Bayle: the man who made it possible for Ritter to indulge himself with his own reflection.

A car paused at the intersection, and its lights poured onto Ritter. He stood quickly as if having been doused with water and darted back into the thicket of darkness toward home.

Streetlights began reemerging and the glistening, wet snake roads leading home rolled alongside him as he ran through the neighborhood jungle. The sidewalk stretched underneath and ahead of him in dim shades of dying yellow leaves until a side street was reached. These areas were lit brighter and the water from sprinklers made the cement strip shimmer like fool's gold.

As he neared the cutoff toward Bayle's house, he slowed to a jog, walk, and then stood completely still, panting. His nose opened wider to pull in more night-scented air as his pupils adjusted to the shimmering pool of light ahead. His lips hung heavy with thirst around his gaping mouth and heavy drops of sweat rolled down the center of his chest where his thick muscles collided together like crashing fists.

The road to Baylor's house moved alongside the road back home for a hundred yards and then ever so slightly began to turn away from it before making a sharp U shape. The place where the two diverged was well illuminated and in no uncertain terms pointed Ritter toward Bayle like the outstretched arm of a panderer.

He knew he had to make a decision before reaching the corner and, for some minutes, he stood in thought. The longer he considered the prospect, the easier it became to concede to it. His feet began moving again, and instead of simply running quickly, they began quickly running toward. The closer he came to the corner, the deeper his claws sunk into the earth. But, just before making the slight detour, he saw movement out of the corner of his eye. He glanced to his right and there, out in the middle of the street, was Beau; his feral eyes twinkled reflectively.

Ritter smiled, stopped, and called out to the animal that was lying in the middle of the warm street beyond the reach of the sprinkler's rattle. The animal was grooming himself and upon seeing Ritter stretched with satisfaction. The two considered one another for a moment and then each called: the human with clicks and the animal with chatter.

Beau sat up with a poetic flow and made as if to walk toward Ritter until gleaming eyes in the distance distracted him. The cat's head turned slightly and looked curiously at the white orbs quickly closing in. Although the animal had been happy out of doors, he had been too preoccupied with the predatory pleasure of chasing birds to notice that he too was prey. He still saw the world around him as a place of only two creations: wonderful things he had encountered and wonderful things yet to be encountered.

Ritter looked over his shoulder, and before he realized that Beau did not know to move out of its path, the five hundred horse-powered beast was too close. There was a momentary squeal, the sound of a breaking melon, and two thuds in quick succession. In only a moment, the world Beau had for so long, so longed to rush toward to be a part of, had in turn rushed toward him and torn him apart.

The four-wheeled monster never slowed. It continued mercilessly down the road until its red eyes disappeared in the distance. Ritter looked out at the carnage and then squeezed his eyes shut tight in hopes of erasing the incident. When his effort to bend time failed, he walked out into the road, collected what was left of his animal, and headed for home.

CHAPTER 27
Happy Last Birthday

Cat rolled her eyes and crunched the cereal in her mouth. "Tres semanas, hija. Es bastante," Cruz said as he sat back in his chair and finished his coffee.

"Oh what," she said, wiping her mouth, "there is a time limit on how long I can stay with my own family?" Cruz shook his head and rose from the table. Of course there was no time limit for how long she could stay there. It was her home as well. But there was a limit to how long she could run from her problems.

"Well, I'm a grown gal. I can decide on that, and besides, tomorrow is my birthday! Good grief, I'll just be back here anyway." Cruz walked back to the table, paused, kissed her on the head, and said quietly, "hoy."

Cat looked over at Paloma who raised her hands up and immediately went to the sink to begin washing dishes. "Mamá!" Cat said with a laugh, "where's the love?" Cruz walked to Paloma's side and the two looked at Cat who looked up in confusion and then smiled.

"If you two lovebirds need some *alone time*, yuck, I'm not even going to finish that. Fine, I'll leave after lunch. I can stay three weeks, but three weeks and one more day is too much! Qué ridículo!"

Cruz and Paloma shook their dark heads and both declared that Cat would begin packing after she finished her coffee. Cat sat stunned for a moment. She then raised her eyebrows, took her coffee cup in her hands tenderly as if it were it were a life source, and slowly blew away its steam with a smirk. She could suckle a cup of coffee for a good hour, a fact both her godparents knew. Cruz sighed, walked to the table, and finished off the cup in one gulp.

Ritter's car was in his driveway, and despite the copious time Cat had had to think of what she would say when she first saw him again, she was struck dumb. As it turned out, she needed to say nothing.

Paul stepped out of his door as she quieted the engine of her truck, and he smiled the smile every teacher has when the school year ends: one of liberation. They hugged and he helped her with her luggage.

"He's not here," Paul said, reading Cat's expression. She nodded silently and hoped he would explain Ritter's absence without her asking.

"He went to New York for a couple days. He missed you pretty bad," he said with an amused tone. "But," he continued more seriously, "he needed to. It kind of smacked him around into being the guy he really is. He was due for a *fine thrashing* as he says! And it gave him time to read like you told him to."

Cat had no idea what Paul was talking about.

"He read the Bible. Like, the whole thing. He read his Jewish Bible and then mine. You didn't tell him to do that? Hmph, well that's a sign of the apocalypse! I'll tell ya what though, Kit, if Jesus is coming tonight, I ain't cleaning my toilet, I can tell you that!"

Cat laughed and as she unlocked the door of her house, noticed the small galvanized bucket that sat beside it on the porch. It was filled with stones. She stooped and looked through them and noticed there was one dated for every day that she had been gone. Each simply read, *Waiting.*

The next evening, just as she had predicted, Cat was on her way back out to the ranch for her birthday. She had been instructed to dress up and assumed the family would be driving together right back into town for dinner. She shook her head at what felt like going around her backside to get to her own elbow.

She stopped at a gas station and went inside to get a snack. Her stomach had suddenly begun to roll with hunger that had been absent for weeks, and she knew she should indulge herself while the desire was present. The clothes that had begun to fit snugly over her curves had once again resumed their previous slump and hung from her shoulders as if on a hanger. She was ahead of schedule anyway. Paloma had said to arrive no earlier than six and it was barely past five.

The freezer case was at the back of the store and, as Cat opened the door to grab a little carton of milk, she saw a familiar reflection in its glass. She closed her eyes, breathed deeply, and grabbed the milk.

The freezer door closed with a hiss and Cat turned. Ashta stood at the end of the aisle in nothing more than a white bikini and flip-flops with a box of wine propped against her very tan and very flat stomach.

Cat turned and hoped to walk away unnoticed but of course she didn't. She almost wished she had frozen like a possum in the frosty air of the freezer case. But her motion caught Ashta's eye the way a rabbit's does a dog's.

Ashta called out to her and sauntered forward like a fertility statue come to life. "Look at you all dressed up! Hot date?" Cat shook her head in response and looked toward the cash register and the doors.

"You're boyfriend's been MIA for a few days. Suppose some jealous lover finally got the best of him? Oh, come on, Cat. It's a joke. You still mad about the deal in the front yard? Look, you gotta just rip a Band-Aid off! It hurts but in the end it's for the best. I hope you can see that at some point."

Ashta hopped to adjust the box on her hip and dropped her purse on the floor. Its contents vomited out, and Cat kneeled to help her pick it up. Among the collection of uncommon, common-girl items was something that, to Cat, looked painfully familiar. It was a river rock polished to a shine. She picked it up and saw immediately that Ritter had written on it: *For the queen of my kittens.* On the back, he had drawn two cartoon cat faces.

Cat stood and, after several moments, realized she had been standing in front of Ashta examining the rock in pained silence. She handed the stone back to Ashta who tossed it up in the air and caught it like a trinket of luck.

"He gave this to me last week," Ashta said with a laugh. "Apparently, he is hoping for another *accident* one day. A double one from the looks of this stupid little rock thing. Uh, no thanks, Rit, one was enough for me! I am glad to be rid of it! Babies are for the bored in my opinion!"

Cat's eyes went immediately to the fallow expanse between Ashta's hip bones. She tried to look through the fecund flesh for a second existence but knew there wasn't one. It had been done. Ashta had sent Ritter a medical bill in the mail and the two were now free to go on living their lives as if a third had never existed.

Cat's throat tightened and she cleared it quietly before nodding a polite parting gesture and turning to walk away.

"Look, Cat, I have done you a favor. I know you are hurt and can't see that now, but I have saved you a whole butt load of heartache!"

Cat stopped and looked down at her feet as Ashta continued. "What Rit wants most from a woman, you aren't going to give him. And as much as he respects you for it now, he will resent you for it later and one of two things will happen: he will leave you for another woman like me or stay with you and still have another woman like me on the side. I know he's charming, Cat! He's gorgeous, has an amazing body, he's brilliant, and an amazing lover! But, what he isn't and will never be is celibate or monogamous! He doesn't have it in him and don't hate him for that. He can't help how God made him. His future is in the shape of a shadow like mine, Cat. Not yours."

Anger welled up in Cat like a geyser and she turned toward Ashta. "God made Reed human and because of that he, we all, have the privilege of making choices, which means the potential to sin. And we all make the wrong choices and all sin because we are human. God also however created us in the image of *His shadow*," she said with emphasis. "That fact reminds us that we always have a light source to go back to that destroys whatever darkness our human choices throw us into.

"You may know Reed and the power sex has over him. But what you don't obviously know is the power of the Most High God who created sex. No matter how filthy that creation becomes in the hands of the sinful, the hands of the Almighty can bring it back to what it was meant to be."

Her heart trembled within her chest and Cat walked slowly toward Ashta still speaking until the two were well within slapping distance from one another.

"It doesn't matter what you believe Reed is or isn't capable of being. What matters is the capability God has to change every one of us into what none of us are capable of being without Him: pure. You may have, or have had it seems, Reed's child. But God will always have his soul, and Reed will always have God's love. You can't change or deflate that truth to fit the diminutive space you have chosen to inhabit! You are a lot of things, Ashta Roth, but none of them are bigger than the thing you are up against.

"Now," Cat said with a low growl through clenched teeth, "I am telling you, stay away from him!"

"You know, Kitty," Ashta said, lowering her head in a predatory posture, "when you mess with the bull, you get the horns. And, little girl, those horns are coming for you. In fact, if it all goes to plan, by this time tomorrow, you will have had two back pockets full of them." Her finger reached out, poked Cat in the stomach, and she made a clicking noise with her mouth.

"Get ready, Rachel Emmanuelle. Sacrificial death is the destiny of white lambs." Her kohl-lined eyes narrowed at Cat, and a murderous smile bled its way onto her red lips.

"I wonder," Ashta said in an amused tone, straightening suddenly to her full stature, "do you suppose if those little lambs knew their fate they would take such effort to remain so white?"

When Cat got back to her truck, she prayed for the Holy Spirit's comfort and the divine strength to not burst into tears. She also thanked the Lord for having made her forget her shotgun at home. Cat wasn't one to waste ammo on the backside of an animal that was more mouth than menace, but she might have made an exception in this case. Ashta had threatened her, albeit not overtly. But in Texas, it was enough to warrant an empty shell casing and a jury of women would never have convicted Cat once they saw Ashta in person and imagined her in a bikini!

"Back pockets full of horns," Cat said to herself out loud, "whatever that means! You don't scare me, Ashta. You are scary! But you don't scare me." She put the truck in reverse and blew air out of her lips in a defiant snort. "Girl, I'd hog tie you and make you put on some clothes," she mumbled to herself as she pulled out of the parking lot and back onto the highway.

Cat pulled up to the ranch, put the truck in park and sat dumbfounded. The barn was lit up with strings of white lights. There was a large white canopy outside and enough bug lamps to electrocute a small village.

She slowly exited her truck and Paloma came out of the house with a smile to greet her. "What is all this?" she asked her godmother with wonder. Paloma smiled, hugged her daughter, and said she had no idea. "Las vacas lo hicieron."

"Ohhhhh," Cat said with a nod. "Well, you know, if you don't watch cows, they will go and decorate a barn." The two laughed and Paloma kissed Cat on the cheek. "Feliz cumpleaños, mi'ja!"

Cruz met them in the barn along with fifty or more guests, half of which were ranch hands and members of their families. "Well, glory, is there anybody left in Mexico?" Cat laughed as she hugged the throng of earth-brown friends. Paul was among the dark-haired crowd and Cat laughed when she hugged him.

"Paul! Well I don't know how the word for *Greek* ended up as *gringo*! You look more Mexican than half the folks here! Why didn't you tell me you were coming! We could have ridden together! Glory, I wish we had! I saw Ashta at the gas station off 2920."

Paul rolled his eyes. Lucky her, he said. He then asked if Ashta was showing much. Cat looked at him for a moment in silence. Ritter had obviously not told him. She looked down and laughed. Ashta was always showing too much she joked and then immediately took the subject back to them riding out to the ranch together.

"Cat! It would have ruined the surprise! I had to go get RJ from the airport anyway." Cat's eyes immediately went to Cruz who pulled his cowboy hat down slightly over his own. Paloma slapped Paul on the back of the head and castigated him in Spanish. Obviously, Ritter's presence was to be part of the surprise at this surprise party.

"Ow!" Paul said with a wince. "You sure you aren't Greek! You hit hard as my *yia-yia*!" Paloma's eyes widened. She wasn't old enough to be anybody's "yeehaw," she hissed as she dragged him away.

Cat stared at her godfather. "So is Reed here somewhere hiding in the cow poop like the prodigal son?"

Cruz hugged Cat. "Todos nosotros somos hijos pródigos. No?" She nodded. There wasn't a person on earth that wasn't a prodigal son.

Cruz looked up and saw the screen door of the house open and smiled. He then kissed Cat on the head and said that he had not invited Ritter. On the contrary, Ritter had invited him.

Cat looked at Cruz in confusion, but before she was able to ask what he meant, a pair of familiar arms wrapped around her and spun her in a circle. When the spinning stopped, she turned to see who she knew was behind her and a different sort of spinning began.

His hair was towel dried but still wet as if he had just gotten out of a shower. In fact, his freshly ironed white shirt had drops of water on it. His face was smoothly shaven, and his hair sprung up in freshly cut curls that seemed angry to not only be short but wet. He was smiling bigger than Cat remembered ever having seen him smile and it was quite obvious that Ritter had no intention of hiding any of the apparent excitement he had in seeing her.

Cat laughed. He had assured her that she would not return to find him a dog, but in her estimation, he looked a lot like an excited puppy ready to wet the floor.

"I'm so happy to see you," he said again before hugging her. "Feels like you've been gone donkey's years," he whispered against her head with a laugh. She inhaled his scent and her eyes rolled back into her head, down her throat and straight way to her knees that were not strong enough at the moment to hold the weight of them. She stumbled a little and Ritter laughed.

"Happy birthday, love," he said, still holding her close. "My, my thirty-five. I'm glad this venue is wheelchair accessible."

Cat laughed and pushed him away. She was thirty she said and intended on staying that way for at least another year. Her stomach growled hard at either the ridiculousness of the joke or its hunger for Ritter, and Cat put her head down on her hand.

"Come on, woman. Let's go get some fajitas!"

"It's pronounced *fa-HEE-tas*, Reed! Not *fa-JIE-tas*!"

"I know, but *fa-JIE-ta* sounds a bit like vagina and that's quite funny don't you think! Oh come on! It's a part of the human anatomy! Okay, *fajidneys*! Is that better? A more suitable organ for you?"

Cat rolled her eyes and followed as he pulled her along by her hand.

Ritter fixed both of their plates and walked outside. There were blankets on hay bales and he climbed up and then offered Cat a hand. When she saw the mound of food he had for her, she gasped. It wasn't humanly possible for her to eat all of it, she assured him. Ritter smiled. He had seen her perform greater miracles, he said.

The two ate in silence for a few moments and Cat thought about the stone she had seen fall from Ashta's purse. She wondered if there was another galvanized bucket somewhere filled with lies etched in stone. It made her sick and she coughed and took a drink of iced tea. Ritter put his hand on her shoulder and asked if she was okay. She nodded and pushed her plate of food aside.

"Why did you go to New York?" she asked, trying to take her mind off her own bitter anger. Ritter smiled, pushed her plate back toward her, and asked how she knew he had been in New York. Had she dared ask about him, he questioned with a wink.

"I had several things to do. There was a medical seminar there for one. And, I met my parents there as well." He took a bite and smiled widely as if he were keeping a secret.

"I told them everything," he said after wiping his muzzle. Cat gave him a confused look and he clarified. "Everything: manky way I've been living, how I have dealt with Reece dying, the baby . . . everything." Cat looked down and wondered why on earth he had told them about the abortion.

She asked what they said and Ritter shrugged after taking another bite. He seemed oddly upbeat in Cat's opinion. Especially considering the subject matter.

"They cried. I mean, what else can a parent do when a child tells them such things! But, I'm glad that I told them. I needed to say it out loud, confess my sins so to speak, and apologize to them for behaving in a way a son shouldn't. And as I suspected, they forgave me, hugged me. For a split second though, I thought they would disown me and it was terrifying. Honestly."

He looked away in thought for a moment and then laughed slightly. "You know, I have always thought that the prodigal son became a different man on his long walk home. But I know now it was the embrace he received once he got there that truly changed him. It wasn't the words, *Please don't go*, but, *I'm so glad you're back.*" Ritter cleared his throat, looked down, and nodded his head.

Cat's mouth was slightly agape in wonder. Ritter was a new man it seemed. Not a different man but the version of himself that was originally imagined. She had never seen him so giddy and his happiness made him oblivious to her obvious shock.

"And when I told them about the baby, my ma cried. But she stopped on the spot when she saw the sonogram. She's massively ecstatic. My da as well. He's generally a low-key sort. I never expected him to peacock about like he did." Ritter mimicked his father and then laughed.

It was then that Cat realized, Ritter didn't know. She looked back up and watched his face as he continued talking. It was animated with an excited expectancy that she knew had been originally conceived from regret, doubt, and fear. But, somewhere amidst the three, Ritter had embraced the gift despite the packaging. He glowed like a new father standing over a cradle completely oblivious to the fact there was no child to be found in it. The hard-gained joy would never be born. It would die in the midst of its expectancy.

"I asked my da for advice on raising a child. He said to be the man I would want my boy to become," Ritter said seriously, still smiling. "I am going to, Cat. I am going to be that man," he said emphatically with a nod. "What is it? What's wrong?"

Cat started to tell him but then stopped. This wasn't the time. And what harm was there in letting him be a proud papa for just a while longer?

"Nothing," she said, shaking her head. "I've never heard you sound so Irish."

Ritter laughed and thought he saw a tear roll down her cheek. This had to be very difficult for Cat, he thought. She, who of all people was meant to be a mother, had lost her child. And now she had a front row seat to someone far less worthy being far more blessed.

Cat wiped her face and asked when he had been given the sonogram. It had been the day before he had left for New York.

"She was going to get rid of it but, I changed her mind. It took a fierce bit of cajoling on my part. Oh, and money. Lots of money, but worth it, wouldn't you say? She'll sign over full custody to me as soon as the solicitors are done with the paperwork." Cat looked at him and smiled. He was even more beautiful as a father.

"What did your mother say?"

Ritter laughed through his nose and gave Cat a wry look as he finished chewing his food. "My ma said that I should marry the girl I'd want my daughter to become and the kind of woman I'd want my boy to find for himself."

He paused. The smile from his face stretched its roots down into his heart, and he looked at Cat. Had she not been so blinded by the pain she knew would be inflicted on him later, she would have seen that he clearly intended to make her the woman of whom his mother had spoken.

"I'm going back to Ireland."

Cat looked up and the expression on her face was one that Ritter had hoped to see. One that said she didn't want him to go.

"I'll be taking the little chiseler back with me after he, or she—don't mean to be chauvinistic there—is born. I've got a job lined up. That was another reason I went to New York. A chief surgeon of a hospital in Ireland was attending the conference as well. I worked with him while he was working in London. Good man.

"Oh, and my parents were oddly enough looking to move back to Ireland soon! I had no idea! So I'll have plenty of nursemaids to help me out. Looks as if God is working out the banjaxed mess I got me self into, doesn't it!"

He looked at Cat for a moment as the smile faded slightly from his face. "They want me to start next month," he said quickly, looking down at his food. He moved it around with his fork not wanting to look back up at Cat for fear that his emotions would get the best of him. He didn't want to leave her.

"I will just have to trust Ashta to take care of herself," he said with a sigh. "She's done it quite well for going on twelve weeks. And I'll come back for the birth."

Ritter looked up at Cat's face and the tears streaming from her eyes crushed the breath out of him. "Come with me, Cat," he said quickly with a desperate yet happy tone. "I'm not that man you left here. I know I hurt you savagely, but I won't again. I know what I have to lose now, and it's more than I ever dreamed of having."

He could see on her face the impact of his invitation and he laughed. He tapped her chin and said a bird would fly in her mouth if she didn't shut it.

"Just come with me for a visit when I go. Meet my parents. Cat, you are the type of woman I want my boy to marry and my daughter to become! I understand if don't want to be with me. But, I do hope you can still be in our lives somehow. You're my mate! My closest mate!

"There are cows in the UK, you know!" he said, pinching her to burn off a bit of the humidity of emotion. "Especially Ireland. It's gorgeous and the people are friendly, albeit a bit more foul-mouthed than to what you are accustomed, but I know you would love it and the people would love you!"

And I love you, is what he wanted to say but couldn't. There was still a gap between them that needed to be bridged before he dared carry something as precious as love across to lay down at her feet.

Cat heard her name called, and she turned toward the source of the cry. "I think they want me to cut the cake," she said in a whisper. "Well, you better leg it then!" he replied loudly with a laugh. "And hurry it up before that shower of savages in there comes out to get you!"

Ritter helped her down, and she stood before him silently looking at the smooth white area of his shirt that would cover the bloody mess that would soon be made of his heart. She reached out and put her hand on his chest and felt the hard push-pull drumming. Ritter picked up her hand and kissed her fingers. "Go, love! It's okay. We've got a lifetime to finish this conversation."

Ritter leaned over and kissed Cat's cheek as the cool tickling sensation of his fingertips danced against her forearm.

"What's all this now?" he asked in a mocking tone, referring to the goose bumps on her skin. She slapped his hand away playfully and, before she stormed off, he pulled her back. In one fluid motion, she was drawn deep into his embrace, her body against his, and his hand was on her jaw raising her mouth to his own. Her body went slightly slack in his embrace and he smiled. He grazed his lips against hers and rolled warm and moist words directly from his tongue onto hers.

"I've got something else for you. But I'll give it to you later." He smiled affectionately and rubbed his nose across her cupid's bow. "Now on your bike!" he said loudly before slapping her playfully on the arm. She yelped from the startle he had given her, and her hand went to her chest to keep her heart from leaping from its nest.

Cat closed her eyes, and when she felt her weight return to her feet, she swallowed hard and then looked at Ritter intently for a moment. Her brain heaved to memorize the look of joy on his face and prayed for God to give him the strength to find it again one day.

She then laughed at herself and rubbed the back of her neck. Despite the wounds he had inflicted upon her, despite the priceless stone he had put into unworthy hands, despite his proneness to wander in spirit and flesh, she loved him. In her heart, he would forever be like all the drawings of him she had ever rendered: the man her heart saw him as being. And like those countless sketches, she wished now she could hold him in her hands, look at him unhindered, and erase anything that would hurt him or convince him that he was anything less than a work of art.

She smiled a last time at him and, as she turned to walk away, whispered, "I love you, Reed," under her breath. She would have climbed to the roof of the barn and howled it out at the top of her lungs had she only known that within twelve hours, she would be dead.

CHAPTER 28

A Silent Ring, a Blaring Horn and a
Deafening Death Knell

Cat awoke the next morning physically rested but emotionally exhausted. Her eyes recoiled from the relentless knocking of the sun against her eyelids and, after a sigh, she pulled the sheet over her head. Her thoughts, which still teetered on the cusp of dreams, went to Ritter. She thought about how alive his face had been when they had seen each other again for the first time. She thought of the water droplets on his shirt, the translucency they had given to the cotton, and the pink cast of his flesh that had shined through. Then she thought of the dark ride home.

As if sensing the absence of light in Cat's thoughts, the morning sun found its way through the thin sheet covering her face and finally goaded her into opening her eyes. When they focused, her mouth cuddled into a sleepy grin. She reached over and put her hand on the book Ritter had given her as a birthday gift. It was a first edition of *Pride and Prejudice* that had belonged to his sister. Cat wondered how Ritter could have known of her love for Austen and chalked it up to a fortuitous guess.

There had been an airline voucher inside the book. It carried a cash value that was more than sufficient to purchase a first class ticket to the UK. Ritter said that she was welcome to use the voucher to travel to whatever destination she would like. But for his part, he hoped she would use it to fly and see him and the baby. He apologized in advance for the amount of crying and whining Cat would endure on her visit. He also added that he hoped the baby wouldn't be intolerable as well.

The ride home and eviscerating truth came soon after. Cat had pulled over onto the shoulder of the road, just a few miles from home, and made Ritter call Ashta. To Ashta's credit, she was honest with him, but Cat was certain it was only because the truth hurt far more than a lie.

Ashta had gotten an abortion the day after the scene on the driveway. Mo had assisted in the procedure and then later gotten a discarded sonogram from another patient to give to Ritter. Both remorseless women felt certain he would tire of what they called a *childish dream* of being a father. Better to be done with it now than later when Ashta's body was irrevocably damaged. A worthy sacrifice, they thought.

Every moment in the car after the call was devoid of pulse. There was complete silence except for the low hum of the motor that rolled like a funeral dirge. At a stoplight, Cat took Ritter's hand but nothing in him suggested that he sensed the touch. He was like a field-dressed animal: warm and beautiful but hollow. All the hope and life-giving joy that had propelled him through the night had been spilled out in a glimmering ruby heap in front of him.

Cat wondered if he would ever be the same. She feared he would go back to being the dead, taxidermic creation she had first met. Maybe, she thought, this would be the death that took: the divine soccer ball to the head that would kill off all that had been killing him for years.

She stepped out of her front door and leaned over to tighten her running shoes one last time and, while doing so, saw a note. It was held down fast by one of the many rocks from her galvanized bucket. *Wake me* was all it read. She folded the note in her hand and smiled as she walked toward Paul's house.

As she passed her truck, she was startled by an unexpected large object. Her eyes focused, and her brain shook trying to make sense of the scene. A blue one-man backpacking tent was set up on her driveway.

Cat removed her shoes and slowly unzipped the tent. She crawled in the small cocoon and then lied on her side next to him. He looked completely serene and beautiful. With the blue fabric of the tent casting its cool tone on his face, Ritter could have passed for dead in the truest sense. The rise and fall of his chest, however, belied his deathlike state just as it had the first time she had seen him nearly three months earlier in this exact spot.

He stirred slightly and Cat smiled. His nose wrinkled and he wet his too-red lips before sighing and falling back into the zero-gravity chasm of sleep. She rose up on an elbow and watched his heartbeat slowly tap his shirtless abdomen with a rhythm. After a moment, she ran her fingers over the pulsating fleshy hollow place at the meeting of his ribs and let her head drop to rest on her shoulder. A flush of warmth ran through her and a soft, high-pitched affectionate moan fluttered its wings and pushed its way free from beneath her heart.

"Are you trying to take advantage of a sleeping man?"

Ritter's voice startled a scream from Cat, and she punched him. He laughed, pulled her close, and kissed her forehead.

"What are you doing here?" she giggled. He yawned and said that it was his tent. What was *she* doing here?

After a moment, he said that he had been unable to sleep the night before. Cat's driveway was as comfortable to him as some people find their beds, and he knew he would rest well there. The tent was simply to keep the mosquitoes from banding together like Lilliputians and carrying him away.

"What time is it?" he asked. "Six thirty," she said before nuzzling herself under Ritter's chin. He in turned yawn and encircled her in his arms with a blanketing, firm embrace. Her bones exhaled and she smiled but then suddenly remembered what it was that had brought her to that spot. She pressed herself against his chest and said quietly, "I'm sorry about the baby." Ritter tightened his embrace and whispered, "So am I."

After a moment, Cat asked if he still planned to return to Ireland. Ritter nodded and said that he did. He needed to begin again in the place he began at the start. He then kissed her head and asked if she would visit. She looked up into his eyes and smiled. Of course she would, she whispered.

Her cheek again rested itself on his chest and she tried to not imagine life without him. Not imagine his car being gone. Not imagine the worn-out places of her fences where he had repeatedly jumped over, weathering and fading to gray. Above all, she tried to not imagine that, in her absence, the feelings he seemed to have for her now would fall to the floor haphazardly like the stone had fallen from Ashta's purse.

"Reed?" She paused for a moment to steel herself, then sighed hard and asked him about the rock. She wasn't sure what she would get in response but a laugh wasn't what she expected.

"What? Oh, how did all this get at sixes and sevens?" he moaned, rubbing his eyes. "She took that stone from my desk, Ginger! That larcenous slag! I had planned to buy a new cat for you. I found a breeder and there were a pair of siblings available. I thought I would buy one for us each to spoil but then I realized that you might not even speak to me again! So, after a few days and a wasted rock, I canceled with the breeder. That's all it was, Emma! Trust me, I want nothing more to do with Ashta!" he said with a wry laugh. *Or any other woman on earth but you*, he thought.

"Wow! That rock business must have made the entire evening last night seem like rubbish."

Cat shrugged and Ritter hugged her. "I'm done with deception, love. From here on out, all you get is the full monty truth. I apologize in advance!"

Cat sniffed a laughed and Ritter tickled her ribs until she giggled in earnest. The laughter turned to mutual sighs and then peaceful silence. Ritter rubbed his hand across Cat's head and then kissed it. He closed his eyes and, with a strange sense of wonderful terror, said, "I love you, Rachel Emmanuelle. I'm blissfully, horrifically in love with you. It's horrible. I blame you completely." Cat laughed and traced her fingers along his collarbone. "I love you too, Reed Jacob." Her face then fell slightly, and she took his hand in hers.

"Don't leave me, Reed," she said, rising up to look at him. "Oh, I'll never leave you, Cat. I might leave the States but not you. I reckon you'll leave me long before I leave you." She shook her head. No matter how far away they were from one another, no matter how long he went without seeing her face, she would be with him.

"I promise you that, Reed Jacob Thomas. I'm yours and will always be with you."

He pulled her close against his chest again and quickly lost himself in the ebb and flow of her breath on his skin. For a moment, he dreamed they were lying together in their marriage bed, in a drunken state of naked exhaustion. He imagined the smell of her, the faint taste of sweat on her skin, and the hot softness of her naked flesh against his.

Instinctively, he spread his hand out to its full expanse over her side. A voracious wave ran through him and he licked his lips as his dream struggled to be born into reality. His breath quickened as he began to reach his other arm across himself to pull her on top of him.

Cat's phone vibrated wildly and Ritter shouted, "Sorry!" Cat laughed and asked what he was sorry for. He looked up toward the heavens, wiped his hands down his face hard, and laughed. "I wasn't talking to you, woman."

Cat shook her head in bewilderment and then answered her phone. Her eyes immediately became serious and, from her tone, it was obvious that something had gone very wrong.

The two pulled up to the ranch and saw several ranch hands spreading hay inside the gate to the pasture. Mort, the bull, had dug his hooves deep into the ground the night before and caused the entire area to be a mud hole. Paloma said that she had heard a commotion in the still-dark morning hours and stepped out to see the animal kicking up dirt and doing what she described, with a laugh, as *La Danza de los Muertos*. She then hunched over and danced herself around slowly, mimicking both the animal and the traditional Dance of the Dead.

The ranch hands who knew the dance joined in and Cat laughed. "You realize of course since I'm in the middle of you all that I'll be the next to die! Go do your *baile* somewhere else please! I'm not in a croakin' mood today! And speaking of death, where is el Señor Muerte." In his pen behind the barn, she was assured.

Cat walked out toward the white-and-brown mound lying several hundred yards away. When she reached the animal, she clicked her tongue and kneeled down beside it.

The cow was lying on its side breathing heavily. Cruz had given the animal several doses of pain killer, but Cat could see it was still in agony from more than one trauma. The heifer had calved for the first time the night before. Then, while in a weakened state, had apparently been attacked by some wild animal although what type, Cat couldn't imagine.

The bloodiest wound was on the side on which the animal lay, making it impossible to inspect. Cruz said that he had tried to turn the animal over with the aid of a four-wheeler, but it cried out terribly.

The blood loss from the obscured injury was considerable, and Cat knew the animal was destined for death. She rubbed the cow's ears, and its large eyes rolled up toward her with desperation. "I know, honey. I know," Cat said compassionately, slipping a sugar cube into the animal's frothy, pale mouth. She then asked for her rifle, put her hat over the cow's eyes, and, with a single shot, put the beast out of its misery.

A party of four set out on horseback in search of the newborn calf. When it was found, Cat gave a whistle to Cruz who was lagging behind with Ritter. The two men were deep in conversation and continued in whispers even after reaching the calf. Cruz repeatedly pointed toward the west and made motions with his hands as if directing Ritter. Then, in a strange gesture, the two men hugged and Cat distinctly heard her godfather say the word *familia*.

Cat and a ranch hand stood over the remains and shook their heads, bewildered as to what could have happened. The calf had been so badly injured that it looked like a ragged, oversized dog toy. The two inspected the limp and bludgeoned body and then suddenly Cat threw her cowboy hat, calling Cruz and Ritter's mysterious conversation to a halt. She then turned toward her godfather and an angry stream of Spanish fired off as if by the aid of gunpowder. The ranch hand's eyes widened and he looked over his shoulder toward the open pasture land.

Cruz took off his own hat, wiped his forehead with a bandana, and called back to the ranch on his cell phone. Ritter had picked up a bit of Spanish in his short time in Texas, enough to know that Mort the bull was apparently responsible for the attack. Cat pointed out a hoof mark just outside the calf's crushed eye. No other hoofed animal would have done that. It wasn't their nature. But Mort was of a different sort. He was not only hostile but seemed purposeful with his violence as if that alone was the reason he had been born. Paloma had been right. She had seen the animal doing the Dance of the Dead, and the two cows must have been the ones for whom the dance had been done.

Cruz and the worker mounted their horses and took Ritter's and Cat's by the reigns. They would drive the truck out to bring the animals in Cruz said. "Por qué no caminan?" he suggested to the couple with a wink. Cat looked at Ritter and smiled. She could use a long walk to cool off, she said, looking out toward the barn and shaking her fist at Mort who was undoubtedly reliving the night's antics with pleasure.

Cruz laughed at her gesture. His eyes then softened and took in the little girl who had grown up before his eyes and in his heart, seemingly over night. He sniffed, dismounted his horse, and lifted his goddaughter in an embrace. For the last time.

The clop of hooves left them behind and Cat and Ritter began walking, hand in hand, back toward the ranch. "Isn't there a pond of some nature out here?" Ritter asked.

"He's not supposed to be in this pasture! Somebody at the party must have, no, nobody would go near him." Cat looked up at Ritter, realizing she hadn't even acknowledged his question. She then smiled and pointed westward and said it would be a good twenty—or thirty-minute walk. Ritter said that was fine. The company was tolerable, he sighed.

The couple laughed and talked and then Ritter asked, "Why did you say Christianity was the child of Judaism again?" Cat gave him a strange, sideways look and then remembered having made the statement. Remembering however didn't explain his question or the timing of it. She joked at the strange digression but saw on Ritter's face that he had asked the question in earnest, wanting an equally sincere response.

"Well, it is. It doesn't stand in opposition to it. Judaism explains Christianity and Christianity completes Judaism. Take away one and you are left with only a partial view and understanding of the other. All the Christian traditions mirror the Jewish traditions. And many Jewish traditions were created specifically to point toward Christ. It makes total sense. Like for example, communion, or mass as I heard you call it, is a Passover Seder. Christ was the Passover lamb. He fulfilled all the requirements for it. Woe, look at all those buzzards!"

Cat looked up with wonder at the black feathered wake. Their dark bodies moved over the reflection of the light in her eyes like ants on a piece of discarded meat.

Ritter looked up and supposed out loud that they had come for the dead cows. "Nah," Cat said. "If that was the case, they would be on the ground picking! If a buzzard is in the air, it's waiting for death. The cows are over there anyway. Why are they above us? Boy, there's a bunch of them . . ." Ritter nudged her and tried bring her back to the subject at hand.

"What? Oh. Sorry. There sure is a bunch of them though! Okay, what else um . . . oh, the Lord's Prayer sounds like the beginning of the Kaddish prayer. Our baptism is like the mikveh—do you hear that?"

Ritter stopped, listened, and said he heard nothing. "Yea, nothing. That's weird! No birds, no dog barking, nothing. There's not a hurricane coming is there? They usually plaster that all over the TV."

"There are birds! Look up!"

"Yea, but they are quiet, Reed! And where are all the other animals?"

"They've all gone on holiday, Ginger, and you've not been invited. I was hoping I could keep it from you." Ritter pulled her forward, and Cat resumed walking slowly, looking around herself for some explanation to the oddity.

"So the men that followed round Jesus, what were they called? His posse?"

Cat nodded her head. "Yes, that was exactly what they were called," she said seriously. "They were originally called the Torah Twelve and had aspirations of being a boy band but figured they would just be His apostles instead." Ritter nodded and said that he had heard something like that.

"So these apostles, after Yeshua died, they stopped being Jewish. They became Christians then?" Cat sighed and said no, that hadn't been the case.

"Well, first of all, the term *Christian* is like the word *Jew*. It was a term other people came up with to lump a group of people together. It was started as kind of a slur but stuck nonetheless and became part of their identity. The apostles never referred to themselves as Christians. They were followers of Christ or followers of *the Way*. But on more than one occasion, we read of some of them still referring to themselves as Jews. Paul did quite often. He was a Benjaminite, which was like . . ." She raised her hands up and gestured as if to suggest something great.

Cat shrugged and then looked up again at the buzzards. "They were Jewish men who knew they had seen the fulfillment of prophecy. They had seen the next step in God's plan for His people. The *Beloved* became the *Bride*. Besides, can you really stop being Jewish? That's like telling you to stop being blue-eyed or dark-haired—"

"Or like telling you to stop being the size of a Guinness!"

A verbal and physical fight ensued and continued playfully until the two reached the pond. Cat stopped just short of the water, but Ritter kept walking.

"Come on, love," he said, tugging at her hand. No, she said. Wet jeans were next to impossible to move around in. "You are the only impossible thing out here, woman. Come on now. This dip has a purpose."

Cat rolled her eyes, took off her boots, and went out toward Ritter who was then waist deep in water. "There are leeches in here, you know," she complained. "Life is full of leeches, Cat. Shut your pie hole."

When she reached him, he turned to her and put his hands on either side of her face. He smiled and said quietly, "Baptize me." Cat looked at him with confusion and said adamantly that this was not something he should do for her.

"I am not doing this for you. You have assured me you love me as I am. And that is in part why I am doing this. Not for you but because of you. You are not my savior, Emmanuelle. But you were enough of the Savior to lead me to salvation."

He paused speaking and waited for the shock of the moment to sink into Cat's brain. He then smiled, pushed her hair back on her forehead and laughed. "HaShem is an ironic One!" he said with narrowed eyes. "I was washing away my sorrows to the point of drowning. And who does He send to dive in and save me? One of the things that was pulling me below the current: a woman! And now, here I am back in the water! I said you would be the death of me and you have been. But it was a part that needed to die so that the rest of me could live."

Reed smiled and then asked if Cat were qualified to do the thing. She laughed and nodded, her face still filled with shock.

"Well, should I get on my knees, then? Don't want to pull you down with me."

Cat smiled, he hadn't been able to pull her down with him thus far. She was fairly certain this would be no different.

Silence reigned all the way up the third heaven as Cat took a deep breath. She then asked Reed if he believed that Yeshua was the promised Messiah and Son of Yaweh. He smiled and said that he did indeed.

Cat declared her actions for all that would hear in the name of the Father, Son, and Holy Spirit and leaned Reed's body back. As the water encased him completely, his weight took hold of hers, and she fell on top of him. They both floundered a moment and came up sputtering and laughing.

"Does it still take?" Reed said with a laugh and Cat wheezed yes through coughs. "So it's done then? I'm clean?"

Cat nodded and said, "Completely." Then, before she was able to utter another word, she was scooped up into an embrace that rocked from side to side.

218

The two shook with tears and, after a moment, Reed said he reckoned they should get out of the water, "what with all the sin floating around."

They laughed then whispered their love to one another as Reed carried Cat from the pond. He put her down gently, and she went to get her boots. "Aargh, I can't move in these wet jeans!" she complained. She slid her heavy socked feet into her tight boots and then shook her head again at the wonder of all that had just happened.

"You know, we need to get us a big ole rock for this occasion!" she said with a laugh, wiping her running nose. "Although there's not many out here."

Cat's breath was taken from her as she turned back toward Reed. He was on one knee with a ring in hand. "I have a rock, love," he said with the smile of a condemned man set free.

"Rachel Emmanuelle Douglas, will you, my beloved, become my bride?"

Cat walked forward slowly as if in a trance. She sat down on Reed's knee and took the ring, looking back and forth between it and his face.

After several uncomfortable moments, the silence on the ranch became deafening to Reed. "You can say no, Emma. My love for you isn't based on anything you say or do."

Cat shook her head and laughed. "I just don't know," she said. "I mean, I haven't even kissed you! What if you are a really bad kisser?"

Reed rolled his eyes and exhaled hard. "Declare yourself, woman!"

Cat looked at the ring and Reed, feigning scrutiny. "Would you wear a kilt at the wedding?" she asked seriously.

"Excuse me?"

"I like kilts. They are handsome and you have nice legs. Does your family have a tartan? Oh, could you wear a plaid yarmulke!"

Reed's jaw dropped and he closed his eyes as he ran his tongue along the inside of his cheek. He then cleared his throat and with obvious restraint said calmly, "No, my dear lady, I most certainly will not wear a kilt as I am no bloody Scotsman! I am Irish—"

"What's the difference?" Cat interrupted and then bit the inside of her lips to contain a giggle.

"Oh, I see. I offer you a rock, and you offer me stick in return! Give me that ring—"

Cat threw her arms around Reed's neck and kissed him. The ferocity of it took him off guard but, once the reality of it settled in, Reed returned the affection. The silence in the air was broken by the sound of their breath and lips as they kissed each other's cheeks and eyes and rubbed their faces against one another.

"Is this a yes?" he whispered against her neck as he dragged his lips along her throat. "It's a definite maybe," she giggled.

Reed threw her to the ground playfully and the two lay on their sides facing one another.

"So what will you give me in return if I say yes?" Cat asked playfully. Reed shook his head and ran his hand over her head. "I've got nothing worthy of you, love. But what little I have on this earth and in this chest is yours." Cat rolled her eyes trying to contain her tears and made him promise that if she said yes he would stop being so *bloody romantic*!

"Only if you stop trying to speak with an English accent!"

They pulled at the blades of grass between them and talked of wedding plans. Reed assured Cat that he would see to it that she had exactly what she wanted minus anything that involved him in a kilt or plaid yarmulke! Her response was a smile and simply, "I only want to end up married to you. We can elope for all I care."

The same thought struck their brains and, within a moment, it was decided. They would elope as quickly as possible and honeymoon for as long as possible. The latter prospect made them both silent for a moment and Reed turned scarlet.

"Does that embarrass you, Dr. Thomas?" Seeing that it did, Cat laughed and yelled out, "I am going to have relations with this man!"

Reed gasped and covered her mouth.

They kissed again and Cat began laughing realizing that she still held the ring in her hand. Reed took it, placed it on her finger, and kissed her hand. After a few more kisses, the excitement of what lay ahead for them became intrusive, and Cat said she had to tell her parents. Reed smiled and decided to not tell her that they already knew.

The two began the long walk back to the ranch with their clasped hands, swinging like wedding bells between them. Within sight of the barn, they heard the warning horn.

Cat rolled her eyes. "Mort's out! Of course! Heaven forbid we have—" Her voice dug in its heels and stopped short as she saw the look on Reed's face. She followed his eyes over her shoulder. There stood the beast twenty yards behind them. The hoof prints in the soft ground showed the animal had been following them for nearly a quarter mile.

Reed pulled Cat close as Death shook its horned head in fury. "We can't run straight to the barn," Cat whispered. "Our jeans will slow us down, and he'll get us. Listen to me, husband. Listen!" she said, jerking the reigns of Reed's fear. "Run right and I will run left. Count twenty steps and cut right toward the tree line. If he is too close to cut right, cut left and get to the barn, zigzag the whole way, and don't look back! Everybody is already looking for us! All we need is a few minutes! You got it?" Reed looked aggressively at the bull and nodded his head.

"On the count of three . . ."

"I love you, wife."

"I love you, husband. One, two, three!"

The lovers struck out in opposite directions as fast as their wet clothes would allow. Reed heard the beast's drumming and angry snorts following closely and the terror slicing through him was only slightly greater than his relief that it was he and not Cat a hoof beat away from death.

On the predetermined number, he cut hard toward the trees. The four-legged demon slipped, trying to make the impossible change in direction, giving Reed just enough time to scale a tree. The bovine threw itself into its trunk, stabbed at the ground with its hoof, and shook his head as if possessed. Reed hung on for his life, hoping help would arrive soon.

A cracking noise sounded from beneath him and Reed looked down to see that he had positioned most of his weight on the one dead limb of the tree. He wrapped his arms and legs around the trunk as the stability beneath him weakened. His body began to slide down and Reed closed his eyes praying for salvation.

Cat's voice cried out and Reed opened his eyes to a horror even greater than what stood beneath him. Cat was trying to distract the bull, clapping her hands and screaming. Reed begged her to go away but the ferocity of his grip on the tree choked out the air from his lungs.

Seeing that her efforts did not distract the bull in its deadly pursuit, Cat decided to come closer. Suddenly, she remembered the folded hunting knife in her pocket. She grabbed it and ran toward the beast.

The thick hide on the bull's barrel gave way to the knife and Cat grabbed it with both hands. The animal convulsed at the shock of pain and for just a moment stood completely still, stunned. Taking advantage of the half second of stillness, Cat jerked the knife upward, hoping the serrations on the back of the blade would tear through the flesh as intended. The ripping drew a gush of blood that poured down the belly of the monster. As the animal cried out and kicked, shiny pink entrails pushed themselves through the gash.

Mort turned and Cat darted behind a tree. As the animal came around close behind, the damp denim of Cat's jeans caused her to stumble. She reached out her hands but, before making contact with the ground, Death's horns hit the back pockets of her pants and propelled her upward.

Her body was thrown into the canopy of trees and her head was dashed against an unyielding oak, crushing a portion of the back of her skull like pottery. The broken shards of bone pushed inward on her cerebral cortex and the memories within it fell into a heap on impact. Before they were able to right themselves, a flooding hemorrhage of blood rushed in and, within an instant, thirty-five years of recollection were left as floating corpses in a sea of red.

A shot from Cruz's gun rang out as Cat began to fall limply through the verdant entanglement. The trees reached out and caught her by the arms before she met with the earth and then, suddenly, there was a hush. All that could be heard was the low crackling hum of the branches as they mourned under the weight of Cat's dead, gently swaying body.

CHAPTER 29
The End of a Beginning

Reed sat in the surgical waiting area alone. He looked around for a clock, found none, and, for the first time, realized why every hospital neglected to put one on the wall. It would only add to the debilitating feelings of helplessness and play cruel tricks with the imagination.

He rubbed his face in frustration and the coldness of it shocked him. The frigid, antiseptic laced air had left his cheeks feeling bloodless and he was suddenly struck with how much in common the waiting area had with the morgue just four floors below. The stress that hung like a mist in the room was slowly pulling the life from his flesh and embalming him.

Cruz and Paloma arrived an hour later, having stopped by Paul's house to get Reed some dry clothing. They encouraged their new *yerno* to change his shirt, get some hot coffee, and walk around. Reed smiled. *Yerno. Son-in-law.* It was a title he prayed he would be able to wear in earnest.

Cat's blood had painted Reed's shirt. It looked like a gruesome Rorschach test and he could see the look of horror on faces as they passed by him and read it. But, it was all he had of Cat. He rubbed his hand over the bit of her heart that rested on his, then put the clean t-shirt over it.

The hospital cafeteria was on the floor just above, but several people walked in the elevator with him, and Reed found himself going down before going up. He leaned against the wall, yawned, and rubbed his eyes trying to listen to other's conversations instead of the steady stream of chatter in his own head.

After the last person exited, the doors closed like a vault and, through the grinding of the elevator's gears, Reed heard a voice that made him want to claw through the metal to escape.

"Hello, Israelite. I told you I'd see you again." Reed closed his eyes and prayed that this was a nightmare. He didn't care how terrifying or gruesome as long as it wasn't real.

Fervent fingers slid down his arm and grabbed his side pocket. "Your trousers are wet, my friend. You should take them off and let them dry. Here, I will help you."

Reed put out his hand and guarded himself. "I was baptized today," he said quietly, hoping that in some way the thought would weaken her desire for him or wake him up.

Lucy recoiled back a step and narrowed her eyes. She then came forward, put her hand against his head and pulled it down slightly as she stood on her tip toes. The seal of the Holy Spirit was on him.

"And so you did. How could I have missed that?" she said with a hiss, looking over her shoulder at her minions standing in the corner. They cowered under her stare.

"Well, you have certainly lived up to your namesake, Jacob, son of Isaac. As he betrayed his own brother, so have you betrayed yours, fellow Jews, for the sake of a myth."

Reed closed his eyes. *Yeshua is my brother, my people,* he thought.

"Oh, speak to me, handsome. I cannot hear your thoughts."

Reed remained silent, still clinging to the quickly thinning hope of Lucy being a part of a lucid dream from which he would shortly awaken.

"Very well then, let us, as they say, cut to the chase, yes? You know who I am, who *we* are?"

Reed glanced quickly over his shoulder and saw Ashta, Mo, and Bayle standing in the corner. He swallowed hard and looked back down at the floor.

"Oh, come now, young betrayer," Lucy said with a condescending laugh. "You did know who they were, didn't you? On some not so deep and dark level, you did. And still you welcomed them into your bed. Or perhaps that is exactly why you did," she said before pausing, letting her seductive tone ferret out his weak places.

"Here is what I propose, my handsome Israelite." Her right hand slid up his chest and the other around his backside. "You are hungry. I can feel it. Celibacy does not suit you." Her nose slid along the line of Reed's trembling shoulder and the alarm of her voice caused the sleeping beast within him to turn restlessly.

"Let me feed your hunger one last time," she whispered into his ear. The words dripped hot down his neck.

Lucy laughed. "Aah, there it is. Sweet hesitation," she said in hopes that his silence was speaking as loud as her own words. "It lives in your soul as the concierge for doubt, keeping all things ready for its inevitable arrival. And it has arrived has it not? Doubt?"

After several deep breaths, Reed whispered, "HaShem will feed me."

Lucy ran a finger down the line of his back and leaned around him to look him in the face. "I think your confidence is counterfeit. Truly, you doubt that God will provide for your needs. He so, so very often has not before."

Reed closed his eyes and maintained silence in response.

"Fine," she said with irritation.

The elevators doors opened and a dark shaft leading to the basement rose up from beneath.

"Throw yourself from the lift. Go on! Your God will save you, will He not? The way He has saved your people from destruction for thousands of years? Jump, good Irishman, jump. I assure you," she said with a wet hiss, "I alone will be at the bottom to catch you. Then you will see!" Her voice had risen to a scream, and she gathered herself before continuing.

"I can give you everything you have ever wanted. Give yourself to me, and I will deliver your little demi-saint from death and into your bed."

Reed's expression changed and Lucy laughed. She brushed her fingers through his hair to add a finishing touch to her synthetic sympathy and spoke in a quieting tone.

"There, there now. Yes, every man has his price, and yours is as selfless as selfish. You will ease her suffering and then I will turn her vibrant heart and body to you. You will have us both and then you will truly have had every woman you have ever wanted. The carnal realm would be yours to rule like a king."

Reed felt his spirit giving way. Not only would Cat be alive, but she would be in his bed where he had wanted her from the beginning. It would be so easy. Just a word and Lucy would make it happen.

He is the father of lies.

Reed opened his eyes and put his hand against his chest. It felt as if a string within him had been plucked and the note sustained leaving behind an echo of an endless, voiceless voice.

Blessed is he whose help is the God of Jacob.

The words resonated within him and pulled the unsteadiness within him to right.

Stand firm and see the deliverance the Lord will give you.

The trembling within him ceased and Reed felt his spirit steadied and made stronger. He felt as if he had been put upon a high place, on solid ground. And from that precipice, he saw something he had not seen before.

There had only been two women that Reed had wanted in his bed that had refused him. One currently had his heart and the other was practicing medicine in Haiti: Adanya Delacroix. They had studied and done their orthopedic residencies together in France. He called her his *fleur Africaine* and was taken with her in every way.

Adanya was brilliant, kind, hardworking, and beautiful. Unfortunately for Dr. Thomas, she was also committed not only to Jesus Christ but her husband. Mr. Delacroix being thousands of miles away in Haiti did not sway her toward infidelity. And Jesus, being two thousand years away in the past, didn't seem a detriment to her faith.

Other than Cat, it had only been Adanya that had been honest enough to tell Reed how lost he was and it was a message to which he had been deaf. Lust rang too hard in his chest for truth to be heard. The more Adanya had tried to bring Ritter to Christ, the harder he had tried to bring Adanya to his bed.

For Ritter, the battle for her had been between two men, and it didn't matter if one was seen as deity. As far as Ritter was concerned, her Jesus was no more than a man and there was no man Ritter felt he could not best. Once his African Flower was seduced away from her deity, her husband would quickly cease to be a problem.

The last time he had seen Adanya, he had backed her into a corner. His skilled surgeon's hands had slid inside her coat around her hips, and he could feel her neck trembling against his lips as her arms pushed back against his body.

"Adanya," he whispered as he looked at his reflection in the metal plating of the elevator. "Yes," Lucy said. "You remember your African Flower. Her dark skin made your mouth water as it is watering now. Do you remember her peaks and valleys?" Lucy took Reed's hand and ran it down her hip. "Do you remember how ripe her mouth was for you?"

Lucy put her hand on Reed's face and turned it toward her. She began kissing his chin and she laughed as his skin broke out into a clammy sweat.

"I do remember her," Reed said, clenching his eyes shut tight like fists.

"Tell me what you remember, Docteur Thomas. *Dis-moi*," she hissed, her French accent accosting him in ways her Caribbean English could not.

"I remember the last thing she ever said to me," he said, opening his eyes and looking down at Lucy. "She said, 'Get behind me Satan!'"

Reed pushed Lucy hard and leaped toward the elevator doors that opened just before his face made contact with its unyielding steel. He could feel claws like hooks tearing at his flesh, pulling him back toward damnation, and he cried out in pain and terror.

The hard smack of Reed's body echoed against the frigid tile of the lobby. "Are you okay, man?" Reed looked behind himself at the closed elevator doors and then up at the voice above him. It was Peter, his great form towering above like an oak tree.

Reed gasped as if having been released from a choke hold and began scrambling up Peter's leg like a cat running up a tree. The scene immediately caught the attention of passersby, and Peter grabbed Reed up by the shoulders and pushed him into the stairwell.

"Dr. Thomas, look at me!"

Reed looked up at Peter's face and saw an internal burning of restrained power in his eyes.

"You have not been given a spirit of fear! The Lord Himself will take hold of your right hand and help you!"

Reed grabbed Peter's shirt as if trying to get a point of reference for reality and asked Peter if he was losing his mind.

"No, Dr. Thomas, you are not crazy. Stand up and stop cowering! You are in the same battle you have always been in. The only difference is that now you can see it. And do you know why? Because you have won and those against us will not stop coming at you until you believe you have lost!

"Do you understand? Hey!" Peter said sharply shaking his charge's shoulders. "Those against us are nothing compared to those who are with us! You know that!"

Reed nodded slightly and closed his eyes, trying to will his adrenaline to ebb. After a moment, he looked up to thank Peter but a raised hand stopped him.

"Don't thank me, Dr. Thomas. Thank the One who sent me. Now go. Cat is out of surgery."

Reed didn't pause to ask how Peter knew Cat was out of surgery nor any of the other questions any other person would ask. He simply raced up to the third floor. This time, however, he took the stairs.

She shouldn't have survived the injury or surgery. Reed was able to immediately begin chest compressions however and keep her organs and brain satiated with oxygen until the medical helicopter could arrive. The paramedics stabilized her and when she arrived at the hospital, the operating room was prepped and ready for her.

The surgery itself went, as the lead surgeon had put it, "miraculously smooth." The head injury was substantial but Cat could recover. She would struggle with some gross and fine motor control, and there would most certainly be short-term memory loss. But therapy would improve her dexterity and she would live to make new memories. It would seem that she, as her nickname suggested, did indeed have nine lives. The greatest concern, however, gathered up whatever lives she might have had left and dangled them over a grave.

Cat had a blood clot in her brain that—due to its size, location, and her current state—was far too risky to remove. The surgeon said that it was old and wouldn't have been caused by her recent injury. But, the blow to her head that morning may have dislodged the clot, making Cat at great risk for a stroke.

The plan was to keep her in a medically induced coma to allow her brain to "hibernate" and recover. It would lower the risk of swelling and keep her blood pressure down, which would hopefully keep the inoperable clot from moving.

After three days, however, she would have to be weaned from the drug-induced coma. Cat had a medical directive Reed wasn't aware of and Cruz had not read until that day. After seventy-two hours, it was Cat's wish to live or die without medical intervention. And, were she to go into cardiac arrest before then, she wanted nature to take its course. On her hospital bracelet were the letters *DNR* typed out in a font larger and louder than her name.

The ICU *fishbowl*, as it was called, was a semicircle of rooms whose glass fronts faced a central desk. Being in it allowed Cat to be monitored constantly and more closely. Unfortunately, it didn't allow for privacy. Reed sat next to her bed holding on to her sheet trying to hold in his emotions knowing that he was being watched as much as Cat. Each time he happened to look out to the central desk, its attendants would immediately look down and start whispering. They knew of Doctor Thomas and his sexual prowess. Most not as much as they would have liked, and one, all too well.

Shame rolled through Reed's chest not only for what he had done but that his reputation was most likely bleeding onto Cat. He looked at her pale face, straightened her nose cannula, and then began to sob.

A nurse quickly walked in and urged Reed from the room. "Doctor Thomas, you need to compose yourself," she said with politely restrained antipathy and little eye contact. "Miss Douglas can hear you and your . . . current state," she said, clearing her throat, "could raise her blood pressure. The room needs to remain quiet and you must refrain from touching her." Reed nodded, wiped his swollen eyes, and looked at the nurse. Recognition wavered like smoke in his brain and he looked down at her name badge. She quickly covered it and walked away.

Paloma came in later that night, and because only one family member was allowed with Cat at the time, Reed excused himself to the chapel. He had never been a man for open displays of religious sentiment, but he had also never been the man he was now.

He sat down on the first bench of the softly glowing room and put his head in his hands. Prayer was beyond him. That would require thought, which would require an energy he didn't have. So, instead, he quietly recited again and again, *El na refa na lah. El na refa na lah.* Please God, bring healing.

A nurse walked by and heard familiar words that were out of place in the cross laden chapel. She looked in the dimly lit room and saw a man in scrubs. *Poor guy,* she thought. *Must be new.*

She tiptoed in quietly and put her hand on the man's back. "Sir, there is a Jewish prayer room—"

Reed turned and she stopped. He had changed out of his dirty clothes into scrubs without her knowing and now she was stuck. She couldn't walk away. She hated him, that was certain, but had enough respect for grief to not simply turn away coldly. Instead, she quickly looked away. After a moment she handed him a box of tissues, nodded politely, and turned to leave.

"Wait," he said. "Please. I know you, but I don't know how. could you please come back?"

The nurse's bottom jaw came forward and she rolled her eyes. Insult to injury. Not only had he humiliated her but he didn't even remember her name. Then she wondered if he had ever known it all.

She turned and he looked at her name tag. *P. Cohen, CCRN.* Nurse Cohen saw his eyes and took off her badge.

Reed smiled and asked her to sit with him. She sat behind him and he knew from the look on her face that she had obviously been a casualty of his previous lifestyle.

"So," he said after several silent moments, "you're Jewish too then?" The nurse looked away and he nodded. "Doesn't get much more Jewish than *Cohen*," he said with a weak laugh. "That name signifies you as a descendant of the priestly tribe of Israel."

The dark-eyed woman sighed. She didn't need a history lesson from him about her own heritage. She smiled a strained smile and rose to leave.

"I'm sorry," he said. "If it is of any importance to you, I'm not that lad anymore."

"It's not," she replied curtly.

He asked her earnestly to tell him what he had done and she shook her head. He hadn't done anything to her that she hadn't agreed to. It was what came after that had nearly ruined her. She ran her fingers over her head and thought that if there had been such a thing as a devil, he would be a big fan of Dr. Thomas.

"The things you said after," she said calmly, "made me a laughingstock around here. I nearly lost my job and would have lost my visa. I came this close from having to slink back to Ontario and telling my dad, the rabbi, I got kicked out of the States for banging a doctor in a supply closet. Oh, you remember now? Yea, I can see it on your face. Did you get any type of reprimand? Did you get a hundred disgusting nicknames thrown at you or filthy notes shoved in the vents of your locker? Did you sit alone in the cafeteria like a secondary-school reject? No. You got high fives. I saw it myself! And to top it off," she said before pausing to wipe her nose, "you haven't looked at me since. The only reason you looked at me today was because you forgot who I was."

Reed looked down and nodded. The nurse sighed and took a step forward. "Look, I am sorry about your friend in there," she said remembering the sting of grief. "I truly am. Don't think she won't get good care because of any animosity I have toward you."

"I don't think that," Reed said calmly. The nurse looked up and made eye contact briefly before turning. "She's not my patient anyway so," she mumbled before walking away.

Nurse Cohen stepped behind the main desk to grab some charts. It was a shift change for half of the staff on duty and there was a low hum of shuffling and mumbling. Suddenly, however, it all came to a stop and silence rang through the air. The nurse glanced over her shoulder and her face went white. Reed was standing in front of the desk and had everyone's attention. His swollen blue eyes rested on hers as he addressed the group.

"I hurt you publicly so it only seems proper that my apology be the same," he said before taking a deep breath and clearing his throat.

"I was disrespectful and misogynistic toward you. And you have been nothing but professional and courteous toward me. In fact, you've even gone so far as to show me compassion. You—" He paused, realizing he didn't know her name.

"You, my good woman, make this hospital a better place. And you've made me a better man by allowing me the opportunity to beg forgiveness. You are a lady and should be treated as such."

Reed then turned and looked at the throng staring at him with gaping mouths. "Perhaps that could be the next rumor to be spread."

The next two days went by all too fast. Cruz and Paloma stayed with Cat, each five or six hours at the time, and then Reed sat with her through the night. While not in her room, he walked and often found himself outside the nursery looking in the window at the red-faced newborns. One in particular had dark curly hair and Reed thought of the dream he had of Yeshua and the twins. The little girl's big brown eyes and thick eyelashes still warmed his heart. He rubbed the back of his neck, almost feeling her tiny hands against it.

Paul came up to be with Reed and begged him to go home, eat something, and rest, but it was a fruitless venture. Reed would go nowhere. He washed off in the restroom and slept next to Cat's bed, holding on to her sheet like a security blanket.

The time came to wean Cat from the sedatives. Her doctor did it slowly and kept her on enough pain medication to allow her to be lucid were she to wake but not so much that it would brazenly go against her medical directive.

As the IV dripped slower, Reed became increasingly nervous and found himself shaking as if with shivers. To gather himself, he went into the bathroom, away from the constant barrage of eyes, to gather himself.

He grabbed a vomit bag from the counter and sat down on the floor. Were it not so weary, his mind would have plundered for the hundredth time what he had gone through in the elevator and then with Peter. But exhaustion, in this case, had been liberating and relieved him of the need to make sense of the world.

Reed laid his head back against the cool tile of the bathroom wall. He watched Cat's bed and the slow rise and fall of her chest, waiting for either life or death. But sleep came to him instead.

The door creaked and Reed opened his eyes. A man stood leaning against its frame, smiling down at him.

"She's dead!" Reed gasped and the man slowly shook his head. The stranger then put His hand on His chest and a low-pitched groan rose up from Him as if He Himself was in great pain.

He smiled sympathetically and sat down on the cold floor in front of Reed. The two looked at each other for several moments. Reed was confused but not in a panic, in fact, he felt deeply at peace. He was still worried for Cat and still hurt for her, but for the first time in days, he felt as if the final outcome, whatever it was, would be as it should be. Above all, he embraced the fact that he was not in control. And it was a relief.

"You're the Counselor," Reed said with a smile. "But you're not water."

The man smiled and shook his head. "No. And you can understand Me now," He continued, answering Reed's next question.

"You saw Me as the means through which you would reach Me. I am as I always have been. It is you who has changed."

The Counselor then became quiet and waited for Reed's soul to speak. When it did, He nodded to affirm that yes, He too was God.

"You're different from the other two," Reed said and the Counselor laughed. "We're all different from the other two. But yes, the same. I heard a pastor say recently that We are three notes that function as one chord and the Father is the note for which the chord is named. Completely different yet harmoniously unified in function."

Reed nodded and then looked down. Sadness pulled at his heart, and he heard the Counselor groan again.

"Bring her back, please? You're God! You can do that! Please, I love her so much! I need her . . ."

"One negates the other, My constant companion. Love doesn't need. It wants, hopes, longs for, but need? No. Love in and of itself is complete and requires nothing from the one it loves in order to exist. And for her life to be the crux of your healing is to nail her to your existence. You are requiring something from her for which she wasn't designed. We alone are made for that burden. The Son has taken that nail. It is Me that you need but not because you love Me. You need Me because I am love, and My love provides for your existence."

"I can't do this alone. If she dies, I will go back to the rubbish I was! I know I will. I can't lose her," Reed cried, burying his head in his arms and heaving with tears.

The Counselor scooted beside the broken man and put His arm around him. "My constant companion," the Counselor said, kissing Reed's head, "you will no longer do anything alone. I call you *My constant companion* because you are. I am forever with you and therefore you are forever with Me. You are the temple in which I reside.

"As for the way you once were, that man is dead. You are free to drag that corpse behind you, but if you do, you will not be free of him. Son, if you hold on to the chains that no longer hold on to you, you are still enslaved.

"Look at me, My chosen one. I know how you feel in a way even you don't understand. I can hear the utterances of your soul that your brain cannot translate and I take those ineffable needs to the very throne of God. Do you understand the magnitude of that? The One who holds the sphere of the earth in place knows your needs and your fears.

"Son, I have given you the gift of faith and that gift will see you through temptations to include the seduction of fear. Has it not already? Don't rely on yourself. You're right, you can't do this alone, in fact, you can't do it at all. You are not in control and were never designed to be. Let that free you, not frustrate you. Give everything over to Me and know that I will never let you come to destruction. To do that, I would have to go against My own nature and that is the one thing I cannot do.

"Reed Jacob Thomas, I know the plans I have for you and they are not plans to destroy you! They are plans to prosper you, to give you a hope and a future! I have ended your captivity to sin and will bring you home to your land. And there, I will bless you with a double portion. Your heart cannot begin to conceive the joy I have planned for you. Trust Me! Know that what I break, I do not leave broken."

A butterfly fluttered into the bathroom and lighted on Reed's knee momentarily before flying up to his ear and tickling it. He looked at it curiously and then up to the Counselor. "What is this?" he asked. The Counselor smiled and kissed his head. "A few moments more, son. A few moments more."

Reed opened his eyes and found his head lying against Cat's bed. He sniffed hard, trying to wake himself and brushed away the tickling sensation at his ear. When he did, he felt fingers. He turned his head and a feeling beyond what earthly words could convey hugged his heart gently.

"You sure are a cute nurse," Cat said in a low, raspy voice. Reed sat up quickly and grasped her hand. She smiled and took a deep breath. The action made her eyes open wide with pain.

"Oh my gosh," she said.

"Oh, yea, I think I broke your sternum giving you chest compressions," he said apologetically.

"Wow, you are a really bad doctor," she whispered with slightly slurred speech and then grinned. Reed nodded. If she was in pain, she was alive, and the fact left him dumbfounded into near paralysis.

Cat's eyes looked around the room and toward the window. "It stopped raining," she said as if recalling a dream. "Ella said it started raining from the time I got here. Every day she told me what day it was and what the weather was like. She told me what happened to me and about the surgery. And she said that I was getting a little better every minute."

Cat squeezed Reed's hand weakly and smiled at him. "She said you were here and that you loved me very much and you would be a wonderful husband and father. She said you were a better man than she ever imagined you could be and that she hoped to find someone just like you one day. And I think, I think I heard you snoring."

Cat sniffed a laugh and then grew silent as if hearing a voice within her say something that troubled her.

Reed put his hand on her face and smiled. "Who is Ella, love?" The disquieting look remained on Cat's face and she made a noise to suggest that she didn't know.

Reed smiled thinking that this *Ella* had been a figment of narcotics. He then suddenly came to his senses enough to stand and say he was going to get her doctor.

"Wait!" she said and asked Reed to keep the curtain in front of them drawn. Reed protested but Cat's face made him acquiesce and sit down beside her.

She raised her hand to reach out to him and found her entire arm rebelling against her command. She looked like a baby wielding its fist like a club.

Reed smiled, took her hand, and kissed it. "Give it time, love. You will be whole again before you know it!" Cat nodded and felt the truth of that statement quickly approaching.

"My precious Odysseus," she said lovingly. "The Father is guiding your sails now. Ithaca is just around the corner, and Penelope is closer than you think."

Reed gave her a look of amusement wondering what other wild thoughts were floating around in the foam of her lucidity. He would remember this and kid her about it later.

Tears filled her eyes and she asked him to kiss her. He did and she immediately apologized for her *coma breath*. It was wonderful, he assured her, and then rose to go to the door. He paused as he put his hand on the doorknob and looked back at her for the last time. "I love you, Emma," he said.

As the door closed behind him, a sharp pain struck like lightening, deep in the right side of Cat's head and the world in her left eye began to dim. She tried to speak but made nothing but incomprehensible slurs.

Her pulse quickened and panic set in as what was human in her instinctively scrambled wildly to hold on to what was left of her life. Suddenly, tranquility gathered up the frenetically flying scraps of her mortality and the parts of her body that had been struck lifeless awakened and became whole. And finally, Cat found herself embarking on the life she had been dying her entire life to live.

CHAPTER 1
(of a whole different story)

Rebuilding Reed

Reed was finishing up the last of his notes for the day when the speaker on his desk clicked loudly. He hated that ancient thing. Its noise was a foreign and intrusive clap that startled him every single time it went off and this time was no different. It caused his hand to jerk and his pen flew up at his face, leaving an ink mark on his nose.

"Your American wife is here," the heavily accented voice said, and then the speaker again clicked. Reed laughed and rubbed his face. If he hadn't inherited her with the practice and she not been the best nurse-turned-office-manager he had ever known, he would have sacked her on his first day and tossed her little, Dr. Who, circa 1960 communication device out with her!

He knocked on the front desk and the vinegar-faced woman looked up. "My lovely bird has a name, Mrs. O'Shannon. If it slips out yer hat holder, then you can just call her Mrs. Thomas. Here is your little Big Brother," he said, holding up the drab green box by the electrical chord like a dead rodent held by the tail. "It fell off the desk and ended up a bit arseways."

The crushed box made a clinking noise as Reed put it on the desk in front of her. Then, as if on cue, the faceplate burst off it and the internal speaker vomited out.

"Well, that's a bloody shame," he said as Mrs. O'Shannon glared at him above her horn-rimmed glasses. "I thought for sure we could fix it. But oh well! It's gone to the Holy Ghost now! Looks like you will just have to ring me at my desk if I'm needed."

He smiled, turned to go, and then stopped. "Oh, and by the way, my wife is Canadian. Not American. Entirely different country there, love. You look nice today by the way, Mrs. O'Shannon. What shade of yellow is that? Clotted cream perhaps? Well, either way, polyester suits you. Be in tomorrow then. Cheers!"

Reed walked out into the waiting area with the smile of a purse-winning prizefighter. He winked at his wife, heaved her to standing, and kissed her. "Come on, my fat little hen."

"Reed!"

"Oh now, you aren't fat, my pet. Let's go."

They arrived early for the appointment and decided to wait in the car. Reed scooted over next to his round-bellied passenger and rubbed her stomach.

"I'm huge."

"You're pregnant."

"With a cow!"

"We Thomas men are a hearty, lusty lot, pet. We need room to flex our muscles."

A sniff caught his attention and he saw that she was crying. Again.

"Oh, my sweet Ella. You are beautiful!"

"But I am huge! You have to admit," she said, blowing her nose. "Molly is twenty weeks along too, and she isn't this big, eh? I am huge!"

Reed rolled his eyes and kissed Ella's forehead then stomach. "Well, you aren't Molly, and I am glad. It's not proper to be married to one's cousin. You are perfect, my pet. Perfect."

Ella composed herself enough to remember that Reed's parents had called. "They are meeting us for lunch after. Some Greek place. *Ithaca*, I think. It's just around the corner from here. And yes, I know. No feta."

She sighed and Reed smiled. His parents lived less than a kilometer away and were calling or visiting daily.

"Are they driving you bats, pet?"

She smiled and said that they were not. "But can you please ask them again to call me Ella. I know your mom think Penelope is a very romantic name," she said dramatically, imitating her mother-in-law, "but I hate it! And I don't even know what your dad is calling me still to this day!"

"Moneypenny." Reed laughed. His father thought himself cleverer every time he said it.

"She's a James Bond character, Ella. And a fit one, might I add . . . okay, okay, I will ask him to call you Ella, but I make no promises for him. Oh Ella, love, no more tears. This is a good day! A right good day!"

He smiled at the welling of hormone laced tears in her eyes and comforted her. He then laughed to himself. Moneypenny was a clever nickname.

They sat in silence for a few moments and Ella asked if he really thought the baby was a boy. He nodded and said for some reason he did. She, on the other hand, had always felt certain that it was a girl.

"Okay," she said, adjusting herself in her seat with a grunt. "I have been thinking and I really want the middle name to be Cohen." Reed nodded and said he liked it. "It would certainly improve relations with your father."

"And," she continued, "I want the first name to be Christian."

"And there goes the improved relations with your father." Reed laughed. "He hates me as it is, Ella!"

"He doesn't hate you!"

"He calls me Haman!"

"With love, Reed. With love! Look, you married his only remaining child, his baby daughter, kidnapped her away to Ireland and then, to top it off, you went and tricked her into becoming a Christian! You baptized me yourself!"

"He really does think I brainwashed you!"

"You did."

The two laughed, and Ella kissed her husband. "Christian Cohen. It's what we are Reed."

He smiled and nodded. "Christian Cohen Thomas it is. That will work for a boy or girl. Well done, you!" he said with a playful slap to her leg.

"I don't want the baby to know how we met," Ella interjected passionately. "Please, I don't!"

The tears began to gather again and Reed held her close. "Once upon a time," he whispered, "two had sex in a hospital supply closet. But those two are dead, my pet. Dead and buried in water. We are the parents of this child. Not those two.

"The parents of this child met at a hospital in America where they both worked. The lad moved home to Ireland and, despite the distance, the couple remained friends. The lass was beautiful, intelligent, patient, easy to love, and, after three long years, the bloke knew that he wanted to be more than friends. And so, he invited the lady to Ireland for Passover. After the Seder, they went for a walk and he told her that he loved her and asked her to be his wife."

"And she said no."

Reed rolled his eyes and sighed, "Yes, she said no."

"Twice."

"Woman, I am telling this story! Okay, the little hateful lass said no twice, but the fine, virile man finally wore her down! She became his bride and, soon after, the bride of Christ as well. And they both love her desperately to this day and beyond."

"And she got pregnant on the honeymoon! You forgot that! My dad thinks we slept together before you know! I look more pregnant than I am married!"

"Oh, please! Did the haggard look on my face during the entire courtship not tell the good rabbi we were being chaste! Worth the wait you know," Reed said as he lifted her chin and kissed her. Doing so, he caught a glimpse of his watch. "Oh, Ella! The time! Come on, pet! Let's waddle!"

The ultrasound gel squeezed out with a *flurp*, and the cold was shocking to Ella's skin. The technician apologized and asked Reed to dim the lights.

The wand moved quietly over the taut heap and a small spine appeared on the screen. It's frail, polka-dotted line moved with jerks and the proud parents gasped.

The technician smiled and asked if names had been decided upon. The couple said it would be "Christian Cohen" whether boy or girl. The wand stopped and the couple looked at the technician.

"Is this your first ultrasound?"

They replied that it was, and the wand began moving again. They were asked if they wanted to know the sex, and they said they weren't sure. The technician laughed out loud as if at a private, very funny joke and said she would put the results in two envelopes. She then giggled again and sighed a long amused sigh.

Reed and Ella sat in the car silently looking at one another. The curiosity was killing them and each held tightly to their own envelope waiting for the other to make the slightest move.

"Let's just do it! Wait, Reed! Good grief! I want to us to find out at the same time! On the count of three, husband! One, two, three!"

The sound of ripping paper echoed in the car followed by excited gasps as they both cried out the results of the sonogram. They exchanged confused looks and envelopes and Ella rolled her eyes.

"Call her back! I guess this is her idea of a joke."

Reed studied the pictures and then realization struck him. His eyes watered and he said there was no need to call the technician.

He held the pictures side by side, took Ella's finger, and pointed it to the top corner of each picture. The first was labeled *A*, the second, B. Ella shook her head.

"So what does that mean? Boy or girl?"

Reed nodded and kissed his wife's heavy stomach. "Yes, Ella. It means exactly that. Boy and girl."

A bruised reed, He will not break.
—Isaiah 42:3; Matthew 12:20

This book would not be complete without my thanking the many people that helped make it happen.

Jeannie Allen (my sister)
Peter Browne
Patti Cogburn
Mark Dawson
Louise Driggers
Jan Frazier
Russ & Pat Hoch (my in-laws)
Lisa Carr Nall
Dale & Doyle Nevins (my mom and step-father)
Kim Norfolk
Patti Peacher
Max Stenger (cover artist)
And pastors Dave Garison & Brandon Forsythe
whose sermons inspired me more than they know.

A special thank you to my sweet husband, Rusty, who never once questioned this and believed in me completely.

And another little double thank you to my precious twins who were patient with mommy being on the computer so much. I never really understood how God loved me, until I had the two of you.

CPSIA information can be obtained at www.ICGtesting.com
Printed in the USA
268548BV00002B/37/P